DOYLE'S LAW

SAM ROBERTS

Marie
Thanks for reading

Cover design by Ken Dawson
Typesetting by Book Polishers

CHAPTER 1:
A FLICKER IN SPACE

Neith Station. Venus Orbit. April 17th 2142.

The warming effect from the drink flushed over Jim Ryburn's face, giving him a dozy smile. He sat at his desk, drumming his fingers in an attempt to predict and match the imaginary rhythm of the flickering ceiling light. He failed at it miserably; the room was spinning faster than the synthochol disc at the bottom his glass... he was good and drunk. Concentrating, he brought his glass into focus as he absentmindedly swirled it around. *Only the dregs left, I shouldn't really...* he thought, but gulped it down anyway. He closed his eyes, waiting for the spinning to stop.

His workstation was a standard four-by-four metre cube in boring grey, the paint flaking away in places, revealing the original cold pressed steel beneath. A cracked panel here and a missing one there; it certainly wasn't the proud and pristine office it had once been, but it was still his sanctuary, his quiet place away from the prying eyes and hustle and bustle of the old station life. Since the caretakers' arrival, though, it had begun to feel like a prison cell – he still had free rein of the station, but it was their domain now.

The four monitors above his desk dominated the room, arranged two by two. They loomed over him casting their long shadow and silently judging him. The top right screen displayed a rotating 3D wire frame representation of the incoming hopper. The top left was broken, a spider web of shattered glass rippling out from its centre, a consequence of the last time a screen got a little too judgmental and met with his prized cricket ball. Various other programmes were running on the lower screens, but the system was mostly idle, and just like Ryburn – waiting.

His desk was the picture of organisational efficiency; whilst waiting he'd organised, reorganised and organised it again; everything in its place. He clumsily reached for his cricket ball, taking it from its presentation pedestal and rolling it over in his hands, the stitching gently snagging on his callused palms. Beside the ball, his only personal items were a photo frame of his long departed wife, the sons he never spoke to and his baby granddaughter back home in York. He smiled at their forever frozen faces. *She'd be ten now* he thought of his granddaughter; the number seemed right, but after a moment's consideration he realised that she'd be closer to twenty now. *Was it all worth it?* he asked himself, rolling the ball over one last time before returning the championship match ball to its pedestal.

He reached for a bottle of water, succeeding on the fourth attempt, and refilled his glass. From his top drawer he took a small foil pouch, fumbled it open and dropped the contents into his glass. The disc slowly sunk to bottom in a fizz of bubbles, releasing synthochol and a gin-citrus flavouring. He watched, with drunken focus, as the disc floated to the surface, reminiscent of the slice of lime which he always put in his drink back home.

That was a real liquor he thought *not this synthetic wash*. The bubbles accumulated on the underside of the disc; looking up at bubbles through glass, he pondered, was something evolution never intended for the human eye. *Bloody hell* he thought, *how many have I had*? He'd lay odds those judgmental screens were keeping count.

He pushed the drink away; it wasn't helping to pass the time. It never did. Sleep wasn't an option either, in case of complications with the hopper approach. *Can't risk the caretakers ballsing it up.*

"Call Benson." he spat at the displays. What was keeping him anyway? A flickering of light on the broken screen and a classic telephone bell rang with slight distortion. "Attempting to connect."

He knew what it meant. "Pick up! You're there. You're always there."

"Dr Ryburn," responded a deep voice with a Tennessee drawl. A pixilated silhouette behind the broken screen faded into view. Ryburn didn't need a clear visual to know it was Benson.

"We have your hopper on filtered visual now," Benson said. "I'll transfer the band. It's moving a bit fast for my liking. Shouldn't you dip it into the atmosphere to slow it down or something? Maybe do another orbit to be safe?"

"Yes thank you. Ryburn out" he snapped and cut the call. "Caretakers should keep their idiot comments to their idiot selves and stick to carving up my station. Leave the important shit to me." Fumbling with the keyboard command he loaded up the visual; an unhelpful yellow-brown haze. *Great!* He closed his eyes to force his thoughts through his synthochol-clouded mind. After some hasty corrections he filtered out the Venus atmosphere, leaving the recognisable praying mantis-like shape of the approaching hopper, with its long, thin body and dexterous looking arms. In its eagle-like claws it cradled the two surface-lander probes tight to its chest. *Don't you dare drop them,* he thought. The hopper's outer skin was scaled with solar panelling to absorb the light particles or reflect them away, depending on capacitor levels. This far into the solar system, light particles were abundant and highly potent; capacitor burnout was a serious risk; it would put the craft adrift without the ability to brake. Alternatively, a chard overload could cause a bright white explosion, scattering debris across the dead space where it had been.

Chards were the units of power; named for the physics engineer who first exploded a light particle, each representing the energy produced by exploding ten days' worth of light particles collected on a one-metre panel through the Earth's atmosphere. As light travelled away from its star the harvestable particles fanned out and lost their potential energy at an exponential rate. Meaningful chard collection on Earth was not viable, but from the inner system, where the potency was strong and the abundance was high, it was a different story.

The hopper glowed vibrantly as it deflected the light particles it couldn't absorb, lighting up the haze all around and interacting with the clouds, forming psychedelic patterns and ripples. In his current addled state, Jim could watch the never-ending swirling for hours. *No time for that now* he thought as he pulled himself away from the hypnotic lure of the trance. From a small pouch on his desk he unclipped a syringe of sober-shot, his own concoction. With a slight pinch of pain the needle pierced his thigh, followed by a shudder and a gasp as the injection gave him the chemical equivalent of an open hand slap across the face, returning him completely to sobriety, along with the aches and pains of his tired old body.

"Fuck!" he said aloud, feeling the sudden cold that his drink had been hiding, squeezing his eyes shut until the shivering spell passed.

With a clear mind, Ryburn made some minor adjustments to the hopper's trajectory, checked over the vitals and set up a small countdown to track the final approach. Ryburn stared blankly at that, strumming his fingers along the desk in time with the decreasing seconds. Only 6984 strums to go: two hours. The swirling patterns of the clouds weren't nearly as enticing anymore and his eyes kept darting back to his glass. *No!*

Ryburn stood gingerly. He wasn't frail, not yet anyway, but had a tired gait as he paced around the room, stretching his old bones. He wore his standard issue communicator on his left forearm; usually he wouldn't have bothered wearing it, but with the incoming hopper he couldn't risk missing any updates from Benson. It was scuffed and worn but still functional. Built more for sturdiness than comfort. He poked at it to check it was still working, willing it to do something, anything. His eyes fell upon his glass again, *No!*

The preparation work for the hopper collection was long completed, checked and checked again; waiting was all that was left to do. Once the hopper was in and the ore processed, the caretakers would start dismantling the collection hub and the work-sphere. They'd been anxious to put their grubby hands to the task for weeks now. His workstation was next on their schedule, of course. The caretakers' job was to strip the station and salvage anything of value. Once the harvest was complete, all the valuables would be loaded into the central sphere; everything else would be abandoned to burn up in Venus' atmosphere. Ryburn had wondered if he deserved a place there too, sometimes.

These salvage contracts were highly sought after. The caretaker firm would have likely bid away much of the potential profit just to secure the contract. Ryburn owned the rights to his research and any resulting discoveries though, that was all he cared about it.

The human footprint across the solar system had been shrinking with each passing year. The old outpost stations dwindled as their scientific efforts were abandoned and not replaced by the inwardly focused governments and corporations. With the exception of chard collection, space was just too expensive.

His uniform was a grey jumpsuit; the yellow "New Ventures" logo displayed on each shoulder. The absence of white chevrons was a constant reminder of his team's Venus missions, labelled "spectacular failures" by his superiors. Ryburn had fallen on his sword for those, words like "negligent", "dereliction of duty" and "gross misconduct" only sharpening the blade.

The wind farm on the surface of the planet was the first failure. The lower levels were unimaginably calm compared to the turbulent upper atmosphere. Solar panelling was installed on the surface, but very little light breached the cloud cover, making a particle farm just as non-viable as the wind farm. *Venus is a write off* he thought, wondering again if he should have cut his losses years ago when all the original investors pulled out. There had been a few owners since then, all lost money and washed their hands of the station.

He considered the incoming hopper and its cargo.

One last roll of the dice.

The official ruling was understandable, even warranted. He had stopped showing an interest and dumped all his Venus responsibilities on his underlings. Neglecting his team, Ryburn focused all his time and energy on his unsanctioned Mercury missions. As those mission failures began to mount, so did his unhealthy obsession with the planet. He'd been unable to deploy a simple band relay into orbit: it crashed. Then came the various attempts to land a probe; these ended in uncontrollable acceleration and fresh craters, framing his failure for all of time.

He had been ostracised, his reputation in tatters. It would not be restored unless the mysterious ore samples proved his desperate theory correct. *Big If.*

He set the diagnostic programme running again. "Scan #23: Operating at maximum efficiency." The systems were poised to analyse the data the moment the ore hit the collection hub. He'd be handling the docking and payload extraction personally; he would have liked to think that it was because of its importance and not the lack of crew.

Ryburn reached under his desk for the boots he'd kicked off some time earlier. They were a military style and took a minute or so to lace up. Scuffed and worn, they hadn't seen polish for months, likely years. He decided he should go down to the requisition cupboard and get himself a new pair. It was a poor excuse and he knew it, but it would kill a bit of time.

The sliding door popped off its rails as he tried to close it and it stuck fast. He struggled with it for a moment but after a couple of frustrated kicks and a few choice words he gave up. The station was long past its prime and had been in a state of disrepair long before the decommissioning process started and the caretakers arrived. Funding, equipment, and crew had begun slipping away years ago. When things broke they just weren't replaced. Occasional replacements came with the supply drops and crew rotations, if you were lucky – but even those dried up.

Leaving the broken door behind him, he stepped out into the dim corridor, skeletal frames of dismantled hardware towering over him and closing in from every angle. After just a few steps from his workstation the hum of his equipment was swallowed up into eerie silence. Even his foot falls made no sound as he walked along the corridor. The rubber panelling fitted to eliminate the constant background noise of the old station equipment was efficient, but very much overkill now.

He headed anti-clockwise along the outer corridor. Neith Station was your typical giant wheel floating in space, the outer corridor the rim. The central sphere sat at its hub and the central corridor connected through its middle.

Ryburn fought the urge to sneeze as the machine dust started clogging and freezing in his nostrils. The background heating was shot and the filtration system had been decommissioned. Everything was either broken, faulty or gone, and as far as Ryburn was concerned, everything was the caretakers' fault. This section of corridor was the "scenic route", since the porthole windows would have offered a breath taking view of the infinite stars and galaxies had they not been obscured by junk, sinking the corridor into pitch darkness. Luckily the communicator had a torch and worked well enough to guide his way, although it needed the occasional slap of encouragement to prevent him walking into a shell or getting snagged on some jagged old frame. He had to step around several piles of dead equipment. Was it so hard to keep a clear path? The junk started to thin out after a while, leading to the section that was home to the collection chamber, where he would be unloading and decontaminating the Mercurian ore.

Ryburn paused to inspect the chamber, allowing himself a satisfied nod; it was exactly as he'd left it on his previous inspection. The chamber was a coffin-sized capsule with a thick glass viewing window looking into the brilliant white vacuum chamber. The controls looked untouched by the caretakers, as was the trolley he'd positioned under the output shoot, ready for the ore.

The next section of corridor was back to complete darkness and Ryburn trudged forward, relying on his temperamental torch. A large shell had fallen over, blocking the corridor; he'd warned them this would happen. Idiots. He stepped up, with a groan of effort, onto the obstruction for a full assessment of the caretakers' incompetence, shining his torch around the edges and relieved to find adequate space for his trolley to pass. Next was airlock-B's section of corridor, where the lighting was fully functional. Ryburn was able to get a good look at the state of the corridor and all the frames ahead.

"Lazy and dangerous. These will topple over at the slightest touch" he said aloud to make his point to no one.

Ryburn pushed against an offending frame; it didn't budge. At least they weren't blocking the breach door anymore. The breach doors were a structural safety precaution: in the event of a major decompression the heavy doors would drop from the ceiling and lock into place. The self-welding mechanics ensured that once lowered they would not open again. Ryburn had had to insist several times that they be kept clear. He took a moment to list off all the examples of incompetence he had seen this morning with the intention of raising them to the head caretaker, "Chief" O'Connor.

He stopped in the alcove where the central and outer corridors intersected. He liked to take in a bit of space-watching whenever he passed, tradition was tradition. He took a moment to recite the various space landmarks that were in view, constellations and far off galaxies and such.

What the hell was that?

Ryburn planted a hand and braced himself against the window

as a sudden dizziness struck him right behind the eyes. For a split second they'd changed focus from looking at the distance to looking at something close up, then back out again. It was an instinctive reaction to something. Was he not viewing the stars billions of miles away but instead seeing tiny stars up close? It was like admiring a landscape painting only to have it pulled away to reveal the real landscape behind it, then flicking back to the painting.

He pressed his face to the window and searched every possible angle for this flicker of something, but saw nothing. Three possible explanations occurred to him. The first was that he was losing his grip on reality, as his former colleagues had all claimed was happening. Absolutely out of the question. The second, a chemical imbalance in the brain, brought on by synthochol and skipping meals. Purple meal bags were disgusting, perhaps he'd skipped one or two along the way. Three, something was out there, lurking. A shiver ran down Ryburn's spine; he found the very notion creepy but still no less plausible. The cold from the window cooled the flop sweat on his forehead, while his heart, which he hadn't until now realised was racing, slowed.

Pressing the red "Emergency" button on his communicator he initiated a high priority call. "Everyone," he said with a nervous and out of breath tremble. "I saw something outside, away from planet, out into space. I was looking out from the fourth inner X junction just a few seconds ago and it was close. Can anyone confirm this?"

"I have nothing Dr Ryburn" said Benson. "I've got no alarms on the proximity sensors, I'm still seeing your hopper coming in, are you sure it wasn't that?"

"No, Benson, this was the complete other way. It must have been close." Ryburn didn't even bother to keep the condescension from his voice.

"Okay okay, so what was it you think you saw?" asked Benson.

"Well..." Jim paused. How did he explain this without sounded cracked? "It was like something was there but I couldn't see it..." He paused to rephrase a more coherent explanation but was interrupted by the giggling voice of McSweeney.

"So let me get this straight, you make a priority one call to tell us you didn't see anything," McSweeney stopped mid-sentence for a spasm of laughter before regaining his composure, "and you want us to confirm that?"

"I saw something. This is serious. O'Connor are you hearing this? Please respond." Calling out the chief caretaker should put a bit of urgency behind his request.

It took a moment for Chief O'Connor's sleep-interrupted response

"Dr Ryburn, I'll look into it once my shift starts. O'Connor out." He cut the call, Benson and McSweeney following suit and disconnecting.

"Thank you O'Connor, your support is appreciated," said Ryburn to the empty call, knowing he'd just been fobbed off. "Ryburn out" he added, impotently. He'd have to run through the sensor data himself.

Exiting the call, he saw his communicator screen was flashing between red and orange. He gave it a slap. The screen was faulty and what it managed to display was heavily distorted, but from the disjointed pixels he made out the word "unregistered". From the context it probably concerned how many communicators his call had reached. As all non-critical systems on the station were being dismantled a glitch in the communicator recognition protocols was not a surprise.

He stopped and gazed out of the window again. Whatever he had or hadn't seen wasn't there now. Even so, he was sure there was something out there. Maybe the proximity sensors had registered it. Ryburn returned to his workstation with haste.

The proximity detection system checked for any gravity-captured objects heading toward Venus that posed a potential threat to the station. Ryburn sat at his desk and combed through its sensor logs; there was nothing to corroborate this flicker in space. He thought carefully about how his eyes reacted, the subconscious part of his brain working faster than the conscious part. He eyes reacted to it, but it appeared and disappeared before he was able to actually see it. Ryburn knew a few things about light and reactions. The human eye was very sensitive, so whatever was out there must have flashed in and out quickly, somewhere between 3 and 5 milliseconds. Sensors were supposed to be able to capture movement faster than that, though. How could they have missed it? Were they looking in the right place? Was the system even functioning? Was it configured correctly? He took a mental breath and stepped back to reassess. "Stop babbling and focus!" he said aloud commanding himself to stay on track. He mulled the word over. Focus?

The sensors had a draw distance. Perhaps the flicker was too close. He brought up the configuration onscreen: a wire mesh representation of the station with a green sphere strobing between opaque and transparent. The sphere represented the sensor range and the pulse indicated the sensitivity. The sensors were not intended to look for objects close to the station; that would be too late. Ryburn made his changes, and the sphere shrunk inwards, closer to the station, with the outer range set to only one hundred and fifty meters. He'd know if anything larger than dust approached.

There was a trade-off for this improved concentration: besides the huge drain on energy, it would be useless for detecting anything outside the new range and anything moving slower than the impossible speed he'd configured. He applied his new settings and leaned back to marvel at his work. *Shit!* He hastily made some corrections, disregarding the warnings about sensor effectiveness and inefficient energy use.

Now he had two events to wait for, the hopper and this flicker. He raised his glass, offering a toast to his screens.

"A watched space never produces an anomaly," he proudly announced before downing his drink... it sounded a lot catchier in his head.

Ryburn gave his useless door a kick on the way past; an

outburst he regretted as he limped away into the corridor, this time in a clockwise direction. *Stupid bloody door.*

The light from the planet below stabbed through the few unobstructed portholes, leaving pillars of yellowy brown light criss-crossing across the floor and illuminating every dust particle floating aimlessly about. Ryburn trudged toward the central corridor staying out of the light, as if by avoiding it he'd also avoid inhaling the machine dust. He swished his hand in front of his face, as if batting away some pesky night flies, to clear the cold and stale air from his irritated nostrils.

This corridor was just like the others on the station, cluttered with dead equipment. He absentmindedly trailed his fingers over a random shell and let out a sigh. It all had a purpose once.

As his path gently curved around, the central corridor junction came into view, as did the silhouette of a figure looking out from the breach door window. It had to be O'Connor, as Benson was too big and McSweeney, well, McSweeney would have been bouncing around listening to some godawful excuse for music.

"O'Connor" Ryburn called out, louder than he intended. He could have kept walking but that would have been too rude, even for him.

"Oh, morning Sir Jim," said O'Connor with a little laugh in his faint Irish accent, "Just taking in the morning Venus."

"Oh yeah?" said Ryburn. *Sir Jim? Was this some knew type of mockery?*

O'Connor stood about one hundred and eighty centimetres tall, with a lean muscular build. He wore the same dull uniform, the only difference being the bright blue shoulder panel of the caretaker division, and the white chevron of his rank as chief. He had a respectable amount of salt and pepper stubble, in contrast to his head, which was almost completely bald, only a few centimetres above his ears and around the back of his head refusing to yield.

My god that's shiny, Ryburn thought, trying not to look, *no wonder he usually wears a hat.*

O'Connor had never been happy about Ryburn's presence on board, an opinion he had made clear to him since day one. Their relationship was professionally polite whilst they engaged in a never-ending verbal battle of one-upmanship.

The window was not large enough for both men to share with O'Connor blocking the view. Ryburn leaned in to bully himself a better position but O'Connor stayed put leaving Ryburn in the awkward position of being a little too close.

O'Connor raised a hand up to his nose and gently scratched it, screwing up his face as he did, then stepped aside allowing Ryburn the majority of the window. First score to him.

"I'm just enjoying the quiet for a moment." said O'Connor.

"The station is always quiet"

"Not like this," O'Connor chuckled to himself. "How's that business with the hopper going?"

Ryburn rolled his eyes. And here was the reason for this chance meeting, the precious caretaker schedule. Typical of the caretakers, never asking about the details of the missions, just the usual questions about how long it was going to take. Ryburn's work and requests for equipment to be left had impacted on the caretaker schedule, and time was money.

"It's still a couple of hours away; I'll give you the clearance to dismantle the hardware as soon as I can. However, I must point out to you that I am not behind on my timings."

"Oh don't worry about that stuff," said O'Connor, "I'm sure you'll get it finished in time."

This caught Ryburn off guard. He had expected the question was another opportunity for O'Connor to make a point about him slowing the progress down; he had not expected the enquiry to be a passing comment or a throw away pleasantry.

"Is everything okay?" he asked, seeing that O'Connor was looking past him, along the corridor.

"I'm fine Jim," said O'Connor regathering his focus, "just fine".

"So what brings you to my window? I thought I was the only

one who stared out into space."

"This is my window, Jim. Yours is on the other side"

Jim? Best of friends now are we? We'll see about that Baldy. "Not wearing your hat this morning?"

"Oh right," said O'Connor, reaching into his inside breast pocket, "I've got it here," pulling the woollen hat over his head smiling in triumph. "My favourite hat, not ripped either"

Ryburn sighed his disappointment, his barb not catching. "Have you had a chance to look into the issue we spoke about earlier?" Even in the bad lighting Ryburn saw the confusion flash across O'Connor's face.

"Yes. No. Not yet," stuttered O'Connor, "but I will have a word with McSweeney. He shouldn't be impeding your important work."

Important work? The sarcastic bastard! Ryburn wouldn't rise to it, though. "Thank you, but he hasn't been that bad of late. I was referring to what I saw outside the station."

"There isn't anything there, Jim. Wouldn't it be best if you concentrated on your work?"

"Perhaps you are right," said Ryburn without any real conviction.

"Look, about McSweeney, has he been moving stuff, taking things away just to be a nuisance?" asked O'Connor

"No nothing like that, he's been-..." Ryburn began.

"Are you *sure* nothing has gone missing lately?"

"No, he prefers just making jokes and getting in the way, he wouldn't take anything," said Ryburn, finding himself in the unprecedented, and uncomfortable, position of defending McSweeney.

"Damn it," said O'Connor through gritted teeth as he raised a clinched fist with freshly grazed knuckles.

"Has he taken something I should be aware of?"

"No, not that I'm aware of..." O'Connor trailed off and the conversation lapsed into silence. "But if he did think it was funny to hide something from you, where would you look first?"

"Hypothetically speaking, well..." said Ryburn leaning arrogantly back and folding his arms. "McSweeney is an attention-seeking clown, but there is nothing malicious in his pranks."

O'Connor scoffed and muttered something under his breath.

"Everything he does is always about wasting time," said Ryburn noticing O'Connor's mouth curl into a smirk, "I would say he would hold whatever it was he had taken close by until you notice it is gone and begin looking for it. Then he would return it to the original position and remain close by to witness the fruits of his attempts at humour."

"Interesting, thanks Jim. Where do you think I would hide something then?"

"Why? Are you planning to take something of mine?"

"No nothing like that," O'Connor reassured him. "I'm just trying to figure him out, that's all."

O'Connor was rubbing his ear lobe. *A subconscious sign of deception?* Ryburn wondered. He looked like he was about to say something but thought better of it. "You've been here since the beginning haven't you?" O'Connor asked.

"Yes I have. It was a grander station back then, of course. During the original phase it was the pride of the system." Ryburn launched into a full history of the station as if he was lecturing at some university. "Three outer rings, three inner, thirty-six work-spheres, and of course the central sphere."

He was proud of the station and hated that it was being dismantled. But it was the life cycle of these old school space stations. It was not the caretakers' fault it was being recycled. Neith was designed to shed the outer rings and spheres as they reached the end of their operational life. The spheres and walkways would all be discarded to burn up in the corrosive atmosphere of Venus. The central sphere had always been at the core of the station. There was only one ring corridor now, where originally there were six: three inner and three outer. All looped around each other, dotted with the workstation spheres, intersected with corridors connecting it all together.

"It was quite a sight," said Ryburn, his nostalgic smile slipping away to one of contempt as his mind returned to the present. Only three spheres remained on the last ring corridor. Once the caretakers' recycling was complete the station would enter its "final phase", the last ring corridor would be cut loose and the central sphere would become a lifeboat for the crew and the all-important salvage.

"It's sad it has to come this," said O'Connor, looking up and down the corridor.

"All things have to come to an end," said Ryburn, turning to look behind him along the same path the chief's eyes had just taken.

"I remember when we deployed the station," Ryburn continued. "Pride of the system; it was going to usher in a new era of energy harvesting; the dawn of a new future."

"How right they were," said O'Connor turning to meet Ryburn's eyes.

Ryburn laughed despite himself. He would not be goaded into an argument about his failures. Nice try though.

O'Connor joined in the laugh, although it did sound a little bit forced. He raised his hand and looked at his wrist communicator. If it were a wrist watch Ryburn would have thought he was checking the time to see if he could make an excuse to leave.

"That's in much better condition than mine," said Ryburn admiringly.

"Don't let me keep you Jim," said O'Connor, standing aside and gesturing toward the central sphere.

"Right you are O'Connor, enjoy the view." They each tipped their heads toward each other in a ceremonious yet casual goodbye and Ryburn started to walk away toward the central sphere.

"And don't worry about McSweeney, Sir Jim," O'Connor called after him. "He will leave you alone to get on with your important work."

Ryburn stopped but did not look back. He wasn't sure who

won that little exchange but O'Connor certainly just landed the last shot. Call it a draw.

Ryburn's muffled footsteps joined the hum of the solar capacitors as he got closer to the central sphere. Upon reaching the crescent shaped bulkhead, the midpoint of the corridor, he felt the vibration of the equipment through the flooring. Some of the more valuable dampeners had been harvested already. Ryburn placed his hand on the bulkhead, as if checking for a pulse. The vibrations could be a symptom of something more serious: capacitor degradation. If a fault was left undiagnosed, the capacitor would soon reach an absolute zero state and fuse, rendering it useless. It was no worse than last time he passed this way, but that wouldn't stop him expressing his concerns to the caretakers.

The rooms beyond the doors to his left had already been stripped bare and restacked floor to ceiling, wall to wall with salvage. To the right stood an empty, makeshift mess hall for crew. A pair of ladders attached to the bulkhead allowed access to the floor above and below. The light seemed to pour down through the hatchway, spilling out into the darkness of the central corridor. Ryburn took a deep, tired breath as he reached for the ladder, then climbed up to what remained of the old command deck. Giving his legs a shake, his thighs thanking him for leaving the ladder.

A powdery metallic odour hung heavy in the air, the tell-tale sign of computer hardware being dismantled. Ryburn stifled a sneeze that announced his arrival.

"All right Dr Ryburn?" greeted Benson with a welcoming smile. He was a big big man and probably tipped the scales at 150kg. He wore the standard grey but with the sleeves torn off at the shoulder, exposing massive arms that were elbow deep in circuitry, wires and grit. And sunglasses. Who wore sunglasses in space?

"Band not working?" he asked as Ryburn continued to walk out the pain in his legs.

"Band is fine Benson," Ryburn replied dismissively. He never extended Benson or McSweeney the professional curtesy he showed O'Connor. His eyes widened as he surveyed the room, aghast by the state of everything. It had once been fitted with computer systems, massive displays, and multiple workstations. Now they were all gone, the buzzing conversation and the excitement of scientific exploration a ghost that haunted only him.

Benson did not really have the time to be distracted by Ryburn's latest fancy. He had a lot of work still to do this shift, having fallen behind trying to chase down and isolate an airlock alerting error.

"So, what can I do for you Dr Ryburn?" he asked, always polite and respectful.

"That was once my terminal you know?" said Ryburn

"Oh right," said Benson fighting the need to apologise. "So what can I do for you?" he repeated.

"Are there any boots left in the requisitions cupboard?" said Ryburn not bothering with the common courtesy of eye contact. "I need a new pair."

"New boots Dr Ryburn?" He was not expecting something so trivial. Keeping the annoyance from his voice and wearing his best grin he answered, "There were one or two, yeah. All the stock from that sphere has been crated and is along the outer wall next to..." He was going to finish the sentence but Ryburn blatantly wasn't listening. "There were a couple Dr Ryburn," Benson repeated with some volume, which snapped Ryburn back to reality.

"Of what?" said Ryburn startled.

"Boots. There are a couple of pairs of boots left," said Benson slowly and loudly.

"Right," said Ryburn dismissively. He was staring intently at the circuitry Benson had stacked up on the floor next to the shell of the old terminal.

Benson didn't know what to say; had Ryburn really forgotten mid-sentence why he was there?

"Hand me that board?" asked Ryburn, pointing and clicking fingers toward the circuitry.

Benson handed it over, easily handling the board in one massive grip where it took Ryburn both of his to keep from losing balance.

"What did you use these terminals for anyway? Judging by the state of the components it hadn't been run for a while."

"It was to manage the communication relays sent to Mercury from here," said Ryburn in the same disconnected tone as before. His attention was still on the circuit board.

Benson struggled to keep his grin at bay, and tried to hide his face by looking down into his work. "There aren't any relays around Mercury," he said innocently, knowing full well that Ryburn had been responsible for deploying those relays and that he had failed in spectacular fashion.

"Just ask your question and be done with it, don't dance around it," said Ryburn.

"Okay, what actually went wrong with the relay missions?" he asked in the most respectful voice he could muster. He was aware of the official accounts and rebuttals, but it wasn't the same thing.

"You want to hear how I failed a simple task? How they kept crashing with no explanation? How I lost the first in a long line of hoppers? Or do you want me to start dribbling on the floor like the crazy old coot that you all think I am?"

Benson looked up, expecting to see outrage, but instead saw an amused smirk. Ryburn had played him.

"The official record clearly states that the hopper transporting the relays crashed into the planet. It was the findings of the investigative committee that Dr James Ryburn incorrectly calculated the approach vector of said hopper leading to an irreversibly sharp decent into the planet surface, leaving all probes and the hopper an irretrievable write off." Ryburn recited in monotone from memory the official account.

"Yeah, I know what they say about it," said Benson. Taking off his sunglasses he tried to slide them into a chest pocket long since ripped away. He hooked them into the rip instead. "I want to know what you say happened, not the official record, they're always bullshit anyway… aren't they?"

"What I said happened didn't matter. They didn't want the truth they just wanted..." Ryburn stopped.

"They just wanted what? What happened?" said Benson, trying to drag the real story from him.

"So… the record is accurate, I admitted that I miscalculated the path and was unable to correct it in time." said Ryburn, staring blankly off into the void

"But you've done loads of relays in your day, come on Doc, what really happened?" said Benson. "Is everything okay? You seem distracted... more so than normal… Dr Ryburn… Dr Ryburn"

"What?" said Ryburn jolted back to reality.

"Maybe you should sit down," said Benson, genuinely concerned. "I'm taking a break for a meal-bag in a minute. Would you care to join me? I'd like to hear about the other Mercury missions."

"No I'm fine, just thinking about something."

"About those Mercury missions?" said Benson, trying his luck one more time.

"Would you mind asking McSweeney to fill you in? I told him what happened a few days back."

"Why would you tell him?" Benson was surprised, and a little insulted. Firstly, that Ryburn would tell McSweeney and not him, and secondly that McSweeney kept it to himself.

"He was up to his usual mischief rearranging papers in one of my folders. I was letting him think he'd successfully kept me distracted"

"Why?" asked Benson.

"I always leave a folder out to distract him; he goes straight to it like an idiot magpie. It keeps him from doing any real damage. But you might want to tell him to lay off. Your high and mighty chief has been asking me questions about him".

"Okay will do, but you know it won't matter," said Benson with an all knowing shake of his head.

Ryburn picked up another circuit board from the scrap heap, his knees clicking loudly.

"What you got there?" asked Benson, looking up from his dismantling.

"Oh it's nothing, just reminds me of something we used in a probe once."

"How about you join me for that bag, you could tell me what the station was like before..."

"Before you and your lot started carving it up you mean?" interrupted Ryburn "No thank you Benson, I've got better things to do."

Benson just stared in disbelief as Ryburn left, amazed at how his mood and attention could swing so drastically.

"No wonder they left you here you miserable old bastard," he said once he was certain Ryburn had gone.

CHAPTER 2: EVERYONE HATES PURPLE

BENSON THREW DOWN the last troublesome metal sheet, skimming it playfully across the floor into one of the scrap heaps. Breakfast time. He dusted himself off as best he could and climbed down the ladder to the makeshift mess hall. The room, like all the others, had been stripped bare and harvested. The long-range communication terminal, their lifeline back home, was all that was left of the room's former glory.

The square table, repurposed from elsewhere, looked very out of place, especially with its four mismatched chairs. A large bottle of tomato sauce sat dead centre of the table, equal distance between the four place settings. "Fair usage" of sauce was closely monitored with the crew keeping each other honest. A tipped-over shell adjacent to the table made for a bench top and upon it sat an external dispersion panel that Ryburn had repurposed into a cooking plate after one day, declaring, "I'm not eating this shit cold anymore."

They did their best to keep this area free of dust and debris, but whoever was supposed to do it last had done a poor job. Benson suspected McSweeney, it was always McSweeney. He gave it a quick sweep whilst berating the laziness of his crew mate. He wouldn't say anything though… he never did. Once satisfied, he returned the broom and walked over to the cupboard. The shelves were stacked high and tight with brightly coloured, vacuum-packed bags.

"Green or purple?" With a bag in each hand he weighed his options. "Do I risk awful fish or dreadful pork?" He turned around to see the chief standing by the ladder trying to peer up to the floor above. "Morning Chief, bit early for you isn't it," he joked. "What meal are we up to?"

"Umm… I don't know." said O'Connor in a carried whisper whilst continuing to look up the ladder.

"Why are we whispering, is everything okay, Chief?" asked Benson, matching the whisper.

"Yeah everything's fine, just looking for Ryburn; was he here?" said O'Connor, backing away from the ladder.

"Yeah, you just missed him. Chief, you always know what meal we're up to."

O'Connor shrugged. "As you say, it's a bit early for me. It's purple, Benson, we're back on the purple now."

"Thanks Chief." said Benson, returning the green bag to the cupboard. He took out a second bag and gestured with it towards the chief.

"No thanks, I can't eat that nasty stuff anymore," said O'Connor "I'll get mine later"

"No wonder too," said Benson looking at the time displayed on his wrist communicator, "I don't usually see you for another forty minutes or so."

"Speaking of up early, Mr Benson," his tone changing, a superior now speaking to his subordinate. "It looks like you haven't been to bed at all. Have you been up all night again?"

He'd been warned about pulling all-nighters. "I'm a bit behind; I wanted to catch up," Benson started to explain, but nervously began to fumble over his words. "You see, I was checking that pressure door on airlock-A. I'm getting some strange readings and minor alarms from it. I went and ran some diagnostics and cleaned up the internals," looking at the floor like a guilty schoolboy. "It took a bit longer than I thought it would. Sorry Chief!"

"Alarms?" asked O'Connor

"I reckoned it's just another system failing, but I wanted to be sure."

"What were these minor alarms?"

"It's the strangest thing, Chief, they were showing an unknown code on the external door."

"On the external door? Well that's impossible, that's another system failing then. We'll have to ignore those minor alarms." O'Connor smiled. "In fact, why not just disable all the airlock alarms? That'll allow you to get back to your assignment area."

"Chief?"

"I'm kidding Benson, just the minor ones of course"

"While we're talking about failing systems, we have sensor problems too, I have…"

"Yeah, you're probably seeing errors in the air pressure too," said O'Connor

"Yes exactly. McSweeney should be able to confirm the details. But the alerts are reporting pressure readings outside of acceptable error margins."

"When did these start?" asked O'Connor.

"First alert was this morning, I was worried it was connected to the airlock warnings so I-"

"More failures, this place is falling apart," interrupted O'Connor.

"Okay but that isn't all." Benson was hesitant but it had to be said, "I'm concerned that Dr Ryburn's hopper is approaching too fast. If he fumbles the collection it could be catastrophic."

"I wouldn't worry about it, Ryburn knows what he's doing."

"Chief?" said Benson. It was *not* the response he was expecting.

"It will all be fine Benson. You worry too much."

"Yes, Chief." Benson sat down and tore the end from his meal bag. He emptied it into his bowl. An unappetising cloud puffed up. He tipped in some sauce and began eating in silence. He didn't think he worried too much, but to have all his concerns dismissed was demoralising.

"Look, Mr Benson, there's something I need to tell you," said O'Connor. Benson looked up from his breakfast and reluctantly met the chief's eyes, preparing himself for a reprimand. The chief had a bit of a temper, Benson had never seen him lose it himself, but at times he'd seen ripples of it behind a strained exterior. There were rumours and stories, but considering McSweeney was the teller of most of them you had to wonder. Now, he looked to be struggling with something.

"I want to thank you for all your work. You're a skilled and highly competent caretaker and a credit to any contract you serve," said O'Connor.

Benson coughed then spluttered, his food going down the wrong hole. The chief never dished out praise. There were the "thanks", "good work today's", but never the taking of a moment for recognition.

"Sorry Chief," Benson wheezed. He thumped his chest, coughing out the last of it.

"I just wanted to let you know how much I appreciate the work you do, it doesn't go unnoticed."

"Thanks Chief, I appreciate you saying so." Then after a silence he put his hand up for a high five. "I'm your huckleberry."

"You're my huckleberry," said O'Connor with a laugh putting up his hand. The clap was loud, and strong enough to rattle O'Connor's communicator.

"Anyway," said O'Connor as he repositioned his com, "I need you to assist Ryburn in the work he will be doing over the next day or so if he asks for help. He's working on something very important. So forget about those faulted out minor alarms, keep up with the schedule as best you can, but assist Ryburn. Understood?"

"Sure thing, Chief."

"Thank you Mr Benson, I knew I could count on you." said

O'Connor. "I'd better be heading off. I'll be back soon for my breakfast bag, so go easy on the sauce. I can't be eating it plain."

"Thanks Chief and will do," said Benson raising his spoon from his bowl in a polite goodbye gesture.

O'Connor was barely out of the room when his voice came through loud and clear on Benson's com. A broad call to everyone.

"This is O'Connor here, I'm having some communicator problems. Could you all please dial up your ranges to maximum?"

"All done, Chief," he replied after making the com change.

"Thank you Benson. O'Connor out"

Benson continued his breakfast, slowly forcing it down; the sauce only worked to a point. He hated it as much as everyone else, but he had to finish otherwise he'd just be hungry later.

"Why are you eating purple?" said McSweeney as he entered the room. A gangly young man with rat-like features. He was never without his grey woollen hat, which covered his dirty blond hair, apart from a scruffy fringe that he was always blowing off his face.

"Why are you on the purple meal bag?" he repeated with an accusing finger pointing at Benson's bowl. "I know you hate green, but we can't skip." His accent was London and his words had an adolescent whine to them.

Benson, spoon still in mouth, stared at his crew mate blankly as he tried to recount the meals from that week. Red, blue, purple, green, yellow… he didn't know, but the chief never got it wrong.

"Chief said it was purple," he said, scooping up another spoonful, letting the runnier clumps drop back into the bowl.

"No," said McSweeney "We're on green. It's fake fish for breakfast today. Green is the only bag that is even remotely edible."

"Chief said purple."

"Bollocks to that," said McSweeney. "It's green and I'm having green."

"The chief said purple."

"He's wrong, I'm eating green. I don't care."

McSweeney stomped over to cupboard, making a show of pushing the chairs aside. He opened the door brushing all the meal bags aside, found his green bag and waved it defiantly at Benson.

"Don't forget to shut the door," said Benson.

McSweeney complied, slamming the door. "There," he declared turning around and locking eyes with Benson. The door slipped off the latch and slowly swung open with a credibility nullifying creak. Benson stifled a giggle. McSweeney spun back around and slammed the door again, a third then a fourth before it finally stayed closed.

"Whoa, whoa, take it easy," said Benson. "What's got you all twisted up?"

"He's wrong" McSweeney snarled back over his shoulder. "It's not purple, it's green."

"Okay," said Benson "Maybe the chief is wrong, does it really matter that much?"

"Sometimes it matters," said McSweeney, catching a ragged breath. He put the green bag back and reluctantly picked out a purple one. He sulkily dropped into his chair opposite Benson. They sat in silence, Benson trying his best not to crack a smile at the silly outburst.

McSweeney filled his bowl, the powdery cloud causing him to cough.

"What was all that about?" asked Benson with deliberate cruel timing, just as McSweeney had raised his first spoonful.

"Nothing, just a dry throat is all."

"Not that, fool. The slamming and the shouting?"

"It's the chief," said McSweeney, still avoiding eye contact. "He just had a right go at me."

"Why? What did you do?" Benson's timing again on the mark.

"It happened like this…" McSweeney begun, looking down at the table as he spoke, looking anywhere except directly at Benson. "He had a pop about my earphones being in, even though he said I could wear them. Then he chewed me out for annoying Ryburn."

"Well, maybe you should lay off for a while."

"That's just the thing though; I haven't done anything for ages. We were talking the other day about one of his Mercury missions but nothing came of it."

"You mean you didn't start to annoy him? At all? Not even a bit?"

"No, I was just asking him about the relays and why they kept crashing. I mean the man is obsessed with Mercury, isn't he?" said McSweeney, finally being allowed his spoonful.

"And you didn't bait him or make fun?"

"No, well not that time, anyway."

"And the chief pulled you up about that? Just now?" asked Benson.

"Yeah, then he starting banging on about me taking rocks." A very confused look washed over McSweeney's face, like he was desperately trying to find the next twist in his little story.

"Rocks?" the story beginning to unravel.

"Yeah it was the strangest thing but that isn't what got to me."

"Oh, there's more," said Benson with mock anticipation.

"Yeah, yeah, he said he had lost track of all the fines against my final fee," said McSweeney eyes looking everywhere except at Benson.

"I'm sure you're exaggerating," said Benson, diplomatically choosing his words. He would have liked to have called outright bullshit, but didn't wish to cause an argument. So he didn't… he never did.

"Dude, come on. He'd never mess with our fees. He may not put you forward for a bonus, but he'd never cut from your contracted amount. That's just not his way."

"I'm telling you man, that's what he said. He was pissed off about something and was taking it out on me. He had me against the wall and everything."

"Oh violence as well, this is getting good," said Benson.

"Then he said he'd just saved my life, whatever the hell that was supposed to mean. I tell you man, he really lost the plot," said McSweeney.

"You've had quite the morning then," said Benson, not buying a word of it. "Did you update your com signal?"

"No why?" replied McSweeney slurping on his spoon.

Benson rolled his eyes, his own worst enemy. "Because the chief just asked us to."

"Must have missed it, had my tunes up."

"Did the chief not mention it during your little adventure with him?"

"No not a word about it."

"Funny that, yet you say this happened just before you came in right?" asked Benson, enough was enough, time to end this before McSweeney dug himself through the hull.

"Oh forgot it then, It doesn't matter," said McSweeney.

"You going to update your com signal then?" said Benson. McSweeney begrudgingly made the adjustments, using his dirty spoon to pry open the hatch on his com.

"What did Dr Ryburn say about his Mercury missions?" asked Benson breaking into the sulky silence.

"What? Has he said something about it?" said McSweeney, far too quickly for a clean conscience.

"He said he had told you all about it the other day, and you didn't want to share, what's that about?"

"Yeah we did, but most of it, most of it I didn't understand," said McSweeney, with a gesture of it going above his head.

"Go on tell me, I couldn't get anything out of him," asked Benson.

McSweeney took another spoonful for dramatic pause; "Something about the gravity being wrong, waiting for another launch window, magnetisms and failure. A lot of failures."

"Anything else?" asked Benson

"He said things about going against the laws of physics… and I understood every word," he made the over his head gesture again, this time with his spoon and splatted the cupboard door behind him. "You're better off asking him about it," he said, spinning around to mop up the mess with his sleeve. "I'd stopped paying attention and was just keeping him talking while I rearranged the pages in his folders."

McSweeney burst into an embarrassing laughing fit, showering the table with his mouthful of food. He was his own biggest fan.

Benson laughed, but not at the prank; poor McSweeney had been outsmarted and didn't even know it.

"So ..." Benson began as McSweeney wiped up his mess, "do you think it was all his fault, like the reports say?"

"Yeah of course it was, when I spoke to him he was, shall we say, synthed up to the eye balls."

"When is he not?"

"Even more than normal; his version was interesting," continued McSweeney. "You know it started off as just getting some relays out to the dark side of Mercury, right?"

Benson nodded. He had finished his meal bag now and had pushed the bowl to one side.

"Well, according to Ryburn, everything about the relay mission was perfectly calculated," explained McSweeney.

"Dr Ryburn," Benson corrected him.

"Ryburn," McSweeney repeated.

"So why did it crash?"

"I'm getting to that," said McSweeney. "Everything was going smoothly, the hopper was coming in nice and slow." He drew his arms up to his chest, mimicking the arms on the hopper. "In one grip was the communication relay and on the other was the do-dah thingy"

"Do-dah thing?"

"The thingy," said McSweeney, searching for the word. "You know, yay long by yay wide," he said measuring out a rough metre by metre in the air. Benson shook his head. "You know, with the big wheels."

"You mean the surface probe, a lander."

"A lander, yes," said McSweeney. "A standard build, but with extra thrusters for the low gravity manoeuvring."

"Low gravity planets like Mercury?" added Benson, nodding as he followed along.

"Right that's just the thing though, it was supposed to have low gravity. This is where Ryburn's version gets really good. The hopper was coming in on a nice angle." Using his spoon and bowl as props, he mimicked the scene. "But when it got too close it changed direction, sharper toward the planet, sped up and crashed. BANG." His spoon plunged into the bowl for emphasis, slopping a few large drops onto the table.

"So what went wrong?"

"Nothing went wrong, everything was planned and calculated correctly… according to Ryburn" said McSweeney, again wiping up his mess.

"Dr Ryburn."

"At the time Ryburn figured that it was a gravity anomaly, or a flash sodium cloud coming up from the surface that interfered. Or the data that came back was just straight up wrong."

"Really? He just discounted the data?" asked Benson.

"Yeah, he said it was all rubbish, said it didn't make sense. He started going on about hundreds of years of science and astronomy being wrong, blah blah. I kind of tuned out during his rant though, I was pre-occupied."

"Messing up his folders, you really got him good with that one."

"I know," said McSweeney with another laugh.

"What's so funny?" said O'Connor, entering the room with a smile.

"McSweeney was just telling me about-" Benson started, but McSweeney cut him off.

"Nothing," said McSweeney shooting Benson a look that warned him not to say anything to the chief.

"Oh, it doesn't matter Chief," said Benson.

"No really," O'Connor repeated. "What's the joke?"

"It was nothing, just forget it," said McSweeney, fiddling his earphones back in.

"Fine, miserable sods," said O'Connor.

McSweeney stood up to leave.

"Not so fast, I need to discuss Ryburn's call earlier."

McSweeney, earphones already in, either did not hear him or pretended not to.

"Oi! I asked you to stay," said O'Connor in a raised voice, but the screeching of music was already escaping from around McSweeney's earphones. O'Connor waved his hands in an exaggerated fashion to get McSweeney's attention.

"What?" said McSweeney, like a sulky teenager, as he removed one of his plugs.

"I wanted to talk to you both about Dr Ryburn. And don't speak to me like that."

"Can't it wait?" asked McSweeney.

"Do you have somewhere to be?" replied O'Connor.

"Yeah anywhere away from you," McSweeney muttered under his breath.

"I'm sorry?" said O'Connor tilting his head offering his ear.

"I've got to fix the air level sensors. They are playing up: minor compression level alerts. I want to isolate them out while they are still only minor," said McSweeney, earphone going back in. "I wouldn't want you to dock my fee for falling behind, now would I?"

"Dock your fee? What are you talking about?" asked O'Connor, but McSweeney wasn't listening. "And what is this about the air pressure? We don't have an oxygen leak do we? McSweeney? McSweeney! Answer me damn it!" he called after him as he left.

The blatant disrespect was hard to watch.

"What the hell is up with him?" O'Conner asked.

Benson considered repeating the ridiculous story McSweeney had just told about the chief. But "who knows?" was the only explanation he offered.

"Hand us a bag would you?"

"Change your mind, did you?" said Benson leaning back and opening the cupboard.

"Pardon me?"

"Oh nothing" said Benson as he passed the bag.

"Not purple again?" said O'Connor, regardless of the colour that was the typical response.

"Don't give me that, I've just had it all with McSweeney," said Benson.

"Right you are, but if we don't follow the order we'll end up eating the same colour each meal."

"They all taste the same after we add the ketchup, Chief," said Benson

"Speaking of which…" said O'Connor as he snatched up the nearly empty bottle.

"Chief, do you know much about Dr Ryburn's missions to Mercury? I mean about what Dr Ryburn says really happened?"

"It's an interesting story. Ask him about it when he's a bit..." O'Connor mimed taking a drink.

"I knew there was more to it. What else happened?"

"Well, he got dragged in front of all the top brass. He put his defence forward and was given permission to send another hopper the next time the planets were lined up, but on the condition that he admitted fault. The board still needed a Mercury relay and Ryburn was the best… and it allowed for a convenient insurance write-off"

"And he just took the blame?"

"Well it was his, whether he took it or not. But he went on record admitting it." He paused to chew a lumpy piece. "He had a long wait though, eight months or so, so he went over and over the available data… you know how obsessive he is?"

"The data he reckoned was wrong?" said Benson filling in the parts he already knew.

"Yes and no, he said it didn't make sense. But it could be easily explained as Ryburn just fucking it up. Which is what everyone believed."

"So what about the next attempt? I know the second mission didn't go any better."

"He refitted the lander, added all the top end mods… and all that went to waste, all that potential salvage." O'Connor took another spoonful, "My god that is nasty, I should have stuck with the green."

"So why did this one crash?"

"He took a high orbit to be safe, much higher than he needed to."

"So he was expecting it to go wrong again?"

"He was never too clear on that part, actually. But I reckon so," said O'Connor.

"Then what?" said Benson, very interested in the story but wanting the chief to move a little quicker.

"He kept it very high in orbit and launched the first lander on a shallow descent. But when it hit the same altitude as the first failure it turned toward the surface and accelerated straight down. He fired the brakes, extended the flaps and readied the bouncers. Nothing had any effect."

"And the backup lander?"

"Same thing, Ryburn didn't care though. They sent back more data. I reckon that's all he wanted anyway."

"What did it tell him?" Benson asked.

"It implied a gravitational attraction well beyond what was physically possible, according to Ryburn, that is."

"According to Dr Ryburn, what does that mean?" asked Benson, knowing what was coming.

In unison they said, "You're better off asking him."

"It's his story after all," said O'Connor. "I think he just fucked it up, personally."

"Even with all the added attention scrutinising his plans?" asked Benson.

"Even with all that." said O'Connor "Anyway… It's time to be getting back to work."

He looked to his wrist to make a show of checking the time on his com, but it wasn't there.

"No com, Chief," said Benson, tutting.

"I've misplaced it."

Benson looked around the floor for a moment or two. "You had it earlier though."

"Yeah. I can't remember where I put it, after Ryburn's stupid call to everyone, old sod woke me up."

"Where'd you have it last?" asked Benson, unhelpfully.

"In the bunk room."

"Probably still there then," said Benson, equally unhelpful.

"Yeah, it has to be there," said O'Connor, mainly to himself. "I'm going to take another look. If you happen to come across it or if McSweeney has taken it to be funny you'll let me know?"

"Sure thing, Chief. I'm your huckleberry," replied Benson as he stood up from the table.

"You're my huckleberry. What does that mean?"

"Means I'm your guy," Benson said with a smile. "I'll keep an eye out for it." He had to make a swift exit before the chief roped him into helping him search.

"You couldn't help me search around for it then could you?" said O'Connor with a sly sideways squint.

"Sorry, Chief I wouldn't want to fall behind schedule," said Benson.

"Good point, best if you knock off early today and get some rest, you know not to tire yourself out with your all-nighters."

"Hey, I'm not the one who's lost my com."

"Well said," admitted O'Connor as Benson left him to finish his poor excuse for breakfast.

CHAPTER 3:
THE HOPPER

Ryburn had returned to his workstation, he'd walked fast enough for a chilled perspiration to bead his brow. He'd been running his chard-induced magnetism idea over in his head, it went against what he knew to be possible, but so did his Mercury missions so in a way it made the most sense.

"Run simulation software," he commanded.

The confirmation tone hung in the air.

"Use voltage threshold testing scenario."

Another "Bing" and all his screens lit up.

He cracked his knuckles and rotated his wrists, then hunched over his keyboard like a protective vulture and began furiously typing in the parameters for the simulation. The bottom left screen showed a 3D block slowly being moulded as he typed. It became a cylinder with two extending prongs. From each prong were small bolts of electricity feeding into a magnetic field, represented by a puffy cloud. Amongst the various numbers displayed a highlighted 10 showed the amount of solar energy, units of chard, being converted to electricity within the simulation.

"Load 1 kilogram of common steel into the scenario."

"Bing." A grey square appeared between the cylinder and the cloud.

"Execute test," he said louder than he needed. The grey square remained stationary.

"Increase to 50 chards, execute again." Nothing, the grey box remained dormant.

He increased to 500 kilochards, equivalent to 18 months' worth of collected energy by Earth standard measures. Still nothing. He cranked the output to 5000 kilochards, 15 years' worth, still nothing. He nodded philosophically to himself. "Load the known data from the Mercurian ore to replace that of the steel."

"Bing."

"Execute again!" The grey box shot forward into the cloud and the word "ERROR" blocked the whole screen. Progress at last.

"Reset to 1 kilochard, execute again."

"Bing" ERROR. Ryburn's smile disappeared into stern concentration.

"Stop. Attach the ore to the capacitor using conventional methods and execute again."

"Bing", the display showed the grey square stationary for a moment before it moved into the cloud. ERROR.

"Stop," he groaned, exasperated.

"Bing."

"And mute that bloody Bing!" he shouted at his screens. *Who chose such an annoying sound?* "Assume an unbreakable mounting and execute again."

The simulation stayed motionless, the only indication that the software hadn't frozen was the animated flow of electricity into the cloud.

"Add a velocity measure and execute again."

The numbers went up faster than he could read and his eyes widened. That was impossible. He stared at the counter, long enough for the simulation to read ERROR again.

"Execute again."

Same result. Incredible.

A knock on his door interrupted him, by reflex he immediately hid the simulation. The unwelcome guest was O'Connor; and he was putting all his strength into trying to get the door working again. "I bet Benson could fix this for you," he said after wedging the door further in the wall.

"To what do I owe this unexpected pleasure?" asked Ryburn with no attempt to hide his irritation. The witty retort he expected didn't come and he was left watching O'Connor as his eyes darted all around the room before finally coming to rest on the blank screens.

"Are you looking for something?" sighed Ryburn whilst gesturing for the chief to hurry up. No doubt the chief caretaker was assessing the room for salvage value.

"Yes I am as it happens," said O'Connor. "How are the experiments going?"

"Experiments?"

"With the Mercurian ore," O'Connor continued. His gaze moved around the desk before meeting Ryburn's eyes. A look of panic flashed across O'Connor's face long enough for Ryburn to see it.

"Is something wrong, O'Connor?" asked Ryburn but immediately wanted his question back. He didn't wish to be dragged into whatever game O'Connor was trying to play.

"No nothing wrong, thanks Jim."

"Okay, well thanks for stopping by," said Ryburn, spinning his chair back around to the monitors. O'Connor didn't take the hint.

"How long before the hopper arrives?" asked O'Connor, after what seemed like forever. Ryburn raised a tired arm and pointed to the screen, showing it skimming along its approach path. ETA 65 minutes.

"Right, that makes sense. And once you get it on board, what are you going to do?"

"Is that really important?" groaned Ryburn.

"Just humour me, please?" said O'Conner.

"Well… I'll take it to the smelt of course, but you know that because you lot are under orders not to touch it without my say so. You haven't started chopping it up yet have you?"

It would be typical, almost expected, of the caretakers to feign ignorance and dismantle it early.

"The smelt is just fine. Don't panic," said O'Connor.

"Good, as agreed, it can't be touched without my say so otherwise I'll make sure none of you work any contracts for us ever again." He meant every word, but lacked the influence now to make it happen. The smirk on O'Connor's face said he knew it. Damn it, he'd overplayed his hand. 1-0

"Oh I'm sure it won't come to that," said O'Connor.

"Good, now if you please I need to get back to my work," said Ryburn spinning his chair back around, closing his eyes willing O'Connor to just leave.

"One final request please, if I may?" said O'Connor after a lengthy silence.

Ryburn groaned. "I don't mean to be rude…" Yes he did. "… But I have very important work to attend to. Is this latest charade just to waste my time or is there some purpose I'm missing? Because if it's time wasting you like perhaps we can talk about the cloud compositions of Venus, or the carbon to iron ratios of the outer Jupiter moons, something pointless like that?"

O'Connor just smiled. "With the uncertain nature of the Mercurian ore, can I get your word that you will not take it to any other areas of the station?"

"It's not that type of uncertainty," Ryburn scoffed.

"Just humour me please. With the uncertain magnetic properties, you do not know what effects it could have if exposed to the main systems, do you?"

"It is clear you don't understand the nature of the ore or magnetic-"

"I agree completely," interrupted O'Connor. "I don't understand, don't understand any of it, which is why I don't want it being scattered about the station."

"I won't be scattering it about the station," said Ryburn.

"I want your word; I want you to promise me that it won't be taken anywhere apart from the collection dock, the smelt chamber and this workstation."

"A pointless request, those are the only places I would take it to anyway."

"So do I have your word?" O'Connor insisted.

"Yes, fine." An authoritative victory for the caretakers. "I solemnly swear that I won't take the ore anywhere it doesn't need to go," said Ryburn, complete with a hand to his heart.

"Thank you Jim," said O'Connor, as if a huge weight had been lifted from his shoulders, "I'll leave you to your work." With a final glance around the room he slipped back through the doorway.

"Magnetic exposure, Bah!" Ryburn scoffed at the absurd suggestion. Hang on, who said anything about magnetism? He spun his chair around but O'Connor was gone. A lucky guess perhaps? Not likely… educated guess? Less likely.

Returning to his work Ryburn put the strange conversation with O'Connor out of his mind. He ran the same scenario five more times to make sure that he had not missed anything. This was big. With a shaky hand he closed down the software. Really big. The simulation results were exactly what he hoped for. They showed that by generating a magnetic field in front of the ore the attraction was strong enough to draw the entire object forward, negating its own mass. Had he just invented a new form of propulsion, with unlimited potential? *Don't go writing your Nobel speech just yet,* he told himself, *it's all still hypothetical.*

It was time to bring in the hopper. He shot back a double disc of synth to calm his nerves and set off. With the caretakers' tendency of dismantling equipment ahead of schedule, coupled with how mission critical it was to him, the collection chamber was at extreme risk of caretaker interference so he had to conduct a final inspection. He could bloody well picture them at it now, all feigned ignorance and apologies. All was in order, but he ran a system check just to confirm. He even tested the wheels of the trolley; they caught slightly but nothing serious as he positioned it underneath the output shoot and continued on his way. Ahead was the green light of airlock-B shining through the gloom, providing him with a beacon. Running his hand along the stacks of equipment to help guide his way, he walked, muttering obscenities at every tipsy bumped knee and snagged elbow. He stopped dead. Ahead of him at the central corridor junction stood O'Connor. Ryburn considered turning back to take the opposite path to the central sphere just to avoid him. Ryburn walked forward guarding his footsteps. O'Connor was talking on his com; he could not hear the conversation clearly but the girly voice had to be McSweeney. O'Connor was whispering but McSweeney was louder, enough for the occasional dropped word to be heard. "Hopper… First… Searching… Airlock…"

O'Connor turned sharply and looked right at him. Ryburn froze, but for once was grateful of the darkness. *What about my hopper? Tallying up more salvage no doubt.*

"Starting now," he heard McSweeney say as O'Connor disappeared from view toward the central sphere. Ryburn loitered at the breach door until enough time had passed to avoid O'Connor, then he continued on toward the central sphere.

He climbed down the ladder to the lower level. The air felt thick with the electric charge. The docking controls weren't always on this floor, but after being "accidentally" decommissioned by McSweeney this was apparently the only viable place for their reinstallation. O'Connor had begrudgingly surrendered the space, which had been ear marked for priority salvage. They were wedged in between the humming chard capacitors that vibrated everything around them. The controls, consisted of several small monitors, a touch pad and a large rubber sleeve, for manually operating the external docking clamps.

Ryburn looked around for something to sit on, but saw only reels of cables and too heavy to move shells. He'd have to kneel, letting out a little groan as he adjusted his weight, rocking side to side until his old body stopped complaining and he found a comfortable spot.

A couple of clicks on the touchpad and the visual feed of the hopper, now on its final approach, was displaying on the monitors He reached inside the control sleeve and took firm grip on the guide handle, positioning his fingers on the pincer controls. He rotated his wrist to check the clamp movements then bent his elbow, the visual on screen showed the external arm matching his movements, with small jets of vapour escaping from the sluggish hydraulic joints.

He took a deep breath in and exhaled slowly. Time was up, the waiting was over, and it all came down to this moment. The pressure he'd put on himself was immeasurable; he had to bring this hopper in and collect the ore. After so many failures from Neith, there would be no more scientific endeavours this far into the solar system for a very long time. Even if there were, he had been so efficiently discredited and shunned that any efforts would not be under his say so. This was his swan song, his final shot at redemption. Perhaps he shouldn't have had that last drink, or perhaps should have had another. Another deep breath and he stilled himself to the task. He would have liked to have claimed to be calm, but his traitorous goose bumps betrayed him.

There had been an ongoing competition amongst the old crew over who could dock a hopper with the least fuel consumption, Ryburn had never won, never even came close. 23% was the record, his best was 40%.

"Lower speed for approach."

The braking thrusters engaged in a flash of red flame as the solid state oxygen began to burn. He glanced at the fuel levels, 36%. This is going to be tight.

"Apply braking, match to zero speed," he instructed.

"Please define zero speed," requested the console in a patronisingly calm female voice.

Shit.

"Define zero speed as station current speed," said Ryburn, forgetting zero speed was a rookie mistake and he damn well knew it.

"Velocity currently below zero speed," dead-panned the voice.

"Well stop the bloody brakes then," Ryburn shouted.

The braking thrusters stopped, but the hopper was already drifting behind and getting further away with every passing moment. The plan had been to match station speed at a safe distance then gently close the gap with steady and controlled bursts. That was completely out the airlock now; there would be no steady, there would be no controlled. His only chance to dock the hopper and he was ballsing it up.

"Increase speed, four seconds full burn." He had to accelerate if it was to reach the station, whilst carefully juggling the fuel consumption. On the four-second mark the thrusters cut out, but it was still falling behind.

"Another four seconds." The thrusters fired again. "Another four seconds, damn it."

"Zero speed achieved."

That allowed a brief respite, he chanced a nervous look at the fuel levels then flinched at the news, 16%. *Shit!*

"Another four-second burn," he commanded with vigour. The distance, ever so slowly began to close. All fuel burned for thrust now would have to be burned again for braking. He had to be very economical.

"Fire thrusters again, full burn."

The fuel levels dropped, He ran the math in his head, it would be on 8% after this burn and everything left needed to brake. If he timed it right the hopper would cruise into range of the docking arm. He rotated his wrist in preparation, his old bones clicked. He counted down the four seconds waiting for the burst to stop. It didn't stop, it just kept on burning. He looked at the visual feeds in confusion, back to the fuel then back to the feed. *Why aren't you stopping?*

7%

Shit!

6%

5%

"COLLISION IMMINENT" flashed in massive red letters

followed by the ear piercing station wide impact siren.

"Shit Shit Shit!"

4%

"Full brake, full burn on all thrusters, no reserve."

The hopper was slowing, but the alarm didn't stop. Ryburn flexed his arm in the sleeve preparing for his move; the collection arm mirrored his movements. The thrusters popped and spluttered as the fuel reached 0%. It was still moving too fast. The damage to the station would be catastrophic. There was nothing more he could do, his mind searched for a solution, the sweat was dripping down his face, his vision closed in from the sides, going black around the edges as he tunnelled in on the controls. He stopped hearing the alarms, only hearing his own heartbeat as he went into a trance of intense concentration. Everything seemed in slow motion, his whole universe shrunk in around him, it was just him and the display, paralysed watching his doom unfold.

Then a voice somewhere in his subconscious screamed a way out. "The landers Jim. Use the fucking landers!"

That was it. "Extend the hopper arms." The arms extended, like the wings of a hulking eagle. "Spin claws one eighty degrees." The claws held the tricked out landers, one of Ryburn's mission modifications being increased thruster power and solid state fuel capacity. "Fire escape thrusters on both landers, full burn no reserve." Jets of bright blue shot slowing the hopper. As the fuel exhausted he released the landers freeing them and sending them clear of the station to avoid them becoming fuel bombs upon impact.

The hopper moved into range. With his eyes swapping between the nose views from the collection clamp to the graphical display, Ryburn braced himself for his final play. "COLLISION IMMINENT"

The hopper was still moving too fast. The sirens were blasting out of every speaker and the warning message would be hijacking every station display. Ryburn jerked his arm, clenching his fist around the controls as he went for his catch. The hopper slipped and ground through as the claw tore thick gouges along its hull before finally getting a solid grip. He leapt to his feet as if he were forty years younger. Still with his death grip he braced himself against the panel with his free hand fighting the feedback through the collection arm. The force of it lifted him up and slammed him shoulder first against the wall as the external arm was swung by the momentum of the hopper. He felt the tremor as the hopper hit the station outer hull before finally coming to a stop. The sirens stopped, the absence of any decompression warning meant that the impact had not breached the hull. Not exactly a text book collection but he would take it. His knees were killing him, his shoulder would definitely be sore in the morning. He needed another drink.

"What's going on down there Dr Ryburn? Was that collision warning for your hopper?" called Benson from the top of the ladder before sliding down. The obscenities being shouted were from McSweeney, followed closely by O'Connor in stoic silence. O'Connor bee-lined to the collection panel to check the status. Benson and McSweeney stood blocking the ladder.

Ryburn allowed adequate time to ignore each caretaker in turn as he found a space of wall to rest against. "It came in a bit quick and bumped us a little." said Ryburn. "No damage, just a miscalculation. Nothing too…"

"Nothing too serious by looks of it," said O'Connor, speaking over Ryburn. His voice demanded respect. Ryburn didn't push the issue this time. "We will need to run checks, see if there's any damage. This, this will put us further behind schedule."

The precious caretaker schedule. Ryburn held his tongue.

"What is so damn important about these rocks of yours anyway," asked McSweeney, speaking very fast. The situation had him rattled "You'd better not have knocked us out of orbit, you crazy old fool," he added, with the dreaded pointing finger.

Ryburn lowered himself to the floor; he needed a minute. The adrenaline had left him. "I don't have to answer to any of you chop-boys."

"Chop-boys?" McSweeney laughed, lowering himself to the floor "Is that the best you've got?"

"I've got plenty of words I could use for you McSweeney," Ryburn spat back.

"We should compare notes," joked Benson, "I've got some good ones for him too."

"Dr Ryburn," said O'Connor, interrupting before the insults escalated. "If we'd known you were in trouble we would have helped, you know we would have." He took a seat on the floor too. "Benson here could probably have dragged the thing in with his bare hands if you'd only asked."

"Sort me out a space suit and catcher's mitt and I'll be out there for the next pitch," said Benson, clapping his fist into his hand. The three caretakers began laughing. Ryburn remained silent; he saw the humour of the situation but he wouldn't allow himself to show it. He wasn't part of their team. His lack of reaction soon had the group in uncomfortable silence.

McSweeney spoke first. "I reckon old Ryburn here would have bumped you from your spot on the team, Benson, if your coaches had seen him on the collection arm just now. Saw it all on the display when that collision nonsense started up. He plucked his thingamajig clean out the air, it was magical," he added with pretend awe and slow shake of his head.

"I need to get those rock samples to the smelt," said Ryburn. He had work to do and refused to sit around listening to stupid jokes.

"Hang on Dr Ryburn," said O'Connor, "we need to establish if our orbit is okay first, what was its speed when it hit us? It didn't breach but we need to be sure we aren't in any danger."

Ryburn let out an involuntary groan of effort as his pushed himself back to his feet.

"Dr Ryburn, how fast was it going?" O'Connor repeated, but Ryburn ignored his questions.

"Dr Ryburn?" he repeated as he stood up.

Benson got to his feet, not knowing what to expect, but preparing to calm the situation if it escalated, McSweeney, with an excited grin of anticipation, was practically wishing for it.

"How fast, damn it, Ryburn? Are we okay or not?" O'Connor repeated, the calm of his previous tone all gone. There was real anger now.

"It was at two eighty six when it made contact with the arm. It slowed down as I swung it round but there would have been a slight angular change in our orbit; it dragged us round with its momentum. Our pivot would be a degree or degree point five off centre now. When it hit the hull it would have been at around fifty or fifty five, at an angle eighty three degrees to the planet and eighty one or eighty two from our central pivot axis. The bulk of the collision force was deflected along our hull so the point of impact wouldn't have breached. At worst I've shortened our orbital life by four and a half hours. As I said…" he paused for maximum effect, "nothing to worry about."

Benson and McSweeney exchanged confused looks. O'Connor nodded quietly to himself.

O'Connor leaned in toward Ryburn and sniffed the air. "Have you been drinking?" he accused.

"Not a factor," Ryburn said, turning his back and returning to the controls.

"What about the capacitor feeds or the panelling, or the releasing systems?" O'Connor said to Ryburn's back.

Ryburn stopped in his tracks, just a step, then continued. He had not considered that.

O'Connor went into damage control mode.

"Benson, get up to what's left of the control deck and check external systems," said O'Connor. "McSweeney, you help him. I'll walk out and inspect the impact area. Report to me immediately if we're in trouble." He stopped. "My com is still missing and the damn spare is gone too"

All eyes instantly fell on McSweeney.

"What?" said McSweeney innocently. "Just run a trace on it."

"Yes, well funny thing the trace isn't working either; getting all sorts of nonsense back from that aren't I? All sorts of conflicts," said O'Connor.

"No one would have tampered with it, even for a joke," said Benson, "The whole station is falling apart. The trace errors are probably just another minor system failure. You know what it's like pulling these old stations apart."

"Thank you" said McSweeney very smugly whilst folding his arms across his chest. "That does sounds much more likely."

"Watch your tone," snapped O'Connor. "Don't think I've forgotten about your little outburst this morning. I will dock you some serious fee if this behaviour and insubordination continue!"

"Seriously, I haven't touched any of them. I swear it. Take my whole damn fee if I have," said McSweeney.

"I'll hold you to that," said the chief, unconvinced.

"I will too," echoed Benson.

"Okay then," said O'Connor, letting his temper cool. "I'll walk out without a com. So if we're in the shit you'll have to come out and get me. It shouldn't take long anyway."

After a quick acknowledgement to their chief, both Benson and McSweeney made their way toward the ladder. McSweeney dashed past his larger crew mate in a rush to reach the ladder first, sniggering something about "not staring up at that for no one" as he scampered up the ladder away from Benson. O'Connor let out a sigh and turned to follow his crew back up the ladder.

"It is really important I get this ore in," said Ryburn almost in a whisper, when he thought he was alone. With a half glance backwards toward the ladder he saw O'Connor was still in the room.

"Keep working on it, Jim"

Ryburn's lip curled into a doubtful smirk. He would never admit it but he was thankful that O'Connor wasn't demanding more of an explanation. This collection business had really shaken him up, he knew he only narrowly avoided disaster.

"But what's so important about the ore anyway?" asked O'Connor.

"You really want to know?"

"Yes I do," said O'Connor.

"I think it could be the future," said Ryburn.

"Well, don't get discouraged, keep at it. It won't be long now," said O'Connor. He appeared sincere, but it was a little too much for Ryburn.

"Don't you dare patronise me! You think I'm mad too don't you? I hear you talking. I know this being nice is just another silly little game of yours. Just let me finish my work in peace as you were ordered to do."

"I'm sorry, Jim," said O'Connor in a hushed voice. "That's not what I meant. I want to know really, please. Why does it have to come from Mercury? Tell me about the magnetism."

"The magnetic properties are indeed baffling," said Ryburn. "It is attracted to solar electricity generated magnetic fields." To further drive the point home he added, "If the attraction could be controlled, it could be a new form of propulsion."

"That's great, but why Mercury?"

"I don't know, maybe it has something to do with the proximity to the sun. But then we would expect to see lesser effects elsewhere..." Ryburn trailed off. "I really have no idea why."

"Okay, don't worry about that now Jim, you can work that out later… I guess. I have to get back to-"

"Yes, yes," Ryburn said, cutting him off. "Checking the hull for non-existent damage? Don't let me keep you from the all-important inspection."

"Yes that's right, I'll be out checking for damage," said O'Connor. With that he left Ryburn to unload the hopper.

Positioning the hopper in front of the collection hub was a struggle, since the botched docking had considerably damaged the arm. The hydraulics were sluggish and the movement jerky. Tendrils of hydraulic fluid were jetting out from every elbow joint and the feedback vibration into the control sleeve told Ryburn something was grinding loose. The best he could do was manoeuvre the hopper into close proximity to the collection hub before the arm seized entirely. The hopper released its storage crate and it slowly drifted toward its target. It was a tense moment; Ryburn watched with bated breath, as it seemed to just hang for an eternity before being drawn into the waiting chute. He slapped the desk in victory and hurried to the ladder.

Upon reaching the middle deck he had a good view in both directions along the corridor. O'Connor, leaning up against the wall, was half-hidden in an alcove. Once again Ryburn considered taking the opposite direction just to avoid him. Instead he set a brisk pace and didn't slow as he passed a nonchalant O'Connor. He offered a quick nod, but wasn't going to stop and waste any more time with idle chat.

Once at the collection hub he made a sloppy attempt to fit the protective goggles over his own glasses, but when they didn't fit perfectly first time he discarded them onto the floor as if it was their fault. He peered through the thick glass into the sterile white of the hub to see his prize: one large crate, space wearied and scared, holding his Mercurian ore. He set the decontamination cycle running. Robotic arms upended the crate and emptied the rocks onto the rollered floor of the chamber. When a flash of intense yellow lit up the chamber, Ryburn turned away to protect his eyes, the image momentary burned into his vision as he watched his shadow lengthen and shrink as the light strobed over the precious samples. When all went dark he pressed the button to release the rocks, and they began to tumble down the chute and onto the floor. He lurched for the trolley and shoved it back into place.

"Who keeps moving my fucking trolley? It's not funny McSweeney!" he shouted.

He picked up the rocks that hit the floor and dropped them

into the trolley, taking a moment to study one. It certainly didn't seem extraordinary. When the last rock had tumbled from the chute he powered down the hub, watching its light fade for the last time. He did not bother with the operational courtesy of removing the crate, nor did he reset the system ready for dismantling. No doubt they would be along shortly, tools in grubby hands, to begin carving it up.

Next stop, the work-sphere. Ryburn manoeuvred along the corridor as best he could. The path, whilst clear enough for walking, was problematic for the trolley. Several times he found himself wedged into the base of an old shell, having to reverse to find clearance. The caretakers got the blame for every delay and the berating continued all the way back to the central corridor junction as more and more hardware shells snagged the trolley. O'Connor was still loitering in the same spot as earlier, only this time Benson was with him.

"Dr Ryburn. *Dr Ryburn*," called Benson.

With no chance of ignoring him Ryburn shouted back, "Yes what is it?"

"We're getting some strange readings on the internal air pressure."

"I'm a bit busy, what is it you want to know?"

"How much additional mass have you brought on board?" O'Connor shouted over. "Sensors are showing a slight increase in air pressure."

"Thirty to forty litres, if you need an exact figure it will just have to wait." It was an empty offer; he had no intention of providing such trivial information.

"Thanks Jim, that won't be necessary," O'Connor shouted back.

Ryburn continued on his way. The next section of corridor wasn't so cluttered, since the equipment graveyard hadn't extended this far yet. He passed the sleeping quarters on his right without slowing, not even a glance at his old bunk room.

The work-sphere was split-level, with a stairwell branching

off to the left of the entrance leading up to hydroponics and the oxygen farms. The trolley bellied out as Ryburn pushed in through the entrance causing it to grind to a halt. Ryburn backed up and, with an overzealous run up that produced a nasty crunching of steel on steel, forced his way in. The room smelled stale, the fresh aroma of purposeful crafting long gone.

It was here Ryburn had refitted and modified his surface probes. The patches of original floor colouring were a tribute to the room's former glory. Only the mini-smelt remained. The outer housing was bubbled and cracked through long service. Various feed and extraction pipes connected it to chemical tanks mounted on the adjacent wall. The machine compressed 9000 years' worth of metallurgical trial and error into a quick and precise automated process. Rocks in one end, catalytic chemicals pumped into the superheated chamber, separated metals out the other end.

Ryburn loaded in a 2kg sample size of the smaller rocks and gave the outer casing an affectionate tap of encouragement as the pressure and temperature started to climb.

Just down the corridor from the work-sphere O'Connor was in the doorway of Airlock-A looking over the sorry state the prep area had been left in. An absolute disgrace. A space suit, which should have been on a hanger, had been kicked under the bench. A helmet was just dumped on the floor and a pair of boots left to lay where ever they fell. There was no doubt in his mind who the culprit was. He opened the cupboard door. There should have been three complete suits at this airlock but there were only two, including the one on the floor. They were red with a coppery shine, thin metal strips formed a mesh allowing some flexibility whilst providing the firmness required in the zero atmosphere. He pulled it from the hanger and started to climb in. He squeezed his legs in first, remembering the knack to getting them on quickly. He clipped and fastened the suit into place before reaching for the boots that had been dumped on the floor. He checked the battery levels on each magnetic heel before pulling them on and locking them into place. Each boot was synced to its pair and as a safety precaution; only one could be magnetically released at a time without manual override. O'Connor awkwardly stood up under the weight of the suit and tested the magnetic locks of each boot. They held fast against the floor and he nodded his approval. He groaned his frustration at seeing the haphazard arrangement of the oxygen tanks. Only one of the four was connected for refilling, one was even loaded in backwards, blocking the refilling valve entirely. This level of laziness was dangerous and couldn't be tolerated. He would have to have a word with McSweeney.

Adding to his annoyance the connected tank wasn't even full. He concluded that it had to be faulty. The dial on his second choice read 42%, which translated to around two hours. It was more than enough. Back in forty, hour worst case, extreme worst... well best not to worry about that.

The tank's self-guiding clips locked into place with a satisfying click and he slowly manoeuvred around and reached for the only helmet hanging up. Once on, the internal visor flickered into life, displaying the expected suit levels, oxygen, boot charge, external heat, and suit integrity. "Communications unavailable" flashed in the corner of his vision, due to the lack of wrist com; he'd have to ignore that. The first breath of air always tasted wrong; stale, chemically and just a touch too cold.

"Everything within acceptable limits, oxygen flow is good. Let's get this done," he said after running through the protocol checklist.

He entered the unlock code with his clumsy gloved finger for the inner door, raising it into the ceiling. He stepped through into the airlock chamber and closed the door behind him then began the decompression.

The floating sensation told O'Connor that artificial gravity had been disengaged and the green light above the door was now red, signifying that current level of the atmosphere in the airlock was zero. The display on the wall showed contradictory information. O'Connor nudged at the screen, trying to get it to work. It flickered briefly then faded to nothing. Another dead system, why didn't anyone report this stuff? He had to be cautious and slowly open the external door. The manual opening lever was set into the wall, so he lifted the hinged covering to reveal the yellow hammer lever, pulled it slowly and raised the door a fraction to test for any decompression. No signs of air escaping under the door, he was indeed in a vacuum. He opened the door all the way.

"There better not be any damage, Ryburn," he muttered before stepping over the threshold into space.

"And what may I ask is the reason for this?" demanded McSweeney with pantomime anger, standing in the doorway of the work-sphere, assessing the scrape marks on the doorframe, hands on his hips and very much the clown.

"I don't have time for a monkey's arse," snapped Ryburn, flicking a dismissive hand gesture at him, "be on your way."

"Tearing up doorframes your new game is it? I'm onto you." The pointing finger punctuating the accusation.

"Not today, I'm too busy. Be on your way or I'll have to report this to O'Connor," Ryburn shot back.

"Whoa! Playing the ace so soon? I'm going, I'm going," said McSweeney, backing away, but his mischievous eyes lingered on Ryburn's trolley.

The refinement process finished and Ryburn opened the cooling chamber the very second it unlocked. The freezing air rushed out making his breath catch in his chest. Once the foggy cold cleared he picked up the flat brick of refined ore. He turned it over in his hands, studying every surface. Grey, cold and heavier than expected. The iron concentrations were greater than he thought. The readout told him the yield was a little over half a kilogram. From the trolley he took a rock of similar size and bundled it up with the ingot, holding them protectively close to his chest. He left the work-sphere and walked briskly back toward his workstation. A highlight of the walk was seeing the silhouette of O'Connor plodding along the top edge of the station, wasting his own time for a change.

Stepping past his broken door, all he saw was flashing light from the proximity sensors, drowning the room in red. He almost fell over his chair scrambling to check the details.

"We have an emergency," he called over the com.

"What is it?" crackled O'Connor's voice before repeating into an echo with increasingly sharp distortion.

"We've got another proximity alert outside the station," said Ryburn after the feedback stopped.

"It's just another sensor glitch," said O'Connor after a pause. "I was… I am outside the station now, checking for damage, remember?"

"Yes, quite right, my apologies O'Connor, that would explain it."

"Chief, stay clear of airlock-B," said Benson. "I'm not sure it's safe; maybe that impact has made it worse."

"Yes, will do," answered O'Connor after another pause. "O'Connor out."

Ryburn exited the call and straightened his dishevelled collar, as if that would somehow absolve his error. He'd just seen O'Connor out on the hull too, how embarrassing.

O'Connor trudged on toward the impact site, unclipping each magnetic boot in turn. The suit did not offer much freedom of movement and he was forced into this shuffling motion. The only sound was his own breathing and that seemed to amplify inside his helmet. He didn't space walk often, there wasn't that much call for it, but when he did he always found it a humbling experience. The vastness of it all made everything else seem so fragile and insignificant; even Venus that dominated his sky line was less than tiny in the grand scheme of it all. It had taken the better part of thirty minutes to reach the impact site, a nicely formed ripple of dented hull plating. He was very thorough in his inspection, checking the seams where the sections of corridor met. He was confident that there was no structural damage, since the bulkhead doors along the corridor would have slammed shut at the slightest hint of decompression. He walked around the entire edge of the walkway checking for any irregularity. Everything was fine.

He wasn't sure which was worse, the waste of time or the smugness he'd have to endure from Ryburn. He wasn't going to waste any more of it by going all the way back over to airlock-A, not when airlock-B was right there. He punched in his access code and swung himself into the airlock. The re-compression seemed to run okay but as a precaution he didn't remove his helmet until he was station side of the internal door. The changing area looked in order, but when he opened the cupboard door to hang his suit up he found it jam packed. There was no room on the shelf for his tank, or his helmet either. Another one of McSweeney's jokes no doubt. He could picture that little sod giggling as he rushed across the station moving all the suits to this airlock.

"I don't have time for this," he shouted out, knowing McSweeney was usually within earshot of one of his pranks. He dumped his suit onto the bench, the boots and helmet kicked under it. "And you can tidy up this mess too."

Ryburn placed the unrefined rock sample on his bookshelf. It had a thick iron vein through its centre and with a spot of polish and cutting it would make for a splendid ornament. His refined

Mercurian brick he placed into the analysis scope. A blue laser grid settled over it and the computer beeped into life, running composition tests to gather accurate data for his simulations. He skim read the results, not concerned with impurity traces, carbon amounts, malleability grade or any of the other data presented. Magnetic properties were what he was after. He smiled, they had been significantly increased by the refinement process.

"Reload simulation," he said.

"Bing." The software complied, bringing up his scenario with the cylinder and simulated magnetic field.

"And mute that fucking bing."

"...."

"Good, now load new data into the scenario and execute." According to the simulation, only 22% of energy was required to achieve the previous result, a significant reduction.

"Load a mass of 1000 kilograms onto the capacitor and execute again."

The simulation was still flawed however: it assumed everything was held together by unbreakable mounts, an assumption that Ryburn knew would not hold true in a live environment. But within the simulation world of perfect structural integrity and unlimited energy supply, the achievable velocity was infinite. He paused, and leaned back from his screens. He felt faint, his breath catching. Faster than light travel? Surely not? A quick drink steadied his nerves and he continued refining his work, adjusting the variables to find a happy medium between sustainable velocity and not being ripped apart. After a time he found the sweet spot, but it was all still theoretical, and useless; a real world demonstration was needed. What to build, what to build? He looked around his room, passing his eyes over everything in search for inspiration for an experiment. He stopped at the glass fronted emergency box fixed to the wall. After shattering the safety glass with his cricket ball he reached in, brushing aside the first aid provisions and pulling out the torch.

"Load exact composition and density of the internal station

atmosphere over the vacuum, include a normal gravity level," he said, whilst unclipping the outer casing from the torch and removing the battery. He adjusted his glasses and read from it, "Add 0.5 chard and a 0.125 kg battery, load the smallest burst regulator specs from the..." he did not finish.

"Call Benson," he reluctantly said to his monitors.

"Dr Ryburn?" answered Benson.

"How's the pet rock?" added McSweeney with his nerve-grating giggle.

"Benson, that unit you were taking apart early, I need to get a certain component from it."

"All the parts are in the heap. What part exactly did you want?"

"Small orange square shape with a black stripe… maybe two stripes. There should have been four or five of them, I only need the one," said Ryburn

"What do you need them for, is your rock hungry?" McSweeney interrupted.

"Yeah sure. Do you have them or not?" said Ryburn, brushing off McSweeney's foolishness.

"You need a burst regulator? There were a few as you said. They'll be in junk crates now, should be near the top if it helps though. Do you want a hand looking…"

"Ryburn out."

"He's a rude old bastard isn't he?" said McSweeney, stating the obvious.

"I'm sure he doesn't mean to be," Benson replied.

"Yeah right! What do you think he wants a regulator for?"

"Don't think it really matters, if he wants one he wants one, they aren't anything to us."

"That doesn't matter. They are our salvage, if he wants them he's gonna have to find them," said McSweeney with a mischievous glint in his eye.

Benson knew what was about to happen, and as if like clockwork McSweeney had starting laughing to himself then, like a cartoon burglar getting ready to creep through a house, he picked up the box of salvage and skulked off toward the ladder.

"Nothing good will come of this," Benson called after him and returned to his work, but only for a minute, as he heard the crash of equipment from down the ladder. "You clumsy bastard, what have you gone and done now?" he called out but when he poked his head down to make fun of McSweeney he saw a very angry O'Connor instead. "Oh hey Chief, sorry about that, I thought you were McSweeney."

"That's alright. Just had a bit of an argument with him myself."

"What type of argument, Chief?" asked Benson.

"He's still messing around with Ryburn's work, I had to reprimand him for it this time. He's taking the proper regulator to Ryburn now."

"Well he's been warned enough times," Benson said, and nodded, as best he could with his head upside down. "How was it out there? Any damage?"

"No, nothing serious. Cosmetic only. Back to work please Mr Benson."

Benson acknowledged the instruction and returned to his dismantling, but not before making a courtesy call to Ryburn to save him the trip.

CHAPTER 4:

WHAT GOES AROUND...

"What do you want with a nine-gauge, eighty-two millisecond, three-gram burst regulator?" asked McSweeney when Ryburn returned to his workstation; he'd been half way to the central sphere when Benson had called. McSweeney sat in Ryburn's chair like some villainous mastermind lying in wait and holding the regulator hostage.

"I would rather the four-gauge," said Ryburn, then noticed some swelling on McSweeney's face and a trace of blood at his mouth. "What happened to your face?"

McSweeney raised a hand to his lip, winching as he wiped the blood away. "It's nothing."

"Indeed, did you bring me all of the regulators then?"

"I think so, but I'm thinking I'll keep this pretty blue one," he added, holding it aloft like some trophy.

"By all means keep it," said Ryburn with his dismissive flick of the wrist.

"But I thought you needed this blue one?"

"No, the one I need is orange, a four-gauge, I'm surprised you even know what they are."

"But the chief said this one," insisted McSweeney, shaking the part at Ryburn.

"What's this got to do with him?" Why was he even discussing this?

McSweeney shrugged. "Dunno, but he said you needed this one."

"Well I don't. But perhaps we should discuss it with him directly. He assured me that you wouldn't impede my work. But here you are, impeding." He didn't have time for the caretaker's games.

"What have you been telling him about me?" asked McSweeney raising a hand to his lip again.

"Is that his doing?" Ryburn asked.

"No, I slipped on the ladder."

"Best I call him, he'll want to know you're injured and make an entry in some important report, probably."

"Don't be like that Dr Ryburn, I was only playing. Here, take them all." McSweeney surrendered all the different regulators from his pockets onto the desk. "Here's the one you wanted," he said meekly.

Ryburn accepted it suspiciously, not sure that he believed McSweeney could be reduced to a drizzling shit at the mere mention of the boss.

"What do you need it for anyway? They're just junk."

Ryburn let out an annoyed sigh. "Junk to you maybe, but I'm going to use it to manipulate the magnetic properties of the Mercurian ore." He'd known as he said it that his explanation would be beyond McSweeney's comprehension. "You do know what magnetism is, don't you?"

He begun to dismantle the regulator, hands trembling more than he liked.

"Yes I know about magnetism. I know about the positive and negative nature of magnets and all about magnetic fields. And I know a little about sarcasm too."

Ah touché. "Well, the properties of what I refined will defy everything you claim to know…" Ryburn trailed off, concentrating on the regulator, his shaky hands struggling with the fiddly component.

"Do you need help with that?" McSweeney asked.

"What? No I don't," said Ryburn without looking up. As if he'd accept help from him.

"So what is it you are going to do? In English this time?"

Ryburn scoffed "The magnetic attraction seems to negate its own weight."

"You mean you can make it weightless?"

Ryburn stopped, such an elegant explanation, he hadn't thought of it that way, but essentially that is what he was intending to do. "Exactly, and anything attached to it."

"So… you're trying to make flying rocks."

"Essentially, yes."

"Okay Doc, if you say so."

Ryburn looked up from his work with the hope of seeing his excitement mirrored, but instead saw an insincere smile and eyes full of pity. How one would look when humouring a doddering old fool. "Best be on your way, or do I really need to call O'Connor?"

McSweeney begged off, but was barely out the door before getting onto his com to make fun. "Magic flying rocks Benson. You're not going to believe this."

Ryburn carried on, pulling out a roll of wire and beginning to cut small lengths. He arranged them into a circuit with the orange regulator and battery. Capacitors, diodes and all manner of other components from his well-stocked drawers joined the collection. Soon little streams of smoke and fumes were rising from his soldering iron and his crude-looking prototype started to take shape. The battery was the dominant piece, its plates removed and wires soldered directly to the nodes, while a circuit board was attached to the regulator. It wasn't his best work by any means, but was hopefully enough to prove his theory. He checked all his connectors to be sure nothing was out of place or cross-wired before plugging it into his workstation. There were some minor flaws in the circuit, output amounts and chard seepage were out, but he made the adjustments to compensate. A few calculations told him 2.4 grams of Mercurian ore were needed.

"That's a very small amount," he said aloud, questioning the figure.

The cogs of his brain ticked it over, it was right, but he didn't have a cutting tool precise enough for such a small shaving. He checked each of his drawers, slamming them shut in turn. He knew who'd have one and he downed his ever present drink to give him strength.

O'Connor climbed the ladder to the top deck of the central sphere. Before he could close the book on Ryburn's botched docking, the station's angle of rotation needed to be checked. "No external damage Mr Benson. It didn't hit with enough speed."

"Yeah, you said," said Benson.

"I came in using airlock-B, all seemed okay."

"Oh, I wasn't sure it was safe," said Benson. "Chief, I must insist that we leave it be, close it up and stick with airlock-A until we're sure. Logs are showing all sorts of false activity."

"Yes, good idea," said O'Connor, fussing about the terminal.

"I'll cycle our access codes too. Maybe the airlock has it locked in memory and something's causing it to trip."

"Yes, fine," said O'Connor.

"I'll put a delay on it too, just to be safe," said Benson.

"Yes, whatever you think is best. And tell McSweeney to stop messing about with the space suits. He's only gone and moved all the suits over to B."

"That's a good one," Benson said with a smile.

O'Connor didn't share his amusement. "He's not as funny as he thinks he is. His little pranks will get him into serious trouble one of these days.

"Yes, Chief."

O'Connor checked their rotational angle and orbit. Before the decommissioning all sorts of self-correcting systems would have been running, but they were long gone. The data showed all was okay, the station's orbit had not changed, the angular spin was within tolerance. The worst thing was that it was exactly as Ryburn had said.

"Why are the external scanners focused in so close?"

"Something Dr Ryburn was doing, looking for his 'space nothing' anomaly from this morning," mumbled Benson. He was holding his cutting tool between his teeth, freeing his hands to wrestle with a stubborn hinge.

"And their frequency is all wrong too," said O'Connor, shaking his head. What the hell was he thinking? "He's only gone and rendered them useless."

O'Connor reset them. The warning was immediate, so quick in fact he almost ignored it as a misread. A gravity captured object, one of the landers Ryburn had used to slow his hopper, was being tracked as a potential collision threat.

The orbital projection showed its calculated trajectory. His eyes flicked over to Benson, who was hard at work; even so he angled the screens away to protect this new information. He had to find out what the risk was. The external feeds would show what had happened during Ryburn's bungled collection; those were always recording. He cycled back to the hopper's approach, both landers were visible in its tight grasp. The footage was a frame every two seconds, enough to get the idea of what had happened. He watched Ryburn's improvised braking manoeuvre, then watched the landers detach and shoot off in separate directions. He followed the inner lander along its path for several more shots. The frame showed a flash. He cycled it backwards for a closer look but the frame looked corrupt, a thick line of white imperfection intersected the image, offering no clues as to what had happened. The next frame showed the beginnings of an explosion and then a trajectory change.

"Everything okay, Chief?" asked Benson startling O'Connor. He'd managed to get right up behind him without a sound.

"Yeah, looks okay," O'Connor lied. There was no sense worrying the crew just yet, not until he knew what to worry them with. He needed Ryburn's expertise on this one, and no doubt he'd have to pay for that. Ryburn's voice suddenly crackled through Benson's com.

"Benson, are you there?" he asked.

"I'm here. And I have the chief with me. What can we do for you, Dr Ryburn?"

O'Connor subtly closed down the tracking programmes whilst Benson was distracted.

"How much of the crafting floor is left?" Ryburn asked.

"Not much to be honest, what is it you need now?" replied Benson.

"Are there any fine-scale cutting torches anywhere?"

"We have something suitable Dr Ryburn," said O'Connor, loud enough to carry through the com. "I'll bring it to you now. We need to talk about your lander dramatics anyway. I'll explain in a moment. O'Connor out." He snatched up Benson's cutter from the bench and headed for the ladder.

"About the airlocks. I'll cycle the access codes yeah?" Benson called after him.

"Whatever you think is best. I'll get the details off you later though," O'Connor called back, already disappearing down the hatch.

Lander. O'Connor had said lander and he wasn't one to mix up names or terminology. If he said lander he meant lander. It sounded ominous to Ryburn as he waited for O'Connor to arrive. The beginning of a new game perhaps? 0-0.

"Dr Ryburn," said O'Connor from the doorway.

"Chief O'Connor," said Ryburn, noting the formal address.

"You wish to speak to me about the landers?"

O'Connor stepped into the door, light footed, with his back to the wall. "Umm, yes I did but it can wait for now."

"Okay?" Couldn't have been that important. "You did bring it, didn't you?" he asked, seeing a distinct lack of cutting torch. O'Connor's blank face didn't help; neither did the sudden look of panic.

"I'm sorry Dr Ryburn, I've gone and left it behind. I'll be right back..." He slipped out in the same peculiar, wall-hugging fashion he had entered.

"And you say *I'm* losing my mind?" shouted Ryburn after him, sipping his drink, not really knowing how to score that particular volley.

The sudden knock at the door made him jump.

"I'm sorry to startle you, Dr Ryburn? Is everything okay?" said O'Connor, looking amused, not sorry at all.

"Yes yes, everything is fine. I didn't expect you so quickly" said Ryburn. *How long he had been staring at the bubbles in his glass?*

"It's a quick walk from the central sphere."

"Yes, quite right. I guess I dozed off," said Ryburn, shaking away the cobwebs.

"You must have," said O'Connor, making a point of staring at the empty glass. "I have a cutter for you, as requested. It is the finest precision we have."

"Excellent, thank you for bringing it to me. Still not found your communicator then?" said Ryburn as he took the cutter.

"No, not yet," said O'Connor as he caressed the empty space on his arm "I don't know what I've done with it."

"I'm sure it will turn up," said Ryburn as he opened the protective covering on the cutting tool, exposing the contact edge. He squeezed the trigger and watched the cutting surface protrude then felt the vibration and gentle hum as the synthetic diamond spun up to its cutting speed. *Filthy, did the choppers ever clean their tools?*

"Dr Ryburn, we have a situation," O'Connor said.

"Oh yes," said Ryburn, picking up his brick of Mercurian and looking it over for the best end to cut his piece from.

"I need to speak to you about one of your landers," said O'Connor.

"You have all the information now, then?"

"Yes you could say that. One of them has been caught in orbit."

The cutter was not loud, but Ryburn ignored him anyway. O'Connor repeated himself, much louder than was necessary.

"I *said* your lander's been caught in orbit!"

This got Ryburn's attention at last. He stopped cutting. "You wouldn't be telling me this unless it's a concern, would you?"

"We caught it on sensors, but lost sight of it as it went behind the planet."

"That's not possible, you're referring to the landers I used for braking… yes?" Not waiting for O'Connor to confirm he continued. "One would have entered a steep descent into the planet and burned up, the other cast out into space."

"Well, normally I would agree with you completely and defer immediately to your expertise on the matter…"

"But," Ryburn said.

"However," said O'Connor "the data cannot be discounted. It's in an orbit and it's going to hit us."

"Ha, rubbish. Nice try through, full marks for effort." 1-0 to him. Ryburn returned to his cutting, shaking his head. There was no way; the lander's angle of descent was too great. If O'Connor had the even the slightest understanding he wouldn't be bothering with this charade.

"Please tell me the data is wrong then," said O'Connor.

"Your data is wrong," Ryburn fired back instantly. "Can I please return to my work?"

"You can't complete your work when we're all dead," said O'Connor softly, gesturing to the displays. "May I?"

Ryburn acknowledged the request with a slight nod. *Might as well get this over with.*

"Load external visual feed and spatial data from the docking today, then play." The visual feed was comprised of many external cameras allowing a decent panoramic view from the station. The spatial data took the information captured and translated it into a three- dimensional map. The display started with the hopper's shaky approach.

"I don't need to see this, I know it wasn't perfect," said Ryburn, wondering if this little dance was just to show how bad his docking had been.

The arms of the hopper extended and each lander fired up before being set free, flying away on their separate paths.

"Angles are too strong. What is it you are hoping to show me?" said Ryburn, folding his arms, unimpressed.

But what happened next explained why O'Connor was seeking his council. The lander in question changed direction, from the steep decline to skimming along the curve of the planet.

"Impossible," scoffed Ryburn, but leaned forward with interest all the same.

"That's not all I'm afraid." O'Connor loaded up the stop gap frames from the cameras. He cycled through them, showing the landers detach, the odd white distortion and the explosion. The single frame made the explosion seem to hang in space longer than zero atmosphere would ever allow.

"Oh my god," gasped Ryburn. "The chances of that happening are billions to one. Trillions to one even."

"What was that explosion?"

"What remained of the solid state oxygen I would guess. The protective shielding must have been breached somehow. Cycle back just before the explosion.... There, that white thing. What is that?"

"Digital distortion. I'd say."

They flicked back and forth between the images.

"Yes, I'd say so too," said Ryburn, not entirely convinced, but what other explanation could there be for it?

There was more to O'Connor's show and tell. He wasn't going to let the scientist off the hook that easily.

"Filter down to last thirty minutes and show final image of the lander," he said, keeping an eye on Ryburn just to make sure he was paying attention. He loaded up the orbital tracking programme, trying to avoid getting too close to Ryburn's breath. *Bloody hell, how many had he had?* "Using available data, show the orbit of the lander and overlay the orbital path of the station."

A classic wire frame representation of Neith set against the murky coloured Venus appeared on screen. A dotted line mapped out their slow orbit and a small blip represented the lander with one of its own.

"Assume both maintain current speeds and trajectory, calculate out twenty two days."

The lines of predicted orbit began to load, one dot at a time. The station's orbit was uneventful, a perfect circle. The lander's was quite different, oval shaped, with the outer point rotating around the planet with each pass. The projection on the screen took the shape of a flower, filling in one petal at a time. On the final pass, the two orbits intersected.

"We have twenty two days until it hits us," said O'Connor, reiterating what the simulation had shown. A collision just as the lander would be reaching maximum acceleration for its elongated loop around the planet; the worst possible time.

"What is the margin of error on this?" asked Ryburn.

"Not enough" said O'Connor, knowing an answer wasn't needed. "Dr Ryburn, can you please tell me this is wrong?"

Please tell me it's wrong.

Ryburn took over the controls. He rechecked the data, and checked it again before offering his expert opinion on the matter. "We're fucked."

O'Connor sighed. "Yes were are. I'm going to request to abort and we all leave early. I don't see an alternative. Can I count on your assistance with the preparations for the final phase?"

"I must finish this, it's very important," said Ryburn shaking his head. Tearing off a strip of sticky tape with his teeth, he used it to fix a small slice of freshly cut iron onto the top of what appeared to be a torn open battery with the top exposed and a load of random circuitry jerry rigged around it.

O'Connor stood in disbelief; he'd clearly given the drunken fool way too much credit. "Right then, you carry on with... carry on with… this." The appropriate words escaped him, although he had plenty of inappropriate ones to hand, or a clenched fist.

"Once I get this working. I'm going to need the rest of the ore processed into Mercurian iron, I hate to ask but if you or your team could assist me just this once. I'll be sure to mention you in the accreditation," said Ryburn as he inspected his assembled junk.

"Accreditation? You think any of us want our names attached to this shit pile you've landed us in? All we want is to get home in one piece." This crazy old fool was talking as if he'd just invented the wheel whilst taping junk together. Actual junk!

"This is important, damn it!" shouted Ryburn. "Your little chop contract is meaningless against what I'm trying to do. You are all are meaningless compared with what I'm trying to do."

"You may be worthless. But my team is worth a hundred of you, you drunken old bastard." He slapped the drink out of Ryburn's hand, sending it shattering against the far wall.

Ryburn just smiled, then casually retrieved another glass and synthochol pouch from his desk drawer, like nothing had happened. "Was there anything else, O'Connor?"

O'Connor couldn't think straight, he was so pissed off. It took all his self-control to not slap that shit-eater grin from Ryburn's face. "I need to get a report away."

He fumed as he turned to the door.

"Very good, now if you don't mind, I'd like to finish my prototype," said Ryburn flicking his dismissive gesture to the door.

"You don't even fucking care do you?" O'Connor turned back "Your crazy obsessions have done this and you don't even care. If you'd done your fucking job properly in the first place you wouldn't even be here now. This is on you. This whole sorry mess is all on you."

He loomed over Ryburn as he delivered his tirade but Ryburn seemed to pay him no mind. His knuckles were white from clenching them so hard; he had to get away from Ryburn immediately.

"If you please," said Ryburn pointing toward the open door again.

"Don't push it," O'Connor warned "You will let me know when you get this junk of yours working won't you? Shame for us all to die for nothing."

O'Connor stormed from the room. Out in the corridor he stood in the cooler air for a moment to regain his composure, resting an arm up against the external wall and pressing his head into his empty forearm. The cold edge of his communicator would have come in handy just then. Deep breath followed deep breath and his calm returned. Then the shame... followed by the guilt for almost letting his temper overtake him. He'd overreacted and Ryburn almost received both barrels. He should really apologise to the sorry old fool.

"I'm sorry about that, I over reacted and let me temper get the better of me. I offer my apologies" said O'Connor stepping back into the room.

"Apology accepted, but I do need to get this done," said Ryburn, not even looking up. The unpleasant end to the previous conversation was water off a duck's back for Ryburn. His skin was thicker than the hull and he'd even scored himself points for driving O'Connor to such a state.

"Do you have everything you need for completing your prototype?"

"I'm fine for now."

"Is that the prototype for your engine?" asked O'Connor, still looking unimpressed.

"Yes this is it. Not much to look at, I know," said Ryburn,

sensing the disbelief, "but if everything plays out like my simulations there will be enough energy to…"

"Generate a magnetic field?"

"Exactly."

"And it will be strong enough to move the entire station?"

"Ha! That would be an impressive first implementation. But quite impossible I'd have to say. I honestly hadn't considered something so grand. Perhaps one day it could be accomplished," said Ryburn, gazing off into the distance.

"Perhaps sooner is better than later on this one. I'm not putting much faith in an early pickup."

"What makes you say that?" Ryburn asked.

"Just call it an educated guess."

"Can you explain your educated guess if you please? Some of us aren't as familiar with caretaker collection cycles."

If this was a new game he wasn't buying in.

"Well, this is the way of it," O'Connor said. "You have three caretakers who, let's be honest, are right at the bottom of the priority list."

Ryburn smirked.

"Perhaps second only to a disgraced scientist."

Ryburn nodded. Well played.

"If you were them, would you pick us up?" It was the economics of business in space. Everything had a cost attached. The reason the planned rendezvous point was with a particle collection vessel was because it was heading back to Earth anyway and wouldn't be going out of its way. They wouldn't wait, not even slow down.

"But there's more you need to know," said O'Connor, again with a hint of reluctance. "Our axis has changed. We're slowly spinning toward the planet.

"Which means?" Ryburn asked, he knew what O'Connor was getting at – just spit it out.

"Entering final phase will have us pointing in the wrong direction; we will end up going the wrong way."

"I see. And you didn't think to mention this before? You just wanted to soften the original blow by not explaining how badly I've doomed us?"

"This wasn't… isn't your fault," said O'Connor.

"That doesn't matter now, it's done," said Ryburn. Apportioning blame wouldn't make the situation go away; it was all his anyway. "I'm definitely going to need more of this iron refined. Perhaps a working prototype will rebalance the scales in our favour and secure us a lift home."

"And you have the right regulator don't you?" asked O'Connor, sifting through the components on the desk. He picked up the blue regulator and read aloud its configuration "Nine-gauge, eighty-two millisecond, three-gram regulator… Dr Ryburn this one's the nine-gauge."

"Yes it is, but it's of no use to me… nor any of the others for that matter. You can take them back." He motioned for O'Connor to help himself.

"Thanks, but I'll leave them here just in case you need them, especially this blue one, it looks very useful."

"What did you do with the rest of the ore?" asked O'Connor as Ryburn continued inspecting his prototype.

"In the work-sphere. Listen, I'd prefer it if you or Benson handled this one. I think McSweeney may feel the need for some ill-placed comedy."

"Yes of course, I'll handle this one myself." O'Connor smiled "But if McSweeney were trying to be funny and hide the ore, where do you think he'd put it?"

"Yes, I've been thinking on that one since you mentioned it earlier. It would have to be somewhere obvious and familiar to achieve optimal annoyance. If I were the target of the prank, he'd stash in here or back in my sleeping quarters"

Ryburn's old room was an awkward subject matter. When he vacated it he made it very clear what he thought of the caretakers, on their very first meeting. "Arsehole parasites chewing at the station" had been a key phrase.

"Would he have hidden it anywhere else?"

"It has to be right under your nose. Have you looked under the dinner table?" Ryburn joked, but O'Connor was serious, overly so for this hypothetical scenario.

"Interesting," said O'Connor, nodding his head.

"He stashes things in hydroponics too, when he is out of ideas."

"Does he now? Thanks, that's good to know. I'd best leave you to your work, good luck with your experiment, Dr Ryburn. Be sure to let me know when you get it working."

"Jim," said Ryburn, turning to face O'Connor. "You can call me Jim. Dr Ryburn is too formal and Sir Jim a bit strong."

"Very well. Jim," said O'Connor, as if trying the name out for size.

"You've been calling me it all day anyway."

"Really? I hadn't noticed," said O'Connor as he left.

Ryburn swigged the last swallow from his glass then absentmindedly ran his fingers around the rim as he pondered where to start.

"What is the total mass of Neith?" he asked his computer.

O'Connor rehearsed what he would say in his report on his way to the central sphere. Cold hard facts, what had happened and what he was asking for. Keep it short. He wasn't certain if it was the drink, declining mental health or pure stubbornness that prevented Ryburn from grasping the seriousness of what he'd caused. Either way, keeping him preoccupied and out of the way with his ridiculous experiment was for the best. Benson and McSweeney he'd keep on a need to know, until an official response from home put his exit plan into place. No one liked losing money on a contract, least of all those two.

Expendable; the word that kept haunting him. Paranoid or not the economics didn't stack in their favour. It would be a boring couple of weeks drifting out and waiting for the collection vessel, but they had provisions to last.

He grabbed the back of the chair and dragged it over to the communications terminal tucked away in the corner. He would have preferred to stand but the awkward height in the corner wouldn't allow it.

"Do we have line of sight with Earth or any of the Earth relays?" he asked the terminal. The relays were a collection of satellites that orbited the Earth and the Moon in high orbit.

"Negative," displayed the text.

"What about Mars?"

"Mars confirmed."

That would have to do, his message would be sent to Mars, most likely one of the Deimos satellites, and bounced onto Earth. The terminal would calculate the targeting. They would be aiming at a moving target from millions of kilometres away that, because of the distance and speed of light, was not where it was when you saw it and would be even further away by the time your band got there. Just thinking about it was hard enough.

"We have a situation here. There were complications docking the final hopper. It hit us at speed. Hull integrity unaffected but debris caught in orbit will now collide with us in a little over three weeks. I formally request to enter final phase ahead of schedule and abort the salvage operation. Can you confirm a revised collection please? Please encrypt reply to me, I don't wish to concern the crew just yet." He played back his message, always surprised at hearing his own voice recorded. It never sounded like him; it sounded more like his dad. The message would do, though. All fact, no opinion nor blame, short and to the point. He hit send and it was gone.

The data band travelled at the speed of light but with the extra distance involved in bouncing off Mars it would take around fifteen minutes to arrive then another fifteen to get the reply. Being the middle of the night Earth time at Lunarbase HQ didn't help either: the corporate decisions makers would be all tucked up cosy in bed. He'd most likely get his answer in morning. Expendable.

"Everything okay, Chief?" said Benson, again sneaking up behind without a sound and again startling O'Connor. One thing they got right when the built Neith was the goddamned soundproofing.

"Benson! You have to stop doing that. How are you getting on with that upper deck?" *Did he overhear? How much did he overhear?*

"I'm a little bit behind but nothing at risk yet. Why do you ask?"

"Because I need to know, usual status update. If that is okay with you of course?" Putting a little bass in his voice and re-establishing the chain of command.

Benson stood a little straighter. "Nothing new to report. Air pressure measures are still faulting out, as I mentioned earlier. Do the priority orders still remain the same?"

"What's this about the air pressure?" O'Connor held his eye, but wasn't sure if he was reading confusion or suspicion.

"It's still faulting up," he said finally and after further hesitation asked, "Are you sure everything is okay, Chief?"

He knew. He must have overheard. "If you have something to say, Mr Benson, just spit it out"

"He was only messing around. He didn't mean to get all up in Ryburn's business, you know what he's like. Nothing serious, he just likes to lighten the mood. He goes a bit far sometimes, but don't log a report about him," said Benson at breakneck speed.

"I'm sorry, what?" asked O'Connor.

"You were logging an official complaint about McSweeney weren't you?"

Benson's concern for his crew mate was honourable, but McSweeney's trivial little jokes were the furthest thing from O'Connor's mind.

"No I wasn't. I was just making a... a personal entry." That was too close a call.

"Oh good" said Benson, with a very wide smile. "I was worried that another mark against him would be enough for him to lose some of his fee."

"Don't worry about that, Benson. Forfeiting pay is only for serious shit. He may bitch and moan but Ryburn has no say in such things." O'Connor dragged the chair back to the table and sat down.

Benson smiled and sat opposite. "That's good to know, Chief"

"Throw me over a bag would you please?" said O'Connor, motioning to the food cupboard and clapping his hands together for a catch.

"And one for me too," said McSweeney stepping out from a bulkhead.

"How long have you been there?" asked O'Connor.

"Long enough to hear Benson begging for my job"

"I wasn't begging," said Benson "What have you done to yourself now?"

"Nothing, just a little accident," said McSweeney wiping at his lip

"You need to be more careful. Accidents tend to follow you around, don't they?" said O'Connor with a raised eyebrow.

"Funny," said McSweeney making a show of moving his chair as far away from O'Connor as the small table allowed.

Benson handed out green meal bags. O'Connor opened his and slopped out the contents into his bowl. A puff of powder and the unmistakable smell of stale egg wafted up and hit him in the face. The crew had exhausted every bad food joke in existence and now resorted to just staring sadly and disappointedly at the nasty food substitute whilst longing for something else.

"How do the food tech guys manage to make it dried out and sloppy at the same time?" asked Benson.

"You got fake egg, count yourself lucky" said McSweeney snatching up the tomato sauce bottle before Benson could get his big bear hands on it. "I got some sort of fake meat." He put his nose over his bowl then flinched away. "Or maybe it's fake fish"

"After you with the sauce please?" said Benson

"Go easy with it, we don't want to be eating this stuff straight," said O'Connor, keeping a cautious eye on McSweeney.

McSweeney handed Benson the bottle, pulling back a few times and leaving Benson's hand hanging, the way he always did.

"Go easy, I said," repeated O'Connor with a little more urgency as dollop after dollop dropped out into Benson's bowl. "Benson, you may as well drink it from the fucking bottle." He regretted his words immediately, he wanted them back as soon as he had said them.

"Don't worry, Chief, I got a little supply tucked away," said Benson. "I gave up some personal space to get some in; it's for all of us, Chief, not just me. I worked a contract once where we ran out. Never again."

"Good man," said O'Connor apologetically, "I should have known you wouldn't be ripping through the sauce without a backup. Next time I'm asked who I want on my crew I'll put you down for sure and I'll even increase your space allocation."

That eased his guilt a touch and seeing the prideful smile return to Benson's face eased it some more.

"You know, when I get back home," said Benson, "I'm going to get those food tech guys to eat some of this..." He raised a spoonful into the air and let it splat back into the bowl, "… and see how they like it."

O'Connor smiled, the idea of force feeding some white coated lab technician seemed a fitting punishment.

"That may be sooner than you think," McSweeney announced "We're leaving early. Isn't that right, Chief?"

"Drop it," O'Connor warned with a deadly dose of eye contact.

"Drop what?" said McSweeney with feigned innocence, ruined by the slop dribbling down his chin. "We're getting out of here early, isn't that what you were just saying?"

"You need to drop it," O'Connor warned again.

"Three weeks ahead of schedule, isn't that what you said?" said McSweeney

"We aren't ahead though, we're behind, what do you mean finishing early?" asked Benson, worry and confusion all over his face.

"Ask him," said McSweeney, grinning into his bowl continuing to eat.

O'Connor slammed his fist down. "Three week fine for insubordination."

That sure as hell wiped the grin from his face

"Three fucking weeks?" said McSweeney standing up and knocking over his chair.

"You want five? I told you to drop it."

"How much is Ryburn getting for that hopper stunt?" said McSweeney leaning over the table, failing to be scary.

"Sit down," said Benson softly.

"Ryburn isn't part of our contract," said O'Connor.

"I want to know what you are going to do about him," said McSweeney, with his pointing finger at the ready.

"Do about what exactly?" said O'Connor, placing his palms on the table ready to stand up if required, a subtle warning for McSweeney to back down.

"McSweeney, can you sit down?" Benson repeated.

"All that business you were talking about just now, collisions and leaving early. Tell the truth or…" McSweeney mirrored O'Connor placing his hands on the table leaning right across into his face.

"Or what? You want to take a swing at me?" said O'Connor.

"That's more your style isn't it, but only when there's no witnesses?"

"Can you sit down, please?" Benson tried again, putting his hand on McSweeney's arm.

"Get off me," said McSweeney, jerking his arm away.

O'Connor jumped to his feet, causing McSweeney to flinch backwards and out of reach.

"That's enough," Benson shouted slamming his fist down on the table, crumpling the leg and sending everything to the floor.

"What the hell is up between you two?" he demanded, before embarrassment took over and he began busying himself with the table leg. The other two just stood in stunned silence, looking at him. O'Connor had never seen him react like that before, he was at loss for words.

"Let me help with that," said O'Connor to Benson, and McSweeney started clearing up the mess splatted about the floor. The leg had buckled in the middle, but once bent into shape the table was usable again, with a slight lean.

"So you overheard my report home?" said O'Connor, it was time to come clean. "Yes, we're going to be leaving early."

"Three weeks early, I knew it," said McSweeney.

"Three weeks?" asked Benson, "we can't finish early, Chief. If anything we could do with an *extra* three weeks"

"We aren't leaving three weeks early," said O'Connor shaking his head "We need to leave in three weeks."

"Three weeks," said McSweeney. "What the fuck?"

"*Why* the fuck?" added Benson.

"We have to leave early because of some complications arising from the hopper docking."

"Whatever it is I'm sure we can fix it, Chief," said Benson. "Panels are still working and we have loads of power in the tanks. Air is good. Why we have to finish up early? How bad can it be?"

"One of the landers Ryburn used for braking has gotten caught in orbit. It's going to hit us as it sling-shots around," said O'Connor, pausing to let the news sink in. O'Connor saw the contrasting emotions on his crew mates' faces. Benson, a disappointed acceptance. McSweeney- just anger.

"The old bastard has cost our full fee and we won't get all our salvage money either, I bet."

"It gets worse," said O'Connor, dreading what he had to say next. "The collection vessel won't be in at the rendezvous until the original date so..."

"It's a float and hope?" said Benson looking down at the table.

"Fuck," said McSweeney, staring off into empty space.

"I'm afraid so." O'Connor let the silence hold before he spoke again. "We'll know what our options are once we get the reply. I'm thinking we should expect one in around eight hours, assuming that they send it straight away, that is. Until then it's work as normal. Any questions?"

"I thought you were just being cheap, when I overheard you," said McSweeney. "I thought you were using Ryburn's craziness as an excuse to rip us off."

That caught O'Connor off guard, and judging by Benson's gasp he wasn't alone.

"What the hell do you mean by that?" said O'Connor.

"I want a promise that we won't get short changed on our fees," said McSweeney.

"Okay, you know that's not my call. I can't see our weekly fee being touched, but the salvage amount will be down."

"And what are you going to do about Ryburn?" said McSweeney.

"With regards to what exactly?" asked O'Connor, knowing that a blame game wouldn't change their situation.

"Oh, I don't know. How about him costing us time and money? How about him messing up our contract from day one? And now his magic fucking rocks. Have you heard what he is trying to do with them?" McSweeney stood up straight and official, then said. "I want to make a formal complaint against Dr Ryburn."

"Sit down," said Benson.

"No I won't," said McSweeney, still on his soap box. "How long before he actually kills us? His hopper came very close, now his lander's going to finish the job. Don't you think it has gone on long enough? His magic rocks. That panic call after another one of his hallucinations. Something needs to be done about him."

"What hallucinations?" asked O'Connor.

"The 'nothing' he saw out in space," said Benson.

"Oh, from early this morning?" O'Connor asked, then nodded.

"And the second one."

"There was a second one?"

Benson and McSweeney shared a confused look.

"He commed everyone earlier," said Benson, inviting O'Connor to remember. "You replied to him."

"I haven't found my com yet. How could I have replied?" He held up his empty wrist. "I was never even on the call." He turned to McSweeney. "Sure it wasn't someone impersonating me, again?"

"Not this time, I was standing right here with Benson when you replied," said McSweeney.

"That's right, Chief, he was," Benson concurred.

"When was this exactly?" asked O'Connor scratching his head, Benson wouldn't lie.

An awful screeching noise came through Benson and McSweeney's wrist coms. All three men tried to cover their ears and distance themselves from the piercing and painful sound. Then it stopped, leaving behind the burned in echo ringing in O'Connor's ears. As his hearing returned, the sound of Ryburn's voice through Benson's com slowly became clear.

"Benson, are you reading? Benson are you there?"

"I'm here, Ryburn. Did you hear that too?" said Benson quietly, as if protecting them all from any unneeded volume.

"Yes. Apologies, I tried to call everyone, and that was the result."

"Must be faulty too," Benson whispered to his two crew mates.

"Is O'Connor with you?" Ryburn asked

"I'm here. What it is?" said O'Connor, just loud enough to be heard.

"O'Connor, a moment of your time please."

"What is it Ryburn?" replied O'Connor tersely.

"You requested that I keep you informed of my progress," Ryburn said.

"This really isn't a good time Ryburn," O'Connor shot back, dismissing the lunacy.

"I've got it working," said Ryburn, his excitement coming through as clear as his words.

"Okay Ryburn, I'll be along shortly. O'Connor out." He gestured at Benson to end the com.

"You really going to see it are you?" asked McSweeney in disbelief.

"I'm going to talk to him again. I thought his work would keep him occupied long enough for our preparations. I'm going to confine him to the workstation. And you are to stay away from him too." At that he stood up. "Then I'm turning in for the night. We have a lot to do tomorrow."

The chief left the room and after Benson was sure he had gone he asked McSweeney, "You don't have his com do you?"

"No Mr Benson, I do not," said McSweeney, in a very convincing imitation of O'Connor.

"That's getting good. Does that mean you do have it?"

"I don't, honest" said McSweeney, with a caricature look of innocence.

"You know you say that a lot, and you're usually lying."

"Yeah, well this time I mean it." He playfully nudged his crew mate. "Reckon the chief has caught whatever is wrong with Ryburn's head? That would explain a few things."

"Ha, yeah maybe." Benson joked back, but held him in a sideways squint.

"You were standing right there when Ryburn called us earlier and we both heard him reply. How else would you explain that?"

"Maybe he used a fixed com point?" suggested Benson, half-heartedly.

"Then how would he have heard the call? He's up to something and it has something to do with his com. And something to do with Ryburn." McSweeney nodded suspiciously to himself, as if starting to make a picture from all the disjointed pieces.

"What? Ryburn and his magic rocks, maybe you've caught it now?" Benson nudged back.

"Yeah, unless that's just what they want us to think. Chief's playing us. Keeps threatening my fee and getting violent. Protecting Ryburn. No, this is all wrong."

"You gotta stop these stories of violence," Benson insisted. "You know he's not like that."

"Not with you, Colossus, but how do you explain this?" said McSweeney pointing at his lip.

"I thought he just held you against the wall and shouted at you?" said Benson, recalling the ridiculous story from that morning.

"No that was earlier, I'm talking about just before, and he punched me."

"Sure he did. But just stop it though, be easier on all of us."

"What do you think he's up to then?"

"Probably nothing; he was just outside wasn't he? Maybe his air tank ratio wasn't set properly. That might cause memory problems," said Benson, grabbing at straws.

"Okay fine, but he says he lost his com! You and I both heard him. It was his voice, from his com."

"Maybe he found it?"

"What? And forgot about it again cause of the bad air? Come on Benson, wake up. They're up to something."

"Yeah maybe," said Benson, his brow creasing with thought.

"And what about how he snapped at you over the ketchup? That wasn't normal was it?" He had his pointing finger out "Why do you keep asking if he's okay if everything's okay?"

Benson offered no reply, he was thinking about the way the chief dismissed his concerns then later claimed to know nothing about it. A picture of his own was forming, and maybe it wasn't so dissimilar to McSweeney's. Did he have his com earlier?

"Fine!" said McSweeney, "I'm signing out, early start tomorrow in hydroponics."

Benson ignored the joke; all the mornings were early starts.

"Yeah catch you later. I want to have that all squared away before I finish," said Benson motioning a wrench over to the heap, he thought better while he worked anyway.

CHAPTER 5: JUMPING AT SHADOWS

O'CONNOR REACHED RYBURN'S workstation and took a deep breath before knocking on the half opened door. He wondered what Ryburn had actually built. He did not know what he was expecting to see; certainly nothing credible, but a part of him was curious to see what the next evolution of Ryburn's craziness would be. Looking through the doorway, he saw Ryburn with a huge smile on his face that seemed more like a rictus. This was the second time today he had seen Ryburn smile in such a manner. Everyone smiles at one time or another but, including today, he had only seen him really smile like that twice the entire time he had been on the station. It took a second or so for O'Connor to stop staring at that unnatural smile and focus on what Ryburn was looking at over the top of his glasses, floating in the middle of the room.

"O'Connor, do come in," said Ryburn, nodding as he directed the chief's attention to the device.

O'Connor saw the small exposed end of a battery, a mishmash of circuitry, and the bright orange regulator that stood out against the rest of the prototype. The lengths of wire that were attached to the contraption gave the impression of a tether connecting it to the terminal. He had to hand it to crazy old Ryburn, whatever it was he was looking at did appear to be floating in mid-air. The little device was letting out no sound at all, at least nothing within the human range. It wasn't giving out any indication of heat either; the fact that the crude construction had not melted was ample testament to that. There was a faint smell in the air, not quite burning and not quite electrical either.

"What am I looking at, Dr Ryburn?" he asked, trying to take in everything he was seeing.

"What?" Ryburn looked puzzled. "What do you mean?"

"I don't understand what it is you are showing me."

"You are looking at an attraction to a chard-generated magnetic field," said Ryburn. O'Connor should have guessed that Ryburn would enjoy the position of knowledge, even more so when he had someone wanting that knowledge from him.

"You see," he continued, "once I refined the ore into iron I found that the magnetic properties increased and my theorised ratio of chard to mass for acceleration was-"

"Sorry Ryburn," O'Connor interrupted "I don't need to know the science behind it all, and to be honest," he continued, letting out a little laugh, "I wouldn't understand it anyway."

Ryburn added a little laugh too, but to O'Connor it didn't sound real. He guessed Ryburn didn't like his lecture being interrupted.

"Okay then, from the controls here I'm changing the amount of chard energy used to generate the magnetic field, the more chard the stronger the field and the greater the attraction."

"So why is it just floating?" O'Connor asked.

"I'm using just enough chard to counter the weight of the hardware and the gravity," Ryburn said, motioning to the workstation. The lower display on the workstation showed a single rectangular dial. "If I lower the amount slowly the unit will descend." He moved the slider and the floating device slowly started to drop. "Increasing it," he continued and moved the slider back up, "will make it go up again."

The contraption rose silently, resuming its original position.

The potential significance of what O'Connor was seeing began to sink in, "This is what you meant by it being an engine? Can this be used on a larger scale?"

"Yes to both, as long as you can get enough Mercurian iron and a large enough chardage."

O'Connor leaned back against the door frame. Could this in fact be a major breakthrough? He was beginning to think that maybe Ryburn was not so crazy after all.

"There are limitations, however," said Ryburn. "We mustn't get ahead of ourselves. You are limited by the structural integrity of anything you attach to the Mercurian iron. However strong you make the magnetic field, the structural strength of the entire unit will need to be even stronger."

"What happens if it's not?" said O'Connor. There was always a "but".

"It will rip itself apart at the weakest points. You see, the overall relationship would be exponentially greater-"

"Okay!" said O'Connor, cutting him off again so as not to be buried with the science. "Can you do more than float batteries?"

"Oh much more, don't worry about that..." Ryburn left the sentence hanging in the air. "Theoretically," he continued, "we have just enough ore to refine enough Mercurian iron to move the station."

"What?" said a shocked O'Conner, "Move it where?"

"Out of harm's way of course, I've done some initial calculations and I think that we may-"

"I don't really have time for the theoretical argument, Dr Ryburn," said O'Connor, putting up a hand to stop him.

"I'm sorry?" said Ryburn, looking confused.

"This is nonsense, Dr Ryburn. Flying batteries is one thing. But moving the station with a fist full of rocks is something else."

Ryburn looked very confused. "You think lunarbase will help us now?"

"Look, I believe that you think you can do it, and that's fine.

But I'm going to wait, they won't just leave us here!"

"So you don't think we're expendable now?" said Ryburn, putting down the hand-held touch-pad O'Connor guessed was probably full of calculations he wouldn't understand.

"I should have a band back from lunarbase by morning. We'll know what is what then."

"You think it will do any good, waiting for their reply?" asked Ryburn.

"They'll at least confirm what our options are." And he'd rather trust that than some crazy idea Ryburn had. Where had he gotten the notion to move the station in the first place? "I'll speak with the others and make sure they are aware of the importance of your work. They won't give you any trouble," O'Connor said. At least this kept Ryburn out of the way.

"They were already supposed to understand the importance of my work!" said Ryburn.

"Reiterating the fact wouldn't hurt though," added O'Connor, "especially to McSweeney. We have to think positively… that they won't leave us here."

"Hmm, interesting," muttered Ryburn under his breath

"And what is that supposed to mean?" said O'Connor, taking immediate offence at the throwaway comment. He was doing his best to accommodate Ryburn, after all.

"You, O'Connor, you are what is interesting. You swing hot and cold so quickly, one minute you are interested in what I'm doing, the next you couldn't care less. One minute lunarbase is going to arrange our collection, the next we're on our own."

O'Connor just smiled a "you have clearly lost your mind" smile. He sniffed the air searching for a hint of synthochol, which might explain Ryburn's mood. All he could smell was the faint peculiar odour from the device. He was not sure where this little rant had come from. Crazy old fool, only heard what he wanted to, that much was obvious.

"Nothing much we can do now anyway. We should have a reply back by morning," he repeated, deciding it was not the time to discuss the crew's frustration; he would wait until he was a bit more coherent.

"Do you want me to stay up working on a solution or not?" said Ryburn, still annoyed. O'Connor got the feeling he was going to work on it regardless. All he could do now was humour him.

"Do whatever you like, Dr Ryburn," replied O'Connor dismissively heading for the door.

"I rechecked our axis," said Ryburn suddenly, "we're still within tolerance."

"Our axis?" asked O'Connor, not understanding.

"The hopper incident. It didn't put us in a spin after all."

"Okay, thanks Ryburn," said O'Connor sarcastically as he left. The comment about the axis was random. Why was Ryburn telling him what he already knew? In fact it was him who told Ryburn that it was okay!

O'Connor instinctively reached for the torch light on his wrist com, but finding his wrist empty he continued in darkness, trailing a hand along the wall to find his way. How many times was he going to reach for his com before it being lost would sink in? *Where the hell was it?*

As he rounded the slow bend of the corridor, the pale glow of the collection hub provided him with the next bastion of light to head for. Ryburn had left in it an awful state. He stopped for a moment to make a mental inventory of any priority salvage from the unit. Now that Ryburn had no further use for it, perhaps he could move it up the schedule. Although, he admitted to himself, the likelihood of that happening was doubtful considering their new circumstances. Even so, he ran the self-cleaning cycle that Ryburn had not bothered to do.

O'Connor had not always been a caretaker but a few unfortunate lapses in his temper had seen him get on the wrong side of his superiors. For too many years now he had been stuck doing these salvage missions. He had been working these high isolation contracts to make amends. One of two more and he'd be back on track.

The flickering green light above the airlock broke through the darkness, offering him his next beacon. He continued to feel his way along using the shells of equipment, which were stacked up along the outer wall all the way from Ryburn's workstation to airlock-B. This meant that despite the fact that he couldn't see his hand in front of his face he was able to walk, although slowly; without the torch he was missing so much.

When O'Connor reached the airlock, he was pleased to see that McSweeney had obviously gotten the message and had tidied up the mess he had left of the airlock prep area. The discarded suits were now nowhere to be seen. There was just a single helmet left out on the bench, which could be forgiven. O'Connor opened the cupboard door.

"Good," he said to himself, the cupboards were no longer stuffed full of space suits, only two were hanging up. There should have been three but he was willing to forgive that too. He left the airlock and continued on his way.

A sudden crashing noise alerted him to something behind him, back along the corridor toward the collection hub. He turned, but the pale white light above the hub gave no clue at all to what had just happened.

"Ryburn? Is that you," he called. The distinct clang of metal on metal was too loud to be nothing. He really missed having his com… and his torch.

"Is that you Ryburn?" he shouted again, but the sound-proofing made his voice sound hollow, an unnatural emptiness in his own ears. "Benson? McSweeney? I don't have a light."

There was no reply; he knew that he would have been heard had anybody been there, the sound-proofing was good but not magic.

"Come on guys, what's going on?" he pleaded with the nothingness. "You want me to fine you a couple of hours work McSweeney?" he hollered toward the collection hub; still no reply. He was not going to be played like this and started walking back towards the hub, determined to get hold of that little creep and give him some of his own medicine. This was one prank too many.

"I'm not in the mood," he shouted. "Have you been hassling Ryburn again?"

Not bothered about getting a reply, he made his way along the corridor, moving very slowly to mask his footsteps, keeping one hand against the wall, with the other checking the empty space in case McSweeney tried to creep past him. The dark was all-consuming except for the white of the hub light, a pale stab into the envelope of blackness. A sudden flicker across the light caused his heart to race.

He quickly spun around as he reached the exact position the figure had been. Nothing. Not wanting to give away his position to McSweeney, he stayed out of the light. They were now on an equal footing since neither of them could see a thing. This was all just a game for McSweeney, but just once he would like to turn a situation around on him and scare the crap out of him instead. McSweeney had got the better of the crew a few times, so many in fact that Benson avoided the poorly lit corridors. But after the nonsense and attitude McSweeney had exhibited today, this time he was going to catch him and make him pay. O'Connor clenched his fist and spun around with his arms high, hoping for an impact. Finding nothing he repeated the action with his feet. He would have loved to catch the little punk, but again his blind swing found empty space.

"I know you're here," he said quietly into the air, "and I will find you."

This had become a game that he didn't want to play and he paced around silently in the darkness for a few moments, throwing the occasional lunging punch and kick at the air hoping to find contact with a face and still expecting McSweeney to jump out and grab him at any moment. There was nothing.

"I don't have time for this!" he shouted. The fun was over and he was getting annoyed. "Are you here or not?"

After a few moments he called again, "Answer me damn it, or I will start making deductions from your fee."

Nothing, nothing at all.

He can't be there he thought to himself and turned back in the direction of the airlock; the red light above, punching that hole in the dark, would show him the direction. He was halfway toward the airlock when the realisation hit him that the light was the wrong colour. Like a shot, he was at full pace sprinting the last few metres but he ran straight into an awkward and lazily placed unit, colliding with it at knee level sending him tumbling over and onto the floor in a heap. He lay on the ground for a moment, considering the stupidity of what he had been doing, jumping at shadows, and chasing phantoms. If it were McSweeney playing silly buggers, he would be gone by now and if he wasn't there no one would have witnessed his embarrassing display.

He struggled back to his feet, and when he finally reached the airlock prep area the light had gone back to green. Another malfunction? Even so, a malfunctioning airlock was extremely dangerous, even with all the fail-safes in place.

He raised his arm in preparation for using his com. He was going to request Benson to run some checks on it, but without the com he was just standing there feeling silently useless. Benson would have turned in for the night now anyway. He would have to check the airlock himself. He opened the inner hatch door, just an inch at first, preparing for decompression, then slowly raising it further into the ceiling. It was safe.

It did not explain the overhead lights though, unless the light was faulty. Occam's razor and all. O'Connor tapped his finger against the wall. He was standing in the doorway sweeping a glance over every corner on the airlock. He didn't know what he was looking for, only that he would know it if he saw it. The displays on the controls were completely blank, even the screen was dead. Usually it would have been displaying valuable information about the environment and, more importantly, it should have been displaying a history of what the airlock had done. However, it wasn't just the screen that was dead. The controls weren't working either. The unit had completely shut itself off.

"Great," he said aloud. This airlock was unusable and probably unsafe to boot. Stepping back through the door, he used the working panel to close the inner door. He punched in the commands to manually lock-seal the door, pronouncing "DELTA OMEGA SEVEN SEVEN TWO" as clearly as possible when it asked for an authority confirmation.

"DENIED" flashed up on the screen

"Damn it." He remembered that Benson changed all the codes, he had not gotten the new code yet. He tapped in the commands for the override, the system should take his personal code and grant him access.

"DENIED" flashed up again.

"What the..." he said, the final word of the sentence drowned out by the thud of his hand against the wall next to the controls. Why wasn't his override code working? He tried again, with the same result. He looked at his empty wrist with disgust, again knowing he couldn't ask Benson for the new codes. There was only one thing to do: fully lock down the airlock. He walked out a little way along the corridor, got down on his knees and pulled the emergency access panel off the wall. Under the panel sat the locking clamps that controlled the emergency release of the entire prep area and airlock. The locking clamps were a last resort; once he pulled the lever the internal and external doors could only then be opened using the emergency explosives charges built into the walls, part of the shedding mechanics of the entire station. He took a deep breath, weighing up his options. The airlock was not behaving, and although the other one wasn't perfect either, this was a liability; too much of a risk to leave as it was. He had to lock it.

O'Connor pulled the lever down and locked the lynch pin. He could hear the charges firing the bolts locking the airlock door into place. The design of the levers meant that he was unable to put the access panel back into place, so he stood up with the panel and walked back over to the airlock. He could hear the liquid being pumped into the door cavities, which warmed to the touch as they filled; they were now locked into place. With a flick of his elbow he discarded the panel onto the bench where it spun like a faltering spinning coin. He left, cursing just about everyone for what had just happened.

After a few steps he could no longer hear the panel rattling on the bench; it had come to rest in the exact spot where he had previously taken note of a helmet being left out… a helmet that wasn't there anymore.

McSweeney couldn't sleep. He was concerned about his fee and angry with the chief for everything that had happened that day. He knew the chief did not believe him when he denied involvement with the missing communicator or playing with airlocks or messing around with Ryburn's work. Maybe he had taken his jokes a bit far, he thought to himself, as he rolled over yet again, punching his pillow to fluff it. He *needed* the money he was due from this mission, all of it, including the weeks that they would lose because of stupid Ryburn and his stupid hopper and his stupid flying rocks.

O'Connor had seriously overreacted earlier, docking his pay was one thing, but the violence was too much. All the stuff about sneaking around the station, why was he accused of that? And again with Ryburn's flying rocks, he didn't even care what they were. *O'Connor's the one up to something not me* he thought to himself and he punched his pillow again, imagining it was the chief's face.

The room was quite large for one person, somewhat of a strange choice, considering the room had two double bunk beds and limited personal space. It wasn't as strange as Ryburn' choice however, who in true unsociable fashion, opted to sleep in his workstation on a roll-out bed instead of his plush personal living quarters next to the crew. Benson and O'Connor had made the smart choice, and taken the vacant senior member quarters.

They were a long way from being luxurious but the sumptuous single birth accommodation for the original senior members had been on one of the outer rings that had been jettisoned many months ago into Venus' orbit for burn up. If McSweeney had wanted he could have taken one of the other empty rooms, but his preference for a top bunk meant more to him.

His room resembled a bomb site. The caretakers did not bring much luggage with them; a few changes of clothes was usually the limit. The small amount of personal items he had brought were scattered across his bottom bunk, leaving the storage cupboard empty.

After a few more tosses and turns McSweeney decided sleep was a pointless endeavour. He was still just too angry. Angry at the chief, angry at himself and seriously angry at Ryburn for jeopardising his payday. Even the big man Benson did not escape the puppy rage, he was angry at him for not being angry at the chief or Ryburn. He worried about his lost fee and worried that the chief's unfounded accusations would continue, which led him back to the anger again.

Since sleep seemed an impossibility McSweeney figured he might as well put in a couple of hours' work and get a head start on his shift; perhaps he would be able to get to the bottom of the pressure readings. He didn't really care too much about those as it wasn't his problem, but what he did care about was getting as much salvage out of those chard cables as possible. If in the process he managed to uncover the cause of the air pressure mystery, well that would be gravy.

His greasy face lit up at the daydream of giving the good news to Benson and the chief himself.

"That would show them," he said aloud.

Perhaps it was a minor leak somewhere in the CO^2 and a block in the O^2. He did not have the technical ability to diagnose or repair any of these problems since his knowledge extended only as far as dismantling the units. Maybe he'd get lucky and save the day or maybe the problem would just go away. If that didn't solve it, then it was something for Benson and the chief to worry about because in all fairness, he wasn't paid to worry about this type of thing. The more he thought about it, the less he cared. Faulty readings, no doubt. It wasn't as if they had suddenly taken on some stowaways this deep into the system was it?

He swung himself down from his top bunk, landing on his feet with a quiet thud. He winced as the combination of cold floor, bare feet, and the impact sent stinging pins and needles across the soles of his feet and up to his shins. He hopped around, unbalanced for a moment, before landing in the bottom bunk in melodramatic fashion. After recovering from his near death experience he looked around the floor for his discarded grey suit; the thought of getting a clean one never even crossed his mind, not for even a second. After finding it he pulled it on in the most awkward, uncoordinated manner possible, arms and legs flailing all over the place as he forced his way into the standard issue suit, not bothering with any of the straps. He looked briefly at his wrist com, which was on the floor next to where his jumpsuit had been. He could not be bothered with it so left it where it was. A few moments later the boots were on, music in hand, and he was ready to sneak out.

He very slowly opened the door: his door was right next to the chief's, and he really did not want to wake him. The chief was a light sleeper, and waking him up was always a bad idea. He would not take kindly to being disturbed, especially by McSweeney and especially after everything that had happened that day.

He closed his door as quietly as possible, keeping both his eyes on the chief's door, looking for the light. The door creaked a little on the rollers but nothing loud enough to cause any problems and then silently clicked into place. Taking his hand off the latch, he made a couple of very soft steps in the direction of the corridor walkway.

"Safe!" he said under his breath. Then he heard it, and his heart sank: the sound of the chief's door opening, he had failed.

"McSweeney," said the chief, "I thought I heard you getting up."

"I couldn't sleep; I'm just heading down to get a bit of work done," said McSweeney spinning around nervously to face the chief.

"Look, I'm glad I caught you I-..."

"I'm not doing anything wrong" interrupted McSweeney, taking a step backwards and away, "just want a head start on tomorrow is all."

"I never said you were."

"You said 'caught' and I'm not doing anything," replied McSweeney, putting a little more distance between them both with another step backwards.

"Will you stand still please?" said the chief, raising his voice slightly. He turned and closed the door behind him obviously not wanting to wake Benson who could be heard snoring loudly.

McSweeney stopped still and stood to attention. He did not like being alone with the chief.

"Look, McSweeney," Chief O'Connor continued, "you and I have had a bad day." McSweeney grunted his acknowledgement and the chief continued, "I think we both said and did some things that we shouldn't have. Wouldn't you agree?"

"Yes I guess things got a bit out of control," said McSweeney, relaxing his footing a bit.

"Right, I apologise for my over reactions and, for the record, I'm not deducting anything from your fee and I'll remove anything negative I've put into the official account since we started on this station."

"Honest?" said McSweeney. He was not quite sure what to make of this sudden change in attitude.

"Honest," said O'Connor, stepping forward and extending his hand.

That just made McSweeney flinch and step back before he realised what the gesture was. The pair of them shook hands and the tension in the air immediately evaporated. McSweeney let out the breath he was not aware he had been holding.

"There's just a couple of provisos," O'Connor added, with a sly smile. McSweeney should have guessed that.

"I know I know, I'll leave Ryburn alone and stop with all the jokes."

"Yes, but I mean it this time," O'Connor added. "And I want to know where you hid earlier in the corridor by the collection hub and airlock-B."

McSweeney returned his own sly grin. "I have no idea what you mean."

"Hmm" said the chief, with mock suspicion. "Okay, we'll leave it at that then. Also my wrist com, I still can't find it anywhere and the one working spare we had is gone too. That isn't your doing is it?"

"No, Chief," said McSweeney.

"Seriously now, no repercussions," said O'Connor.

"Honest. That's nothing to do with me either. I swear it." Why wouldn't the chief just believe him?

"Where's yours tonight?" said O'Connor, with a nod to McSweeney's empty wrist.

"In there, on the floor. I was going to put it back on..." How much trouble was he in for that?

"I don't care about that," O'Connor cut him off. "It's the least of my worries now. I have your word you don't know where my com is?"

"I swear it, Chief. I have no idea where it is." The truth was that McSweeney had no more idea what was going on with the com than the chief did.

O'Connor took a deep breath in. "Okay then, thanks for this little talk. We'll put it all behind us then?"

Relief flooded through McSweeney. "Thank you, Chief."

O'Connor nodded. "I appreciate that you are putting in the extra work tonight. We should have word back very soon from the lunarbase. In the morning we'll know how much time we have left to complete the salvage."

The two of them parted ways; the chief returned to his quarters and McSweeney, with a refreshed hop in his step, put his headphones on and continued down toward hydroponics.

Hydroponics was the top floor of the work-sphere, stacked wall to wall, and floor to ceiling, with shelves of the high-density plants that kept the station supplied with oxygen. The plants had been genetically modified to produce more oxygen than their natural, earthbound cousins. The room was quite a sight, the vibrant green of the plants contrasting against the bold white of the shelving, the bright light source fixed above each shelf gently spilling out between the greenery. An immediate calm would wash over anyone who entered the room. It was a small touch of Earth in the dusty and decrepit old station.

The air from the oxygen farms tasted strange, the hint of chemicals made it a touch too cold and a touch too crisp. The first breath of the direct air always induced an involuntary cough as the cold hit his lungs. The plants were producing much more oxygen than was required for the crew; even with only two thirds of the room functioning it was too much. Now, with the tanks at maximum storage, it was time to decommission the middle third of the room. McSweeney had spent the last week stripping out the chard cables from the dead third. It was a time-consuming task but the payoff was huge due to the concentration of the cabling in the equipment. There were once other organic spheres on the station that grew fresh fruit and vegetables, but they had long been discarded along with the outer rings.

Lucky sods, McSweeney thought jealously as he imagined the amount of salvage those spheres would have yielded. He was in good spirits. He felt like he had turned a corner with the chief and all the unpleasantness of the day was behind him. "He's a good guy..." he said aloud to a shelf full of plants, bobbing along to his music. "Just has a bit of a temper."

He set about collecting all of the tools that he had casually thrown around the floor because, of course, he now needed them to start his work. There was some basic prep work that needed to be done before the next third of the oxygen farm could be dismantled. It involved sealing off all the nutrient supply lines to each plant bed and all the extraction lines for the oxygen they produced.

McSweeney stood at a small display screen fixed to the wall between the two large storage tanks, wrench in hand, all set to close the water supply to the drip pipes. However, the screen had all sorts of warnings flashing upon it. He tapped the screen lightly with his wrench, an uncouth method to use on the touch screen, tapping rapidly through the high priority warnings and ignoring the information regarding changes in the station's air pressure: both oxygen usage and carbon dioxide creation twice the expected rate. That last one caused him to pause, before dismissing it all as another broken system.

His money was on an internal leak, which would explain the increased pressure and usage… but not the carbon dioxide levels, unless that measure was wrong, causing more oxygen to be pumped out.

"Supposed to be super sensitive and super accurate," he scoffed, giving the screen a hard tap with his wrench for good measure. That was as far as his diagnostics ran, however.

"I wonder if this will solve it?" he said aloud as he shut off the water to the plant bed. He was thinking that he had a 50/50 chance of solving the problem with the air pressure; his thoughts then digressed into a day-dream about the praise and admiration he would get from his crew mates. It was an anti-climax however; the plants never just withered and died immediately, that would usually take days. He closed down the nutrient and carbon dioxide lines next, and the screen began to show the same warning again, a new warning flashing red to alert him that he had shut down an entire bay; he closed the unhelpful message.

There was a set procedure to follow for shutting down the farms, but bollocks to that. McSweeney shut down the remaining components in the order he randomly selected. A little victory against the authority. The same warnings popped up again, they were becoming an annoyance. They used to be localised to only this display but as of that morning they were being escalated to the central sphere, thus inviting Benson to offer an opinion.

"We're creating more oxygen than we should be and using

more oxygen than we should be," would flash up on his screen, and he would follow up with the chief. In McSweeney's mind that translated to "not my problem".

He reminisced about all the jokes he had played on his crew mates over the last few months; perhaps he had taken some of them a bit far. He recalled the time he had scared the living daylights of the chief by hiding in the airlock and the countless times he had messed around with Ryburn's simulations. That never grew old. Neither did swapping wiring on the doors so they would lock instead of open; that was always fun. All that would have to end now, a fresh start.

He went about his business for another twenty minutes, which included the unnecessary flaming down of the redundant plants. Eventually tiredness got the better of him and he decided to call it a night, again. He had made some good progress, got a few more metres of cable extracted and rolled up, and had cleared the air with O'Connor. With that weight lifted from his mind he actually felt like he could get some sleep now.

The station was peaceful late at night after everyone had finished for the day. It was early morning if you went by central Earth time, but with the station being in a fixed orbit around Venus, the outside influence on the day/night cycle was non-existent. McSweeney had not long turned in; Benson was snoring away in his room and the chief had just managed to get to sleep. Ryburn, on the other hand, was wide-awake, working, putting calculation upon calculation together to fine-tune his device. A welcome side effect of his sober shots was the occasional spell as a high functioning insomniac. He had named his new device in typically grand fashion, celebrating it with a drink and an announcement to his workstation: it would be called The Mercurian Magnetic Manipulation Propulsion System: the 3MP.

Naming it was the easy part.

"Damn it all!" Ryburn shouted at his screen, running the chard dispersion controls for his prototype. He had gone over every component piece by piece, reconfiguring each one to what should have been nano-degree perfect throughput. Even so, the prototype wasn't behaving as it should. It was functioning but generating a chard back loop, meaning that it was firing on and off repeatedly instead of producing a continuous flow. It was too rapid for the human eye to see but the fluctuations would generate undue stress on the system. This needed a solution!

Ryburn was already reassessing the situation, though. Perhaps that back loop did not matter for his prototype as the concept was proven. But if he was going to implement his technology on the grand scale required to move the station it would matter. The simulations indicated that the stress would rip through the energy reserves and burn out the chard cabling, which meant that it would not work, or at least not for long. The 3MP was not going to be taking them anywhere, was not going to write his name into the history books, was not going to change the world… not in this state.

He gulped down the last swallow of his drink and slammed the cylindrical glass down hard on the desk top, hitting just the right resonance to send a crack spiralling around the glass.

"Damn it all!" he repeated as he threw the glass hard against the wall.

He looked longingly at his synthochol supply. He wanted that drink, but knew another one would not help; he liked to ride the very edge not topple over it. The synthochol effects of a couple of drinks helped him think. Unfortunately, a couple more made him think of nothing but more drink. He took another glance at the simulation and calculations he was running.

It was an ambitious plan to say the least, the heart of which was to take advantage of the large chard reserves. They would need to refine all the Mercurian ore and build custom regulators and dispersion units. They would need to utilise some of the recycled chard cabling that the caretakers had salvaged. However, the whole scheme was a non-starter if he could not solve the back loop problem. He needed to work this one through again from the very start.

Not wanting to cut himself on the broken glass, Ryburn brushed the shards that landed on his desk to the floor. Standing up, he pushed it all to the corner with the side of his boot. He sat back down, mumbling the calculation steps to himself. His hands wanted something to replace the glass he had been fondling. He needed a new comforter or, as he preferred to think, a new thinking aid; something to roll around in his hand while he worked. His eyes searched the desk for his cricket ball but landed instead on the bright blue regulator.

He picked it up and started rolling it over in his hands, running the calculation and component settings through his head. Faster and faster his mind began to work, the equations and calculations dragging him down a complicated path further and further away from his destination. It was like running along the edge of a widening chasm searching for a bridge that could be just around the next bend. The realisation hit him like a comet.

"Of course!" he said to the object in his hands, "the gauge is wrong."

He had built the entire scenario to rely on the three-gauge regulator, and even though he had adjusted the other settings of the regulator to handle the chard levels, the gauge was fixed. That was his mistake. He could have kissed that little unit at that moment. Of course, with the benefit of hindsight it was so obvious, he had taken the fixed value as fact and had not even considered making it a variable by simply using a different component. *Idiot!* He ran through the adjustments, then loaded the figures into his simulation to be sure. He needed a nine-gauge to balance it all out; he'd have to get all the components back from O'Connor, there was bound to be a nine-gauge of some variation in that pile he had taken away, the nines were usually blue.

Ryburn looked at the sky-blue piece in his hand, carefully reading aloud the configuration "Nine-gauge, eighty-two millisecond, three-gram." That was spooky; what were the odds that the only regulator O'Connor had left him would turn out to be the exact one he needed? He rolled it over in his hands thinking on the likelihood some more. He had taken all the others away and made a point of leaving him the "bright blue one". It was also the same component McSweeney had been teasing him with. What was it that little toad had said? "The chief said you needed a nine-gauge". That recollection sent a shiver down his spine, how did O'Connor know?

A lucky guess? No, they both told him to use the nine-gauge. That was too much of a coincidence. Something felt wrong about it, so Ryburn checked the regulator to be sure it was genuine, even ran a quick diagnostic over it. It was fine, a little worn but nothing to worry about. "Just highly improbable," he muttered to himself as he prepared to incorporate the nine-gauge to his 3MP prototype. "Besides, he didn't outright tell me to use it," he continued, trying to convince himself that it was just a fluke. However, it did not sit well: it was too convenient, and scientists did not believe in coincidences.

"There!" he exclaimed with satisfaction once he had fitted the new regulator. A couple more minor adjustments here and there but before he knew it the prototype 3MP was running without the chard back loop. To the naked eye the behaviour was the same, the device still floated silently in mid-air, but from a chard circuit point of view it was now running significantly smoother and with an improved yield from the chardage.

Ryburn was about to start applying his new finding to the station scenario when he became aware of a methodical, dull, clanging noise just breaking through the silence. He had been hearing it for a few seconds before it registered and now he actually started listening to it. He stood up from his chair.

"I don't have time for this ridiculousness," he muttered as he stepped out into the corridor to investigate. The clang came from the direction of the collection hub, he started walking toward it. He waited for another clang, but it never came.

He could see the collection hub light just a little in front of him when his foot hit something soft, the hard rubber padding on the floor had suddenly given way to something that crunched under his step, so he bent down to pick it up. It was a woollen hat, and wrapped inside he found the sharp edges of something cold to the touch. He could not see clearly in this light but whatever it was it was sharp enough to tear through the hat. His fingers slid through the small hole in the side. He carefully tucked the hat into his inside breast pocket, to look at it in better light.

He did not have time to think about what happened next as it all happened so fast. A loud explosive noise and a vibration along the flooring. Then the air in the corridor rushed past him and swept him off his feet, his arms flailing wildly as he instinctively tried to grab hold of something as he was sucked along the corridor.

The piercing wail of the decompression siren was blasted deep within his ears. Ryburn knew, even though he couldn't hear them well, that the alarms would be screaming out from every junction until it filled the entire station; there was no place the sound wouldn't be heard.

CHAPTER 6: DECOMPRESSION

O'CONNOR WAS THE first out of his bed; he was already awake after something had disturbed his sleep. But that annoyance was quickly forgotten when the decompression alarms began. He almost tripped over as he tried to run, get dressed and open his door simultaneously. He all but jumped to the status terminal positioned centrally in the conjoining corridor that connected the sleeping quarters. The terminal was displaying exactly what the problem was: Explosive decompression.

"Benson! McSweeney! Get out here now!" he shouted, his voice barely audible over the alarm. It didn't matter; his two crew men were already behind him dressed only in their underwear. McSweeney and Benson were polar opposites in every physical sense. Both stood half asleep and unaware what was happening or why. Neither had been in a decompression situation before and likely didn't appreciate the seriousness of it all. Although the fact that they were all there and breathing and not already sucked out into space meant that the situation could have been much much worse.

"Can we shut that off?" Benson shouted back with his hands over his ears, before muscling his way to the controls like a sleepy bear.

"About time," said McSweeney as the noise stopped.

"We've lost airlock-B corridor," said the chief, looking over the information onscreen. His ears still ringing.

"What do you mean 'we've lost the corridor'?" queried McSweeney.

"See for yourself," said the chief as he gestured towards the screen.

"The whole airlock-B corridor is gone," O'Connor reiterated, pointing out the entire segment of the corridor that was flashing red, from the central corridor junction down, past airlock-B, toward the collection hub. Two blast doors had fired, sealing off the corridor, one at the collection hub end and the other and the central corridor end. Everything in-between was lost. A third blast door, a few metres along the central corridor, had also fired.

"Damn!" said McSweeney, whilst keeping a nervous distance from O'Connor.

"Did the airlock give way or something? I was getting odd readings from it yesterday," Benson suggested.

"Couldn't have, I hard locked it last night, after my codes didn't work."

"I changed the codes, Chief, remember?"

"Yeah I know," he said with frustration "but I didn't have the new ones, and I thought the whole airlock was malfunctioning so I hard locked to be safe."

"Good move!" agreed Benson. "Do you want your new codes?"

O'Connor could see McSweeney's eyes fixed on him.

"I'll get them off you later," said O'Connor. "I'll get over to the far side. Make sure that section is secure, Benson; we need to know exactly what happened. Can you get back to the command deck and get as much out of the system logs as possible... ...what is it?" he said to McSweeney finally unable to ignore the venomous look on his face.

"Nothing," came the grunted reply, as McSweeney changed his gaze to avoid eye contact.

"Okay then, McSweeney, you check this side. See what you can see. Check both of the doors that fired. The central one must have faulted, but we can't be sure. Check they are both closed and check for leakage. I'll update Ryburn too; that crazy sod can't have slept through this unless he hit the synth extra hard again last night."

He thought that McSweeney would acknowledge the cheap shot at Ryburn, but there was nothing; the young man continued to look away.

"What are you sulking at?" he asked, but his question went unanswered. He thought he had cleared the air with him earlier but something was up with him now.

"Ryburn's not answering his com," said Benson after a failed attempt to reach him.

"A relay could have been cleared out," suggested O'Connor, he again reached for the com that wasn't on his wrist.

"I'll run a reroute sequence at the central sphere," said Benson.

"Where's your com?" O'Connor asked McSweeney.

"Don't you fucking dare!" said McSweeney, shuffling closer to Benson.

"Fine, let's move," said O'Connor, ignoring the grumpy little outburst.

"Yes, Sir, straight away, Sir," said McSweeney, adding a mock salute. Benson put his gorilla-like arm across his chest and pulled him back from the chief, before the two were nose to nose. McSweeney put up a little bit of resistance, but it was likely just for show.

"What's wrong with you, I thought we were all cool?" said O'Connor, not understanding McSweeney's reactions.

"Really? After the shit you said to me last night?" said McSweeney from behind the barricade of Benson's massive arm.

O'Connor was even more confused now, he thought they had settled their differences and moved on, obviously not. He could feel the beginnings of his anger brewing just beneath the service, he was aware of the tension in his fingers wanting to clench a fist and only too late aware that he had squared his feet. Taking a slow breath and relaxing slightly he said through almost gritted teeth.

"I meant every word of it!"

"So why don't you say it again in front of Benson?"

"What I said was for you, not Benson," said O'Connor, embarrassed and determined to hide it. It had been hard enough for him to apologise in the first place, but getting this reaction after he thought everything was okay did not sit well with him. The slimly little sod was playing games and was definitely up to something; was he behind this decompression? He was in the corridor last night despite his blatant denial.

"That's exactly my point!" said McSweeney. "It's all smiles and jokes when Benson's around isn't it? Good work team and blah blah bullshit. But it's all an act." He pointed his accusing finger, the way he always did.

O'Connor stood in silence completely blown away. He was not at a loss for words, just trying to stop himself from lashing out and smacking the two-faced little turd right in the face.

"Now's not the time for this," Benson interjected, "We've got to secure the station, remember?"

Benson pushed McSweeney in the direction of his assignment, a big flat palm across the back forcing him to walk or land flat on his face. McSweeney broke into a light jog and disappeared around the corridor.

O'Connor stood for a moment, trying to wrap his head around what just happened, he breathed slowly, letting all the pent-up anger wash away until his calm returned.

"Don't let him get to you, Chief," said Benson. "He's just trying to push your buttons for a reaction."

"I try Jerry, I really do," said O'Connor, "that could have gotten ugly if you weren't here. He only ever acts up when you're here to hide behind. Sometimes I could just smack him, you know?"

"Yeah I know, I'm sure, but you won't though," said Benson, and then added with a note of seriousness to his voice, "Will you, Chief?" It was a question but carried the hint of a warning. "Just don't let him wind you up so much."

"Thanks Jerry," said O'Connor, "I appreciate what you're saying. I'd better get over to the far side and check on that door, and Ryburn."

He took off in fast jog. After all, he did have to get to the far side of the station.

McSweeney could see the orange flashing lights emanating around the curve of the corridor as he approached the central junction. The way to the central sphere was blocked. The blast door had indeed fired, sealing off the access. He gave it a tap with his knuckle as he pondered what could have set it off. He looked through the porthole window but there was nothing that would indicate the decompression of the corridor. *Another false alarm*, he thought to himself; that would be typical of the decaying station. He had to check the next breach door towards airlock-B and the state of the corridor that was supposedly lost. He shook his head, blaming O'Connor for wasting his time, and Ryburn for good measure too. It had to be another false alarm.

When he got to the breach door, though, McSweeney stared. This door had slammed shut too, but unlike the other one, the view through the window into the corridor beyond showed clear and unequivocal evidence of a decompression event. It had not been completely jettisoned, as the readout had shown, but it might as well have been. The emergency flashing light provided enough contrast between the internal walls and the outside starlight to show a clear and jagged hole where airlock-B had been. The entire airlock was gone. There were a few of the large empty hardware shells floating around in the zero gravity, bouncing off each other but the rest had been sucked out of the airlock by the force of the decompression.

The stray hardware shells and other debris floated by obstructing his view, but in the gaps between, McSweeney could see small jets of air dissipating out of some broken pipe ends and the occasional white sparks of a chard line shorting out. He pressed his face up close to the window, then used his com torch to improve his view and take in the full extent of the damage; it was significant to say the least. The entire airlock and a sizeable portion of the surrounding ceiling and floor was gone. McSweeney stood in awe; he had never seen this level of destruction before.

Toward the bottom of his view he could see that one of the larger, empty hardware shells had been flung sideways, wedging itself horizontally across the corridor between two support beams. Just above the spot where it had come to rest were some deep scratch marks where the unit had been forced downward, along the beam. It sure was in there tight.

His eyes snapped back to it as the realisation clicked into place that this was not right. There was nothing behind it, nothing fixed anyway that could have caused this by collision. The direction of the scratches on the wall was certainly not in the direction of the decompression. He knew a thing or two about intentional damage, and recognised the signs. He twitched his head left and right, taking in as much as he could regarding this anomalous hardware shell. He saw his own calling cards, indicators of his lazy work. The shortcuts taken when stripping down the units were obvious to him: haphazard cable detachments, hammer indentations along the joins, the ragged cuts, he might as well have signed it. He had harvested the cabling from this unit and placed the shell here because of its awkward size, and he had hidden in there once while winding up the chief. He remembered that he had dumped it further along the corridor, towards the airlock, and had laid it flat along the floor. There was no way a decompression would have put this unit in its current place, further away from the hole. It had been deliberately moved before the event, but why?

"Mother fuc..." he said slowly before trailing off, leaving the obscenity unfinished. It had to have been the chief. He had been in the corridor last, and he was playing around with the locks, he already admitted that. McSweeney started concocting the elaborate schemes through which the chief must be plotting to swindle him out of his fee. He started rocking again, backwards and forwards slowly, in his twitchy paranoid way. He raised his fingernails to his mouth and started to bite; his teeth found whatever obtruding edge he could, stripping the cuticle back to the skin before spitting each little strip onto the floor. Not that there was much point, as his nails were already chewed down to bloody stumps. He quietly admitted to himself that his scenarios did not make sense and were just getting more and more outlandish. Nevertheless, what remained as undeniable facts was that the chief was the last one in this corridor and he had been the last one to interact with the airlock.

"Benson," he said into his com.

"Yes McSweeney, what's the damage?"

The reply made McSweeney jump, he had been half expecting the coms to not be working. He didn't think Benson would have had a chance to reroute the communications yet.

"Damage is bad, not a false alarm, but from this side it is secure and contained. The corridor's still there, but the airlock has gone."

"And the doors?" Benson asked.

McSweeney made a quick visual scan around the outer edges of the door, and placed his hand against the joints. They were warm to the touch, which signified that the internal blast/melt lock had triggered as designed.

"The outer corridor door this side is solid, central corridor looked solid, but I think it was a misfire."

"Any clues to what caused the decompression?" Benson continued, his voice crackling slightly over the speaker, routing must still be non-optimised.

"Besides the massive hole where the airlock should be? No…" he hesitated and was about to share his other findings but Benson spoke first.

"The chief should be on the other side by now, he is still

without his com, no word from Ryburn. Can you get back here in a hurry please? You need to see something and I can't say this over the coms." Even with the communicator crackle Benson's voice sounded a bit nervous. Benson was never nervous.

"I've got something to tell you too. I'll be there soon, got to take the long way though haven't I?" said McSweeney, slipping in that little joke before ending the call and heading off; he was anxious to share his suspicions with Benson.

O'Connor had run all the way round to Ryburn's workstation. "Ryburn!" he called out as he stepped sideways around the half open door into the workstation. He was expecting to see an inebriated Ryburn slouched over his desk, oblivious to the world, but he was not there. The room was vacant. O'Connor eyes were drawn to the floating prototype, which was hanging in the air, suspended by nothing, with only some cables tethering it to the desk. He had to admit he was a little bit curious about this device. Ryburn had once been a very well respected man before his Mercury missions… and his slight issue with the synthochol. What caught his eye about the floating device was the sky-blue regulator. The vibrant colour stood out against the rest of the parts, looking out of place. He leaned right in to get a clear look at what was actually happening. He gave it a gentle push and watched it bob up and down. He knew a bit about chard dispersion circuitry but his level of knowledge was nowhere near Ryburn's, not even in the same ballpark. It looked ridiculous with its electrical tape holding the battery in place, cables split and rewired with the bare wire exposed, and random parts added here and there that, to the best of his knowledge, would have no apparent function. It looked to be the work of a rank amateur… or a madman. Even though Ryburn claimed that it worked, which it did, the thought of this stupid little contraption, held together with spite and bad breath, being able to move the station out of the path of the stray lander was delusional.

Where the hell was Ryburn? His makeshift bed was empty and he hadn't used his actual sleeping quarters for ages so there was no reason to think he would be comatose in there.

He looked over the desk for any clues as to where Ryburn could be. The four screen displays offered nothing. One was flashing blue with what could only be a proximity warning of some sort, tracking some event that happened around five minutes before, most likely the decompression. The other display appeared to show schematics and plans involving the entire station, with nothing of immediate use for locating Ryburn. O'Connor left the room, with a lump in his throat at the possibility that Ryburn was no longer aboard the station. Protocol said that they had to check on the breach door first; that was the priority.

The light from the emergency alarms provided a thin orange beacon for him to follow through the graveyard of hardware shells ahead of him. He had to navigate his way around them; some were in precarious positions that needed stabilising for safety. The smaller units he pushed out the way to clear his path. The blast door was immediately in front of him as he tipped the last of the frames out of the way. He could see Ryburn sitting down against the wall.

"Dr Ryburn!" called O'Connor. Even in the poor lighting, it was obvious that Ryburn was not okay. The angle of his slump told a story of someone without the energy to stand up. He hastened his step the last few metres and crouched down next to him, shaking him by the shoulder. In that moment, he feared the worst.

"Ryburn, are you alive?" he said, leaning in to check for breathing. He caught a whiff of the synthochol on his breath, then stood up in disappointment. "You are drunk again aren't you?"

The doctor stirred slightly then slowly sat up. He looked around slowly, getting his bearings; he gave a startled flinch seeing O'Connor standing over him.

"Decompression!" he shouted with belated "raise the alarm"

urgency. He stretched out a hand for the chief to help him up, letting out a groan as O'Connor pulled him to his feet.

"The decompression, what happened?" he said again, after steadying himself.

"I'm not sure what caused it yet, but the entire corridor from here to the central corridor has been sealed off," said O'Connor. He carefully watched Ryburn, who seemed coherent enough, maybe he jumped to the wrong conclusion about Ryburn being drunk. "What happened to you?" he continued without giving Ryburn a chance to react to the news.

"I was heading this way…" began Ryburn but he trailed off. "There was a noise, a banging…" he continued, his eyes drawing along the corridor. "I found something..." He tapped his chest where he had tucked the hat, "Then I heard an explosion, I was being sucked out. I managed to get a grip on a seam in the wall, but only for a second. Then it stopped." He turned around and put his hands on the blast door. "Still warm too," he added as he felt the gentle heat on the door's surface. "I must have gone unconscious when I fell."

After checking the door was secure, they took it in turns looking through the porthole window of the breach door at what was left of the corridor. The collection hub was still there for what it was worth, but beyond that they couldn't see.

"The initial information said the whole corridor was lost, but it might be just the airlock," said O'Connor.

"It couldn't have opened by itself?" said Ryburn, looking at O'Connor for confirmation.

"That airlock was faulty, I had to hard lock it myself last night to be safe," said O'Connor, still peering through the window.

"Hard lock, what made you decide that?" asked Ryburn. There was an accusing note to it.

"The system wasn't right, it was showing incorrect readings. There were signs that it was in use when it wasn't. Benson had reported irregularities too," O'Connor added, feeling the need to explain himself. "My codes had been changed so I couldn't just disable it either; hard locking seemed the prudent course of action."

"Quite right," agreed Ryburn, "under the circumstances. An imperfection in the locking seal perhaps. If the external door had even a minor failing, or even a non-uniform dispersal, then the hard lock could have been compromised. If the doors weren't maintained then it could have triggered an epicentre of stress loading..."

O'Connor gave him a pointed look. This was no time for the finer details of the door mechanisms.

"Both airlock doors must have failed," Ryburn finished.

"What would cause both doors to fail, without us getting a warning? That's impossible," said O'Connor. He was sure there should have been stress warnings, unless of course that system had also failed.

"No," said Ryburn, "not impossible, just very improbable."

Again, O'Connor gave him a hard look. This wasn't time for being pedantic either.

"Well," Ryburn said, "if you would please excuse me, I've got to get back to my work; you'll be pleased to know I've just cracked a, shall we say, a little hurdle. A little more refinement and we'll be ready to start preparing the station."

Ryburn was very unsteady on his feet as he tried to step without the support of the wall. The decompression must have lifted him up into the air, then dropped him hard on his side. His poor old body just could not take such an impact and he needed some help to walk the aches away. O'Connor offered him his shoulder to lean on as the pair of them slowly made their way towards Ryburn's workstation.

"I've solved quite a major setback on the prototype," Ryburn repeated after a couple of steps.

"I heard you the first time, Ryburn." O'Connor had deliberately ignored him, not wanting to be drawn into a pointless discussion about the magic space rocks.

"Well then, you will be pleased to know that we should be able to fly the station clear."

"I'm sorry, what?" said O'Connor, almost dropping Ryburn where they stood.

"I need to do a little more fine tuning," Ryburn continued steadying himself by gripping O'Connor's shoulder more firmly. They awkwardly got through the half open door and Ryburn collapsed into his chair.

"You're going to fly that station clear with that?" said O'Connor, flashing a disgusted nod of the head toward the floating collection of junk. It still seemed like a drunken fantasy.

"No, not that of course, but with the rest of the refined ore… how are you progressing with that? I should be ready for it very soon."

"Progressing with what?" O'Connor asked, not understanding.

"With refining the ore."

O'Connor shook his head. "I'm sorry Dr Ryburn, but you aren't making any sense."

"You were going to process the ore for me," Ryburn said.

O'Connor reached out and placed his hands on Ryburn's arms, just below the shoulder, in a reassuring yet authoritative manner, the way a parent would with a confused child.

"Ryburn, I made no such promise. Now I really think you should just rest for a moment, have you taken a knock to the head?" he added offering Ryburn a dignified retraction from the conversation.

Ryburn didn't take it, though. "No! You said you would help, you assured me that you and your team would help. I have only done what you have requested. At first I thought it too preposterous, I admit that, but then I got to thinking on it. It can be done. My simulations weren't producing the favourable results, but then I changed the regulator to the one you left behind…"

He brought his hand up touching the outside of his jacket. He took the hat from his jacket and emptied the contents onto the desk.

O'Connor frowned at the sight of a hat full of what appeared to be discarded regulators. "I didn't leave you any regulator, I've had nothing to do with your work."

Ryburn just gave him a confused look.

"Let's get you back to your the sleeping quarters so you can lie down," said O'Connor. He was worried about just how badly Ryburn's mind seemed to be falling apart.

"I'm okay really; I just need to finish what I've started," said Ryburn brushing away O'Connor's concerns.

"I don't think you are. Please take a moment to rest." O'Connor was beginning to wonder if Ryburn had in fact cracked his head during the ordeal.

"Is this not your hat then?" snapped Ryburn, clenching the hat in his fist and waving it at O'Connor.

O'Connor quietly withdrew his hat from his pocket and pulled it down onto his head, answering the question without speaking.

"That isn't your hat, that one isn't torn," said Ryburn sounding so sure of himself. "I remember seeing the rip clearly!"

"My hat has never been ripped Ryburn."

"Take it off and show me," Ryburn demanded.

"Okay then," O'Connor agreed, handing him the hat and staring at the two as Ryburn compared them. The hats were identical, black in colour, both standard issue. The only difference was that one had a fairly lengthy rip across it. O'Connor's did not.

"And what's all the junk?" O'Connor said as he took his hat back, and pointed to the pile of broken parts on the bench.

"These are the regulators you took back to recycle," Ryburn said.

O'Connor just looked at him blankly.

"Are you also saying you know nothing of these regulators either?" Ryburn demanded.

This was getting crazier by the moment. "I'm sorry, but I don't know what you're talking about. Now I think you need to lie down Ryburn, that fall must have knocked something loose."

"I told you I'm fine, the simulation shows that we can move the station. I will just need some help from the others in getting everything into place."

O'Connor rolled his eyes again. Flying the station clear? Really? "I'm sorry Ryburn, but I can't have you taking up the crew's time, we have precious little time left as it is."

"But it was your idea," Ryburn protested.

"What was?"

"Moving the station!" shouted Ryburn, losing his temper.

"Ryburn, I never suggested such a thing and I don't know why you would think I did," said O'Connor calmly. He wasn't angry. In fact he was nearly laughing, the extent of this man's synthochol-fuelled delusions had hit a new level.

The two of them just looked at each other quietly for a moment or two.

"Why are you being like this? I thought you understood," said Ryburn.

"I'm not being like anything," replied O'Connor.

"You told me that we had to come up with our own plan, because the folks at home won't help us."

"You mean the reply to my message?"

"Yes."

"The message that they haven't replied to yet?" said O'Connor.

"Yes...no, I don't know. But you told me we're on our own and asked if the 3MP could fly us clear."

"What the hell is a 3MP?" asked O'Connor, his disbelief was impossible to contain now.

Ryburn sounded as though he was getting more and more confused. This had to stop.

"Ryburn, please," said O'Connor, raising his hand up in a calming fashion. "I honestly said no such thing to you; perhaps you misunderstood what I said or something, why would they leave us here?"

"I'll show you," said Ryburn and he turned around to his workstation terminal, tapping the screen to bring it back into life. But the screen was not the schematic display of the station; it was a blue alert on the top right screen, where he had the high intensity proximity detection running. It had picked up something, and not just once but several distinct and separate proximity events concentrated around the airlocks.

"It's all just glitches; we've been getting all sorts of messed up readings on everything." O'Connor didn't care about that. His mind was on the message home and somehow getting out of this mess with everyone alive.

"No these are clean," said Ryburn, "Something is out there, I saw it, well, didn't see it."

"Your ghost?" asked O'Connor, rolling his eyes.

"Don't you dare mock me, I saw something," said Ryburn, then pointed at the screen, "and this proves it."

"What do you want me to do?" O'Connor countered "That whole section is gone! There's nothing to check."

Ryburn dropped his head disappointedly, raising his hands up in a brief indication of surrender.

"I'll see what Benson has figured out about the airlock," said O'Connor placatingly, "and we should have the message from home very soon." He looked at his wrist again without finding his com. "Would you mind calling Benson to let him know I'm heading back to central sphere. Tell him that there is no immediate danger."

"I'm not your secretary!" Ryburn snapped.

"Please, Dr Ryburn, I have no communicator."

After he received a begrudging agreement from Ryburn O'Connor left the room.

Ryburn gathered his composure before making the call to Benson.

"Benson, are you there?"

"Benson here, how are you Dr Ryburn?"

"I'm fine Benson, thank you," Ryburn said after a moment's pause, "O'Connor has just left and will be with you shortly. He says that there is no immediate danger this side."

"Oh that is good news," Benson replied before Ryburn cut the call off

"McSweeney," Ryburn said into his com, as he initiated another call.

"Yes, Ryburn?" McSweeney replied, the surprise at receiving a direct call from Ryburn evident in the tone of his voice. "I'm nearly back at the central sphere, can this wait?"

"I need you to listen carefully McSweeney; this is extremely important," said Ryburn slowly and clearly.

"Is something the matter with the pressure on your side?" asked McSweeney immediately.

He must have thought that this was regarding the breach door situation. To his credit it was not an unfair assumption; however, it was still wrong.

"Yesterday, with the regulators, you were sure I needed the blue one. Why was that?" asked Ryburn, focusing on what he needed.

"You needed the blue one?"

"Yes, Yes! But how did you know I needed the blue one?"

"The chief said you needed that one. Why?"

Aha.

"Are you certain? He specifically said the nine-gauge, the blue one?"

"Yes. He pulled it out of a pile and handed me that exact one. Why is that important?"

Ryburn was too busy thinking to answer that.

"Ryburn are you still there?" asked McSweeney at last.

"Thank you. Ryburn out," said Ryburn. The pleasantry of ending the conversation without simply cutting off the line wasn't second nature to him, he had to force it.

How did O'Connor know what regulator needed to be used for the prototype to work efficiently? Why was he lying about it?

CHAPTER 7: DOESN'T ADD UP

McSweeney had just poked his head up the ladder when Benson grabbed him by the collar and dragged him up the last few rungs.

"Quickly we don't have much time," Benson whispered as he dragged the poor struggling McSweeney over toward the terminal that he had been using to diagnose the decompression and establish the overall safety of the station.

McSweeney didn't bother to attempt to free himself from Benson's death grip; he knew it would be pointless, so he just let himself be dragged along. Whatever it was that had Benson spooked must be serious. Benson was not that good an actor, nor was he prone to dramatic exaggeration, he wouldn't be behaving like this without reason.

"Okay, okay, let go," McSweeney returned in a whisper, but Benson didn't let go until they were all the way to the other side of the room and in front of the terminal.

"Check this out," Benson whispered as he tapped on the interface to bring up the screen showing the data he had been looking at and then pointing to the scrolling text going up the screen. "These are the records for the airlock," he added, pointing out here and there in the logs as each time one of them, mainly McSweeney, had used the airlocks to jettison old hardware.

"So?" asked McSweeney, still puzzled.

"Yesterday the number of actions increased."

"I don't get it!" said McSweeney, still whispering.

"Yesterday the number of entries dropped to nothing," said Benson.

McSweeney still didn't understand, and his confusion must have shown on his face.

"The airlocks are always self-checking their safety, all day every day. Like clockwork," Benson explained.

"Like clockwork because it is set to run on clockwork," McSweeney added. He couldn't help the sarcasm.

Benson very quickly hushed him with a "Shhhhhh!" with a finger up to his lips and a nervous look over toward the ladder.

"Sorry dude!" whispered McSweeney. Benson had never been this serious before.

"I started looking at the airlock data here," said Benson, pointing at the screen again. The time stamp showed when he had started running his checks along with his name against his access code. "Here are the routine checks."

Again, he pointed out the data entries. McSweeney spotted something.

"Whose code is that?" McSweeney asked, pointing to at an "access failure" log entry.

"Exactly! That is the chief's new code, *before* it was activated," said Benson, leaving the statement hanging in the air for a moment to allow McSweeney to take in the impossible statement. "See," said Benson, pointing to the place in the logs where several hours later the entire system was updated with the new codes.

"Are you reading this right?" asked McSweeney, still not entirely sure what he was looking at.

"Of course, but that isn't all." Benson pointed to a spot immediately after the failed entry working code was used.

"What's logging level zero?" asked McSweeney.

"Means that nothing will go into the airlock records regarding anything they do."

"So the chief disabled them?" McSweeney thought he

understood now, and it was a worrying thought, given everything that happened.

"Yes, but why? I spoke to him about the faulty readings I was getting and he basically forbade me from looking into it any further."

"And did you?" McSweeney asked.

"No, I stopped, it was the chief. He said I was wasting my time and I was behind already and I didn't have any reason to disobey his order…" Benson stopped himself mid defence.

McSweeney would have looked, but he couldn't expect that from Benson. "How are you even getting this data? Shouldn't it all be locked down, access control rubbish?"

"No, it's just barebones data now and all the protocols and restrictions were reset to allow for a smoother dismantling process. We have access to everything left…which is only the logs and diagnostics of the systems, including the logs from the central authenticator."

McSweeney nodded, but Benson mustn't have been sure he was following, because he kept going.

"So any time a code is used we know exactly what system was accessed. So even though the airlock logging was set to zero, we still know when it has been accessed and by whom, we don't know what it was used for exactly, but we know it was used."

"It's an airlock," said McSweeney, unimpressed. "It's either open or closed."

"Yes, but let me show you this…" Benson typed in a cross reference search for all of O'Connor's access requests and then explained to McSweeney the data on screen, the time stamp the location and code owner. He walked McSweeney through the log entries, showing that O'Connor, or someone using his codes, had been periodically using airlock-B every few hours the previous morning.

To McSweeney, it made no sense.

"External door!" McSweeney said in astonishment. "He's been leaving the station?"

"Entering the station, look at the sequence," said Benson in a whisper. "The external door is always first."

"These must be wrong," said McSweeney. "It has to be a problem somewhere. What's he doing? Going out for a stroll then coming back in a few hours later? No, no way!"

"Same again in the afternoon," Benson said, scrolling through the logs showing the same access pattern.

"That one says code had expired," McSweeney said, pointing out a single "denied" message.

"But it's immediately followed by accepted," continued Benson. "Someone left the station using his new code. But I haven't given him his new code yet, or the delay instructions for that airlock; there is no way that code could be a memory glitch unless it had been entered first," said Benson, lowering his voice again and nervously looking toward the ladder.

McSweeney could understand that nervousness. If the chief showed up now…

"But check this out" said Benson as he showed McSweeney the records from the evening. They showed that the internal door was accessed, then the external door; the same backward sequence as the entire day. Then four expired code failures from the station side of the internal door.

"That's messed up," said McSweeney. "What the hell is he trying to pull?"

"Then later the manual blast release of the airlock was activated and all these access ports went dead." Benson transitioned the display to another entry that showed the timings of the manual release. "That is captured in a separate system here."

"He accused me of being in the corridor last night around those times," said McSweeney pointing to the four failures. "I reckon he is setting me up for something, another bastard reason to take more fee off me."

"We don't know it's the chief, all we know is that his code is being used."

Trust Benson to defend him. McSweeney spread his hands.

"If not him then who? Ryburn? What would he do outside the station?"

"What if he was out looking for that ghost of his?" said Benson.

"No way, he can barely walk as it is," McSweeney countered. "It's the chief, and he's up to something seriously dodgy I reckon."

"Any idea what it could be?" whispered Benson, motioning for McSweeney to keep his voice down too.

That was the difficult part. "I don't know, but listen to this, one of the old hardware shells had been wedged across the corridor just past the breach door."

"When the corridor decompressed?" asked Benson.

"No, it couldn't have been. It was that old XB82 shell, you know, the really big one, and it wasn't where I had left it. It had been dumped over deliberately; there were big gouges in the corridor beams where it was stuck into place. No way was that done by decompression," said McSweeney resolutely. "That's what I've been telling you… The chief is trying to set me up for something."

"You think he set this up to blame you?" said Benson, giving another nervous look over at the ladder,

"Yes! He's got it in for me I tell you," said McSweeney, almost shouting. He couldn't help it. After all of this, he needed someone to believe him.

"Shhhhhh," Benson replied. "The chief is past due. He's expecting reports on the decompression."

The idea that he might walk in at any moment wasn't a pleasant one, McSweeney had to admit.

"What are we going to tell him?" asked Benson.

"We just tell him he's crooked and we're on to him." said McSweeney.

McSweeney's logic was simple enough. He figured that if they called the chief out on it that whatever he was up to he would immediately stop.

"On to him about what though?" asked Benson.

McSweeney's silence spoke volumes, neither of them had a clue what they would even be accusing the chief of.

"Do you think it has something to do with his secret calls back to lunarbase, and us losing some contract fee?" whispered McSweeney, as they both took another nervous glance at the ladder. Then, accusingly he declared, "He's trying to screw me out of my entire fee by pinning this airlock crap on me. Bet he fines me for it and then pockets the rest."

Benson shook his head. "I don't think the chief would do that."

"His actions are pretty suspicious though," McSweeney insisted.

"None of this makes any sense," Benson said.

"Has he had a reply back from them yet?" asked McSweeney. Maybe that would change things.

"Yeah it came through a little while ago."

"Well what did it say?" said McSweeney

"It was encrypted; we couldn't open the chief's messages anyway."

"Bollocks to that" said McSweeney as he reached for the input panel and brought up the message. "All we need is his password and you know that don't you?" he added. Of course Benson would know it.

"I don't know his password," Benson insisted.

McSweeney didn't believe that for a minute. "But all that access control stuff? Surely it's in there?"

"No! Two different things"

Damn it. "Can we guess it?" suggested McSweeney and typed in backstabbing, money stealing bastard. Predictably, it didn't work, but it made him feel better.

"His birthday?" Benson suggested

"What's that?" McSweeney asked.

"No idea."

At that moment the small icon above the message changed from new to old; someone had just read it.

"Shhhhhh! He's gotta be down there," said Benson pointing to the floor below.

The clang of a foot on the ladder echoed up the hatch and across the room. At that moment it could have been the most frightening sound either of them had ever heard. Benson reached over to the input panel and McSweeney guessed that he was ready to remove everything from the screen.

"No," said McSweeney. "He's got to see this, he has to know that we know."

"Benson…" O'Connor called out as his head popped up from the hatch, "…and McSweeney, good. How are things looking?"

"Reports show that the breach was at the airlock, two blast doors at either end were successfully activated, a third looks to have misfired, but it is sealed too." said Benson, not looking at the chief. McSweeney wasn't so subtle.

"On the far side I couldn't see anything. Ryburn is okay. He got caught up in the decompression. Poor old bugger got picked up and dropped." O'Connor switched his attention to McSweeney. "And what did you see?"

McSweeney wasn't going to shrink from him this time. "I saw a big gaping hole where the airlock used to be."

"That airlock was playing up last night," said O'Connor looking directly at McSweeney, "do you think it caused the breach?"

"How should I know?" replied McSweeney defensively, taking a quick sideways glance at Benson for reassurance.

"I know you were over there last night; did you see anything that could have indicated any problems?" asked O'Connor.

"See!" said McSweeney to Benson, "What did I tell you?"

"What is that supposed to mean?" snapped the chief.

"It means I knew you'd try to pin this on me," said McSweeney, as twitchy as ever.

"Why? Do you have something that needs to be pinned on you?" O'Connor pressed.

"Show him, Benson" said McSweeney, folding his arms

smugly, anticipating his victory.

Benson gave him a "what the hell are you doing?" look.

"Show him what you found." McSweeney repeated, with a lot less smug and lot more desperation in his voice. He knew full well that he could not bring that information back if Benson didn't want to show it, and that would just leave him further out on the limb he'd just stepped onto.

Benson stepped out from blocking the screen on the terminal and with a gesture of his hand invited McSweeney to the controls. O'Connor stepped in with intrigue.

"Benson, please!" said McSweeney, begging now for help. He couldn't be alone on this.

Benson's eyes shifted from O'Connor to McSweeney and back again, as he desperately tried to work out what to do. McSweeney should have guessed this would happen. Benson hated confrontation too much.

"Yeah Benson, please," said O'Connor, openly mocking McSweeney.

"Fine!" agreed Benson, "I'll show you the logs for airlock-B."

"Logging had been disabled," O'Connor interrupted. "I saw that last night when I manually locked the entire airlock."

"Logging was disabled by your code," said McSweeney, arms back across his chest.

"That is impossible; I never disabled the logging. Is this one of your games?" said the chief, plainly accusing McSweeney of foul play yet again.

McSweeney wasn't standing for it this time, though.

"Oh there is more!" McSweeney added whilst staring daggers at the chief.

Benson sighed. "I referenced the access control database to see who had been using that airlock."

"I didn't know you could do that," said O'Connor, crossing his arms and steadying his feet. "What did it tell you?"

Benson brought up the airlock-B access records and McSweeney took over the conversation, quickly turning it into an interrogation. "This is your code opening both airlock doors," he said, pointing at the first two entries, "This is your code failing to lock the doors."

"This is rubbish, that airlock was playing up. These are mine!" countered the chief, pointing to the failed attempts to lock the door, and the anonymous entry about manually locking the door, "but the first two aren't mine. My code didn't work."

"I changed the codes earlier," said Benson.

"And I didn't get my new code yet," replied O'Connor.

"Well someone tried to use it before it became active, so I say you knew what your new code would be and you are just playing stupid, trying to hide some crazy plan to screw us out of our fee," said McSweeney in the manner of an a lawyer presenting a closing statement to a jury. He needed to get O'Connor to admit it.

"What about the last entries, Chief?" asked Benson very calmly, interrupting McSweeney.

"This is wrong," said O'Connor, matter of factly. "This is all wrong. I was nowhere near the airlock when it happened."

He took a step back from his two accusers. To McSweeney, it looked as though he was getting ready to run.

"You were with me at the terminal outside the sleeping quarters, moments after it happened."

"You were there yes, but how do we know you didn't set that up?" said McSweeney with his arms folded, "or perhaps you set the corridor to recompress and ran back to meet us." Turning to Benson, he asked "Is there anything in those logs about disabling the alarms?"

"That is nonsense and you both know it," said O'Connor. "And if I knew my codes why would I use my old ones just to get them denied, explain that one you smart little..." he tailed off. "Is there anything in the logs that I can use to assure you both that the airlocks were playing up and that this had nothing to do with me?"

"I know the airlocks have been playing up," said Benson.

"So what are we arguing about?" O'Connor said with a forced

fake laugh to punctuate his statement.

"Because you told him to ignore them and to forget about it all," said McSweeney with his pointing finger up in front of his face as Benson just nodded quietly in agreement. He wasn't going to let O'Connor talk his way out of this.

"Put that finger away or I'll take it off you," said O'Connor with an icy calm. "When am I supposed to have told you to do this?"

"Yesterday before you came back for breakfast." said Benson, hesitating. McSweeney willed him not to give up.

"Before I came back? I didn't see you until I had breakfast yesterday!" said O'Connor, shaking his head.

"You have selective memory, don't you?" said McSweeney.

"Just come out and say what you want to say!" said O'Connor, and McSweeney could hear the anger there. He kept going anyway.

"You have a convenient way of forgetting things. You threatened me yesterday before breakfast, I guess you don't remember that either?" said McSweeney, his finger pointing more than ever.

"You're just making this up now," O'Connor said, looking at Benson as if expecting support.

"You told me to ignore the airlock warnings and you dismissed my concerns about Ryburn's hopper," said Benson.

"Yeah, the hopper that got us into this mess!" said McSweeney. He'd forgotten about that part. "You set this entire situation up, didn't you?"

"This is ridiculous," said O'Connor.

"And what about earlier when you assaulted me?" said McSweeney, choosing the word "assault" to make it sound official.

O'Connor was just shaking his head in disbelief.

"Do you believe any of this?" he asked Benson.

"I don't want to, Chief, I really don't."

"And where do you think this came from?" said McSweeney, pointing to his split lip.

"You probably just fell over or smacked you head on your bunk, what the hell has gotten into you McSweeney? I thought we settled all this last night anyway."

"You think that is funny do you?" snapped McSweeney. "What's your angle? How much are you trying to scam out of us?"

"You better put that finger away!" O'Connor warned.

"Or what? You'll deduct some more of my fee away? Do we even have any left?"

McSweeney squared right up to the chief doing his best to look intimidating, he did after all have the safety of knowing that Benson was there if anything actually happened."Stop it." Benson shouted, "This isn't helping."

"Fine." said O'Connor stepping down, "but you both better toe the line with me if you want me to forget about this little misunderstanding."

Benson's huge arm was in its usual position across McSweeney's chest, pulling him away from the chief.

Meanwhile, Ryburn, still glued to his workstation, punched in the last few adjustments to his plan and transferred the schematics to the work-sphere. There were a couple of custom parts he would need to craft, nothing extreme, nothing that would take too long. He waited impatiently for the little icon to confirm that the plans had been uploaded. It was taking longer than it should have and he quietly cursed the caretakers for this problem, blaming them for pulling out the wrong power cable or wrong data junction somewhere during their grave-robbing process. He reached for his personal data card and pushed it into the slot on his desk. Nothing important was on the card so he wiped it and was about to click the export command when the original icon flashed confirming that the data transfer had gone through to the work-sphere.

Standing up, he turned toward the bookshelf in the back

corner of the room. He was not looking for his favourite book but for the hip flask he had stashed there, to make sure it was still there. He did not want a drink as he needed a very clear head for now. The conversation with the chief had really confused him and he wanted to be sure he had not "accidentally" drunken his stash. It was still there and, by the weight of it, the contents were untouched. So many things did not add up. Could it have been the drink messing with his head all along? Did he unknowingly knock his head when the airlock blew out? He ran his hands over his head searching for any bumps before dismissing the notion. His head had never hit the ground; he was sure of that, and he did not even lose his glasses.

Once again, he did not bother to try to fully open his door as he sidled through; nor did he bother trying to close it behind him. There had been a time when he would have been paranoid about people coming into his workstation but the unfortunate open door policy that had been running since the door was damaged forced him to get over his paranoia. There was also the fact that no one had believed in any of his work these last couple of years in any case whilst the three caretakers just didn't understand it.

He turned left and started along the corridor. He was a few metres in before realising his mistake, this direction was, of course, now sealed shut but by the blast door. "Focus," he said to himself as he turned around to take the other direction. The portholes along the walls were left uncovered and the shells of equipment this far around had not been affected by the decompression. They all remained stacked high to the ceiling, leaving only enough of a path to walk through on the outer side of the corridor. *Must have been Benson's work* Ryburn thought to himself as no one else would have bothered to leave the portholes clear.

He reached the blast door alcove where he had spoken to the chief the previous morning, but had he spoken to him? He thought he could remember the conversation but it all just slipped away as he tried to reach for the details. The chief had been very annoyed with McSweeney for something, and he was not wearing a hat. That damn hat! He was so sure that it was the chief's hat he had found in the corridor full of the spare regulators, but now he was not so sure. Time was growing so short and he quickly passed the T-junction that led to the central sphere, where he knew the three caretakers would now be comparing notes and sharing stories about crazy old Ryburn and his magical flying rocks. He scowled with disgust at the thought of them all mocking him but smiled again when he thought that they would not be laughing when he moved the station clear. The thought was quickly followed by a flash of guilt when he remembered he was having to do this because of his little incident with the lander. He wondered whether they were plotting their revenge.

The light from the window suddenly darkened, causing him to turn around, as a shadow was briefly cast across the walkway. He saw a flash of floating metal disappearing upwards as the lighting returned to normal. *What the hell was that?* He thought as he rushed into the alcove to get a look at whatever it was. He scanned all around but could not see anything except his breath condensing on the window before evaporating away. He pressed his face right up against the reinforced glass in order to get the best angle possible to see upwards outside and along the station but still could not see anything. *Must have been some debris from the other airlock stuck in close to the station,* he thought to himself, *I wonder if that will divert the lander?* It wasn't a serious thought. The speed at which the lander was moving would annihilate anything in its path without it even slowing down.

A little way down the corridor he could see the familiar green light on the airlock chamber that meant the compression was on. This side must have been McSweeney's corridor, because equipment shells were stacked high to the ceiling and very close together. There were obvious signs of scratch and bend damage to the racking and shells leading Ryburn to the fair conclusion that the dismantling had been carelessly done. To McSweeney's credit, however, everything was stacked securely, with no danger of anything falling over. Ryburn could not let him get away without some form of criticism however, and that criticism was for the actual positioning of the equipment shells. Luckily the lighting was functioning along this stretch of corridor so he could navigate the maze that was left for him by the placement of the hardware shells. He cursed McSweeney as he went for causing him to have to walk from side to side; then he cursed the chief for not processing the remaining ore for him.

Ryburn knew full well that he often stopped listening mid-way through conversations, usually when he felt like he was talking to an idiot, which unfortunately for the caretakers was most of the conversations they engaged him with. There was a very strong likelihood that the chief had never actually agreed to process the remaining ore, but he was stubborn and equally admitted to himself that the likelihood of the chief being awkward and unhelpful was also possible. Reasoning out his side of the argument he concluded that it was realistically unfair of him to expect the caretakers to help him with anything after he had probably cost them a large amount of their salvage and contract fees. Having admitted this to himself, his mind then swung back the other way, belittling the caretakers for not being able to grasp the magnitude of what he was trying to do and what it could mean for the future. O'Connor was the only one who seemed to understand, at least he did yesterday, but this morning he could not care less. Very strange behaviour.

He's the one with the problems thought Ryburn, as his mental zigzag of blame finally landed back on the chief.

He kept one eye on the green light as he approached the airlock since they were all the same age and any potential failing could affect this one as easily as the first. He sincerely hoped it would not fail any time soon, but not from fear for his safety. Part of his plan required a space walk. His concern was that now that this was the only airlock on the station the plan would need to be taken back to the drawing board if it were to fail. He dismissed the thought as his own paranoia. The chances of it failing were effectively zero.

His attention was drawn to one of the windows again. Out of the corner of his eye he thought he saw something, but nothing met his eyes when he turned his head and all he saw was the darkness of space. He continued to run down the caretakers as he sidestepped around yet another equipment shell.

"Son of a… no no no!" he exclaimed as he quickened his step to the hardware in front of him. It was the crafting unit he was intending to use at the work-sphere. Those damn caretakers had not told him that this unit had been moved and decommissioned. "Damn them!" he said aloud and placed both hands on the top of the four-foot tall, bench-like casing. "Why would they even need to move this?" he muttered as he ran his hands over the unit checking for damage. It all looked in order, apart from the cabling connector along the base. The system was an enclosed robotic assembler and was the primary unit he had used for crafting the pieces for the landers he used for the Mercury missions. It housed several robotic arms and laser torches for the precision-crafting of chard-based equipment. Using non-magnetic materials to build the internal systems of the last landers was somewhat of a breakthrough in engineering but, like nearly everything else about the Mercury missions, was lost on everyone.

Ryburn pressed his shoulder against the side of the large, box-shaped unit making a very feeble attempt to move it. It did not move, not even a fraction. There was no way he was going to be able to get this back to the work-sphere. He was going to have to ask the caretakers for help… again, which was not ideal considering O'Connor's speech about staying out of their way and leaving them the hell alone.

"Fine," he said to the machine, quietly swallowing his pride. He was going to ask them for help; no, this time he was going to have to *beg* for help. He shook his head and slapped the top of the assembler in outright disgust at the realisation that it would probably mean losing the final shred of his pride. Most of his dignity was long gone before the caretakers got to the station for the decommissioning phase, but he always had his pride. Having to go begging to O'Connor for help with something the chief had absolutely no belief in was not going to be a pleasant experience, especially considering the conversations they had already had on the subject where he thought the chief was behind him and understood the importance. He gave the top of the assembler another slap. The chief must have been just humouring him in each of those conversations about helping and understanding the concept. Still, that did not explain how he knew about the regulator, unless McSweeney was in on it too.

Ryburn walked away from the hardware he had finished inspecting it. Without being able to fully power it up, he could not tell for sure if it was functioning, but there was no evidence that the case had been removed. The only sign at all that it could be damaged was the hatchet job that someone (McSweeney?) had done in separating the cabling block at the base from the main chard feed.

He walked along the corridor with his head down; he was not feeling very confident about the conversation he was going to have to have very soon. They didn't have much time left before his lander collided with them. He had to get everything in order before that so his 3MP could fly them clear, but that was not going to happen unless he could get the crafting unit operating again. The alternative was entering the final phase of the station early and floating out into space, hoping to be collected, for which there was no hope.

The smelt was still in the centre of the room. Luckily, those useless choppers had not touched it yet; he knew how much they wanted to get their hands on some of the more intricate power units within. Although it did not count for much now, Ryburn could imagine that they would still want it dismantled out of spite.

To his disappointment, the smelt was in the exact state he had left it: a mess. He was used to the old days, when there were people responsible for the daily cleaning of these units; it never crossed his mind for a moment to clean the smelt himself. Those days are long gone. He sighed to himself; he'd be needing the smelt to process the last of the ore into the Mercurian iron. He looked around the rest of the room and the empty spaces on the floor where the other works equipment should have been, looking specifically at the spot that should have been filled with the assembler unit.

Ryburn walked over to the smelt and brought up the display, the screen of which was in a thick casing, to protect against the heat. He brought up the previous settings and added an adjustment for the increased weight. The chemical drums made familiar sounds as they filled with the pressurised liquid used to catalyse the reactions and the noise slowly built up into a solid hum as the various chambers reached their required temperatures. He turned to the spot where he had left the trolley full of the ore, then panned the room again left and right. Always his eyes returned to the spot where the trolley should have been, desperately trying to find it. The trolley was gone.

A brief glimmer of hope that the ore was in the entry chamber for the smelt was quickly gone when Ryburn lifted the hatch to find nothing and for a second he thought that perhaps the chief had processed the ore for him after all. That conversation had happened, he thought again, trying to convince himself that he wasn't going mad or didn't imagine it after a drop too much synth. He walked over to the area by the door where the ore was, certain it had to be there. Turning around in the empty spot looking around the room, a puzzled look crossed his face. He wasn't wondering where the ore was; he was blaming the choppers.

Everything was against him; those fools did not understand the significance. Ryburn beat at that drum again inside his head as he paced around the room checking each and every dark corner for the ore, with or without the trolley. He figured that the metal in the trolley must be worth a buck or so, picturing the idiot grin on McSweeney's face as he imagined him turning out the ore onto the floor, discarding it for junk, whilst appraising the potential value of the trolley. He walked around the room several times, each cycle interrupted partway round as he was drawn back to where the trolley had been. He could not let go of the thought that it should be there. Something so stupid had McSweeney written all over it.

"At least they haven't removed the internal coms yet," said Ryburn acidly to himself. He reached for the small unit attached to the wall. There weren't too many of these left but, by design, they had been patched into everyone's wrist communicators while the caretakers had been at work, a good thing too since he had left his behind.

"Benson," Ryburn said as he pushed the emergency "call everyone" button. Benson was always his first port of call. "Benson, Benson are you there?"

Ryburn's voice came through the com. He couldn't have known about the conversation that had just taken place between the three caretakers, but Ryburn's call could not have come a better time for Benson.

"Benson here," he replied with his thick arm around McSweeney, holding him back from launching into an ill-fated physical attack on the chief. "What is it, Dr Ryburn?"

Restraining McSweeney took zero effort for the big man and he was able to activate his wrist com without a struggle. McSweeney might have wanted to get his hands on the chief, but wasn't strong enough escape Benson's hold.

"Benson? Good! Where are my rock samples? They were next to the smelt but now they are gone."

Rocks? "I don't know Dr Ryburn, I have my hands full at the moment."

"I need the rocks back, has anyone moved them, by accident or purpose. I don't care, but I need them back."

"The smelt hasn't been touched yet to my knowledge," Benson replied feeling the insignificant resistance from McSweeney lessening as he gave up and relaxed a bit.

"Someone has been in here!" replied Ryburn. "The crafting unit has been moved! It's down by the airlock and I'm going to need some help getting it back in here and set up."

"That was moved weeks ago," McSweeney whispered, raising his hand to his ear and spinning his finger around it. "He's losing it."

"Is McSweeney there? We need those rocks back."

"You've commed everyone Dr Ryburn," said Benson, thinking it odd Ryburn hadn't realised that. "He can hear this."

"McSweeney are you there?" Ryburn asked.

Benson let go of McSweeney, freeing his com arm and allowing him to reply but McSweeney just said in the hushed voice meant only for the two people in the room, "I don't know what he's on about."

"McSweeney!" said Ryburn, raising his voice, but obviously trying not to shout. "This is not the time for you to be messing about with my work!" Silence followed for a moment or two. "Benson?" called Ryburn at last, "He's not replying."

O'Connor grabbed McSweeney's arm and, with a speed that caught both McSweeney and Benson off guard, pulled the smaller man towards him. The look on McSweeney's face said it all, for all his bravado he was terrified of the chief. Before Benson could react the chief had McSweeney wrapped up in some nameless arm-shoulder hold. With his free hand the chief pushed the button on McSweeney's wrist com.

"That's enough Ryburn!" O'Connor's voice demanded respect. "A crew wide com is for emergencies only."

"This is an emergency. We need those rocks. How many times do you need me to say it?"

"Do either of you know where they are?"

McSweeney struggled out of, or was more likely released from, the hold that the chief had on him, but O'Connor still held onto the wrist com, maintaining a steely glare on McSweeney. He shot him a challenging look that demanded the truth and insisted on immediate answers.

"I don't know anything about any stupid rocks," said

McSweeney, snatching his hand away and cutting off his end of the conversation.

"Where are those rocks McSweeney?" O'Connor asked again.

"I never touched them."

"You'd better not be lying this time."

"Or what Chief… or what?" Just like that the focus was back on the chief, back on the fee and the accusations of the deductions. "You'll take money off us?"

"Not us, just you!" O'Connor clarified, his eyes meeting Bensons.

"Now where are those rocks?"

"Why do you even care?" McSweeney replied, edging slowly toward Benson for protection. Benson stood there, like a big hulking statue, raising an arm motioning McSweeney to stand behind him. This had gone far enough.

"I want your word McSweeney, your fucking word!" said O'Connor, "And I want yours too!" he added shifting his stare to Benson "I want your word that he hasn't touched those rocks."

Benson guessed that this had gone beyond being about the rocks now. It was about who was in control.

"Hello?" crackled the voice of Ryburn over the coms system again.

"Dr Ryburn, Benson here. McSweeney knows nothing about your rocks, I'm sorry but none of us do."

"Ryburn out." The crackling noise went silent.

"What was in the message, Chief?" McSweeney asked, punctuating his words with a shake of the head.

Benson had been hoping he wouldn't do this now.

"The message?" said O'Connor, unable to stop the worry from flashing across his face. "The message… the message was just confirming the adjusted schedule from home, we need to leave early. But we already knew that."

Something about the way he said it made it impossible to believe, and O'Connor had to know that. He was certainly giving Benson enough strange looks.

"What else was in the message, Chief?" McSweeney asked with an exaggeration on the "Chief" that made it clear to Benson that he didn't think O'Connor was anyone's chief anymore.

"Can we hear the message?" Benson asked.

"This is not my fault," said O'Connor, picking up on the blame being directed at him. "None of it."

Benson and McSweeney's eyes met for a moment.

"It was Ryburn's damn accident," O'Connor insisted. "Forget all these damn machine errors and logging nonsense and get back to work, this station is falling apart at the seams and we're going to need to launch into final phase early."

"How early, Chief?" Benson asked, not convinced at what the chief was telling him. He did not want to believe that the chief was trying to defraud them all out of a fair contracted fee but it was certainly beginning to look that way.

"That lander is still going to hit us, so we need to get out of here before any other pieces start falling off the station. Three weeks; that hasn't changed, so we need to get all the good stuff finished and down below ready. Can you both run some checks on the final phase scenario? We need to get that ready too."

Benson didn't exactly jump into action. He had too much to think about.

"Now!" O'Connor snapped.

After a moment's silence as Benson and McSweeney started to look busy, O'Connor climbed down the ladder. McSweeney shot up a middle finger to the chief's back. He had a mischievous grin on his face but as his eyes met Benson's the grin went flat.

"You have Ryburn's rocks don't you?" He asked with a cold seriousness.

"Yeah," McSweeney answered as if it was obvious. His grin flashed up again, but only for a second. Benson's seriousness killed it off.

"What? He's lying to us! Why should I tell him anything?"

Benson shook his head with a sigh. "I need to start running checks on the final phase prep if we're leaving in three weeks."

CHAPTER 8:

A POSITION OF POWER

O'Connor headed toward the work-sphere. The light carried to the end of the corridor and to the blast door where the porthole window in the door let in little starlight. He walked quickly to the end of the central corridor and turned right, he could see the red light of the airlock at the apex of the corridor. The corridor itself was a mess. He had run through this section during the airlock decompression emergency in order to get to Ryburn and had to side step around the equipment shells and frames but he certainly hadn't taken in the state of some of them. It wasn't a big issue as this was one of the "junk" corridors that would be detached and set free into space as part of the station shedding process just before they entered the final phase. However, some of the bigger hardware frames moved and swayed when he pushed lightly against them. That was dangerous. How had he not spotted this earlier?

O'Connor navigated his way along the corridor. He didn't immediately notice the strange smell in his nostrils as he walked closer to his destination. It was a dusty, electrical odour that somehow smelled cold. The odour was not one he knew, but he recognised it from somewhere. It made his nose twitch uncomfortably, as if he was on the very edge of a sneeze.

The empty shells were in a terrible state. They should have all been stacked close to the walls and tight up against each other. 'Lazy' was the word at the forefront of his mind, closely followed by 'McSweeney'. There were obvious scuff marks along the wall in the few places that did not have hardware piled up against them. It must have been McSweeney getting a bit over eager with moving some of the shells. The corridor curved around to the right and the walking space widened on the far side of the airlock but even then, there were thick gouges taken out of the rubber flooring and walls, with some deep enough to the show the metalwork underneath. The dull lighting caught these, making them more visible against the otherwise dim illumination. O'Connor reached down to run his fingers along one of the deep cuts. A chunk of the rubber flooring that had been cut out was not too far away, it seemed fresh.

Another damage mark on the wall caught his attention: an impact mark. He could picture McSweeney trying to force the badly loaded mini-fork unit along the corridor, scuffing the walls and digging into the floor. The rubber had been split and crumpled up on one edge. Again McSweeney's laziness got the blame for this. He must have got something stuck and then moved it backwards in order to cause this damage to the floor since all the scuff marks were facing the wrong way with respect to McSweeney's dismantling of the oxygen farms and his moving the harvested equipment out to the corridors.

The smell was noticeably stronger at the smelt door.

"Ryburn?" he called out, more of a question to the empty space than an attempt to get someone's attention. From the door he could see the room clearly and Ryburn wasn't there. The air in the room felt thick and the smell, that cold smell, drew him directly to the far wall of the room where it was at its strongest, right in front of the crafting unit. O'Connor was puzzled. Hadn't Ryburn said something about needing help with reattaching the crafting unit? The unit was in position and running although he couldn't see what it was doing since the display units had long since been removed. Following the cables along the floor he could see that a single panel had been forcibly removed and a clip placed into the chard line that was supplying power to the smelt. He had to hand it to Ryburn here since he certainly knew his station. From a caretaker's point of view they just disabled systems and stripped out the chard cabling. They didn't need to know the exact path the cabling took, they just disconnected one end and dragged it out from the other. He would never have known where to lift the flooring to find the clip point. He took a moment to study the positioning, mentally trying to picture where the cabling would be under the floor. The clip points were not spaced at regular intervals and the cable was not even in a straight line from the main junction box to the smelt unit. He would never have known it was there. However, Ryburn did and the crowbar device that Ryburn had obviously used had been left haphazardly on the floor next to the upturned floor panel. It was not the type of behaviour he would have expected of Ryburn, more like the calling card of McSweeney. The crowbar looked like one of McSweeney's tools too, which had been brought the short distance from where he would have been using it in the oxygen farm.

The cold smell was becoming less noticeable and the chief wondered if it was just dissipating or whether he was subconsciously ignoring it. He turned back toward the crafting unit for a closer look. He could hear the cutting laser being engaged underneath the hood but still had no idea what it was making.

What is Ryburn doing? he wondered as he drummed his fingers across on the top of the unit. He was not familiar with the actual internal operations of these machines but he knew that they were for crafting electrical equipment. It was a fully automated system that you either sent instructions to from the controls, or they collected the instructions from a data card input. His eyes panned over to the space where the controls should have been: they were half missing, and even if they were complete the touch pad was not functioning. There was a data card sticking out of the slot. He pushed it slightly to release it and it came out. "New ventures" was stamped on the side and he turned it over before putting it in his pocket. The card itself offered no clues as to what Ryburn was crafting, but it was Ryburn's card; more madness probably, but O'Connor would ask him and bring the card as proof of his delusions. He still wanted to speak to him about the message too and once again reached instinctively for his wrist com to make the call, cursing his mistake yet again. He left the crafting unit churning and buzzing away and walked back to the entrance to use the coms panel. The smell he had followed was now only faint.

Probably something to do with the crafting unit anyway, he thought, dismissing it completely.

O'Connor pressed the coms button, but something was wrong. The button did nothing and the unit was dead. He pushed the button again, a little harder this time. The unit on the wall gave slightly and he knew that that should not have happened. He looked more closely. It had recently been pried open. There were obvious marks where it had been forced. O'Connor removed the cover to inspect it, just in case something simple had come loose.

"What the hell?" he spoke aloud after he had removed the casing only to find the unit had been deliberately broken. The wiring had been ripped out and left loose.

Why would he have done that? he thought, wondering what could have possibly possessed Ryburn to do such a thing. O'Connor had seen the smashed up monitor in Ryburn's workstation, which hinted at a temper, but this was something different: this was calculated vandalism. He had a final sniff of the air before leaving the chamber, the smell had completely gone now. He was none the wiser about what it was, he just knew it was familiar. He still needed to talk to Ryburn about the situation and the message from lunarbase but without his com or the hard wired system he was going to have to go all the way around to Ryburn's workstation.

Stepping out of the smelt into the corridor he headed back the way he had come when the smell hit him all over again. He sniffed in the air and let out a loud dry sneeze, violent enough to whiplash his arms and make his hands feel a bit numb. He slowed his pace, taking in the smell. Cold, electrical, burning? What the hell was it? He recognised it but could not place it. Checking the walls and floors for anything that could be the cause he found nothing. It was a burning smell, he was sure of that. O'Connor took in another deep noseful of the air, following the action with yet another sneeze. It was getting stronger the further along the corridor he went. He wasn't really paying attention to the path in front of him as he inspected the walls and floors for smoke or some other tell-tale sign.

An equipment shell had fallen sideways across the corridor.

"For fuck's sake!" he said aloud as he reached the unit that had blocked the path. O'Connor couldn't believe what was in front of him. It was not a single unit blocking the corridor; it was several units, all stacked so as to deliberately block the only way out of this part of the station. The final phase flashed to the front of his thoughts and a bit of panic set in. That smell, was that something to do with final phase preparations? No, that wasn't it. Even so, O'Connor was now trapped at this end of the station. Ryburn was the last known person down this way, but McSweeney was always up to nonsense and he clearly had a grudge of some sort against him.

O'Connor ran his hands over the end of one of the units. He could slip a hand into the gap and could see out the other side where the green light from the airlock was colouring the floor. He checked the end of each of the two shells turned end up in front of him and then the ones stacked on top of each other. Ryburn or McSweeney couldn't have done this. Benson was the only one with the physical ability to move these so quickly, even with the mini fork lifter, but the fork lifters were broken?

Benson wouldn't do this though, he thought but then recalled the look on Benson's face during the confrontation in the central sphere. With all his strength O'Connor pushed on each of the units but none of them moved. Peeking through the gaps he could see another unit tipped over and pressed up hard against the base of all the others, placed deliberately there to stop him pushing them out the way.

"Hello?" he shouted through the barrier. "Who's done this?"

There was no reply but he was not really expecting one and the sound proofing would prevent his voice from carrying far enough to be heard. After a few repeats he gave up and slumped to the floor to collect his thoughts. Once again that strange smell was disappearing.

O'Connor took a deep breath from his position on the floor leaning up against the damn equipment shells blocking his path. Usually this wouldn't have been that big a problem as the station is circular. However, with the blast door down, he was trapped. Letting out his breath slowly he allowed the moment of despair to pass and then pushed himself back up to his feet. The corridor was dimly lit, any extra light being blocked out by the hulking wall of equipment in front of him. He just needed a bit of leverage. Panning his eyes around the entire unit, he took in the details, this time with his mind working on a solution instead of the problem.

Cutter he thought. If he could cut out just a small area off the corner he could get a bar or something behind it and hopefully leverage out enough of a gap to squeeze through. He stopped there, ending the thought in mid-flow as he could feel the anger boiling up again. Both Benson and McSweeney must have done this!

A crowbar had been left out in the middle of the work-sphere and McSweeney would have a cutter up on the hydroponics floor. His messiness would be his undoing and it was almost too perfect to believe. He ran the few metres back to the work-sphere.

O'Connor shook his head, his quiet satisfaction and expected disappointment visible as he reached the top of the small stairs and saw the state of the oxygen farm. Exactly as he had anticipated;

McSweeney was predictable in his laziness. All over the station there would be bent bolts and snapped fittings, from where he would not finish dismantling a unit properly and would instead reach for one of his trusty crowbars to finish the job, which ironically required more effort.

The smell of the recently incinerated plant life still hung in the air. The cold metal benches that had once housed the plants had been burnt down and stripped of their cables, all but one row, which wasn't even necessary any more since the "go home" oxygen tanks in the central sphere were full, the oxygen storage in this room was all full and even with four people on the station this single row of the plants were producing enough to keep them steady. That is what should have been happening, anyway. O'Connor tapped his finger on the gauge of a tank that should have been full. The digital readout showed that it was not at 100%, but these tanks always had an error tolerance. However, even accounting for the airlock breach there should have been more - a lot more. They were not in any danger of running out, that thought did not even cross his mind as he looked at the other storage units. It was more of a curiosity than a concern at this stage, but they were going through the air almost twice as fast as they should be.

I bet that crafting unit is patched in wrong and somehow leeching off the air, he thought to himself as he tried to picture the thin duct system that moved air around the station. It was a long shot, and it did not even matter, apart from that breech they were not losing air into space. He picked up the cutter, a pistol shaped grip with a drill like tip and then went quickly back down the stairs to collect the crowbar.

With the O^2 issue still annoying him he decided to take a quick look at how the crafting unit had been plugged in. The room was silent, meaning that the unit had finished doing whatever it was doing. He walked to the point in the floor where the cable had been latched onto the primary feed, and checked carefully for an O^2 leak, again amazed at the precision of knowing exactly where the join was under the floor panels. He passed his open palm over the space to check if any air was escaping but felt nothing, not that he expected it to, but he didn't really know much about it.

Why the hell I am trapped in here like a rat? he suddenly thought to himself and firmly gripped the crowbar, as if testing its strength. He visualised tipping those units out of the way after using the cutter to loosen some of the corners.

"What the hell is the purpose of this?" O'Connor asked aloud. "Another one of McSweeney's jokes?" But this didn't seem to be playful, there was an intent here O'Connor didn't like.

It was clear that he and McSweeney were having troubles, but he thought that had all been cleared up with their little talk the evening before. They had both walked away from that conversation with different understandings, obviously. McSweeney had always been the joker, enjoyed playing pranks on people but this was borderline malicious. His attitude this morning and the confrontation were so very close to getting out of hand and yet O'Connor still showed restraint, although not as much as he would have liked, he quietly admitted to himself.

Then there was Benson. What was Benson's beef? All this nonsense about codes and changes with the airlocks. Would McSweeney go as far as to falsify the logs to intentionally implicate him of something to get Benson onside? That train of thought came abruptly to an end. It was not McSweeney's modus operandi. Stupid pranks, yes, but nothing even slightly clever. They both thought he was hiding something from them, which he was. So that left Ryburn. Ryburn was single-minded, although, in O'Connor's opinion, whether that single mind was entirely there was questionable, but with all due consideration of Ryburn's eccentricities, this type of nonsense was beneath him. Forgetting about the who or even the why, though, there was the how. How did they block the entire corridor off like that? Those things were heavy! It just didn't make any sense. Many things in the last 24 hours did not make sense to him and he was now seeing an overwhelming paranoia from his crew mates over the message.

"Yes," he considered, "it is definitely best to keep the contents of that to myself for now."

The crowbar device sat on the floor where Ryburn must have left it, almost as if it were left intentionally, almost arrogantly, for him to see. He pictured Ryburn on his knees connecting the cables to the junction, miming extending his arm in the direction of the tools that were well out of reach, on the opposite side of the uplifted floor panel. He looked again at the cable and the junction connector at the end of the main cable and pictured Ryburn doddering around like an old fool, slightly hunched, turning back on himself as if forgetting why he was there, talking to himself... and placing the tool down, not dropping it, but carefully placing it down, without really paying attention to what he was doing. However, even then there was no way anyone could have known the exact place under the floor where the cable junction was. He corrected his thinking from the last time. This had to be a guess, but then again Ryburn never guessed anything. There were the scratch marks on the floor panel that showed where the crowbar struggled to get a grip on the edge. Looking around at the other panels he couldn't see any other such markings. Nor was there any evidence that the cutter was used. *Very odd.*

O'Connor slipped the pistol-shaped cutter into his pocket and followed the cables out of the floor and over to the crafting unit to where they had been attached to its base. Slowly walking the few steps over to it he could see that this was a rough connection too, looking hastily done. It had been just good enough to get the unit to do what it had now finished doing, whatever it was. Now it was silent and a green light was flashing underneath the area where the display had once been. He lifted the lid and the entire top lifted up and slid away on hydraulic rollers. The contents offered nothing apart from the obvious, they were Ryburn's: two light grey coloured roundish units, each roughly fist-sized. Rolling the first over in his hand, it was cold to the touch, there was a series of what appeared to be random numbers and letters.

Ryburn's pedantic numbering system, thought O'Connor. The random numbers would only make sense to a lunatic. Each unit was identical, a star-shaped cluster of prongs protruding from each end, narrow and tight together. O'Connor gathered them up.

Something to do with his flying rocks experiment! he thought, and could feel a flash of anger building up at the thought of Ryburn wasting his time while they were all in danger. There was nothing to be done about that now, though.

He put the two unknown pieces of hardware in his trouser pockets, one on each hip. He still needed to speak to Ryburn about his previous ramblings about a way to get home. Saving him a trip back to this chamber might loosen his tongue, or more importantly sharpen up his mind and allow a little focus. Either way, there were also the comments regarding the message from home that needed some clarification. How did he know what was going to happen? He really needed to speak to him and not be barricaded down this end of station; time was short. He pulled the lid of the crafting unit, the small bit of resistance from the hydraulics made a comforting cushioning sound as it slowly landed in place.

O'Connor walked back along the corridor at a reasonable pace. There was the yellow/brown tinge from the planet below just starting to shine through the small windows; this side of that ridiculous barricade had not had the portholes covered up. His focus however, was on the barricade. He withdrew the cutting tool from his pocket. Like a pistol, it had a trigger in the typical spot that activated the cutting edge on the barrel end. He pressed it tightly against the top edge of the hardware shell. It was here that he had previously identified a weak point caused by the manner in which it had been wedged into place. It was at the very top of his reach but he turned his head away as he pulled the trigger. The vibration combined with it being at the limit of his reach caused the tool to bounce slightly as the edge found its grip and begun eating its way through the metal. Stepping along the barricade he drew the cutting tool along toward the centre. It was a slow process and very uncomfortable but he was making progress. There were sparks flying off, not carrying enough heat to burn him, but still uncomfortable to look directly at. Somewhere at the back of his mind the light from the planet below began bothering him.

The jagged strip of metal begun to hang down, like a limp tree branch, before finally becoming completely detached and dropping to the floor. With a dull thud it bounced off the rubberised floor panelling and O'Connor then wedged the edge of the crowbar under the base of the unit. It took a fair amount of effort but now that the top edge had some clearance from the ceiling he was able to get about ten centimetres worth of grip and slowly applied some downward pressure until the whole unit tipped up, reaching about 20 degrees. He pushed the crowbar in a bit deeper having to release the weight for a split second, to improve his grip, before catching it again. He felt the pressure on his hands as the weight took hold again and adjusted his grip on the bar, bending his knees as he prepared for a final push.

"If anyone is behind this thing they had better move!" O'Connor shouted out, as loud as he could, but it still came out in an out of breath pant, thanks to the weight of the unit and the strain he was under. The unit made a couple of small rises and on each small movement he re-steadied his stance, letting out a groan of effort as the top edge scraped along the ceiling and the whole unit reached its tipping point. It toppled over, hitting the floor with a thud.

"Job done," O'Connor thought in quiet satisfaction as he admired his handy work and discarded the crowbar and cutter whilst he walked over the unit as if it were a bridge, letting them clang against the back of the other unit that was blocking his way. The adrenaline was still high and he had thrown the tools harder than he had intended, both clanging off the dead frames.

"Rise above it," he said letting out a calming breath as he

walked along the corridor past the airlock, the light of the planet beneath them still glowing through the small windows. In the back of his subconscious mind O'Connor knew that it was different, somehow it was not right, but it had not reached the forefront of his mind as he walked on without giving it another thought. He needed to speak to Ryburn.

The door to Ryburn's workstation was in its stuck-halfway-open position when O'Connor got there but he still paid the courtesy of knocking. Ryburn was at his desk frantically typing away and mumbling to himself.

"Ryburn," he said as the old man turned around in his chair, meeting him with a rather wide smile. "I've received the message from home."

"You have my new regulators?"

"Did you not hear me?" O'Connor replied, "I got bad news from home."

"Yes, Yes, We're on our own," replied Ryburn, strangely dismissive of what the chief considered rather grave news.

"I'm sorry?" said O'Connor in disbelief.

"You already knew that!" said Ryburn, the smile disappearing this time, replaced by a glint of confusion.

"How did you know that?"

It was true that O'Connor had suspected the worst from the planet side clowns back home, but he was sure he never shared those suspicions.

"You said so yourself, remember? When I showed you this..." said Ryburn, pointing towards the prototype device.

"You said you would have my regulators," said Ryburn again, with his hand outstretched. The confused look on O'Connor's face must have given him away. "You said they would be in your pockets? One on each hip..."

"Oh these, from the crafting unit, yes," he said as he pulled out each regulator one by one and handed them over. "The crafting unit you said wasn't even in the room..."

Ryburn nodded. "You said you would fix it. Thank you. It is important, I assure you."

"When?" said O'Connor in disbelief, but Ryburn was already drifting away into his own world of data and schematics.

"When what?" Ryburn drifted back in.

"When did I say I would fix it?"

Ryburn had half an eye on his monitors, not really listening to the chief. He was harmless but clearly was not all there.

"You have the ore too?" Ryburn asked.

"Ore? No I don't have it. We just went through this. Remember?" The sharpness of his tone changed from aggressive to soft. It was clear to him that Ryburn was losing his marbles.

"You said you would solve it," Ryburn said.

"Are you drunk again?" asked O'Connor and leaned in to check for the smell on Ryburn's breath.

"No I'm not," Ryburn insisted. "At least you had the regulators, I suppose."

"Yes I have them, but how did you *know* I would have them?"

"You said you would have them, after you said you would reconnect the crafting unit and get the ore back from McSweeney."

"Oh my god," O'Connor said in frustration. Where to begin correcting that statement? "Whoever connected that crafting unit knows way more about the chard lines than me," said O'Connor, thinking again of the precision of the lines under the floor. "That would be you! McSweeney doesn't have your ore, you've just lost it, and third I said nothing about any regulators."

The elderly scientist was clearly delusional, hearing and seeing what he wanted to. It was the only possible explanation.

"Quite frankly Dr Ryburn," O'Connor said, in a formal tone now, "you are a danger to this crew and I feel I have no option but to confine you to this room. You are not to have any further interaction with the crew."

"I did not imagine it," said Ryburn firmly. He stood up and

added, "You said you would bring me the regulators and here you are."

"It was your card that held the schematics," said O'Connor withdrawing the card from his pocket and handing it to Ryburn.

Ryburn took it and, silently turning to his workstation, brought a particular window to the front of the display.

"Oh dear," he said.

"What is it?" said O'Connor, seeing on the screen the slow, spinning schematic for the regulators.

"I never exported the schematic to my card."

He clicked the export command and after an icon popped up to show that the data had been successfully transferred to his card, it popped out of the reader. He stood with this card in one hand and the card O'Connor had handed him in the other.

"This isn't my card," he said, waving the one O'Connor had given him, and then holding up the one he'd just withdrawn from the reader. "*This* is my card."

O'Connor reached out to take the card back but Ryburn recoiled holding both cards up to his face for a closer look.

"This is very good copy," he said after comparing the two identical cards. "The scratch and scuff marks are all a perfect match."

"Are you sure you don't just have two?" asked O'Connor dismissively.

"Yes I'm sure," Ryburn insisted and showed the chief how each card was exactly the same.

O'Connor was not convinced. "So they look the same, they both have your name and codes on them. It is because they are both yours?"

"Where did you get this from?" demanded Ryburn.

"From the input on the crafting unit, where you left it when you crafted your regulators."

"No, because mine is here," he replied emphasising the card in his hand, "and I already told you crafting unit wasn't ready. It wasn't even in the room."

"Well how else do you explain it then Ryburn?" said O'Connor.

"I..." he hesitated, "I don't know."

He sat back down.

"You better just stay in here from now on," said O'Connor. "The rest of us have a lot to do if we're to enter final phase and get to the collection point."

Ryburn inserted both cards into the reader and clicked a couple of screens, bringing up the attributes of each card.

"This doesn't make any sense," he said. "They are the same card."

"What does that even mean?" said O'Connor. He was losing his patience. He did not have the time to humour this old fool now.

"They are the same card, and I mean exactly the same card."

"It's just your spare Ryburn, it has to be," he said, hoping that it would put an end to the pointless discussion. The old fool had forgotten he had already done the work and had redone everything.

"No. Both cards contain the same schematics for the regulators and both have the same time stamp."

Sure enough, the time stamp on both cards were identical. Ryburn picked up one of the regulators, turning it over to show how the version number printed on the side matched the creation time of the schematic.

"This can't be falsified," he said, showing them to O'Connor, showing the matches and showing him how the regulators that he had collected from the crafting unit twenty minutes ago, which would have taken at least twenty minutes to craft had a unique code printed on them from just seconds ago.

"They are the same," said Ryburn, handing O'Connor's one back and putting his own "real" one on the desk.

"Okay fine, they are the same," said O'Connor, thinking that this whole situation was ridiculous. He snapped the card in half, and discarded it onto the floor. "This doesn't change anything.

You are to stay in here until I figure out what we're going to do." *And more to the point figure out how I'm going to explain this to McSweeney and Benson without an outright mutiny.*

"Yes, exactly," said Ryburn, springing back into life once more. "With the new tilt we need to be out of this position in three hours, which gives us just enough time."

"Just enough time to do what?" said O'Connor, shaking his head with utter disbelief.

"To get set up to fly us clear." said Ryburn again as if it was an obvious answer to a stupid question.

"Oh I see," O'Connor rolled his eyes. We're back to that again, are we?"

"Why do you keep doing that?" Ryburn asked, "Making me repeat myself over and over again. We've been through this already, we've got three hours."

"Three hours?" O'Connor said in astonishment "Where the hell does three hours come from? We have three weeks."

"The new axis tilt and orbit position, caused by the airlock-B incident," said Ryburn as if it were common knowledge.

"Okay, we can work around a new tilt, we just have to get the spin timings right," said O'Connor, the pieces suddenly slotting into place. The light from the planet below was brighter than normal because the station was sitting at a different angle. If they were spinning they would be on a bad direction for final phase separation and clearance acceleration. Which would mean that the three weeks might have to be shortened. He would have to go back to the central sphere and make the calculations himself, away from crazy Ryburn.

Both men stared at each other for a moment, each equally stubborn.

"But we've been through this," said Ryburn now looking to be also losing his patience. "How is McSweeney coming along with the ore?"

"McSweeney doesn't have the ore! We've just been through this."

"Oh good, because we will be needing that."

"Didn't you hear me? McSweeney doesn't have it."

"You said he did!" replied Ryburn and the conversation deteriorated into another loop.

"That is enough," O'Connor snapped. "McSweeney doesn't have the ore; he never did have the ore. He swore to me that he didn't have it and I believe him. I don't want to hear anything more about it. You stay in here out of the fucking way, and count yourself lucky I'm not having you sedated.

"Chief!" came the voice of Benson from behind the half opened door. "How did you get here so fast?"

The door was too narrow for Benson to fit through so he gave it a little push, then when it didn't move he flexed his arm and gave it a proper push, grinding it into the wall and popping it back onto its rollers. He pulled it forward and back to test it. The door moved with a clean rolling action.

"I'm glad you are here," said O'Connor. "Please tell the good Doctor Ryburn what McSweeney told us both about the ore."

"That he will go put it back in the work-sphere," Benson said, standing up straight like a solider. O'Connor looked at him in shock. Where the hell had that come from?

"What? No he swore he didn't have it."

"Chief, are you okay?" said Benson, looking concerned and confused.

"I'm perfectly okay. Stop asking me that," growled O'Connor. "And I need a word with you both. What was all that in the corridor blocking me in?"

Benson looked over toward Ryburn but the scientist merely shrugged.

"I don't follow you, Chief." said Benson.

"You and McSweeney blocked me in down the end of the station."

"I don't understand what I'm being accused of here," said Benson. He was not lying; O'Connor knew him well enough to see that.

"Oh forget it then," said O'Connor. "What are you doing here anyway?"

Benson looked again to Ryburn for backup.

"You told me to come and help Dr Ryburn."

"What?" said O'Connor, raising his eyebrows high and tipping his head forward slightly, as if to trying to hear better.

"Don't worry, he's been doing this to me all day too," said Ryburn dismissively.

"What are you guys playing at?" O'Connor asked, turning to look at Ryburn so as to include him in this.

"What are you asking Chief?" Benson asked calmly.

"All of this. You accuse me of tampering with airlocks, block me down the end of the station and keep telling me I've said this or I've said that. McSweeney seems to be on the edge of doing something stupid towards me over God only knows what," O'Connor quickly enumerated whilst going red in the face with anger and frustration. "Are you just messing with me? Because if you are I fail to see the joke!"

"Chief, you aren't making any sense," said Benson after sharing a look with Ryburn.

O'Connor took a deep breath to calm himself. "I want to know why you are all doing this."

"Chief, I don't think you are yourself, are you sure nothing is wrong?" asked Benson.

"Not yourself…" Ryburn repeated.

"Maybe you're feverish," Benson said stepping forward. "Do you need to lie down for a spell?"

"Perhaps he should be the one confined to quarters, we've got a lot of work to do…" said Ryburn, standing up. "…and fucking sedated."

O'Connor looked around him. The imposing figure of Benson coming toward him, yet still standing in front of the doorway had him trapped now. Ryburn standing up was not a threat but his instinct took over, and that instinct told him to get out of there as something bad was going to happen, something was not right with the entire situation and it was now clear all three of his crew mates were in on it.

"To hell with all of you, I'll check out this new axis and decide what we need to do," he said, moving toward the door. He needed to get back to the central sphere and away from those two. He pushed past Benson; the big man hardly moved, but let him pass. He was half way along the corridor when he saw McSweeney heading toward him, bouncing along in his carefree manner holding something in his hand.

"Chief!?" said McSweeney in great surprise turning to look back along the corridor. "How did you... do that?" he looked back at O'Connor with a grin, like he had just seen a magic trick.

"Are you in on this too?" O'Connor shouted at McSweeney.

"What?" said McSweeney, surprise crossing his face. "I've done nothing, I've put them back in the work-sphere just as you asked, and I've got that thing for Ryburn, how did you get..."

"You better not be talking about what I think you are talking about," interrupted O'Connor, his fist clinched at his side. McSweeney was turning back down the corridor. Something was bothering him. Was he looking for something or someone, or for Benson to hide behind?

"What did you put back?" O'Connor demanded, knowing the answer, but needing to hear it.

"Ryburn's rocks… just as you asked" said McSweeney, the smile slowly leaving his face.

"You lying little..."

"This is another set-up, isn't it?" McSweeney said stepping backwards and looking down at what he had clenched in his right hand. "You've set this all up, you swore on your life."

O'Connor just saw red. The ore that McSweeney had sworn blind that he did not have. It was the blatant lying to his face that angered O'Connor the most.

"So you hid the ore and you lied to me." It was a statement of fact not a question.

"This is a set-up," shouted McSweeney back to him, still

edging slowly backwards. "Why do you do this? I'm only doing what you asked." He turned as if to run off down the corridor. "Benson!"

The call to Benson was pointless; the soundproofing swallowed it all up.

Everything that McSweeney had done over the last day was passing through O'Connor's mind. The accusations, the lying, the jokes, the shouting, and the attitude; he was like a powder keg waiting to be lit so he could explode. The vein in his neck was raised as he stepped towards McSweeney, stalking him. McSweeney stepped back keeping that distance.

Everything happened so fast. McSweeney lifted his arm to use his com, O'Connor read this as an act of aggression and slapped the arm away. McSweeney instinctively stabbed forward with what he was holding in his right hand. A looping right hand punch from O'Connor swung and landed very awkwardly on McSweeney's shoulder in a flopping motion. O'Connor staggered off balance and collapsed to the floor in a heap taking McSweeney to the ground with him. He tried to get to his feet but stumbled back to the floor. His arms and legs were not doing what they were meant to. He felt the pain in his side and he carefully moved his sluggish arm to it and pulled out a syringe.

What the hell was this doing in my side? was the thought that flashed through his mind, quickly followed up by feelings of blame and anger directed at McSweeney for, what was so apparent to him now, sedating him. He had lost full control of his arms and legs, and was just lying in a heap. He was aware of McSweeney scrambling to get to his feet, dulling impacts on his chest he assumed were McSweeney's feet kicking frantically to get out from under him. All he could hear was his own breathing, slow and steady but very loud to his ears. It was the only thing he could feel. McSweeney was standing over him shouting.

"You set this up too," he shouted down at him and landed a stiff kick to O'Connor's ribs. "What do you get out of this?" he shouted again in time with another kick. "I swear you're going out the airlock now! You promised it was over!"

O'Connor didn't feel any pain; he was aware of the kicks landing but did not feel them. Again and again the kicks came in and so did the tirade of abuse and accusations and the threat of being put out of the airlock. His hearing was fading out as the sedative took full hold, but the accusation of "setting this up" and "having it all planned out" continued for a little while longer before it finally stopped. He was aware of McSweeney picking him up by the shoulders, just enough to drag him behind a large equipment shell.

"I'll leave you here where you won't be found," he said punctuating it with another kick. The last thing O'Connor saw before his vision completely faded away was McSweeney's legs hurrying off toward Ryburn's workstation.

Neither of them saw the figure standing in the shadows looking on with disappointment.

O'Connor was drifting from a state of complete unconsciousness into being semi aware of his surroundings and back again. Footsteps, voices, the hard floor; he was always aware that he was on the floor. Was he being dragged? Whose voice was that? It was familiar. Was it the voice of his father? No, that would be ridiculous. He tried to see but with all his effort he couldn't open his eyes. He was lying down, he had to be. Was there any way of knowing? That voice again and then another. The second voice; was it Ryburn? There was a long pause between voices... or was there? There was the sound of a voice, but he couldn't process the words. He still couldn't open his eyes. A flash of light, then dark again. Now he was still, then shortly after moving again. He was sure of it this time. Had he been floating? He was being dragged, he could feel the pinching under his armpits as the material caught the skin. Upright. He felt upright again. Did his head just clonk on the floor? He felt his head shudder like it had, but didn't feel it hit. He was still on the floor, eyes still refusing to open.

What is going on? he thought, but his mouth didn't move so it stayed in his mind. Underneath his eyelids he could see the light pass to dark then back again. That voice again. Still not able to pick out the words. He felt safe, or at least he was not aware enough to feel in danger. Then nothing, he was unconscious again. Silence, then a tugging on his jacket, his head suddenly cold, then warm again.

Who's there? He wanted to say because someone was there, but his mouth still was not moving and he said nothing. Silence, a pale white glow to his right. A pinch on his arm. He felt that. Then the familiar voice again. It sounded strange in his ears, but he knew it. The voice was gone but the sounds it spoke echoed in his head, slowly becoming clearer and clearer and his mind processed it into words.

"This will wake you up."

What had happened? Floor, he was on the floor, his eyes slowly opened, no he was on a bench. He still could not move but he could see, it was all blurry, but he could see. Slowly but surely the movement returned to his body and he reclaimed control of his limbs. He remained on the bench, still very hazy about what had happened or why he was there. His vision slowly came back into focus and he became aware of his surroundings. He slowly got to his feet. He was in the airlock changing room. What had happened? How long had he been out? Why the hell was he here?

The big hand of Benson grabbed him by the shoulder and spun him around, almost sending him back to the floor. O'Connor flinched and instinctively tried to swat the hand away.

"Sorry Chief. Didn't mean to startle you," said Benson. Ryburn was there too.

"I'm fine," said O'Connor, steadying his feet. "Where's McSweeney?", and then turned to Ryburn, who seemed to be winking at him, looking at him with one eye, then the other.

"Why are you winking at me?" O'Connor asked Ryburn

"Nothing," said Ryburn, "just checking something."

"Where's McSweeney?" O'Connor repeated.

"Oh don't worry about him," said Ryburn.

O'Connor could not remember why, but did not want McSweeney anywhere near him.

"Good job you're all suited up. We don't have much time, you've got to come with me," said Benson.

"Suited up?" O'Connor repeated, not following what was going on.

"Only one left," said Benson, opening up the cupboard taking the final suit out. He gently placed the suit onto the bench next to the chief, who was now sitting on the bench looking very confused. Benson collected gloves, boots, and a helmet from the rack.

"Come on Chief!" Benson said in his thick booming voice, and started putting on his space suit. O'Connor sat on the bench trying to process everything that was going on. Benson was in his suit fairly quickly considering how big he was and how small the suit was. The big man reached for a tank and checked the reading. It showed there to be only 35 minutes left. Benson paused for a moment, checking the reading of O'Connor's tank.

"I guess this will have to do; it will be enough."

"Enough for what exactly?" said O'Connor. The thought to object did not even enter into his still slightly sedated mind.

"To angle the prongs to…" said Benson, the end of his reply muffled as he helped O'Connor with his helmet. The new oxygen tasted cold and caused him to take a double breath.

"Why am I in the airlock?" he asked as Benson shut the door behind him and punched in the commands to normalise the airlock chamber with the outside vacuum.

"Benson! Benson?"

There was no reply, nothing. Without his wrist com, he could not talk in the space suit either.

The outer door opened and he followed Benson through to the outside of the station.

He felt Benson knock on his helmet. He turned round to look at him and tapped a finger to his own ear and shook his head. Benson turned slowly, the magnetic boots holding onto the external wall of the station.

Benson was making "hurry up" gestures with his arms as they both walked back along the outside hull of the corridor in the direction of the central sphere. O'Connor was concentrating on his footing, not really taking in anything around him and still not questioning the reason they were outside the station.

They reached the central corridor and Benson stopped. He tapped the oxygen readout on the outside of his suit and pointed along the station in the direction of where the rest of the corridor should have been, but it was gone. What happened to the corridor?

Inside his suit Benson was talking on the coms, but of course that wasn't getting through to O'Connor.

O'Connor tried to follow but Benson stopped him and pointed him in the opposite direction.

O'Connor started walking the other way, still not clear on what was going on. As he slowly walked around the circumference of the outer wall, he could see that some serious damage had been done to the station as there appeared to be nothing left of the outer ring. The part of the walkway with Ryburn's workstation was completely gone. He could see it off in the distance along with huge chunks of station floating off toward the Venus atmosphere. *Had something gone wrong when they entered final phase?* The yellowy brown from the planet below dwarfed everything else in his vision as he slowly walked along the length of the station, still not sure why he was outside.

The clipping vibration of his magnetic boots releasing and attaching was the only thing he could feel. It was completely silent apart from the sound of his breathing. His mind was clearing and he started to question what he was doing out here. He stopped and turned around to see where Benson was and could see the big man at the far side of the station. He was holding the end of a pole that was sticking out of what was left of the corridor.

No that couldn't be final phase, if it was the only thing left would be the central sphere he thought as he continued walking along the outer wall.

Benson had reached his destination, he slowly stepped the 90 degrees all the way around on the flat edge of the breach door. He hated those big steps; they seemed to go on forever before the magnets in the boots locked on again. He could see the "spike" sticking out of the porthole in the middle of the door. The pole had diamond cabling coiled around it.

Could have been worse, Benson thought, thankful that all that was wrong was some loose cables. He reattached the cables to the pole before climbing back up onto the roof of the walkway. He looked up to the far end of the station to where O'Connor was heading. He could see that he had cleared the central sphere and was on the central corridor nearly at the junction. He looked at his oxygen gauge: 25 minutes left. Did he have time to get over the far side and back? He toyed with the idea for a moment.

"Sorry Chief, you're on your own," he spoke into his helmet.

"I've got this Benson. Don't worry about me, you get back inside," came the crackling sound of O'Connor's voice through the headset.

"Chief, I'm nearly out of air, I gotta get back." Looking back over again he saw McSweeney approaching. "McSweeney must have been sent out to help us I see him coming up from the airlock" McSweeney waved back, then tapped the side of his helmet.

"Right you are I see him," came the chief's reply. "I guess his helmet isn't working either."

O'Connor's mind was clearing but he still did not know what the task was he was out here to do. He looked back toward Benson, who was walking back along the corridor. Then saw McSweeney approaching him and motioned for him to go back. He pointed to his oxygen read out; he was trying to tell him something. O'Connor checked his: the bar was in the red. If he had been more alert perhaps he would have realised it. In contrast McSweeney showed his readout, well into the green.

It was very unMcSweeney like. The selfless gesture felt like a throwback to the old team spirit when they were all friends. He did not argue. McSweeney was right, getting back to the airlock was going to be close. Basic training here was for him not to hurry back, just make his way over at a normal and steady pace. Looking at the readout he found he had 10 minutes left, and it would take him a good five to get back and through the airlock. A quick look over his shoulder showed him McSweeney flipping over to the edge on the outside of the blast door. He hated that "big step" and preferred to "climb" over and down instead.

McSweeney had more than enough air to get back, so he did not enter O'Connor's mind in that context again. But what did enter his mind, or returned to his mind was his recollection of events leading up to "being drugged unconscious by McSweeney" which came flooding back like a torrent. He felt his breathing rate increase. He had to calm that down, but he struggled. The threats of putting him out of the airlock were too clear. Then the waking up in the airlock. Rather than being selfless, was McSweeney planning to kill him?

He continued along the top edge of the station and past the central sphere. Slow, calm breaths. He was going to have to get to the bottom of this once he was back inside. It was all slotting into place. McSweeney must have dragged him to the airlock, then been scared away by Benson. He had to get back to the station before McSweeney. He looked behind him and saw McSweeney already back on the walkway. All McSweeney needed to do realistically was slow him down for a few minutes. He had no com so no one would be coming to help him. The panic set in now, he felt helpless. The alarm in his helmet triggered to show that his breathing rate was way up and he was not even having the bonus of moving faster toward his destination. He looked back over his shoulder again, McSweeney was gone. Had he gone to the other side of the station? He took some deep relaxed breaths in and finished the walk over toward the airlock. The outer door was open as expected and he swung his legs through. This was a good sign. If McSweeney had gotten there first the door would have been shut.

O'Connor hit the button to close the door and re-pressurise the chamber. He had beaten McSweeney back. He took off his helmet and took a deep breath in of the fresh station-side air. He felt safe again. He reached out to the airlock controls to open the door but the controls were locked out. He pushed the button again with the same result. McSweeney was on the other side of the glass window, already out of his space suit. He must have ducked over to the other side of the walkway whilst they were outside to get in before him. McSweeney had anger in his eyes: the same pure hatred that he remembered while he was kicking him in the ribs. McSweeney had a mean streak, especially when in the position of power - which he undoubtedly had now. There was not a shred of remorse or mercy on his face.

O'Connor knew what was coming, and had just enough time to stuff his helmet back on before the outer door exploded outwards. He would have already been dead except that in that split second he was able to reattach his air supply. He desperately tried to grab hold of something as he was blasted out of the airlock but it was all over too quickly. He was flipping around and spinning wildly, flailing at the emptiness. On each spin he was getting further and further out. The no oxygen alarm was blasting in his ears now. Even if he was able to regain control with the small suit thrusters, and if he had more than just a few seconds of oxygen, he would still be unable to get back into the station. The external door was gone, meaning that the internal one would already be blast locked. His lungs rasped for air as the last of the tank emptied. He was a long way out now and getting further away. He held the last of his breath and calmly closed his eyes accepting his fate. McSweeney had killed him.

CHAPTER 9:
FLOWERS

A SUDDEN IMPACT forced O'Connor to open his eyes. He had collided with something that had slowed his uncontrolled spinning and the shock caused him to take an involuntary gasp for air. To his surprise, he was breathing. His lungs gasped deeply as he took in the newly-found oxygen, which was hot and burnt slightly. Nevertheless he was breathing. He was not dead.

As his momentum spun him around, he saw a suit that he didn't recognise. The mysterious figure, an impossible man, had grabbed hold of him and somehow made him breathe again. He raised up his oxygen display to find that he now had twenty minutes worth in his tank. He tried to turn his head to get a good look at his saviour but he was always just outside his field of vision. His spin was slowing and each revolution gave him a slightly longer view of the station. The central sphere and central corridor were all that was left. Ryburn's workstation, the sleeping quarters, the work-sphere and what was left of the outer corridor were all drifting silently away.

A flash of blue light filled his vision as the peculiar prongs sticking out either end of the broken central walkway lit up. Their intensity dulled, then brightened again, as if it was fighting to exist. By the time his next spin had brought him around again there were two bolts of electricity slowly snaking through space toward the front of the station. What the hell was it? After his next spin the arc was gone, but the prongs were still glowing, brighter than ever. The station was moving! With the planet below dwarfing and distorting everything, it was impossible to gauge distance, but it was moving. On his next spin it was definitely further away.

Judging by the way he had stopped and was staring in its direction, his mysterious rescuer was equally fascinated by the sight but they were both being drawn toward…nothing. He caught a glimpse of a cable that was attached to both of them but it wasn't leading anywhere. O'Connor tried to look in the direction the cable was taking them but his eyes wouldn't focus. It was like they were straining to look at something that wasn't there. He looked away, looked at his new-found friend.

The stranger's suit looked nothing like his own, it was obviously of a much better, more expensive, design. Just looking at how it was put together showed a freedom of movement and flexibility not possible with his own suit.

"Who are you?" O'Connor asked. "Why have you saved me?" He paused and then continued "Thank you for saving me." Even knowing he wasn't being heard, O'Connor found this very humbling.

The mysterious figure pointed in the direction they were heading in, then moved his hand across his helmet, showing the motion of covering his eyes.

O'Connor nodded his understanding, although it was in his helmet; from the outside the suit didn't move. The man put his hand back up across his eyes, pointed at the direction, then pointed at O'Connor. The only thing he could think of to indicate he had understood was to give a thumbs up. The stranger replied with a thumbs up of his own.

O'Connor watched the man tip his head down into his chest, looking like he was preparing to protect his eyes from something. O'Connor pulled his protective visor down, tucked in his head and closed his eyes, not knowing what to expect but having no choice in the matter. Gravity took hold and he dropped onto a hard surface in a heap. He opened his eyes, very slowly lifted up the visor and sat up slowly wondering what had just happened. He had many questions for his new friend, who was now standing over him without a helmet.

Short brown hair, a haircut style he hadn't seen before, he assumed it was "fashionable" and therefore didn't like it on principle. His face was very smooth, he would have guessed mid-twenties, and his eyes had a purple metallic shine to them that gradually faded back to a normal brown. The man had a very excited, almost childlike, grin and was bouncing around like it was Christmas. He extended a hand, mouthing words that O'Connor couldn't hear.

O'Connor took the hand and pulled himself to his feet, difficult in the heavy space suit. He could see the man was talking but he couldn't hear a thing. O'Connor unclipped his helmet from the oxygen tank, noticing a strange grey device attached to the side of the tank. It had a red exclamation mark printed on the side, with "Emergency" in bright yellow underneath it.

"You are Chief O'Connor right?" The man said again, with an overbearing enthusiasm. Now, O'Connor could hear it.

"Yes," replied O'Connor, finding his feet and looking around at the room he now found himself in. The external and internal doors clearly showed it to be an airlock.

"Who are you?" he asked still looking around.

"Sorry. I'm Anderson. This is…" he said stepping back "… very, surreal, you look just like the pictures."

O'Connor continued looking at his surroundings. He decided that this had to be some special unit ship come to save them after all.

"Just Anderson?" O'Connor asked.

"Yes," replied Anderson, still staring with awe at O'Connor.

"No rank?" O'Connor asked hoping to get some clue as to who this man was working for.

"Rank? I don't follow you."

"What ship is this?" O'Connor interrupted, still trying to take in his new surroundings which he considered very non-standard.

"There are actually two, and one of them is made of many ships. This is the Caution of King John but we're latched..." he dropped his head with a slight smile of embarrassment. "... onto the O'Connor."

"The O'Connor?" said O'Connor, thinking to himself that it was a stupid name for a ship. "I'm not familiar with that name. What company are you with?"

The names of the various contractors were running through his head as he tried to match him up with the best fit.

"I'm not really with any company anymore," said Anderson as he motioned to O'Connor to follow.

The controls on the door were like nothing he had ever seen before. Anderson reached his hand out toward the flat slick black panel and an intense blue light flashed, before a small 30 cm square screen slid forward in front of the panel. It was touch sensitive, Anderson pushed his fingers into the display and spun his hand around. The door opened into the ceiling and the screen disappeared in an unnecessarily flamboyant flipping over and shrinking to nothing.

"Lancers?" asked O'Connor marvelling at the technology. The Lancers were a rival caretaker firm, who had just recently bought out the Neith Contract. O'Connor had never been on one of their ships, although he had heard that they were impressive.

"The Dynasty?" said Anderson in astonishment then with disappointment asked. "You work for the Lancer Dynasty? Doyle said they started around this time?"

O'Connor had not heard that term before, but whatever this Dynasty was, he was no Lancer.

"No I certainly do not," said O'Connor screwing up his face. "Do you work for them?"

"No" said Anderson, visibly insulted by the question. His brow creased and scrunched up his nose, and his lip curled as he answered. It was obviously a touchy subject.

"Maybe they aren't the same firm," O'Connor said, trying to placate him.

"No they are the same, they make you learn their history in school. You can leave your… suit here." Anderson was now looking O'Connor's suit up and down, he wasn't impressed.

"What type is yours?" asked O'Connor, "I thought mine was top of the line!"

"I guess they must have been," Anderson replied, not answering the question.

They took their suits off. Anderson's came off a lot quicker than O'Connor's, who hung his suit on one of the hooks in the cupboard and looked around for somewhere to attach his oxygen tank.

"Just leave it there," instructed Anderson pointing at the floor while wrinkling his nose.

"I'm sorry about the smell," O'Connor apologised. "After a long time in space we tend to get a bit whiffy."

"Don't worry about it," said Anderson.

"Is this the extra oxygen?" O'Connor asked, feeling the small narrow canister that was sticking out the side of his tank.

"Yeah, that's it. Never used one before. Surprised it worked," said Anderson making a stabbing motion in the air that painted a mental picture of how he must have used force to break the tank's surface. "I was expecting your tank to be much stronger and I almost hit it too hard."

The canister fell off in O'Connor's hand.

"I can fix it if you really want to keep it," said Anderson. "I suppose it might be worth something to a collector." The way he made the offer implied it was junk which, looking at the gaping hole in the back of the tank, it was, since the emergency air device had punched right through the outer-casing using technology that he had never heard off, let alone seen.

"Does your head get cold like that?" said Anderson, bringing attention to O'Connor's baldness.

"Yeah it does," O'Connor replied, tapping his breast pockets, looking for his hat whilst thinking that it was an odd and rude thing to say. His hat was there but he quickly found the large rip in the side of it. "Damn it," he said, "My favourite hat." He folded it over trying to hide the tear.

"Barely noticeable!" commented Anderson as the two of them set off along the corridor.

O'Connor continued to look around surprised at the small things he had never seen on a ship before. There were pot plants and flowers everywhere. It was very unusual and yet they somehow did not look out of place. Then there were the big things like doorways into rooms filled with obviously advanced equipment which nevertheless looked antiquated, dull, scuffed and well used. It was the same with the walls: everything he saw made him think the ship was old, but the design itself was rather futuristic.

"Is this a station?" he asked.

"No, it's a ship! Do you like it?"

It was an odd question, out of place when talking about a ship, more like being asked if you liked a friend's house. "It's different," he said as he ran his finger along the panel on the wall. A ripple effect emanating out from his touch and bouncing back once it hit the ceiling and floor. "What does this do?" he asked watching the ripples bounce around, over each other and back again.

"Nothing!" said Anderson.

O'Connor was not impressed; why have something with no purpose on a space ship? It merely added weight, complexity, and chard usage. "And why all the flowers?" asked O'Connor, looking at a huge display of small blue wild blossoms that almost covered the wall of the corridor.

"For air of course," replied Anderson, "and filtration."

"Really?" O'Connor responded whilst thinking that there was no way that these flowers could be producing oxygen in significant amounts, even though they appeared to be in every available space.

"Really!" Anderson said, continuing to walk, but still taking the occasional look at O'Connor as if he was an oddity that he needed to check was still there.

"So you don't have a hydroponics suite?"

"Not as such," said Anderson slowly, as if he were holding back information.

"Short range then?" O'Connor continued, trying to put the pieces together and establish what firm this man was with, and what his purpose was this far out. There was no way they could be this far into the system on oxygen tanks alone and, judging by what he had seen so far, the ship was far too big to be a runner class attached to a big freighter.

"We're as long range as you get," said Anderson, laughing.

"What does that mean?" O'Connor snapped, irritated by the condescending tone.

"I'll let Doyle fill you in on that one. I'm still not 100% sure of it myself."

O'Connor took that to mean that this "Doyle" person was in charge and stopped asking questions; Anderson wasn't very forthcoming anyway.

The two men walked in silence. Anderson kept looking over at O'Connor with fascination whilst O'Connor, although it was beginning to get on his nerves, pretended not to notice. At the end of the corridor a short young man in a very tidy dark grey three-piece traditional suit was standing to the left of an archway door. The man had a very blank look on his face and nodded in a submissive way when O'Connor made eye contact. A shiver ran up O'Connor's spine when their eyes met and he could feel the goose bumps rising on his arms. Anderson didn't acknowledge the man at all as they entered the room he was "guarding".

It was a very comfortable-looking room fitted with several padded arm chairs set around a coffee table. *A coffee table?* O'Connor thought to himself in astonishment as he couldn't even remember his last coffee, let alone a coffee table, what a waste of weight.

"What type of ship is this?" he asked again, horrified at the blatant unneeded niceties of this room. It was a long way from being decadent but even so it was a far cry from the bare essentials he was used to. Anderson motioned him towards a sofa.

A sofa thought O'Connor incredulously *in space*? The sofa was fitted against the wall, filling up the space perfectly, its red fabric worn in places you would expect to be worn after a long period of extended use.

"Wait here," said Anderson.

"Okay," said O'Connor. "Should I remove my shoes as well?"

"Sarcastic too," said Anderson. "You two will get along perfectly."

The door slid shut as he left the room, his silhouette clearly visible through the frosted glass until the outline of the smartly dressed man obscured it as he stepped over in front of the door.

O'Connor sat down on the sofa, at first on the edge testing it out, and then sinking right back into it. He hadn't sat on anything like that since he left Earth many years ago. He looked around the room; it was what he would have normally called a sitting room. There were plant pots all around the edges of the room although these ones weren't flowers and, since he was never much of a botanist, didn't have a clue what they were. The longer he sat there the more out of place everything seemed and the more questions he had for this "Doyle" person.

The lighting in the room was brighter than on Neith, and it hurt his eyes. On the wall opposite him was a large screen. At first glance it appeared to be a painting of a girl on a swing underneath a tree, but it kept changing and after a short period it was a boat on the edge of a lake.

Perhaps it'll help, thought O'Connor thinking that it was a computer access terminal or something. He got up and nearly fell over the coffee table, practically falling as he touched the black panel next to the screen. A blue screen appeared in front of his eyes, just the same as in the airlock. He pushed his fingers into the display in the same way Anderson had done and his fingers felt cold and tingly. He moved his index finger ever so slightly and the painting on the screen flashed into something else, he moved his finger again but this time the painting moved to the side, sliding off the edge of the screen and disappearing. Intrigued, he tested what affect different motions of his fingers had on the screen. He managed to flip a painting of an old lady on a chair upside down, then have a dozen or so paintings all on the screen at once before somehow manipulating it back to showing a single picture, this time two horses running along a beach, but it was displayed sideways. It was obviously not a computer and even if it was he did not know how to use that weird blue screen control thing properly. He walked around the room, touching the leaves on the plants, and then sat back on that very comfortable sofa wondering why he was being kept waiting.

The door opened and Anderson stepped back in, followed by a tall lady with a lot of curly black hair.

"Doyle, may I introduce you to–..."

"Chief Jake O'Connor," she interrupted, extending a hand toward him, "the actual Chief O'Connor."

O'Connor stood up and accepted the handshake, which was firmer than he was expecting. Doyle was an attractive lady, mid-thirties O'Connor guessed. She had a fairly round face but the beginnings of wrinkles around her small nose gave the impression she was on the verge of frowning. Her curly hair was cut short to her shoulders. She had the same amazed look on her face as Anderson and unfortunately the same recoil to his odour *Such a great first impression I make* O'Connor thought to himself.

"He's got the bald," said Anderson.

O'Connor turned to glare at Anderson. "That's a very rude thing to say," he barked, his dislike of Anderson growing even more now that he knew he was not in charge. Without knowing who they were or who they worked for it was clear enough that he outranked Anderson, Doyle he was not so sure of.

"Please pay him no mind, we don't have bald people anymore," said Doyle.

"You don't have bald people?" said O'Connor. He wanted to ask "what the hell does that mean?" but held his tongue.

"Please let me try to explain," she continued, sitting down next to him on the sofa. Her proximity made him feel awkward as he was expecting her to sit on one of the other chairs in the room, ideally one across the table from him and not in his personal space.

"First, may I ask you for the Mercurian ore?" she continued, a wide and satisfied smile on her face. Anderson leaned in toward them both in anticipation.

"I don't have anything like that," replied O'Connor, confused at the question.

"You have a sample of the rocks that came back from Mercury do you not?" said Doyle, her smile replaced with a look of overwhelming worry.

"No I don't think so," replied O'Connor slowly, surprised at the question. It was the last thing he had expected to be asked.

Anderson covered his mouth, and produced an electric static noise.

"No, I believe not," said Doyle in response to Anderson's noise, did she understand it? "Sir Ryburn gave you some, did he not?" she asked O'Connor.

"If you mean Dr James Ryburn then, no, he didn't," said O'Connor. *Sir Ryburn, indeed.*

"No, he did. Please check," said Doyle, "I'm sure that you are mistaken."

O'Connor started to unenthusiastically pat down his pockets.

"Please check all your pockets," said Doyle, getting a bit frantic. O'Connor stood up.

"What's this all about?" he asked, with a slight laugh as the others moved in to pat his pockets. He was being frisked and patted down by his two new friends. They were rather aggressive, desperate for him to have this rock on him.

"You don't have it!" said Doyle, turning her back and walking away from him to pace around on the other side of the room.

"We've changed it," Anderson said, his eyes and voice lit up with excitement.

"Nothing changes, we've been through this," Doyle said as

she dismissed his suggestion.

"He doesn't have the rocks?" Anderson said again, as if it was the only conclusion possible.

"We've changed nothing, nothing ever changes, it doesn't work like that," Doyle said. O'Connor got the impression that whatever it was that never changes had been discussed before.

"Why not, though?" Anderson asked again, with a profound look on his deceptively young face.

"Because it happened, the way we know it happened," replied Doyle, rolling her eyes at yet another pointless question.

"But what if we do?" he said it as if he were onto some major breakthrough that Doyle had not considered.

"But we can't have done," she replied, the turned up corner of her lip showing her annoyance at being questioned again, "because we wouldn't be here if we had."

"What do you mean?" Anderson asked.

O'Connor watched them argue, listening to their words and their slightly twisted accents. It didn't make much sense to him.

"Oh for goodness sake Andy!" Doyle said with mock anger. "If we had stopped the Neith Incident we wouldn't have come here would we?"

Neith Incident? O'Connor thought.

"But what if we did change something?" Anderson said, not letting go of his argument.

"We didn't, whatever happens happened, nothing can change, otherwise it wouldn't have happened the way it did. The facts are the facts, we can't change them because we didn't change them."

"What about the message back to Sir Ryburn and the others, did you say what you said?" she asked, looking straight at O'Connor who had been trying to follow the conversation.

"He was out of air when I got to him," Anderson answered for him. "Seconds from death I would have thought, and spinning out of control. I had to use an airshot canister to get him back."

Doyle, who had started pacing again stopped and turned to look at Anderson and then at O'Connor as if it were his fault.

"Say that again!"

"He was out of air. I had to get him… no other choice..." Anderson explained.

Doyle put her hand up in front of Anderson's face to stop his explanation.

"Did you call your crew and say your goodbyes?" Doyle asked again of O'Connor

"Did I call the crew?" replied O'Connor, repeating the question with confusion on his face. "I called no one. I was too busy being blasted out into space and suffocating."

"You didn't say anything to your men?" asked Doyle as if it were an interrogation.

"No! Even if I could breathe I didn't have my communicator."

"Oh this complicates things," said Doyle, slowly lowering herself into the chair behind her. She didn't appear to be worried or concerned, more like she was mentally assessing a Plan B.

"No matter, we'll think of something," she said at last with a smile.

Anderson, however, was not taking this apparent bad news as calmly. He looked on the edge of having a mental collapse and had also dropped down onto one of the chairs, but with his head slumped forward onto his chest. O'Connor looked at Doyle, then Anderson, then back to Doyle, who was still looking at him as if he was some strange object, a curio of some type.

"Doyle?" he asked quietly. "Just Doyle?"

"Yes, just Doyle," she smiled. "We don't have ranks here, you see."

"Yes, so your colleague said." O'Connor was keeping as polite as he could but this meeting was very surreal to him. One moment he was in space floating away to a quiet death, the next here he was in a strange flowery ship, sitting around a table with two strangers who just would not stop staring at him.

"You are certain you don't have the ore?" asked Anderson.

"Yes," O'Connor shot back, with growing annoyance. "I'm sure I don't have it."

Anderson covered his mouth again and produced more of that white noise, was he talking?

"Please stop using that, Andy," said Doyle. "No I don't think he is lying, he has no reason to. What happened on the station Chief O'Connor?"

Anderson begun moving his hand up to his mouth again, but his motion was cut short by a snapping look from Doyle, he spoke normally "We know what happened."

Again, he was stopped by a look from Doyle.

"Please," said Doyle leaning forward to give O'Connor her full attention. "What happened? You were all in danger, why?"

"We had to leave early," explained O'Connor. "The station was in the path of an unplanned orbital."

"The small Mercury craft? The lander?"

"Yes," said O'Connor, surprised that she knew that already. "I was going to put us into final phase early as an airlock explosion was changing our angle against the planet." O'Connor paused and then added. "My crew turned on me!"

"Please continue," said Doyle, still all attention.

"I don't remember," said O'Connor, his eyes moving unseeingly around the table, his brow wrinkled in concentration as he tried to recollect everything that had happened. "McSweeney drugged me, then I was outside with Benson, doing something. But I didn't do it, McSweeney did it for me."

"You gave the order to alter the shedding mechanics to allow Sir Ryburn to fly you home," said Doyle.

"I did no such thing," said O'Connor, looking up, his line of thought broken. "McSweeney got back before me, and wouldn't let me back in. He tried to kill me."

"He did kill you," said Anderson. "Then they all flew home and you became a heroic martyr."

O'Connor's initial dismissive smirk, slowly changed to match the more serious look on Doyle's face.

"You aren't joking are you?" he asked slowly. "You both think I'm dead?"

"That is not entirely accurate." said Doyle. "You are not dead, but it *is* complicated." For a moment she seemed to think about how she was going to phrase her answer and then continued "You are not physically dead, but you are dead from a historical reference point of view."

"What the hell does that mean?" said O'Connor, not bothering to hide his frustration at their riddles and stupid statements anymore.

"I really wanted to ease you into this slowly," said Doyle, "but I guess we can't. You have already guessed that we aren't from around here?"

O'Connor nodded.

"We're from the future," Anderson interrupted, like an over excited child who couldn't keep a secret.

"Of course you are," said O'Connor, standing up. "I don't know what angle you are trying to pull here, but if you want to steal the salvage I won't help you. You may as well put me back out into space." Then, clenching his jaw, he added, "But I guarantee I won't go easy."

Awe-struck smiles and a stifled giggle was not the response he had expected.

"Is something funny about this?" O'Connor demanded.

"Your temper, it is just like the records say" said Doyle, making a hand gesture for him return to his seat. "Please sit back down, I'll show you, then if you don't believe us we'll take you wherever you want to go."

Anderson shot Doyle a look, a look as if to seek some clarification on what she had just said. O'Connor saw that look, and the look she gave back in return.

"You two are lying," he said. "Your story is impossible."

"Please," Doyle said disarmingly, again motioning for him to sit. As he sat, she stood up and turned to the screen behind her, the one showing the sideways picture. She brought up the same blue screen that O'Connor had and pushed her hand into the light. The screen flickered into something that looked more in common with the computer displays he was used to and the screen displayed a graphical picture of the Neith station with Venus behind it.

"What is that control system? I haven't seen it before," asked O'Connor.

"No, you wouldn't have," replied Doyle. "It wasn't invented until the middle of the 26th century."

"Fine," said O'Connor rather rudely, because he saw no point in being polite if they were going to mock him. "Can you please get to the point?"

"Right you are," said Doyle and the picture changed. "This picture shows the Neith station, in a low lunar orbit."

The picture indeed appeared to show what was left of the Neith station in the lunar approach area above the base.

"These are our three heroes, Sir Ryburn, McSweeney and Benson, at a press conference moments after they were cut out of the station… we have a bit of video on this one."

A brief video played. Judging by the body language Ryburn was in charge. They answered the typically useless media questions but anything even remotely technical was answered by Ryburn. When asked about O'Connor, Benson gave a very moving tribute explaining how he had selflessly given his life making final adjustments to Ryburn's design. Wiping away the tears he spoke of the heartfelt goodbye their chief had spoken as he was drifting away into space.

"I said no such thing. This is nonsense," said O'Connor dismissing the charade in front of him, but Doyle continued. A series of pictures appeared showing his crew mates gradually ageing.

"Shortly before the 40th year reunion McSweeney made a deathbed confession admitting to being at the airlock door when you were killed."

Another picture appeared showing a very frail Ryburn. "This is Sir Ryburn at McSweeney's funeral." Another picture appeared. "This is Sir Ryburn's funeral procession. The whole system stopped for a month of mourning."

"Sir Ryburn?" said O'Connor in amazement, "Are you telling me they knighted that crazy old fool?"

"Yes… for his 3MP invention. It took us to the stars, for better or worse. Only Benson was around for the 70th anniversary." The photo now on the screen showed an elderly looking Benson, with the same wide grin but the face of a very old man looking very dignified and stately. "There wasn't an 80th, but the day of the Neith Incident was celebrated as O'Connor Day."

"O'Connor Day?" said O'Connor, shaking his head in complete rejection of what he was being told.

"Here, look," said Doyle, switching the screen to a view of the Neith station. "This is what they are doing now." The screen showed the station moving away into space.

"Are you telling me that Ryburn's rocks actually moved the station?"

"Yes and he flew it back to Earth, well the moon of Earth." said Doyle.

"You mean Lunar?" said O'Connor, correcting her, "No one calls Lunar the moon anymore."

"Okay Lunar," agreed Doyle. Anderson nodded in agreement but his agreement was neither required nor acknowledged.

"And you three have time travelled back to save me?" asked O'Connor, folding his arms across his chest.

"Three?" queried Anderson.

"That little guy out there," said O'Connor, pointing to the silhouette of the smartly dressed man standing behind the closed door.

"Oh, don't worry about him, he's just an indentured servant and came with the ship," answered Doyle very dismissively. "No, we came for the ore from Mercury, which you were supposed to have. Saving you was a bonus."

"How very good of you!" said O'Connor sarcastically. "So why not just go to Mercury and get some, or better yet go to Mercury in your own time and get some?"

"We can't take anything from Mercury now," replied Doyle. "We don't have the equipment. Anyway the burning sun is far too hot, and the method that Sir Ryburn used is not something we can replicate."

"Okay, first stop calling him Sir Ryburn, 'cause I'm not having it," O'Connor interrupted. "He's a delusional angry old drunk. He's no hero of mankind, or any of that other nonsense. And second, why can't you replicate what he did if you are all knowing from the future?"

"We don't go to the original system anymore. In fact we don't go anywhere," She replied placidly. "Some unsanctioned ventures supposedly went back several decades ago but the reports were that they couldn't get close to Mercury. The most recent venture reports were that it isn't even there anymore. No, our time is not an option and trying in the future is too much of an unknown."

"I see," said O'Connor, playing along with her story. "What happened to it?"

"Sometime in the twenty-fifth century the sun went into a very violent cycle, far beyond the normal maximum that was known at the time. It has lasted for centuries. It is supposed to be past the tipping point now and calming down a bit but we're still a few hundred years from even trying to reclaim the Earth." Doyle paused on the final word, then adding "That's the short version anyway."

"So you came back to get some of the Mercury rock, from me?" said O'Connor.

"It's the only time we found in history where the rocks had been taken from the surface before full mining started and this area became crowded."

"Well I don't have it, so now what?" said O'Connor, returning his arms back to their crossed position over his chest.

Anderson started to put his hand up over his mouth, white noise coming again.

"Andy if you use that again I will remove it myself" said Doyle. Perhaps too quick to accept defeat the weight of the failure was already sitting heavy on Anderson's shoulders.

"Yes, now what?" he said again for O'Connor's benefit.

"We haven't failed yet," said Doyle with a smile. "We have plenty of time."

"Oh very funny," said O'Connor, not amused at all. "How do I get back onto the station? I would like to return home with my crew."

"You can't go back with them," said Anderson. "You're dead."

"Dead from a historical stand point," Doyle corrected, "but nonetheless you didn't go back, or won't go back with your crew. History says you didn't, so you don't."

"But *your* history says I have a rock, which I don't," O'Connor rebutted.

"Yes that is interesting. Sir Ryburn wouldn't have lied," Doyle said.

O'Connor had to agree with her on that point. Ryburn was many things: drunk, miserable, cantankerous, delusional, and very bitter, but never a liar.

"Right," said Doyle, clapping her hands together once and pointing at O'Connor with a touch of excitement. "Talk, say something… anything."

"Such as?" O'Connor asked.

Anderson looked equally confused as Doyle put her hand back into the blue light and started moving stuff around.

"Anything! Tell us about the fall of the Common States."

"The fall of the Common States?" O'Connor asked in astonishment.

"Oh, hasn't that happened yet?" she turned back from the screen and it was clear that everything was now being recorded. "Anything, recite a song, anything please, humour me, why have you stopped talking, where's all that denial and anger?"

"What did you say about the Common States?" O'Connor asked.

"At some point in the next hundred years there will be water shortages; some of the biggest rivers on earth will be dammed but this will create serious water shortages downstream which will lead to conflict and the eventual break-up of the Common States," explained Doyle.

"You mean the United States, the USA?" queried O'Connor.

"I'm sure that they were called Common States," said Doyle looking away.

"I don't know about any common state, but the USA won't ever break up, there hasn't been any fighting there since the Civil War, 300 years ago… well there was a bit of a standoff when they started buying Canada but the rest of it followed on peacefully over the next few decades. Mexico and Cuba joined almost overnight after that," said O'Connor.

"Well whatever it was called, it was a long time ago," said Doyle, "but the way we were taught was that their religious differences resurfaced when the dams were built."

"Religious differences? You probably mean the Middle East Union," said O'Connor thinking that they needed to get their story straight.

"What is a Middle East?" asked Anderson.

Doyle motioned for O'Connor to answer, she still needed him to talk.

"Fine," said O'Connor willing to play along. He proceeded to give an encyclopaedia style summary of what he knew of the Middle Eastern Unions. The peaceful union between several countries Pakistan, India, Afghanistan, Iran and the other surrounding countries up to the Chinese boarders, and the countries of North Africa.

"There were many separate countries?" asked Anderson in astonishment "I thought there were only a few big countries."

"You might be thinking of land masses," said O'Connor helpfully. *Idiot.*

"Countries were the tribal territories. Lines on a map," said Doyle, to Anderson. "And they all had separate laws and governments, like the orbs that ran their own laws before they were collected."

"Hang on!" said O'Connor, somewhat offended at the remark. "They are a little different from tribal territories."

"Right that's enough." said Doyle bringing up the blue interface again. The screen cycled through various screens again. "Okay listen please, this is the famous final message of Chief Jake O'Connor."

The message played.......

"That isn't me, and Benson doesn't sound like that either," said O'Connor. "What was all that noise at the end?"

"A distortion over the communicators as Neith flew away, interference from the magnetic field interfering with the devices of the day," Anderson explained.

"Whatever! That's not me," O'Connor repeated. None of this made sense. "Sir Ryburn? Mankind's hero? McSweeney forgiven?" his fists were balling up in his lap at the mere thought of it. "That little stain tried to kill me, no way would I forgive him."

Doyle nodded, the screen displayed "primary match confirmed" showing quite a flattering historical picture of O'Connor alongside a far less flattering second picture taken only moments ago, of him sitting at the table.

"That's just wrong; I never said any of that, but credit for Ryburn's voice. That sounded good," he mocked, with a short round of applause.

"This is the most sophisticated voice recognition software ever produced. You can't fake this," said Anderson.

"Secondary match confirmed," announced the computer. All three looked to the screen, the surprise on Doyle and Anderson's face was too real to be fake and O'Connor noticed it. The pictures showed an unknown, shadowy silhouette, representing something from the recording, and the other was a picture of Anderson.

"Why is my voice on there, Doyle?" asked Anderson with childlike innocence.

Doyle put her right hand up for silence, and via the blue light told the computer to isolate out the secondary match. It was the inaudible white noise at the end. She applied the ship-specific clean up algorithms and decryption methods to the sound block, whilst explaining to O'Connor how their current communications are encrypted, masked, packet split, digitised the sound at the wave level, and typically just failed to arrive at any type of recording or transmission. But they had another layer, custom built for extreme secrecy that even with their future technology needed the exact key to decipher it.

"What? It was word perfect."

There it was, Anderson's voice clear as day, an impossible message hidden away in the famous recording.

"What does it mean?" asked Anderson.

"I have no idea what it means." said Doyle. "But it does mean that you somehow got your voice onto the recording with that thing in your neck."

Anderson raised his hand, covering his mouth, and produced some of the sound again.

"Yes that one," said Doyle.

"Oh come on," said O'Connor, not accepting this newest attempt to confuse him. He stopped when he saw the look on their faces again. It was like looking at a ghost in a photo, an impossible something that shouldn't have been there, something that couldn't have been there. Doyle was as white as a comet and Anderson just looked confused, very confused. In that moment, O'Connor started to believe the time travel story; no one could fake that reaction, they were telling the truth.

"How old is this recording, from your point of view?" O'Connor asked after a quiet moment of observing his new friends and realising that they hadn't actually said "when" they had come from.

"Eight hundred years or thereabouts," answered Doyle sheepishly, her mind already on other matters.

"And this is the famous speech heard by billions of people?"

"Billions, probably everybody of this time and everybody since then," agreed Doyle. "So why only now are you hearing him?" said O'Connor pointing at Anderson who was staring blankly at the screen. "It couldn't have remained hidden for that long?"

"It's unique to this ship, our computer knows the decryption key for it, that's the only reason it got picked up now."

"Anyway," said Anderson, still visibly shaken, "why would anyone need to check that it was you? No one ever questioned it before, and who would have guessed it would have been yourself questioning it?"

"Can you run it again?" asked O'Connor. "I still never said any of that!"

"Nor me," Anderson added, crossing his arms in defiance.

"Never said any of it yet," said Doyle. "We're going back. If you could please show O'Connor to his quarters, I'll start the calculations for us to leave in the morning."

A twitch of the hand in the controls started a comparison running as she walked straight to the door and left the room. The screened flashed up a second confirmation, then a third, then a fourth before Anderson stood up and stopped it. It was a fact, O'Connor's and Anderson's voices were on the recording, the famous and historical last words of Chief Jake O'Connor, 2099 – 2142.

CHAPTER 10: RUNNING WATER

"I HAVE PREPARED a room for you Mr O'Connor." said the smartly dressed young man from the doorway. He motioned along to the left of the room and bowed slightly, taking on the demeanour of a very polite and humble hotel porter.

"Thank you..." said O'Connor, searching for a name.

"Radcliffe, Sir."

"Thank you Radcliffe," O'Connor said awkwardly. He wasn't used to being addressed in such a way.

Radcliffe filed in behind, as Anderson led O'Connor out of the room and along the corridor. The flowers started to thin out the further they got away from what he had determined to be the middle of the deck. They walked in silence; O'Connor had a million questions but none of them were forming into sentences that he could put to Anderson. The corridor widened showing a magnificently large viewing window, stretching the full height and length of the walkway, but what grabbed his attention was a brilliant view of the sun.

"I can't get enough of this view," Anderson said, with a smile. "The burning sun is amazing, don't you think?"

"I know what you mean, we can go months without even seeing it," replied O'Connor remembering how much he missed the feel of the sun on his skin.

"Months? Up until when we got here I'd never seen it."

"Never?" O'Connor asked in disbelief.

"I've seen stars, plenty of them, but never the actual burning sun."

"So you live in space?"

"Yes, we all do now"

"All? Are there more people on this ship…" he tried to remember the name. "The O'Connor? Is the ship named after me?"

"Not this one, this is the King John" Anderson said rather proudly before adding with a touch of embarrassment "but the battery ship we're attached to has your name."

"I'm flattered," said O'Connor, sharing the embarrassment. "So how many people are on board with us?"

Anderson seemed happy to change the subject. "Just the three of us now."

"And him," said O'Connor, flicking his head back over his shoulder toward Radcliffe.

"Okay four with the indent," Anderson agreed dismissively.

An important question had formed in O'Connor's mind, one, he dreaded to ask but knew he had to. He was already getting a sense of what the answer will be.

"You mean all of mankind, don't you? When you say we all live in space?"

"We're pretty much all in space now," Anderson's reply was without any emotion or regret.

"What happened to Earth?"

"You are looking at it," Anderson said. "The burning sun got hotter and hotter."

"When?" O'Connor asked in disbelief, thinking of all the people.

"Hundreds of years ago," Anderson replied, then, after a thought, he corrected himself, "or rather hundreds of years from now. They say it happened slow enough to give us time to move out to the colonies."

"You've found liveable planets?" O'Connor asked with

excitement.

"Nothing we can live on naturally, but there were early colonies on the rocky planets and moons that were found, when people left the original system. There are some who believe they are still out there, but if they are, they've been out of contact for hundreds of years so I doubt it."

"Any alien life?"

"No, just us," Anderson replied half mockingly, like answering the questions of a three year old.

They stood at the viewing window for a time. Anderson fascinated by his "burning sun" whilst O'Connor still wanted more of the history lesson.

"So what's left of Earth then?"

"It's still there, apparently. Those who didn't make it onto the orbs stayed, but the burning sun kept getting hotter."

"The orbs?" O'Connor asked. *It's like getting blood from a stone.*

"Sorry, I find it hypnotic. Apparently there were a lot of people who remained on the Earth planet who didn't want to live in space, they moved to the poll."

"The poles," O'Connor corrected him, it was obvious that he did not know enough about the future history to retell it with any accuracy.

"The polls, what were the polls?" Anderson asked, showing an actual hint of enthusiasm.

"The north and south poles, they are the very top and bottom of the planet, the coldest places."

"Oh that makes sense then."

"Are they still there?"

"They probably cooked to death as the sun got hotter; Doyle knows more about history than me, ask her to show you the history."

"Or you could show me how to work your computers," said O'Connor lifting up a hand and moving each of his fingers as if moving them inside the blue controls. He didn't like not knowing how to work basic things.

"Mr Anderson," interrupted Radcliffe's soft voice. "I wish to remind you of Miss Doyle's schedule."

"We'll get to the computers in due time, I'm sure," Anderson said, a touch too dismissive for O'Connor's liking. Anderson must have heard what Radcliffe had said, but didn't offer him any acknowledgement of it.

This Radcliffe person made O'Connor nervous, he had to keep a close eye on him but couldn't say why. However, when he turned to look at him he was still looking towards the floor.

They left the corridor and the window, leaving the view of the sun behind them.

"You haven't asked how we got here," Anderson asked after the direction of the corridor began to lead them back to the centre of the ship and they went up a circular stairwell.

"I just assumed it was some fancy futuristic drive that I would have zero chance of understanding." It had never actually crossed his mind, for a little while he thought they were working some scam on him and so didn't believe any of it, then like a switch in his head he accepted their story as fact.

"Ah, it's surprisingly simply, just needs a lot of chard."

"How much chard do you need to punch a hole in time?" O'Connor said with deep interest.

"An impossible amount," Anderson said. His timing was perfect as he had just led O'Connor into a small room with a viewing window that looked to the rear of the ship onto a structure consisting of hundreds of large cylinders stacked high and deep. It took up most of the window.

"Are those your chard tanks?" O'Connor said in awe.

"These are the best chard storage units ever built," Anderson began to explain, "each cylinder tops out at a little over an octillion chard."

"How many zeros is that?" O'Connor said, just wanting a real number.

"Twenty-eight."

"How long did it take you to gather all that?" O'Connor

asked, thinking of the sheer difficulty of gathering energy.

"Ninety four seconds," Anderson said with the cheeky grin, that slowly faded and his eyes teared up briefly before he wiped them. O'Connor was still taking in the individual size of each unit and the collective size of all the units, it was ominously massive.

Radcliffe prompted them to keep moving. They walked the rest of the way in silence. O'Connor was deep in thought trying to process everything that had happened in the last hour or so, it was after all a lot to take in.

They arrived at the room that had been allocated to O'Connor; Anderson passed his palm over a dark grey reflective panel just to the left of the door which slid open with a hydraulic sound. The room was much bigger than he had expected. Actually he had not known what to expect but it certainly wasn't what he saw. Along the far wall was a double bed, an actual double bed. O'Connor couldn't even remember the last time he had seen a double bed, let alone slept in one. The blanket on top of the bed had seen better days and it was evident that it had been repaired numerous times over the years. The wall to his right contained an exceptionally large screen built into the wall itself. He got the immediate impression that this wall was to be used to display various scenic backgrounds. He wandered over and pressed gently on the mattress. It was soft; he was not aware how tired he actually was and the thought of sleeping on a real bed for the first time in years made him immediately yawn. This he suppressed as best he could by clenching his jaw.

O'Connor continued to look around the room in amazement: there were two wing-backed armchairs around a small table that was fixed to the ground. The chairs at the table were a complete contrast to each other, probably from different time periods centuries apart. Just like the bed, the chairs were worn in places and showed signs of repair on the upholstery. The table had a blue light emanating out about 20 centimetres from a small pad in the centre, O'Connor assumed it was for controlling the display wall opposite.

"How do these work anyway?" O'Connor asked, pointing to the blue light.

"It reads these," Anderson replied tapping at the bracelet fitted tight around his wrist. "The blue is just the user interface so you can select what to display onto the screen."

"So the data isn't stored. It's all in your personal device?" said O'Connor.

"Yes and no. It is all on your personal device, but your personal device is set to sync up with the data-store."

"I guess I'll have to get one of those?" O'Connor asked to test the waters. This all seemed well and good, very impressive. However, was he on equal footing with his two new crew mates? Would they be willing to share their information and technology with him?

The answer to both was a quick yes as Anderson replied, "I could get you one copied up; however we don't have the facilities to install them on board. But once we're back in the present we'll get that taken care of. The bracelet will have to be surgically attached and the process is irreversible."

O'Connor swallowed at that thought.

"Radcliffe here will see to you this evening and will collect you in the morning once you have freshened up," said Anderson. This was the cue for Radcliffe to enter the room, again with a submissive bow of the head.

"I trust this is to your liking?" Radcliffe said just as if he were some hotel maitre d' showing a guest to a lavish presidential suite.

Radcliffe was a short man in his mid to late twenties. On closer inspection his suit was worn in places and showed signs that it had been mended. When the man looked up from his bow he still had that vacant look on his face, as if day dreaming or looking off into the distance. Something about him though made O'Connor very uncomfortable, to the point of giving him goose bumps up his arms.

"What's through there?" O'Connor asked, pointing to an archway leading to a walled off corner of the room.

"Radcliffe will be able to answer your questions about the room. Radcliffe does not know why we're here. Apart from your name, he does not know who you are and nor does he care," Anderson said, "I must go and assist Doyle. Radcliffe. Mr O'Connor is new to space travel and he may ask a lot of questions about how things work. You are to answer them all. Is that clear?"

Radcliffe nodded his head.

"That will be your private shower room Mr O'Connor," Radcliffe answered in his usual monotone, accompanied by a tip of the head.

"How much time do we have Radcliffe?" Anderson asked.

"Approximately thirty minutes, Mr Anderson."

"You can turn in for the evening," Anderson said to O'Connor. "Radcliffe here will come for you in the morning, please remain here until you are collected."

O'Connor nodded his agreement without objection and Anderson left the room. O'Connor was more interested in the prospect of a shower anyway.

"A shower? A shower with water?" he asked Radcliffe, barely able to believe it.

"Yes, with water," Radcliffe answered. If it weren't for the vacant expression and dulled voice, his response would have seemed sarcastic.

"You use water for personal cleaning?" O'Connor asked half amazed half horrified at the very notion, water was very precious.

"You do not? That would explain your aroma."

O'Connor had been in space for many, many months of physical work. The personal odour of the crew was something everyone grew accustomed to and simply stopped noticing. O'Connor let the comment pass.

"Is that not a terrible waste?"

"There is no waste, sir. A hundred percent is recycled, even the moisture out of the air," Radcliffe answered.

"Can I have a shower now?"

"Yes, of course, please do," Radcliffe said very politely. "I have placed several changes of clothes for you in your footlocker." He motioned with an open palm to a sleek black box pushed tight against the wall. "I shall lay one out for you for the morning if you wish?"

It was always the simple things that everyone tended to miss during these long contracts in space. High on the list for O'Connor was always a nice hot, steamy shower. He peered round the archway to get a closer look at the shower, as if to check that it actually existed.

"I'll leave you to your ablutions Mr O'Connor," Radcliffe said. O'Connor wasn't really listening, so Radcliffe politely cleared his throat to get his attention. "Will you require any assistance dressing?"

"No thank you," O'Connor answered, surprised. It wasn't a question he had ever been asked before.

"Very good Mr O'Connor, I'll be just outside your door throughout the night. I will knock for you in the morning."

"Yes, thank you Radcliffe." It was not O'Connor's intention to sound rude, but he did, however Radcliffe either didn't notice or didn't care. He stayed vacant.

O'Connor had his shower, and it was heavenly; he could have stayed in it forever. He reached for a towel and stepped out through a curtain of steam a new man, refreshed and clean. "Hundred percent recycled," he said to himself, still amazed at the concept and after a second thought a little bit disgusted as well thinking back to the colour of the water when it first ran off his body. The extractor fans started to take the steam away and the words "water capture in progress" displayed in bright green flashing lettering against the pristine white wall.

He enjoyed the shower so much he had another one when he awoke after a curiously good sleep which had started almost before his head hit the pillow.

"Mr O'Connor, are you ready?" called Radcliffe from behind the door, accompanying his call with a knock.

O'Connor bade him enter and stood up from his seat at the end of the bed. He thought it strange that with all these futuristic conveniences there was not a doorbell.

"You slept well I trust?" Radcliffe asked.

The smell from the tray Radcliffe was carrying hit O'Connor. It was food, real food. He replied politely, silently wondering if he had been drugged. However, it was hard to think of anything but that tray as he tried to see what the food was; it certainly smelled of what he remembered real food to smell like.

"I've brought you a modest meal to break your fast," said Radcliffe as he placed the tray down on the table. "Miss Doyle insisted that you would be hungry."

O'Connor practically inhaled the meal that was placed before him. He had lived off those god awful meal bags for so long he had wondered if he would ever see real food again. It was plain and simple food but to O'Connor it was like an extravagant and luxurious banquet.

"Please forgive the simple nature of the meal, Mr O'Connor, I'm afraid it is not a traditional morning meal, but as I said, Miss Doyle insisted I prepare this."

"Nonsense," O'Connor said, while embarrassingly spitting some food out as he spoke "This is perfect."

He was sure the orange stuff was mashed carrot, but he hadn't even seen a carrot since he was kid. Several slices of white meat he guessed was some bird. The smell, the texture, and the taste were intoxicatingly rich. There was a pile a soft white fluffy mashed potato, he knew this as it had been his dad's favourite, and some small green stuff; he couldn't recall if they were peas or beans. Finally there was a thick steaming brown sauce of some type poured all over it.

"You are too kind," Radcliffe said in his monotone blankness.

O'Connor continued to wolf down his meal; it didn't bother him that it was not a traditional breakfast style dish in the least.

It wasn't grey slop and that was what mattered.

"Can I assume Miss Doyle was correct about you being hungry?" said Radcliffe. "She will be pleased."

"Yes, thank you."

I could get used to this O'Connor thought as he scraped up every last morsel from his plate and licked the brown sauce from the knife and fork. Gravy, it was called gravy.

"I trust you found the clothes to your liking?" Radcliffe asked. O'Connor stood up and gave a twirl to show the fresh black jumpsuit.

"Very nice, Mr O'Connor" Radcliffe said, the clothes were identical to what Doyle and Anderson had been wearing.

"Is this a uniform then?" O'Connor asked.

"It is a thermal controlled pressure suit; it automatically adjusts to your surroundings and body temperature."

"Do you not have one?"

"I wear it under my duty attire."

"Duty? What is your duty, Radcliffe?"

"My duty is to serve this ship and crew for my term of service."

The goose bumps returned along O'Connor's arms, when he said "term of service", something about this strange young man made him uneasy.

"Are you a robot?" O'Connor asked very innocently. It would make sense of a lot of things if he was.

"No Mr O'Connor I am not a robot. I am serving an indentured period for wrongs I performed in my past."

"Wrongs?"

"Unlawful conduct. I do not know the crime. I do not know the length of my sentence. Only that I am to serve the Caution of King John until the end of the said period. I cannot answer any questions about it. I just do not remember, part of the process I am afraid. You understand Mr O'Connor?"

"Not really, but hey, it's been that sort day," O'Connor joked, overcompensating for his unease.

"Very good, Mr O'Connor," Radcliffe said. His eyes remained

blank and his face expressionless.

"Does it do anything else?" O'Connor asked, talking about the suit again, extending his arms to the side looking up and down each sleeve in turn.

"What else would you have it do?" Radcliffe asked "It is just a jump suit, designed out of convenience and practical use. It is not fashion statement. Not so different to the jump suit you were wearing as I understand it."

"So then," O'Connor said after a moment's pause. "What happens now?"

"I will escort you back to Miss Doyle and Mr Anderson; they will be in the observation dome."

Radcliffe took what must have been the direct path to the "dome". The walkway was very wide, with doors and corridors branching off to left and right. Was this a converted cargo bay? Many things about this ship didn't quite add up. All this junk scattered around implied a salvage operation. Was looting something that happened in the future? O'Connor had not seen anything in the realms of lasers or space torpedoes. Anderson and Doyle didn't even have side arms. There had been no mention of gun turrets and the ship was missing any indication of company branding. On Neith you could not help but know who built it and who was running it. It was the same with every other station and space craft he had ever seen, but on this ship there was none of it. Nothing but the flowers and plants, and they were everywhere. This area of the ship appeared to be very dense with plant life, yet it was contained, it was not out of control or wild.

"Tell me Radcliffe," O'Connor began, "what's all this for?"

"They were unpacked with haste, my apologies Mr O'Connor I haven't straightened it up as of yet."

"No I mean the plant life."

"It has a psychological effect on the mind, as well as creating the oxygen," Radcliffe said.

"And you grow your own food here too?" O'Connor asked, recognising a tomato vine, overwhelmed with ripe produce, clinging to a wall.

"Some of it grown outright, yes. However most is compiled using organic matter," Radcliffe said motioning for O'Connor to take the lead as they entered a very incongruous looking stairwell that looked to be a different design and style to the walls surrounding it. As they emerged onto the floor above, O'Connor recognised to his left the "sitting room" from the previous day.

"The dome is this way, Mr O'Connor," Radcliffe said, directing O'Connor to move along. The corridor joined the base of a twin winding staircase left and right, both leading to the same point doubling back on itself to a floor above and the entrance to the dome where Anderson was waiting for him.

"I trust you feel well rested now O'Connor," Anderson asked, not offering any acknowledgment to Radcliffe.

"Yes thank you, I slept very well... a little too well in fact."

"Yes we all do, it's part of the evening air cycle in your quarters."

"I was drugged?" O'Connor asked, not knowing exactly what he thought about that, although he certainly felt refreshed.

"The air is carefully constructed, you will find yourself awake and alert through most of this ship."

"So, I guess you need help collecting Ryburn's rocks?" O'Connor said, noticing Radcliffe disappearing from his side and back down the staircase.

"Yes, that is right. Then we go back to our time, find out where it all went and explore the galaxy," Anderson said reaching out his arms and extending his fingers for dramatic effect.

"Our best bet is to intercept the hopper coming back from Mercury, it has your-"

"It's never going to be that simple," Anderson interrupted with a shake of his head.

"And why is that?" O'Connor demanded, once again taking offence at the condescending tone. "It's what you need and it will be right there for the taking. It's what makes the most sense!"

"Oh I agree with you one hundred percent, I even suggested

the exact same thing, however, Doyle said that was never going to happen."

"Why wouldn't it work?" O'Connor asked.

Anderson smiled. "I'll let Doyle explain it to you, I had the same questions and didn't quite understand her answers, perhaps you will understand better than I did."

"But how can you be so certain it won't work?"

"Doyle is certain and that's enough for me."

O'Connor was impressed by the loyalty. It was not demanded, as that was not the nature of the relationship; the loyalty seemed to be given freely.

"She is waiting for us at the dome, we had best hurry," Anderson said; pointing ahead up the remainder of the stairwell.

"What's the rush? Surely we have all the time in the world?" O'Conner joked.

"Yes, but the longer we wait the further we will be from the exact time and spatial coordinates that we need to cut to, and the further we're away the more chard we will burn getting there."

The heavily scuffed door at the top of the stairs slid to the side, opening into a small trench in the floor of a huge circular room which was bathed in the yellowy brown hue that Connor immediately recognised as light reflecting up off the thick atmosphere of Venus. O'Connor climbed out of the trench onto the floor of the dome itself and was able to take in the full majesty of the room he found himself in. It was very impressive. The entire room was a perfectly circular viewing platform, offering an unprecedented view of the outside. Venus dominated the view, with the sun just beginning to show over its right-hand edge. O'Connor wondered what type of visual dampener was being employed since the sun looked dull and certainly not as intense as he knew it should be. Superimposed over the glass was tracking information, highlighting various moving objects. Off in the distance were planets with brief labels giving their name, distance and speed. Behind them were stars and galaxies that he'd never heard of, highlighted with descriptive text. Asteroids and comets millions of kilometres away were all being tracked and displayed across the ceiling and highlighted in bright red. A bright green circle highlighted Neith station travelling away at a very respectable speed; a blue line showed where it would intercept with Earth's orbit.

"Welcome to our dome, Chief O'Connor," said Doyle loud enough for her voice to carry across the expanse of the dome.

"Very impressive," O'Connor said in amazement, still trying to take in all the various details flashing around in front of him.

"Everything is tracked and everything is traced," Doyle began. "How fast we're moving away or toward everything from galaxies to small dwarf planets, from moons to space rocks. The directions of everything and the gravitational influence of everything on everything else, where everything is going and where everything has been."

"And what about this one?" O'Connor asked, pointing to the brightly flashing red asteroid.

Doyle stepped up onto the main floor. Keeping an eye on O'Connor's asteroid she walked over to the desks. Pressing her wrist firmly against a handrail the fluorescent blue screen appeared beneath her fingers. "Expand section 92," she said loudly. O'Connor was still staring up at the ceiling when the entire view zoomed in on his asteroid. The sudden change of focus made him dizzy for a moment.

"An impact threat. It will cause quite a panic about 40 years from now. I wouldn't worry about it."

"Impact what? The Earth?" O'Connor asked in horror.

"It doesn't hit; it gets stopped, but it will be a close call by the looks of it"

"What do you mean," O'Connor asked, with urgency in his voice. "Should we do something about it?"

"No, that's not what we're here for, and besides, nothing we do will change anything." Doyle paused for a moment to read the text that was displayed on the ceiling. "Oh very interesting, turns out it was stopped using a weaponised version of Ryburn's engine, probably the first real practical application of such an atrocity." The outright disgust in her voice was obvious.

"Resume normal view," Doyle spoke and unclipped her wrist from the rail.

"Weaponised?" O'Connor asked as the panoramic view returned to normal resolution, it made him close his eyes for a moment.

"I'll take this one," Anderson said smugly. "They basically just accelerate as fast as they can and plough right into whatever they want vaporised."

"With a colossal waste of the Mercurian ore," Doyle added.

"Is this common?" O'Connor asked.

"Unfortunately, it was. Quite a few potential planets and moons were lost and hundreds of exodus orbs were destroyed."

"We're cleared to power this down," Doyle said flicking a dramatic finger at Anderson who was already over at the central control area.

"Do you pilot from here?" O'Connor asked. It seemed a reasonable question to him that didn't warrant the scornful laugh he received from Anderson.

O'Connor shot Doyle an unimpressed look, as if to say "are you going to tolerate this type of behaviour" but it didn't matter; he saw that Doyle also doing her best to hold back her own giggles.

"Why is that such a stupid question?" O'Connor asked the pair of them.

"This is a viewing dome, Chief O'Connor" Anderson replied stating the obvious, but not answering the question.

Doyle at least picked up on this. "This is just a window O'Connor. You understand?"

"Right," O'Connor, said slightly embarrassed, thinking he would be better off keeping his questions to himself for a while.

Doyle looked over to Anderson. "Calculations are complete and the clock is running Andy, I've transferred the timings and details to your area."

She turned to O'Connor.

"We use the dome to work out exactly where we need to get to but the calculations take several hours, which is why we couldn't leave straight away."

"Even with your technology?" O'Connor asked.

"Yes," Doyle said. "For a bit of perspective, if we were to use the most powerful computer system from your time the calculations would never be completed."

At that moment all the grids and display information on the panoramic ceiling blinked away. Anderson had shut it down.

"It is important to shut the viewer down, you see," Doyle started to explain. "Once we pass through the cut everything will be in a different relative position to now. The system doesn't recover well from massive input changes so it is best to turn it off and restart it once on the other side."

"The other side of what?" O'Connor asked, silently kicking himself for the question.

"You probably understand it best as a wormhole," Anderson added quickly. O'Connor didn't need to see his face to know there was a smirk on it.

"Yes, thank you Andy," Doyle said. "We use the chard, a *lot* of chard, to cut a hole in existence and create a portal to where we want to go. We keep pumping it with chard until the correct distance is reached. The further we want to go the more it takes. Once the distance is correct we stretch the portal until it is big enough for us to pass through. Third we pump in exactly enough chard to make the wormhole deep enough to reach the calculated point in time we wish to exit. That third release is the time travel and the real drain on power. The more we pump in the further in time we go. But as we're only going back two days this won't be so bad. Not as far back in time means not as much distance either, so less chard on both accounts."

"Okay," O'Connor said, not even trying to pretend he understood. This was the type of conversation Ryburn would like to have. "And do you have enough power?"

"We have enough," Doyle said.

O'Connor thought she had pretty eyes that somehow looked more purple than dark brown.

"We may have to adjust our trip back by a few light years or a couple of months, depending on how you look at it," Anderson said.

"We will have to either get out early or get out short," Doyle added for clarification.

"Makes sense," O'Connor said, and nodded; that part at least did make sense to him.

"It's better than going back empty handed," Doyle said.

"Yes," Anderson added. "As great as it is to meet you in person and save your life O'Connor, we can't exactly cash you in when we get back."

The three of them left the dome and were now walking with purpose toward the flight deck, O'Connor was anxious to see what type of technology was awaiting him, his mind full of holograms, virtual intelligence systems, psychic interfacing, teleportation and a dozen other wonders yet to be invented.

"I'll see you on the other side," said Anderson, with a mocking flick of a salute. O'Connor shook his head; it was all he could do not to groan and roll his eyes.

"Good form," said Doyle, acknowledging the humour as they shared a "Good luck", along with a hug that worried O'Connor, and brought him crashing back to reality, since it seemed very much like an "in case we all die" embrace.

"O'Connor, you're with me," she said.

"What's happening?" O'Connor asked, anxiously.

"Anderson will be balancing the chard levels and controlling the throughput... and we cannot assist him," she added, putting a reassuring hand on Anderson's shoulder.

"Good luck," O'Connor added, the atmosphere of adventure and excitement gone, replaced with tension and foreboding.

Doyle and O'Connor continued toward the front of the ship.

"Why are you so worried?" O'Connor asked.

"We're about to cut a hole in the universe and then pass through it into another point in time and space. If we get it wrong it could create a black hole."

"I'm sure it will be fine" said O'Connor, awkwardly stopping himself from putting a reassuring arm around her. "I bet you've done this loads of times."

"I'd take that bet," Doyle said. "This will be the second time we have attempted this."

"What?" said O'Connor, coming to a stop and grabbing hold of Doyle's arm.

"This will be the second time we attempted this," she repeated.

O'Connor had had it in his head that they were seasoned veterans of time travelling.

"Time travel takes ridiculous amounts of energy and isn't something you can really practice."

"Oh my good God," O'Connor muttered under his breath. "So when you guys first got here it was the dry run of time travel?"

"Well actually no," Doyle grinned, "the first time was when I received a small box containing a brief note from myself saying simply "it works", six hours before I wrote that note and sent it back to myself. Then I wrote another note to myself saying, "It still works," and sent that to myself, I picked that note up the next day, but then had to explode a chard tank so I could explain to the auditors where the energy had gone. However when we got here it was the first time we had both actually travelled in time."

The flight deck was not as impressive as O'Connor had hoped; it paled in comparison to the observation dome. It was cramped and, unlike everything else he had seen, looked to have been purpose-built. There were two egg-shaped pods, which resembled the type of thing O'Connor had seen in simulator booths. Each pod was a dull, faded and dirty grey but with a vibrant green light pulsing around it. The front of the deck had a large window display with various data superimposed over it via a transparent screen; either side of the pods were standing work stations with various display screen showing more read-outs.

The signs of wear and tear were obvious. On closer inspection one of the pilot pods had a large crack along the top of the shell, there was loose cabling running down the curved ceiling above one of the terminals and evidence of fire damage that marred the once slickly polished wall and ceiling. Not a single flower or plant was in this room; every surface was clear and clean although scuffed up in many places, and some of the surfaces had glaring holes where buttons or some piece of unnecessary equipment was missing. It suddenly struck O'Connor the room was probably older than he was.

One of the large displays showed a 3D representation of the two ships. The King John was significantly smaller than the O'Connor and wasn't shaped at all like he had expected it to be. He was used to seeing collection tankers, thick cylindrical blocks of metal completely lacking character or variation, solid juggernauts slowly moving through space. The King John was oval shaped with four overly large feet that he would have said were hydraulic but assumed were doubtless some futuristic technology instead. The dome platform, perched toward the back, looked like it had been stuck on randomly whilst three prongs that extended out from the front of the ship looked like they were not part of the original design. The O'Connor was big, a mass of chard storage cylinders. The pair of them attached together resembled a beetle trying to carry a brick.

The display showed dull yellow sections over the hulls of both ships which O'Connor felt compelled to ask about as Doyle busied herself around the right-hand controls.

"The outer shell system is absorbing and bending a portion of the light spectrum around the ship, the colouring means we need to run a discharge. It's nothing to worry about as we're only absorbing the low frequency and visible."

"Absorbing visible light, does that mean we're invisible?"

"Invisible yes... undetectable no. We hoped that we could not be detected by your primitive systems but Sir Ryburn reported some strange things in his original account, which he later retracted. I think that was us running discharge as we would then appear very briefly."

"You're Ryburn's ghosts?" O'Connor laughed. "That explains a few things."

"Ghosts? Plural" Doyle said. "That is interesting. We can shut the system off for the moment." She tapped on a couple of the icons and then pulled a sliding lever down to a full off position.

"What type of ship is this?" O'Connor asked after a few minutes of studying the display and vainly trying to work out its purpose.

"This was one of the original parasite class latch ships," sighed Doyle. "They were designed to chase down the original Earth exodus orbs out in deep space and bring them under Dynasty control. Using a technique called proboscis docking, the ship would clamp down hard on the hull, splitting it, before sealing the gap to stop any decompression, and then through the resulting holes the ship would be flooded with soldiers. No one really knows how many orbs were attacked and their pioneers…" Her voice trailed off. "Murdered?" O'Connor asked quietly, receiving a dejected nod of agreement.

"They have always denied it of course, saying that the swarms, as they called them, were sent out to shepherd the orbs back to the new planets."

"And that ship," O'Connor asked, pointing to the O'Connor, "what was it for?"

"Built for its purpose. The most ambitious chard collection mission of all time. When I saw the name I knew it was a sign from the universe, a good omen if you will, that the battery ship was the one."

Doyle smiled, she was very pretty, O'Connor thought again, with a diabolical twinkle in her eye.

"After the chard collection was complete I triggered an evacuation." Doyle's smile widened. "Anderson flew in with the King John and we took the O'Connor."

"But where did all that chard come from?" O'Connor asked.

"VY Canis Majoris, the largest star we've ever found, went nova."

O'Connor's jaw dropped. This was a remarkable statement. "That's 5000 light years away."

"Yes, it took a little while to get there. The nova gave off more chard than could ever be collected from all the combined suns we know of until the end of the universe," Doyle said almost proudly.

"And you really collected an…" He hesitated as he recalled the 28 zero number Anderson had quoted, "octillion chard?"

"Yes, per tank give or take, and we only gathered up the tiniest of tiny fractions of it too, before we reached the upper limit of the storage capacity and they are as close to pure light particles as you can get without actually living on a star."

"That is incredible," O'Connor said, as he attempted to do the math in his head about how long it would take to gather this from Earth, but stopped trying when his units of measurements became thousands of billions of years. In practical terms they were sitting on what was effectively an infinite amount of power, it would be able to sustain a population forever.

"But it all counts for nothing you see," continued Doyle, the sombre tone returning to her voice. "Without the Mercurian metal, we can't go anywhere. The Dynasty control all the travel now. And they don't want to go anywhere."

There was an air of desperation in everything Doyle had said. She seemed sad. She was certainly not from some utopian future; the ship was a testament to that, the flowers, the wear and tear, the sections of the ship that were obviously not part of the original design. This was the ship of disparate people desperate for a better life.

"So it is stolen?" he asked nervously, not sure if he wanted to hear the answer.

"You can't steal sunlight, it belongs to the universe," Doyle said, then after a pause added "But yes, we stole the O'Connor and its cargo."

"You are going to need to sit down for this part," Doyle said pointing toward the left hand pod whilst settling herself into the right. O'Connor sat down; it was comfortable, it seemed to mould to his body.

"Andy, are you there, Anderson?"

"I'm here and ready, let's get this over with," replied Anderson.

"Synchronising the countdown," said Doyle as O'Connor sat back, in the deep recline of his pod, still in awe of the new technology. She had placed her right arm into a sleeve device that seemed to lock her entire forearm arm against the controls. She fitted her hand into a glove and, after flexing her fingers, rotated her wrist. A small panel opened beneath her hand and a floating sphere emerged. Small tendrils of brilliant bright blue light shot out from the ends of her fingers and connected with the ball. The pod trembled.

"What is that thing?" said O'Connor casually as he placed his arms on the sides of his pod until the tremors had slowed to a stop.

"I should have warned you. This is what we use to move through space. The control sphere is our relative angle. I have set the zero plane to match the plane of this system. That tremor was just a quick calibration."

"So, instead of a steering wheel, you have a steering ball?"

"I guess you could say that," she said, whilst still concentrating heavily on the task at hand. Her other arm was free to work the controls on her left side, but O'Connor could not see exactly what she was doing. The displays showed that they were slowly turning and moving forward although he now felt nothing.

"Are we moving?" he asked cautiously.

With her free arm she reached above her head and adjusted some of the dials, the concentration on her face enough for O'Connor to stop asking questions.

"Yes we are," Doyle said after a moment and a few more control adjustments. "Andy, how are we doing? We're approaching the target position."

"All ready down here," replied Anderson.

"Right," said Doyle, "this is it."

She adjusted a few more of the controls, a large T minus kilometres and T minus seconds appearing over the front viewing screen: 0.4 kilometres 24 seconds.

"Ready to begin, Andy, making our approach."

"Ready to go on your mark," Anderson replied.

O'Connor felt useless in the situation as all he could do was watch.

"Okay, mark," Doyle said firmly.

"Releasing chard now," said Anderson, his voice showing the strain."Two hundred metres and twelve seconds to go," said Doyle.

O'Connor could see the energy began to build up. The prongs extending out from the front of the ship began to glow, from the base the light begun to spiral around toward the tip, forming a ball of energy. The spiralling energy started to pulse as its speed increased. The light was intense, even with the window's shielding it was too bright, and O'Connor had to turn away.

"Look away if it is too much," said Doyle, "I'm sorry. I forgot your eyes wouldn't have been fixed. We'll get that arranged for you once back in normal time."

O'Connor didn't ask what that meant.

The streams of light were now pouring out of the energy balls, focusing 150 metres in front of the ship.

"Cutting first and starting second," said Doyle as the countdown reached 100 metres and 6 seconds.

"Confirmed, depth chard release to burn for set duration," said Anderson, sounding out of breath.

"Here we go," said Doyle as, with her right hand, she tipped the control sphere forward very slowly so that both ships matched the angle. The focal point shifted from their seated perspective, from directly in front to a 45-degree angle toward the ceiling. O'Connor guessed that this was to achieve a minimal vertical clearance area of both ships but did not ask for confirmation.

The countdowns both hit zero at the same time and stopped.

"What's happened?" O'Connor asked. The intense light was

gone. Nothing had happened.

Doyle jumped out of her seat to the left side dashboard where the light-bending controls were housed and powered them up to maximum.

"Just a precaution, while we get our bearings."

"What happened?" O'Connor asked again.

"Congratulations, Chief O'Connor you have technically just become the first time traveller."

O'Connor did not much care for the time line technicalities of who was first and who was not.

"That was it? Nothing happened," he said in disbelief.

"What were you expecting?"

"I don't know, a vortex and bright light, something. I felt nothing."

"A bit anticlimactic I agree, but what did you really expect to see? A measurable gap in reality?"

"He wanted to see floating clocks all around us. No, no, no, he wanted to see everything moving backwards really fast," laughed Anderson through the connection. He was in obvious good spirits.

"How did everything go on your end?" Doyle asked a swift change of subject.

"Reservoirs are above expected levels, the depth chard release didn't consume as much as planned. I've locked it all down and I'll run some checks."

"Good form Andy; we'll meet you at the dome."

"But how do you know it worked?" O'Connor said, still not seeing any evidence of time travel.

"There's a reason for you," Doyle said pointing back toward the viewing screen. "I'll reduce the filter so you can see it."

She flicked another dial on the dashboard and there was O'Connor's proof. The completely intact Neith Station back in its Venus orbit.

CHAPTER 11:
ECHOES

THEY HAD ALL gathered back on the observation dome, Radcliffe was there too, standing guard at the top of the stairs. "So…," O'Connor began, looking up at Neith, "there's another me over there right now?"

"That's right, but not another you, the same you, just earlier." Doyle pointed over to an empty area of space, where the earlier King John must have been. "And there is an earlier us too."

"Do they know we're here? Can they see us?" O'Connor asked.

"Who?" Doyle asked with surprise "Our earlier selves?"

"Now you've done it," Anderson said with a smile, popping his head up from under the desk where he was busy at work restarting the dome's viewing platforms and predictive tracking systems.

"Done what?" O'Connor asked innocently. Doyle did not look impressed by Anderson.

"You get the lecture about how we won't because we didn't," Anderson said, still grinning.

"Well we didn't did we?" said Doyle, joining in. "We know that our earlier selves won't detect us because we didn't detect us when we were them. When we were them we weren't even thinking about having to travel back again."

"And look how that turned out," said Anderson as he sneaked back under the desk.

"But we can detect them?" O'Connor asked. "Even with your invisibility thing?"

"We know where we were, so yes, we can detect them. We were only bending some of the light at the time, so if we were to search the background space for the full spectrum, we would see an 'us-shaped' empty space. Once we're back up and running again I'll show you."

"Or we could just scan for our beacon. We still have it on," Anderson said, from underneath the desk, where he was purging memory as a prelude to restarting the system. "Hey I bet that's why we picked up our beacon echo."

"Picked up what?" Doyle asked in horror; the fun atmosphere was gone in an instant.

"I caught an echo of our beacon, nothing serious," Anderson said, looking a bit worried now.

Doyle rolled her eyes "An echo? You mean when we were them?" pointing out toward their earlier selves. "And you mean now for them?"

"Maybe yeah," Anderson said. "I didn't think it mattered."

"Were there any more of these echoes?" Doyle asked, accusingly.

"Actually there were, there was a double echo a few hours later, really quick though lasted less than a minute."

"And you didn't think to mention this? Foolish!" Doyle said. She started working at the controls on a nearby workstation.

"What does it mean?" O'Connor asked as Anderson busied himself back under the desk.

"I think it means we detected ourselves but didn't know it. Here it is," Doyle said pointing to the display in front of her. "We started detecting a beacon that matched ours, it lasted for nineteen minutes forty four seconds." She shot a look over to the desk Anderson was quietly, very quietly, working under. "Nineteen minutes! Then it disappeared."

"Why did it disappear?" O'Connor asked.

"I'm guessing we turned it off... will turn it off," said Doyle with a thoughtful glance at the screen. "Andy! Find the beacon, shut it down NOW!"

"Don't you want this started up first?" Anderson asked, poking his head up from his bench.

"No, get to that beacon; you have a little less than five minutes."

"I don't know where it is," he said, jumping up to his feet.

"Radcliffe," she called out. "We need your assistance please."

Radcliffe walked into the room, still in his smart and formal dress, "How may I be of service, Miss?" he asked, dipping his head as he did.

"Do you know where the beacon is?"

"It is not a single piece of hardware, Miss Doyle. It is several interconnecting signals interlaced deep within several of the core systems."

"Why so complicated?" O'Connor asked. He was thinking a box with a flashing light that you might just unplug.

"To prevent it being illegally removed or disabled, Mr O'Connor," Radcliffe answered.

"Okay, but can you stop it casting a signal then?" Doyle asked.

"That would be an illegal modification, Miss. I cannot be a part of illegal activities," Radcliffe said with his no-emotion blank face and monotone voice.

"Fine, yes." Doyle's voice had a flash of panic and urgency to it.

"Can you take us to where it casts from?" O'Connor asked. Both Doyle's and Anderson's heads spun towards him.

"Yes, Mr O'Connor," Radcliffe replied.

"Andy go with Radcliffe," Doyle said. "You have three and a half minutes."

"Why three and half minutes?" O'Connor asked after watching them leave, Anderson running with purpose and Radcliffe very awkward and upright, trotting behind.

"In three minutes twenty nine seconds it will be exactly nineteen minutes and forty four seconds since we travelled back."

"But Anderson said there was another echo," O'Connor pointed out.

"Yes a detection of a double echo," Doyle said pointing to the display. "Or perhaps the same echo twice. Interesting. I don't know what that means. Maybe something else goes wrong, we can't solve that now though. It could be a glitch, as Andy originally thought." She sounded very unconvinced, although O'Connor thought she was trying to convince herself and not him.

"What happens if they don't shut it down in time?" O'Connor asked after a brief pause.

"They do because they must have," Doyle said. Her smile was back, obviously not putting too much thought into something they have no control over.

"But what if..." O'Connor started but was very quickly cut off

"Would you like a wager Chief O'Connor? If you are unsure?"

She pushed some buttons on the dashboard and brought up the screen display, showing the "fully functioning" beacon.

"Oh no, I'm not taking that bet," O'Connor said. No way was he going up against her on this. Sure enough, as Doyle counted down the last ten seconds aloud, right on zero the beacon stopped.

"That's spooky," O'Connor said, shaking his head. "How did you know? I mean how did you *know*?"

"It made sense: nothing is ever a coincident. Our original selves stopped detecting the echo exactly when Andy stopped the beacon casting. We knew that something caused the beacon to stop because we have it in the logs. That's how I knew it would stop casting and it did stop just as the clock said it would." Doyle jabbed a finger at the logs on the screen again.

"So you can detect where you were with the beacon thing?" O'Connor asked.

"Yes and the parts of the light spectrum we aren't bending. But we don't need to detect our earlier selves because we know where we have been."

Doyle started dragging the displays across the desk and pressing buttons."I'll upload our locational data for where we were when we were our earlier selves." She drew her finger along a glowing yellow touch panel to complete her work.

"There!" she said looking up at the ceiling. A white graphical 3D outline of their ship, their earlier ship, was now taking up a fair portion of the screen. The King John by itself was small enough, but when attached to the O'Connor it took up quite a chunk of the visible space.

"We'll park ourselves over there on the far side," she said, pointing to the area of empty space on the far side of Neith, exactly opposite to where their earlier selves were.

"We had a decompression incident on that side; we'll have to watch out for that," O'Connor said. With all the excitement he had almost forgotten about McSweeney. There was no doubt in his mind that McSweeney was in the walkway that night, up to no good. The little shitbag had killed him after all; maybe it was not the first attempt he had made. His blood boiled at the thought of McSweeney plotting and scheming. He took a deep breath to calm himself. It was all in the past now, kind of. "You guys didn't cause that decompression did you?"

"No, we were still over there," Doyle said, pointing to the graphic of their other selves, "but we know exactly when it happened, so we can avoid it. It was quite something to see," she continued. "It changed the entire rotation of the station."

She was putting in place some type of check for them to get away from that area when the time comes. "The hull of that area of the station got caught up in the atmosphere and burned up. We didn't notice any odd trajectory that would suggest it hit anything, or hit us..." she trailed off and she looked away in deep thought.

"What is it?" O'Connor asked.

"Oh nothing, at least I don't think it is anything," she answered dismissively.

"Okay so we move over to the far side, I enter through the airlock and grab Ryburn's rocks, simple."

"No, he gives them to you," Doyle corrected him.

"Maybe that never happened," O'Connor said. "I'll get over there, take the rocks and come back."

"If you say so," Doyle said, crossing her arms.

"What's wrong with that?" O'Connor asked.

"I don't think it will happen that way," Doyle answered.

O'Connor knew there was no sense arguing with her on this, and so let it drop.

"Can you see where everyone is on the station?" O'Connor asked. "That would make it easier to work out what everyone is doing."

"No, we tried already. The heat output from the antique panels caused too much dispersion to get a clean reading of anything inside the station, not unless we knew what we were looking for. Do you not have any personal communication tools, or any signal generating implants?"

"Implants?" O'Connor said, and laughed. "No, nothing like that. We do have communicators, but they are uncrackable."

"Maybe with your technology," she scoffed. "How do they work?"

"They use ID handshake code to establish heavily encrypted communications."

"We can use those," she said. "May I take a look please?" she said extending her hand cupping her fingers, obviously expecting something very tiny.

He raised up his empty wrist, where his com should have been. "I lost mine a couple of days ago, plus it wouldn't work anyway. They are all set for internal short bands only. The signals piggybacked off the central systems. The signals wouldn't reach out this far unless they were all switched over to a wider distance, which has to be done manually."

A disappointed air hung between them for a moment as they both tried to think up a different approach.

"How much range are they set to now?" Doyle asked.

"Twenty metres, thirty tops. We're never that far away from a com check receiver."

They were never intended for off-station use.

"What about the space suits?" Doyle asked.

"They have separate systems that the local coms connect to, like a signal booster," O'Connor explained.

"Okay so we somehow have to get your crew to boost their signals to be able to reach out this far."

"How can we do that?" O'Connor asked.

Doyle's sinister smile returned. "You're the chief. You *tell* them to do it."

"And how am I to do that, when I don't even have my wrist com anymore?" Again, O'Connor pointed to his empty forearm.

"Face to face then."

"Face to face?" O'Connor wasn't sure he was hearing this properly. Was she being deliberately confrontational?

"Yes, you just tell them plain and simply. You're the chief, why would they refuse?"

She had a point; there would be no reason for them not to obey his orders. He didn't like the idea of doing it face to face, as another version of him was walking around, no, he needed his wrist com.

"Or I could get my wrist com before..."

"Before what?" Doyle asked, "Before you lost it?"

"Yeah, before I lost it."

"Good form!" Doyle said. "Where was it last?"

"Well, I was in my bunk; Ryburn was talking about some nonsense over a broad com to everyone. So I turned it off and put it on my shelf." He left out the part about violently turning it off and throwing it onto the shelf. "Maybe it dropped down on the floor, because I couldn't find it when I went looking for it."

"Interesting," Doyle said. She had that glint in her eye again.

"What is it now?"

"Do you think you couldn't find it because *you* stole it?" She pointed at him to make her point.

"No it was McSweeney and one of his stupid jokes again, although he denied it of course, I mean that little..." he stopped himself again as he felt himself getting angry at the thought of that worm again. "He lied right to my face about it too."

"What if he wasn't lying? What if he was telling the truth? You say he denied it. Maybe he never took it, because *you* did."

O'Connor thought a moment on it and honestly, as silly as it sounded, that made more sense: it was on his shelf, and then it was gone. If anyone were going to steal it, they would have had to know exactly where it was. It would have been a stretch for McSweeney to risk waking him up just to take it.

"You may as well bring one off those wrist com things back here too, so we can keep you appraised of everyone's movements, assuming we can hack them, of course," she said, with a hint of sarcasm.

"I can't, the spare was missing too. After I lost mine I was going to use the..." O'Connor shook his head as he understood. "The spare was missing because I'm going to take that too, aren't I?"

"Beacons disabled," Anderson said, walking back up on to the dome floor.

"Yes, we know, right on cue too," Doyle said. Anderson looked a bit disappointed at the lack of fanfare upon his return.

"Right then," Doyle said, "we have a plan. Andy take O'Connor back to the airlock. He's going back to Neith."

"Did you ask her about intercepting the small craft with the raw Mercurian then?" Anderson asked.

Doyle shot him a hard look. "Don't be ridiculous Andy, that could never happen."

"Oh yeah, I forgot about that" O'Connor said. "Why can't we just intercept the hopper before it gets to Neith?"

"Tell him why it wouldn't work," Anderson said.

"I never said it wouldn't work, I said it never happened," Doyle replied. She clearly knew what Anderson was trying to do. "Anyway, O'Connor has a better plan now, He's going to get his com, tell everyone to update their communicator setting, or whatever those cans and string need so we can track the crew…"

"Cans and string?" Anderson asked, obviously not understanding the reference.

Doyle continued on as if he never spoke "He'll get the spare tin can and bring it back to us to decrypt."

O'Connor was sitting down on the bench just outside the airlock chamber, the space suits that he and Anderson had discarded on the floor had since been hung up; his dark metallic red suit was noticeably bigger and bulkier as it hung in the rack, taking up more than its fair share of the space. Anderson, Doyle and Radcliffe were all there, presumably to see him off.

"What happens if I bump into myself?" O'Connor asked, feeling nervous about what he was going to do.

"If you bumped into yourself you would remember it, wouldn't you? Not the type of thing you would forget I would say," Anderson answered in a slightly patronising tone. "Did anything like that happen to you?"

O'Connor shook his head.

"Good," Doyle said, cutting in. "Then you don't have to worry, do you? Because you already know it isn't going to happen," her sharpness cutting off any further questions.

"Your old clothes Mr O'Connor," Radcliffe said, placing the nicely folded caretaker jump suit onto a small bench. O'Connor knew they had not been washed because, unfortunately, he could smell them.

"Wow," Doyle said, "Well that's just… wow."

"Gets you right in the face doesn't it?" Anderson added. "You forget about it then it hits you fresh, Bang!"

"Indeed," Radcliffe added. "My apologies, I have not done a laundry cycle as of yet." Even his face looked like it was about to crack. "I will go and collect Mr O'Connor's antique air tank now."

Doyle nodded her approval and Radcliffe slipped back out the doorway.

"Hey, it's not funny," said O'Connor, turning his face away from the odour as well. "I've been out here a long time, and we can't waste water on cleaning clothes."

"But don't you have a rotation of uniforms or something? You must have more than one?" Anderson asked.

This was an uncomfortable conversation for O'Connor, as it would have been for anyone. "Yes, I stink, can we please move on, I'll collect a spare suit while I'm out, and we don't even notice it anymore."

O'Connor stood up and started to peel off his current black jump suit until he was down to his shorts, which were also made of the same slick black material yet surprisingly cool.

"Oh, you can leave those on I think," Doyle said, with a blush.

"See something you like, do you?" O'Connor said.

"What does your artwork mean?" she said changing the subject to the elaborate tattoo on his arm.

"Doesn't mean anything that I know of," he said, straightening his arm. "It's a family tradition. My dad had one, although his was messed up on the forearm, so I don't know exactly what it was to look like, his dad had one too, apparently."

"And you would force your children to have these printed on them?" Doyle said, doing her best to sound offended, but O'Connor wasn't buying it.

"No, he'll choose to have it, one day if I ever have a…" He stopped as he noticed that Doyle was no longer listening to him, instead she seemed to be looking over his chest. He paused long enough to catch her eye.

"Your chest is bruised," she said. Perhaps that was why she was staring. "We should get that taken care of."

They were the marks left behind from McSweeney's boots.

"It's nothing really," O'Connor said, although his ribs were still a little tender.

"If you two are finished flirting, shall we continue?" interrupted Anderson.

Doyle turned away from O'Connor to look at the tank Radcliffe was carrying.

"Good form Radcliffe," she said, leaving O'Connor standing in his shorts before he quickly pulled on his old grey jumpsuit after the moment had passed. He sat back down and pulled his old boots on, which felt a bit damp but familiar.

"I have refitted the patch over the hole," Radcliffe said placing the tank by O'Connor's feet.

"Refitted?" O'Connor asked, thinking it was an odd word to choose.

"Yes Mr O'Connor, there was already a patch covering a hole."

"There shouldn't have been a hole, and if there was it should never have been patched, once damaged they are to be scrapped, for safety reasons," O'Connor said, shaking his head.

"Maybe someone forgot to scrap it? Nothing gets scrapped now, we reuse everything," said Anderson, making a little jab at what was obviously a wasteful period of history.

"I do not know what further explanation I can offer on the matter," Radcliffe replied so robotically that it was hard to remember that he was human. "The bonding will hold, Mr O'Connor, I have tested it thoroughly. I would not and cannot put any member of this ship in danger."

O'Connor still did not trust Radcliffe; something about him was just wrong.

"Radcliffe is right," said Doyle. "If there were any doubt he would not allow the tank to be used."

"Okay then, I'll use the tank, but I'm going to bring a new one back."

It was a statement of intent, and was not open for discussion. He ran his fingers along the edges of the patch; it was barely noticeable, definitely a good patch job, the colours matched exactly. "Okay, let's say I believe you, it was already patched. Who patched it? It certainly wasn't done on the station."

"Whether you believe me or not is irrelevant, the tank was already patched," Radcliffe said with zero emotion. "I removed all trace of the previous bonding, so it was a clean mend. It will hold I assure you."

"What else can you tell us about the previous patch?" Doyle asked Radcliffe.

"From what I could tell from the metalwork, Mr Anderson's air canister punctured the previous patch, directly into an existing hole that had been cut clean through all the layers on the antiquated tank."

"That's quite a coincidence," Doyle said making a point of looking at O'Connor.

O'Connor acknowledged the eye contact, and Doyle's opinion on coincidences.

"That would explain how easily the air canister went in," Anderson said.

"How fresh was the previous patch, would you say, Radcliffe?" Doyle asked.

"A day, perhaps two judging by the viscosity and colouration of the bonding material."

"So it was our bonding agent?" Doyle pressed.

"It was the same," Radcliffe concurred.

"And the patch material, can I guess that was ours as well?"

"Yes, Miss Doyle" Radcliffe answered blankly.

"Does that mean it's the same patch…" Anderson began but was cut off by Doyle.

"Maybe the tank hasn't followed the same sequence of events as the patches."

Silence hung in the air, as they all tried to make sense of Doyle's statement.

"I'm still getting a new tank," said O'Connor, finally giving up on trying to follow the implications of the conversation.

"There is nothing more of value I can add to this," said Radcliffe, as blankly as ever.

"Very good Radcliffe," Doyle said. "You may go."

O'Connor climbed into his old space suit. It was so tight and uncomfortable. The dark red of the suit certainly looked out of place with everything around him; it had a coppery shine to it that seemed to glow against the pristine white that surrounded him. He clipped the boots on, testing the magnetic trigger panel above his toes and then stood up whilst Anderson helped him strap on the tank.

"This will hold won't it?" said O'Connor doubtfully, running a thick glove over the patch. He still wasn't sure.

"It will hold, you can bet your life on it," Anderson said.

"I pretty much am, aren't I?"

Anderson took a moment to consider the statement "Well," he said "we never found a dead body floating out here, and neither did you guys, so I guess that means you don't die."

It was a poor version of a Doyle speech and did nothing to convince O'Connor.

"How about, we know it must hold because you were, and will be, using it when we collected your earlier self, and that event hasn't happened yet," said Doyle, "but it has happened to the tank."

"We'll go over procedure again," said Anderson. "To the left of the door are the tethers and jump boards."

"Yes, yes I get it," O'Connor said.

"Remember," Doyle said, "we can't talk to you yet, so you are going to have to be ready."

"Bend your knees like this," Anderson said showing him exactly how to stand ready for the launch. "The tether will stop you just short of the Neith hull."

"I can get in from there," O'Connor said. "We're good to go."

Anderson passed O'Connor his helmet and connected it to the tank. O'Connor checked over everything before stepping through into the airlock. This old tech was new to Anderson and he had to be sure it was all fastened and connected.

"Remember five seconds after you give the signal I will launch you," said Anderson as O'Connor pulled his helmet on.

All O'Connor could hear now was his own breathing, the air tasted cold and fresh. He saw that Anderson was still speaking to him but he could only hear a muffled noise. It was the tether that he had just connected to his waist. He gave him a thumbs up signal after picking up the tether and giving it a quick pull to test it was secure. The airlock door slid closed and O'Connor stepped slowly into the middle of the room. He stood still, feeling his boots grip the floor as he clicked the magnets on. He felt himself go weightless inside his suit as gravity was shut off and the atmosphere removed from the airlock.

The outer door opened very slowly and he could see the station, his target, a hundred metres away. He walked over to the door and pulled himself out onto the external hull of the ship.

There was a walkway of sorts leading out to the jump pad and he made his cumbersome way over to it. It did not make sense to him for it to be so far away from an airlock door. However, after seeing the rest of the ship he made the guess that the airlock and the jump pads were not originally from the same ship. Doyle had explained the sinister purpose of the King John while going over the plan for him to re-enter the station and he supposed that the jump pads had the similar dark purpose.

He stepped onto the jump pad; it was a clearly labelled panel with two yellow footprints painted on it. He shuffled his feet inside his boots then bent his knees ready for launch and gave the thumbs up, knowing that Anderson and Doyle were watching and waiting. He started counting back from five, and took a deep breath in, not really knowing what to expect. He released the magnetic grip from his boots when his count reached one and the next moment he was flying off toward the station. He was travelling very fast; if his tether didn't work he was going to hit very hard. It felt exactly the same as when McSweeney had blasted him out the airlock but this time he was shooting toward the station, not away. The feeling of being completely powerless was still there and he tried to steady his breathing rate, but it was impossible. When his flight reached the half way mark he felt himself being pulled from behind as the tether began to tighten. His velocity slowed to the point he was almost at a complete stop as he reached his destination. He spun around putting his feet out toward the station and very slowly drifted in and made contact, his boots locking onto the station's external wall. He unclipped the tether and gave another thumbs up back in the direction of the now invisible ship and the cable retracted, disappearing into the nothingness.

He made his way over to the airlock door, the very same door that had decompressed, losing the entire corridor.

"McSweeney!" he could imagine his twitchy ugly little face laughing with his bad teeth and boss eyes. O'Connor had to put that thought out of his mind; it was not going to do any good losing his temper at McSweeney now. He took another look back in the direction of the King John but saw absolutely nothing, not an outline, not a blurring against the stars, nothing. He was alone.

He pulled open the control panel next to the airlock door and entered the only code he knew, the code he had before Benson changed it. As that event had not happened yet, his code was valid.

"Access granted," announced the bright green text on the display. O'Connor did a little fist pump at this little success and smiled at the thought of good old Benson following procedure to the letter with the code changes. It was dangerous times for the caretakers doing these decommission contracts as the safeties, firewalls and consistency checks were usually the first things that had to be removed from the internal systems. After that, the bare systems were all there for easy access and unfortunately that meant things were more likely to go wrong.

After evacuating all the air from the internal side of the airlock he pushed the appropriate button and the door slid open. He manoeuvred himself into the station and entered Neith. He was nervous, mindful of the fact he did not know with any real certainty where anyone was apart from his earlier self, who was asleep in his bunk. O'Connor cycled the airlock and removed his helmet then poked his head out of the prep area and looked up and down the dark corridor. The only light was from the planet below, which barely lit up the porthole windows. The shells and frames of equipment were stacked high just as he remembered them last time he was in the corridor.

He wanted to get this over with as quickly as possible; it felt very unnatural being back over in the station almost haunting it.

He quickly discarded his space suit, leaving it on the ground, and did not bother to plug the tank in for refill. Without thinking, he took his favourite woollen hat out from his breast side pocket, pulled it onto his head and then took another nervous look up and down the corridor. There was still no one there. Benson was probably in the central sphere, McSweeney most likely in hydroponics, and Ryburn almost certainly drunk in his room. The only certainty was that his earlier self was asleep in his bunk.

He stepped away from the prep area and crept off into the darkness, towards the sleeping quarters. In his mind, he was playing over exactly where he threw his wrist communicator after Ryburn's call. It had to be on his shelf, so he just had to get to it before his earlier self awoke up and started searching for it.

O'Connor crept along the corridor, taking note of the large equipment shells which, last time he had seen them, were floating off into space after the entire corridor had been lost. The breach door that had sealed this end of the walkway was just ahead of him and the large shell that had been wedged in against the bulkhead was leaning against the wall, looking as stable as ever.

The station seemed even quieter than normal. O'Connor reassured himself that with only the four crew on board, five if he counted himself twice, there was little chance of running into anyone. Doyle had assured him that nothing would happen, but he still felt he was somehow trespassing.

He poked his head nervously into the intersecting corridor as he reached the T-junction leading to the central sphere. The corridor was empty so he continued sneaking along toward the sleeping quarters. As he approached the alcove that lead to the bunk room he shared with Benson, he could hear Ryburn's voice coming through a wrist com there. Knowing that someone must be on the other side of the door he pushed himself flat against the wall, held his breath and listened.

"No, Benson, this was the complete other way. It must have been close," said Ryburn.

"Okay okay, so what was it you think you saw?" replied Benson.

"Well," started Ryburn, but then lapsed into a silence that seemed to last forever. O'Connor's mind began to race into panic. What were they talking about? Had Ryburn somehow seen him?

"It was like something was there but I couldn't see it," Ryburn continued at last.

"So let me get this straight," said the equally distorted voice of McSweeney. "You make a priority one call to tell us you didn't see anything." McSweeney laughed before regaining himself, "and you want us to confirm that?"

That stupid laugh grated on O'Connor's temper.

"I saw something," said Ryburn, his tone becoming irritated, "This is serious. O'Connor, are you hearing this? Please respond."

O'Connor remembered this conversation. He was in his bunk half asleep; it had woken him. His heart skipped a beat when he heard his own voice start swearing and he remembered the tirade of abuse he had hurled at Ryburn before he reached for his wrist com.

"Dr Ryburn," said O'Connor's earlier self. "I'll look into it once my shift starts. O'Connor out."

The terse communication was followed by a thud and a light crashing sound and O'Connor knew that this was his wrist com hitting and clearing the contents of his shelf.

He stood deadly still against the wall for a minute to be sure his earlier self had gone back to sleep before making his move. He gently pushed open the sliding door. It was very surreal for him to see himself in the flesh. He took a few steps closer then stopped dead as the sleeping figure rolled over to face the wall. His heart was racing as he stood there for another moment staring at his sleeping self, hoping that he wouldn't wake.

It was one thing to understand Doyle's theory about not actually meeting his past self but quite another to be in the same room, where any false move could force it to happen. He looked at the shelf and almost to his surprise there was his wrist com, exactly where he knew it always should have been. His sleeping self stirred a little and reached up to scratch the back of his head, displacing his woollen hat in the process and revealing his bald head. He leaned over his sleeping self, coming close enough to hear his breathing, to feel his own breath on his face. It was a strange sensation, more like watching a video of himself than merely looking in a mirror.

He retrieved the wrist com and it suddenly dawned on him that he had an opportunity to swap his ripped hat for the non-ripped one his past self was wearing. As he attempted to grip gently between finger and thumb his sleeping self rolled over onto it, forcing him to let go. He backed away slowly and saw the cupboard where he stored his clothes. They included a spare hat, not his favourite, but at least it wouldn't be ripped. The door to the cupboard was wide open; he was a tidy person and the door being open bothered him, he would have closed it before he retired to bed.

He rifled through the clothes, but there was no hat, everything but a hat in fact; perhaps he never had a spare after all. Ryburn had presented him with a hat after the decompression event he recalled, but it was ripped and full of his rubbish. Forgetting himself, he slammed the cupboard shut in irritation. His sleeping self stirred a little but that was all. He imagined Doyle brushing her hair out of her face as she delivered a "he didn't wake up because you didn't" explanation. Not wanting to push her theory, he exited the room as quietly as he could, blaming McSweeney for his brief loss of composure. He pulled the wrist com on. Why did it feel like he was stealing?

He crept along the corridor, periodically looking over his shoulder until he reached the archway to the work-sphere. Thinking of the duty roster he remembered that McSweeney should be in the oxygen farm on the upper floor, while Benson and Ryburn would be elsewhere. He entered the work-sphere, wrinkling his nose at the odour of chemical, dust and burnt residue. The mini smelt was where it always was; the crafting unit that had caused so much fuss earlier was nowhere to be seen. The floor panels were all back neatly in place and there was no sign of any ripped up cables. This time travel is confusing, and O'Connor shook his head at the absurdity of his own expectation that it would have been as it was the last time he had seen it.

He quickly retrieved the spare com system. It was the same model as his one, only with much less evidence of wear and tear. He gave it a once over to be sure everything was in working order and found that the only thing of note was that it had a missed direct call and recorded message from an unknown and unregistered communicator. He played the message.

"Stop, Stop what have you done, idiot?" The message made him smile, it was undoubtedly his voice, most likely from when the caretakers were preparing their inventory for the Neith assignment. No! That was not right, it wouldn't have been from the unknown com if it was his voice.

He tried calling it back but the return signal he received indicated that the reference point of whoever he was calling was gone. Although it was very strange, he had no time to deal with it and so put it out of his mind. He turned off the spare unit to prevent his earlier self being able to locate it.

The butterflies in his stomach started fluttering wildly. It was time to make the call to everyone but what was he going to say? He rehearsed it aloud a couple of times, flipping back and forth between overly polite, or aggressive and finally settled on keeping it short; identify himself, state the problem, make the request and end the call. He took a deep breath and spoke:

"This is O'Connor here, I'm having some communicator problems. Could you all please dial up you ranges to maximum?" In order to stop anyone replying, he ended the call without adding the usual "O'Connor out".

"All done, Chief," came Benson's reply, so quickly it made him jump. He had to say something now, otherwise they would be suspicious.

"Thank you Benson," he replied and then stuttered, "O'Connor out."

He was surprised at how nervous he had been about this little part of the task. He had goose bumps up and down his arms and he could feel his heart pounding in his chest. He took a moment to steady his nerves but it was job done and he could breathe more easily.

He decided to take the same route back to the far airlock in order to avoid everyone again and was about to step out when he heard the screechy and muffled sound of music coming from the stairwell. He ducked back into the shadows just before McSweeney, bobbing his head and silently singing along to the god awful crap whilst making a ridiculous double step every other step, danced his way through the door. O'Connor stepped out from the shadow and everything washed over him.

There was no holding himself back this time. It was time for revenge for the little runt's mouthing off, threats, accusations, and in particular the drugging, the beating and the attempt at murder. He was in a white hot calm as he pictured the almighty beating he was about to administer. He usually would never jump someone from behind but McSweeney didn't deserve any mercy or courtesy. However, when he entered the corridor he saw something that made all his bad intentions disappear instantly: he saw his earlier self holding McSweeney up against the wall by the collar. He ducked behind his side of the bulkhead wall, sure that neither McSweeney nor this other self had seen him.

"I know you can hear me, I know you are behind there and I know what you are thinking and this is our way of stopping you," said the other O'Connor.

"What are you doing?" said McSweeney from his position, stretched up to his tiptoes with O'Connor's forearm pressed across his neck.

"And you, stay away from Ryburn."

"I haven't been near Ryburn," said McSweeney, trying to wriggle free.

"Don't lie to me. We've put up with enough of your crap over the last day." He spun McSweeney around and up against the side of the arch, so that he was virtually back to back with O'Connor hiding on the other side.

"Didn't we?" the other O'Connor added, thumping McSweeney back against the wall again for good measure. "But it isn't all your fault, putting me out the airlock isn't your fault. We're to blame too!" he said adding the last bit louder. "But you have to leave Ryburn and especially his rocks, alone."

O'Connor, crouching behind the wall, was stunned. He had no memory of this? As far as he knew his past self was still in the sleeping quarters, asleep.

"I don't know anything about any rocks; take your hands off me you psycho piece of…" he heard McSweeney argue back, still struggling to get free, but completely outmatched.

"Say it!" said the other O'Connor. "I dare you, push me, it will cost you. I've taken so much fee off you now that it doesn't matter. Right, I've said my piece and I know it won't change anything, and you have what you've come for. I'm going to count back from ten and you are going to go. Ten…"

"Go where, you …" McSweeney started.

"Shut it! I'm not talking to you!" the other O'Connor interrupted. This sent a chill right down O'Connor's spine. Was his past self talking to him? That was impossible.

"Nine… move Jake!" the other O'Connor said again; it was very clear now who he was talking to. O'Connor took his cue and left. He heard the count reach seven before the sound proofing swallowed it up. What the hell just happened? He had never had that altercation with McSweeney.

He slowed his pace as he passed the sleeping quarters and could hear himself in his room repeatedly saying "Where is it?" with varying curses and swear words punctuating each repetition. But how could that be? He has just seen himself; something was very wrong. He had to get back to Doyle immediately.

He made it to the airlock and sat for a moment to gather his thoughts about what he had just witnessed. Two distinct versions of himself, one he remembered and one he didn't. All sorts of paradoxical and multi-dimensional thoughts were popping into his head. Had reality fractured around him? Was he now seeing alternative versions of what might have been? Time travel was just not meant to happen.

How could his past self speak to him? His lip curled angrily at the thought of his missed opportunity for revenge on McSweeney; he certainly wasn't finished with him. Using the terminal in the changing room he logged into the reporting system and recorded a deduction against McSweeney's payment. One month was the maximum he could deduct at any one time. It seemed such an impotent punishment and it did nothing to ease his need for vengeance.

He put on the space suit, picking it up from where he had left it on the floor, tucking the spare wrist communicator inside his jumpsuit. He pulled down a fresh air tank from the shelf, placing the patched one up in its place and carefully angling the patch toward the back of the cupboard, out of sight. Why use a potential faulty system if you didn't have to? Besides, with the air tank over here and out the way there is no way anyone would use it and it would be lost in the decompression event that would be occurring later that day. Unless he had changed something… he really had to get back to Doyle.

CHAPTER 12:

I DON'T LIKE THIS GAME

O'Connor exited the station making sure to re-pressurise the airlock behind him so as not to raise any alarms, especially with the curious Benson who had been, or would be, investigating strange readings from the airlocks. He looked out in the direction of where Doyle's ship should be to see if he could make it out against the backdrop of distant stars but there was still nothing. He raised his arm and gave a thumbs up, the signal for Anderson to shoot over the tether cable for him. He felt a bit silly standing there outside the station giving a thumbs up to nothingness, until he saw an object moving towards him. The cable hit the hull of the station; if it hadn't been for the vacuum of space he guessed it would have made quite a clanging noise and anyone station-side would have heard the thump, but the corridor was vacant.

Upon impact the line went slack leaving him just enough time to gather up the cable and clip it onto his suit. A thumbs up later and he was being pulled through space away from the station and back to the King John.

Pain shot through his eyes, all the way to the back of his head. He likened it to being stabbed in the eye while staring straight at a flash grenade. He'd forgotten Anderson's warning to keep his eyes closed as he passed through the light-bending focal point. All that light suddenly hitting his eyes stung as he passed through the blanket of darkness into the lit bubble containing the King John. His eyes were twitching underneath his eyelids and his head was pounding as the tether continued drawing him in. He was aware that gravity had taken hold and dropped him onto the floor with a thud which seemed to have an aftershock causing his head to rattle inside the helmet and his brain within its skull. He lay on the floor in the foetal position hoping that he wasn't blind and hoping his new friends could take the pain away.

"Quick he's been lighted," Doyle said, rushing into the airlock and recognising the tell-tale signs. Anderson followed in just behind her and the pair very slowly and carefully pulled O'Connor up into a sitting position before carefully unclipping and gently removing his helmet.

Doyle leaned in close to his ear and whispered "You'll be okay in a few minutes, the effects wear off, don't worry."

O'Connor heard the words and started to relax, it wasn't long before the sound of his breathing began to fade from prominence and his eyelids loosened up enough to blink, then open wider.

"Are you okay now?" Doyle whispered again.

O'Connor nodded and tried to get to his feet, which he did with Anderson's help. Still unsteady he partially collapsed as the room started to spin, letting poor Anderson take all his weight for a moment, before slowly returning to the floor.

"What was that?" he asked.

"Visual overload," said Anderson.

"Visual cortex overwhelm," Doyle corrected. "It's when you pass through the refraction horizon of the invisibility system. Just keep your eyes closed next time." She shot a dirty look to Anderson. "Andy should have explained that to you…"

"It's okay he did, but it slipped my mind with all that just happened," said O'Connor.

"Very well then, how did it go?" she asked with great anticipation.

"Give me a moment" said O'Connor, his eyes settling back into a normal blinking rhythm. After a pause he started to explain. First he unclasped the front of the space suit and took out the spare wrist communicator. He handed it to Anderson whose face clearly showed that he was not impressed with what he was seeing.

Doyle took it instead. "This technology is ancient and overly large," she said, unimpressed.

"Things certainly have changed over the years," said Anderson, with a quick glance to his own, surgically implanted, equivalent.

"I've got my one too," O'Connor added as Doyle helped him out of the sleeves of the space suit, letting the air tank clunk loudly on the ground behind him. "I left the patched one over there," said O'Connor as Anderson picked it up to inspect it. "Better safe than dead…again"

"And the range issue you spoke off?" asked Doyle, getting back on point.

"It's taken care of. Benson has done his, I don't know about the others yet, but they will."

"Good," said Doyle "historical records will only get us so far."

"But there is more, much more" said O'Connor putting his hands up as if to steady his own head.

"Did you get a change of clothes?" said Anderson; the smell of his clothing had hit them all again.

"No, I didn't. This is more important, we've changed something, what we spoke about happened, I saw a different past me over there, doing things I don't remember doing," said O'Connor as he pulled off the space boots.

"A past you doing something different?" Anderson repeated "I knew it! Something has changed."

He gave Doyle an "I told you so" grin, which she just dismissed with a shake of her head, as if to say "that's not how things worked."

"Another you? " Doyle asked, urging O'Connor to continue "A you who you don't remember being?"

"Yes, he was… talking to McSweeney."

"And the you that you do remember being, was he there as well?" she asked.

"Yes, he was asleep in my bunk; that part went according to plan."

"And this new version of you," she continued, "did he know you were there?"

"I don't think he saw me, but he knew I was there. He spoke to me"

"What did he say, exactly?" asked Doyle pressing for the details.

"He knew why I was there and he was there to stop me. He said I had what I'd come for and I had to go."

"And this was after you'd got everything?"

"Everything but the change of clothes," Anderson added but no one was listening.

"Yes," O'Connor confirmed. "I got the coms and called everyone about the range. I'd done everything and was heading back."

Doyle needed more though. "Was there anything else? Details Chief O'Connor, the details matter. Why were you going after McSweeney?"

"I was going to get him," O'Connor admitted, "but I didn't get that far as the other me was there instead."

"So basically, the other you got to McSweeney first, very intriguing."

"Yes, but I was so close," said O'Connor.

"Did this other you beat McSweeney?" Doyle asked.

"No he just talked," said O'Connor.

"And stopped you from 'getting' McSweeney," said Doyle, using O'Connor's words.

"Yes, that is the short of it, what do you think it means, what have we done that has caused the change in the past?" asked O'Connor.

"Yeah" Anderson added. O'Connor saw he wanted answers too. Or at least for Doyle to acknowledge she was wrong about not being able to change the past. "It's changed, that's the only explanation. So if I wanted to change something..."

Doyle took a disappointed breath in and rolled her eyes at Anderson. "Nothing has changed! We can't change anything. There is no paradox; there is none of this multiple time line nonsense, parallel universe, or multi-dimensional cross over, okay? Anything you do will affect the mission, yes that is true. But whatever you do or don't do won't affect the final outcome of you being in that airlock. Nothing will change; it already happened."

"If nothing can change, how do you explain the other past me?" asked O'Connor. "I didn't just make that up, I saw him."

"I don't doubt that for a moment, but that other you was a future you. Think about it. He knew you were there, he knew what you were going to try to do. There is no other explanation... which unfortunately confirms what I have suspected: this won't be our only trip in time to Neith."

Her statement left another one of her foreboding silences in the air.

"But," O'Connor said, "if my future self stopped me getting to McSweeney that means I never did what he was there to stop, so why was he there to stop it if it never happened?"

"Oh, yeah," Anderson said, swinging his gaze back to Doyle.

Doyle paused, she didn't have an answer, not immediately anyway. "Nothing can change, but the other you must have had a reason."

Anderson was repeating the paradoxical loop under his breath to himself, with hand motions. "He did it, so he went back to stop it, so it didn't happen, so he didn't stop it, so it happened, so he went back to stop it, so it didn't happen, hey what if..." Anderson began to say to the others, but Doyle quickly interrupted.

"No! There is no what if."

"But it's still just a theory," O'Connor added "Will you concede that? You don't know for certain that I can't change what happened to me."

"No I will not" said Doyle standing up and folding her arms

"History says you were blasted out of that airlock! You yourself have lived through that. It happened!"

"Just say it's not certain," said O'Connor, trying to get to his feet again but stopping short.

"I will not," she said firmly. They were at an impasse, eyes locked together. "I'll be in the dome, getting this ready," she finally said breaking eye contact and shaking the wrist com at them before turning around to leave the room.

Once he was able to stand without the room spinning O'Connor and Anderson headed toward the dome. More flowers, still finding them out of place but very soothing, the effects of being "lighted" were all but gone now. There was the odd flower here and there that he didn't recognise and he stopped to take a closer look at one particularly bright purple bunch.

"That one, we took as part of a trade," said Anderson, "It was altered to live in the dry air. It shouldn't be purple, but it is."

O'Connor had leaned over to smell the fragrance, but jumped back at the mention of if being altered.

"You mean it's been genetically engineered?"

"It won't bite" said Anderson, with a giggle.

"That's not funny," said O'Connor. "There has been a global ban on genetic engineering since several generations of Africans had side effects."

"Doyle wanted to add a bit of colour," Anderson explained as they crossed into the central part of the ship. O'Connor could tell that it was part of the original ship because of the distinct change in style. The walls, floors and ceilings were different, the once pristine white of the previous section replaced by the more homely use of cream and magnolia walls and flooring that looked to resemble old Earth tiling.

"So, this part is the King John?" asked O'Connor taking a good look around and seeing where old and new had been melded together. "Where did the airlock part come from?"

"I'm not sure when that was fitted," Anderson said. "The ship is quite old and it was already there when we took over ownership. I think it was from the same ship as our bedrooms, The Gilded Lily; there is a plaque on one of the walls near my room. It was quite a big deal once."

"Why do you keep adding to it? Why not just have fresh build?"

"Ha," Anderson laughed. "We don't have that kind of money, not yet anyway. Our major addition was the dome. You should have been there. It was..." but he trailed off, laughing boyishly as if something had embarrassed him.

"What is it?" O'Connor asked, worried now.

"Let's just say it didn't go according to plan and leave it at that," said Anderson with a sorrowful sniff.

"Oh, I'm sorry," said O'Connor. "What was the name of that ship?"

"It was from a first observation post on the outskirts, I don't think it had a name."

O'Connor didn't press the point, he could tell Anderson didn't wish to talk of it any further.

They entered the observation dome to find Doyle standing over the desk looking over the wrist com. The design was basic, tough and very hard wearing designed for use in space and able to send and receive communications through all types of interference. However, since the caretakers never had to go anywhere they were dialled right down.

"Oh good," she said looking up. "How does this tin can work?"

"They are basically a telephone, you have to press buttons," he started, but after seeing their faces he stopped. "What?"

"What is a telephone?" Doyle asked.

O'Connor looked at her to see if she was being serious.

"A really old version of this," he answered. "There is a small menu system, you select the ID of the person you wish to call and it calls them."

"We will need to be certain not to use our encryption bolts when we use them to talk to you," said Doyle looking at Anderson. "Make sure yours is working, I think you'll be needing it before we're done here."

"Encryption? No, that is all taken care of internally, you just talk and I will hear you," said O'Connor.

"No, I'm afraid that won't work" said Doyle. "If we used them it just wouldn't work" said Doyle flicking the side of her throat with her finger. Obviously another "enhancement". "An information security precaution," said Doyle. "If you had to make the plans that I did you'd need to keep your secrets secret."

"Show me," said O'Connor curiously. After showing Anderson and Doyle how to use the communicator to make a call to him they spoke. And all he heard through the communicator was a faint distortion.

"And only we can decrypt it," said Anderson, rather proudly.

"How does it work?" asked O'Connor, having never seen anything like it.

"It digitises the sound at the wave level, changing the vibrations of it. If there is no decryption signal upon receipt it stays scrambled. We haven't used them since we travelled here."

"So why even bring it up?" O'Connor asked.

Doyle just smiled and indicated that O'Connor should continue with his demonstration of his communicator.

"It sends a bounce signal to each number every so often, measures exactly where the reply comes from and so gives us their exact location," explained O'Connor, "At least that's the theory."

"Okay then," said Doyle.

"That's where you guys come in," said O'Connor.

"I got this one," said Anderson, making an attempt to brush O'Connor aside, an attempt that failed. O'Connor conceded and stepped aside.

"I just need to know what to send each unit to register a 'bounce'," Anderson continued as he instructed O'Connor to place his wrist com at one end of the desktop, and put the spare wrist com at the other end. From the centre of the desk a thin, black, featureless panel rose up and turned on its side before beginning to glow a faint blue. It meant nothing to O'Connor but Anderson seemed to take it as a good sign. "Call that one," he said to O'Connor.

"Hang on, I need to turn it on first."

"How primitive," said Doyle, as if looking at some exhibit in a museum.

"I have to change the identifier codes too," O'Connor said.

"Why?" asked Anderson.

"So my crew can't call them; they will have their wrist coms set up with the current identifier for me."

O'Connor quickly turned it on and made the adjustments, then returned to his place on the table.

"I've just started to call it," he said.

"Got it," said Anderson, O'Connor had barely pressed the command before Anderson begun his critique. "Very basic stuff; I'm surprised it even works. I've got it now. Okay call the other units."

"But they'll answer," said O'Connor, cautiously.

"No, we'll dampen the signal," said Anderson, making some adjustments on the screen "unless they are within two metres they won't get it."

O'Connor cycled through the three crew members and when Anderson confirmed he had read the info he needed out of the encrypted signal, the panel on the desktop retracted.

"Uncrackable was it?" Doyle said with a smile.

His secure communication system had been decrypted and turned back on itself, cracked like an egg.

"It's hundreds of years old, remember," she added, putting a reassuring arm on O'Connor's shoulder as they quickly followed Anderson around to another workstation area.

"There you go," said Anderson, looking up at the ceiling at Neith. A series of lights flashed. When they flashed again five seconds later each light had a name attached.

"There is your crew."

Benson was at the top floor of the central sphere, McSweeney was in the hydroponics and Ryburn was in his workstation.

O'Connor gave a grunt. "I could have guessed that already," he said. "Where is the other me though?"

"You lost your wrist com remember?" said Doyle.

"No not the past me, the future me," O'Connor corrected. "He had my or his wrist com on."

"Sure we just need you to call it, same as the others," Anderson said.

"I don't know the identifier he's using. Can't you crack it or something?"Anderson shook his head. "It doesn't work that way I'm afraid. Without knowing the exact identifier we can't find him."

"If your future self wanted to talk to you, he would," said Doyle.

O'Connor was sure there was some logic buried in her statement but couldn't quite find it. "It's a shame there's no way to see where the first me is, if there was you'd probably see me searching for my com."

"Perhaps there is a way," said Doyle, tapping her index finger to her chin. "What if you were to tag yourself, how would you do it?"

"That depends how big the tag is," said O'Connor, crossing his arms, theoretical discussions never amused him. What was she getting at?

"Small. Size of your thumb and light; you'd never notice it."

"I'd slip it into his, my, left leg pocket I guess, I never use it anyway."

"When would you tag yourself?"

"I'd do it when I go to sleep later," O'Connor answered. "That's the next time I will stop long enough to… why?"

Doyle smiled.

"No that's too late. We would miss all of today, and you can't recall your exact movements?"

"No, why would I? I was all over the place throughout the day searching high and low for my lost communicator."

"Andy, do we still have those tag-lozenges we used for that track and trace business out on Eradani?" asked Doyle

"Yes we still have them. It took me ages to get them just right, I wasn't going to scrap them. Shall I send Radcliffe to collect them?"

"No need just yet, if you remember their classification numbers?" Doyle continued.

"Of course," Anderson answered.

O'Connor felt as nervous as he looked. He didn't like where this was going.

"It's looking pretty obvious now that we will travel back again. The new O'Connor, the second beacon echo," Doyle started to explain. "Let's say that when you do go back, you tag yourself, when you were asleep this morning? Before you reclaim your com. Andy see if you can detect one of your lozenges on the station."

"Unbelievable," said Anderson after a couple of adjustments. A solid blue light appeared on the ceiling, depicting the original O'Connor moving along the outer corridor of the station.

"It's cause and effect," said Doyle "but we get effect first, and have to worry about the cause later. There's another signal with us in this room with us too, I would bet."

O'Connor thought for a moment, piecing it all together. He reached down into his left leg pocket. At the very bottom he found a thumb sized cold metal disc.

"I don't like this game," he said handing it to Doyle.

"I don't like it either," said Anderson, echoing the sentiment.

"So we know where everyone is now, mostly," said Doyle, summing everything up as the three of them discussed their next move. "We can see Sir Ryburn's hopper coming back." The ceiling of the dome showed a green line tracking, around and behind the planet, the path the hopper had taken. "It's in a fast orbit now so Sir Ryburn will soon have the ore on board. That's our opening."

O'Connor agreed and took over the run down, "The hopper

comes in hard, but Ryburn collects it and then takes the rocks directly to the work-sphere. He smelts a sample of it down but leaves the bulk of it there but McSweeney," that name said through gritted teeth, "takes it."

"Or does he?" Doyle asked.

"Yes he does… he confessed."

"It went missing though, right" Doyle asked.

"Yes," O'Connor confirmed, "it did."

"That was probably you then," said Doyle dismissively with a shade just short of blame.

"I want to stop the lander," O'Connor suddenly belted out, making the other two stop and take notice. He put up a hand to cut Doyle off from giving her favourite speech. "I want to try, I want to change it."

"But..." Doyle tried to start,

"I know what you are going to say," said O'Connor. "If you're that certain it will fail then you have nothing to lose do you?"

Doyle was speechless, if only for a moment.

"Very soon Ryburn will use the two landers attached to the hopper for brakes; once they are spent he will release them. One of those landers is the reason we had to finish the contract early. But that hasn't happened yet, none of it has," said O'Connor. "Look I don't buy into this "'can't because we didn't and won't because we don't' crap." The statement was for Doyle but he was looking to Anderson to back him up. Anderson was now looking very awkward at being brought into this, he looked to avoid all eye contact and shifted his feet nervously

"Well I don't really know enough about..."

"Stop it," said O'Connor, raising his voice. "You don't buy it either."

"Nothing is for sale," said Doyle, her voice raised now as well.

"It's just a phrase," said O'Connor. "It's just we think we can change things."

"We?" Doyle asked, "Oh stop it," she said to Anderson as he was now busying himself at the controls doing nothing.

"I mean…" Anderson started to speak, very nervously "… what's the point of being able to time travel if we can't change anything?"

"Thank you," said O'Connor, walking over to Anderson, standing united against Doyle.

"It's agreed then, we will stop the stray lander from hitting the station," said O'Connor.

"You do realise that the lander thing never hit Neith, don't you? What do you hope to achieve here?" Doyle asked, her hands on her hips, obviously not liking being dismissed to the background of the planning.

"This won't change much," O'Connor assured her. "Just a little tweak. Stopping the lander will mean there is no panic. Ryburn will still have the rocks and will still be able to invent his engine... but I won't be killed because none of that part will have to happen."

"Fine then, let me know how it turns out," said Doyle, leaning against one of the railings, folding her arms. "This is going to be good."

"I guess you are on your own," said Anderson.

"Oh no," said Doyle from her railing. "You help him on this one."

She had her condescending smile again; did she know something they didn't?

"But when this fails," Doyle added, "we do things my way!"

"Agreed," said O'Connor.

"So how are we going to do this?" asked Anderson.

"We move the ship into its path, we're only a little way out."

"No way are we doing that! Sorry but no absolutely not, that will kill us," said Anderson

"What about the O'Connor?" O'Connor asked, grabbing at straws.

"You want to risk a particle containment collapse? There are trillions upon trillions of chard there. Who knows what that would do to this solar system, or even region," said Anderson.

"That's a very bad idea," Doyle's voice echoed from the back.

"But it didn't because we would have seen it," said O'Connor.

"Oh no, you can't say that," said Doyle, inserting herself into the discussion again, "You are changing things remember?"

"Right," O'Connor agreed, begrudgingly.

"But risking the O'Connor is too much," said Anderson, looking over to Doyle for backup. She ignored him.

"Can we shoot it down?" asked O'Connor.

"With what?" Anderson asked, he wasn't being much help.

"I don't know, don't you have a laser or a blaster or something?" asked O'Connor looking around for some type of inspiration.

Anderson shook his head and Doyle let out a very loud "Ha!"

"How good is your aim with the tether?" asked O'Connor.

"Yes, that could work," Anderson said, showing a bit of enthusiasm now.

"We'll need to be within five hundred metres, and we'll need to calculate the exact trajectory," said Anderson.

"You don't need to calculate it, we already know, we would have tracked it when it happened," Doyle said from her casual observer position. "But that's all the help I'm giving you."

Anderson started to bring up all sorts of information on the small screen in front of him, before mirroring the information to the ceiling. A green image of the hopper appeared on the screen, and two blue images representing the landers that Ryburn had used for makeshift brakes. Two distinct dotted lines extended out from the hopper indicating the trajectory of the discarded landers.

"That's our one," said O'Connor excitedly, pointing to one of the lines.

"And we will need to be here, and hit it with the tether *here*," said Anderson pointing to where in space they would need to be. "We need to move the ship out to be able to get the clean shot," he continued showing the rotation of the ship in relation to the airlock and tethers launching system.

"Okay then, let's do this!" said O'Connor.

Anderson looked toward Doyle for permission. She nodded.

"Go ahead Andy, I can see where this is going."

"I've transferred our positional destination to the flight deck," said Anderson.

"Let's go then," O'Connor said and, accompanied by Anderson, quickly left the dome.

Thirty minutes later Anderson had gently moved the ship to the ideal position. The flashing icon representing the original O'Connor had been moving erratically as he searched for his missing communicator. The Ryburn blip had moved along the corridor from his workstation and was now stationary at the bottom of the central sphere, preparing for the fumbled collection. Benson had remained in the central sphere.

The sun was just beginning to show over the horizon to the left of the planet. The lack of brightness was the first thing to catch O'Connor's attention when he and Anderson returned to the dome, both looking very proud of themselves. He wondered again what type of visual dampeners ran on the windows to make the sun look dull. But questions like that could wait, he had a future to change.

Anderson jogged over to one of the panels and prepared to shoot the tether.

"We've put a harpoon on the end of the tether," said O'Connor, to a disinterested looking Doyle.

"Yes, it will punch right through the lander and we can reel it in," said Anderson as he continued the preparation

"Well good luck," said Doyle and then added, "I hope this brings you closure and we can move on."

O'Connor ignored her words. This was going to work.

"It's all set up and ready," said Anderson, "coordinates are locked."

The McSweeney blip and the O'Connor blip had started moving very fast along the corridors, heading toward the central sphere each taking opposite directions.

"I remember this," said O'Connor, "I was looking for my com when the impact alarms started going off."

"Can you zoom in on the hopper please Andy?" Doyle asked.

The hopper had just extended its arms and the landers had started to fire for brakes."This is it…" said O'Connor, as the engines burned out and the landers detached and went off in their separate directions. Their target had been outlined in red. It passed the station following the dotted green line showing the trajectory, from when this event was first witnessed, toward the "target place".

"Harpoon is away!" shouted Anderson, slapping a hand on the desk. He was obviously looking forward to proving Doyle wrong at last.

Anderson adjusted the zoom for maximum dramatic effect, and they watched with anticipation as the two objects on the ceiling moved toward the convergence point.

"It's too late to stop it now," said Doyle.

"Good!" grunted O'Connor.

The harpoon hit the lander, causing a small explosion. O'Connor's arms shot up in the air as he celebrated the perfect hit, but as the flash of the explosion disappeared he knew he had failed. The mental tingling sensation of déjà vu crept over him. It had unfolded exactly as he had seen before, but this time it was a live video and not static stopgap images he had shown Ryburn. What he had previously thought was an imperfection on an image was the harpoon just before impact. The impact must have punctured the tank and ignited the remaining fuel vapour. The thought of it all made him nauseous.

"Here is its original path we traced when it first happened," said Doyle, as she zoomed the view right out to show the whole planet. She added a green line looping around Venus forming a petal display before crossing into the stations path. "And this is where it was going before you interfered." A blue line this time showing a path out and away into space. "And here is the path it is on now," said Doyle indicating a line tracking exactly the same path as the green line, colliding with Neith, just as it was always going to do. "Good form to the both of you," she said with a mocking tone. "Now, can we get back to getting the ore?"

"You knew this was going to happen, didn't you?" said O'Connor with a raised voice, a finger of blame pointing at Doyle

"Of course I knew," Doyle shot back "And so did you!"

"But, how?" asked Anderson.

"Because it had already happened," said Doyle loudly. "You can't change anything. How many times must I say it before you learn?"

"Learn? This is all just a game to you isn't it?" accused O'Connor.

"Does it look like I'm having fun here? Do you know what Andy and I have done to get here?"

O'Connor shook his head in frustration. "So if I'd done nothing it wouldn't have happened, is that what you are saying?"

"If you'd left it alone it wouldn't have happened," Doyle repeated to herself as she collected her thoughts, "If you left it alone you wouldn't have ever been in the position to leave it alone. It was your actions that started the sequence of events that put you in that airlock. And that led to us coming here, for the ore you should have had. It's a circular logic and it can't be broken"

"You can't know that," O'Connor insisted.

"Sure," Doyle said. "What if it didn't happen? Maybe Sir Ryburn wouldn't have invented his magnetic propulsion. Maybe you and your crew would have moved on, and I bet you and McSweeney would have become the best of friends. And maybe the Lancer Dynasty wouldn't have taken over everything and plunged humanity into darkness stranding us all under their boot. But all this did happen and we're here. Nothing can change."

Neither O'Connor nor Anderson spoke a word; they had well and truly been put in their place.

"It happened because it always happened," she said "We came back to get the ore that was supposed to be in your pocket."

"I'm sorry," said O'Connor putting his hands up in front of his chest, retreating in defeat.

"Good, thank you! Now let's move on. Andy, please get us back into position alongside the station."

CHAPTER 13

...COMES AROUND

"How is it looking?" said O'Connor, nervously testing the waters as he entered the dome. Doyle had stayed in the dome as the ship returned to its previous position, following the slow orbit of Neith. They had missed a prime opportunity to get O'Connor back on to the station whilst the crew were all gathered on the lower deck of the central sphere after the hopper dramatics.

"We're good O'Connor," she said. "No need to tiptoe."

"Thanks. I'm sure Anderson will be relieved."

"*He* should've known better" she said, looking away to hide her tired disappointment. "Besides, it always happened that way. Curious how events really unfold, cause and effect backwards. Who would've known it was us all along?"

"I still feel responsible," said O'Connor, somewhat subdued.

"And so you should," she replied, "just because it always happened doesn't mean you didn't have a choice. I hope it's lesson learned so we can move on."

"It was a complete waste of time," he said.

Doyle smiled at the bad pun, a smile that turned into a laugh and before they knew it they were both doubled over laughing about the absurdity of the situation and the circular events that led them there.

"So," said Doyle, finally returning to business, "I've been

following their movements and Sir Ryburn has been on this walkway," She pointed up at the station, "for quite a while."

"That would be the collection hub," said O'Connor and explained how Ryburn would have emptied the rock samples into the chamber for decontamination since it was the only way to get the rocks on-board without physically walking out to get them.

"Afterwards," Doyle said, "he headed toward the work-sphere, stopping very briefly for a moment, only four or five blip cycles. I suspect he was talking to Benson, as no one else was nearby."

"What have I been doing?" quizzed O'Connor.

"Don't you remember?" she asked and pointed at his blue light. "You've been back to your room, again, and now you are in the airlock prep area."

"Where is McSweeney?" he said coldly.

"He's been in the hydroponics area, nowhere else."

"He's not gone anywhere near Ryburn?"

The display showed the two blips at separate places on the sphere, one on the top deck, and the other on the bottom.

"They are both in the same sphere, but have been on separate floors."

"This is our time," said O'Connor, "I walked across the entire station and came back in airlock-B. I can get in and over to the work-sphere, when the other me comes back from outside. I remember I went to the central floor and spoke to Benson as soon as I got back station-side, after that I spoke to Ryburn about his bloody landers. I won't need to worry about running into anyone but only if I go now, while the other me is outside."

The plan was reasonable and Doyle offered no objections. What could possibly go wrong? It sounded simple enough.

O'Connor was eager to go back to Neith and gather up the rock samples from the work-sphere so practically sprinted to the airlock and got into his space suit.

"You sure you won't see yourself?" asked Anderson who had joined him in the airlock.

"Not if we're quick. Plus I didn't meet a future me when I was space walking earlier, so he won't see me now, right?" O'Connor said.

"You're sounding like her now," said Anderson.

"I have to be quick," O'Connor reiterated as he clipped on his helmet and stepped into the airlock. He wasn't so confident after all.

Anderson cycled the airlock for him and once in space, O'Connor used the jump pads and tethers to return to the station, landing on the perfect angular blind spot, keeping himself hidden from his past self, who was also on the hull of the central sphere.

"All is clear, O'Connor," said Doyle through the com. "You are good to enter."

O'Connor hurried inside, then got out of his space suit as fast as he could even though he knew his past self was quite a way behind him. He put his boots into their correct position and noted that there were a lot of boots at this airlock now; he must have arrived midway into McSweeney's "move all the suits like an idiot" prank.

He opened the cupboard and squeezed his suit in next to the others, remembering how his past self would be opening it to find it in this terrible state. The uncomfortable sense of déjà vu gave him the shivers once more. He put his tank up on the shelf, wedging it in between the other four that were there and noticing that the patched tanked was on the end, still turned the wrong way around, just where he had left it.

"Sir Ryburn and McSweeney have left the work-sphere, so you are all clear." said Doyle, her voice sounding loud and raspy through the coms.

O'Connor acknowledged and then promptly dialled the volume to a more reasonable setting. It had seemed louder than ever before probably as he was so mindful of being as quiet as possible. This time he walked confidently around the dark corridors, not needing to creep or sneak as he knew where everyone was, apart from the possibility of his future self who may or may not have been here too. The realisation put him back on edge and he sped up as he passed the central corridor junction and again at the sleeping quarters just to be on the safe side.

"Entering the work-sphere now," he announced as he gave a final look up and down the corridor.

"We see you," Doyle replied.

The room smelled of the chemical fumes of the catalyst agents used in the refinement process, O'Connor wrinkled his nose. Suddenly Ryburn's voice boomed from his com.

"We have an emergency!"

O'Connor couldn't help wondering why Ryburn was calling everyone but before he could resolve the question he heard his own voice crackling in his ear.

"What is it?" said another O'Connor, accompanied by a faint feedback echo.

"We've got another proximity alert outside the station."

There was a long pause before the other O'Connor spoke again.

"It's just another sensor glitch."

He never made that call; he was outside the station with no com, something the mystery O'Connor must have realised too.

"I was… I am outside the station now, checking for damage, remember?"

"Yes, quite right. My apologies O'Connor, of course you are, that would explain it." Ryburn replied, sounding a touch embarrassed.

"Chief, stay clear of airlock-B." Benson had joined the conversation. "I'm not sure it's safe; maybe that impact has made it worse."

There was a long silence before the mystery O'Connor replied: "Yes, will do. O'Connor out."

O'Connor immediately called Doyle. "Doyle did you get all that?"

"Yes. Good thinking with the space walking."

"That wasn't me, I didn't say a word and it wasn't the old me either."

"Our friend from the future perhaps," said Doyle.

"It must be. Can we trace his com?"

"No," answered Anderson, "the equipment wasn't running. I'll leave it running to see if he calls again."

"What about the tag in his pocket?" asked O'Connor.

"You mean the one you removed and left up here?" answered Doyle sarcastically.

"What should we do?" O'Connor asked, leaning back into the shadows nervously.

"Stay the course," answered Doyle "We can't change it, nor do we know what your future intentions are. The future you knows how to reach you so it's all up to him."

O'Connor sighed. It was strange to be thinking about his future self as a separate person.

The smelt was still hot, when O'Connor ran his palm across the top, and it hadn't been cleaned after use, an omission for which he silently admonished Ryburn. He couldn't see Ryburn's trolley.

"Where was he standing exactly?" he asked Doyle

"You're on the spot, exactly."

"I can't see it. Where else did he go?" said O'Connor, urgency back in his voice.

"He paced around the room a bit but didn't leave," said Doyle.

O'Connor started to search the room although he had already thoroughly searched it when he was looking for his lost com.

"It's not here," O'Connor called back, the anger in his voice starting to trickle through. "Are you sure McSweeney hasn't got to it already?"

"The signals flashed in and out. He would have had to have moved from the doorway to the ore and back to the doorway within one blip cycle. That's highly unlikely."

"Where is he now?" said O'Connor after assessing the distance quickly and agreeing begrudgingly.

"He's in the central sphere, with Benson."

"And the other me?"

"Still outside, and Ryburn's in his sphere."

"I'm going to have to ask McSweeney," said O'Connor. "I'll be able to tell if he's lying face to face. Radio silence until I call you please."

"What does that mean?" asked Doyle.

"It means don't call me unless you absolutely must, I can't have you calling through and risking the others hearing."

"Okay then. Starting now."

O'Connor shook his head and laughed to himself at Doyle's words; they weren't strictly wrong, but they weren't right either.

Once again O'Connor found himself pacing around the work-sphere, rehearsing what he was going to say to McSweeney about the ore. The same approach as before was called for, quick and to the point. Above all, he had to control his temper.

He walked along the corridor, past where his future self had had McSweeney by the scruff of the neck, and past where he had been mysteriously trapped behind hardware frames, the offending frames all neatly stacked, flush against the walls. The floor was clear of the deep gouge marks that had puzzled him earlier, or would puzzle his past self later. His mind went back to the strange metallic smell that had been in the air. What had that been? He was sure it was connected.

A little way past the airlock was the crafting unit that had been, or later would be, in the work-sphere. The sheer size of it told him it was heavy and he wondered how Ryburn had managed to get it back to the work-sphere.

His confident walk slowed to a crawl as he turned the corner toward the central sphere. McSweeney and Benson were just up the ladder ahead. Suddenly McSweeney slid down the ladder with a crate of components under his arm. The sight of him and his stupid grin was too much. O'Connor only lost his temper for a second, but a second was all it took for him to punch the little creep squarely in his ugly, greasy little face, sending him crashing back against the ladder and falling awkwardly to the floor in a heap, sending the crate from his arms and scattering the circuitry all over the landing.

"Put me out the airlock will you?" said O'Connor as he flexed the fingers of his punching hand. "You ever do anything like that again and it will be *you* going out the airlock."

He reached down with both arms and dragged McSweeney back to his feet.

"What the hell is your problem?" McSweeney squeaked.

"Where are Ryburn's rock samples?" demanded O'Connor, banging him back against the ladder, in the exact same manner as his future self.

"Not this again! I don't know, what's it got to do with me?"

"Don't bullshit me McSweeney, I know you've been messing around with him and his work. Now where are they?"

McSweeney was struggling to get out of O'Connor's grip, a familiar position that he had already been in once that day. O'Connor saw a flash of primal anger in McSweeney's eyes: the same look that he'd seen on the other side of that airlock window.

"I don't have his stupid rocks," he shouted right in O'Connor's face, showering him with a good film of spit. O'Connor flung him onto the floor amongst the scattered circuitry.

"One month," he said wiping his face off, he was going to take away a month's fee. It was an empty threat, but he knew it would get to McSweeney.

"You've lost it, you've fucking lost it," said McSweeney looking back up at O'Connor. He didn't argue about the fine, though. He looked away breaking eye contact and started gathering up the circuitry quickly stuffing them into his pockets.

"Stop getting under Ryburn's feet, leave his damn rocks alone," said O'Connor as his eyes were drawn to the small sky-blue coloured component among the other pieces, that same sky-blue he had seen on Ryburn's prototype. That prototype had not been built yet. He reached down and picked it up just as McSweeney was reaching for it, causing him to flinch away.

"Now, you listen here," he said as he held the piece in the cowering man's face. "You take this, this piece right here, to Ryburn now."

He dragged McSweeney all the way to his feet again and pushed him on his way down the corridor.

"Now!" he yelled after him as he watched McSweeney half run, half stumble away. *To hell with forgiveness*, he thought, *I'm not finished with you yet.*

"You clumsy bastard, what have you gone and done now?" called Benson from the floor above and poked his head down the ladder. "Oh hey Chief, sorry about that, I thought you were McSweeney."

"That's alright. Just had a bit of an argument with him myself," said O'Connor.

"What type of argument, Chief?" asked Benson, concern washing over his expression.

"He's still messing around with Ryburn's work, I had to reprimand him for it this time. He's taking the proper regulator to Ryburn now."

"Well he's been warned enough times. How was it out there? Any damage?" asked Benson.

"Damage?" O'Connor thought, there was no blood, so McSweeney couldn't be cut... his mind desperately retraced what Benson could have been talking about, did he guess he had just smacked McSweeney? *Space walk*, he remembered. His past self was out checking for damage to the hull. "No, nothing serious. Cosmetic only. Back to work please Mr Benson," he said, short and to the point. At least he got that part right and he stepped away from the ladder.

What a complete disaster that was he thought, as he headed away, that could not have gone any worse. He'd lost his cool with McSweeney and was unnecessarily rude to Benson, who didn't deserve to be spoken to in such an abrupt fashion, McSweeney however, well he had it coming.

"Doyle, Anderson," he spoke into his com, once he was in a quiet alcove along the central corridor.

"Go ahead O'Connor, we're here."

"McSweeney was no help, he says he didn't touch it and doesn't know where it is," said O'Connor, despair in his voice, "I don't think he's lying either, not yet anyway."

"Okay," Doyle said, "we'll have to think of something else. Are you coming back?"

"No, I'll keep looking, but when we come back again, maybe we can tag the trolley in advance."

"Good form, it will probably save us some time." said Doyle.

O'Connor shook his head at the bad joke he himself had made before and was sure he heard Anderson groan too.

"Maybe we have already tagged it," suggested Anderson, but then followed up with, "No, I can't detect it, maybe that's not what we do?"

"I'm going to have to ask Ryburn," O'Connor said. It was the only option available although he wanted to avoid any unnecessary interactions with the crew.

"Sir Ryburn… really? He will be working on the first iteration of his propulsion by now, how exciting." said Doyle.

"Save it will you?" replied O'Connor, still in good jest, but with a hint of venom in his words. "I know what you say his legend is, but I know the man and he's a drunk, and a forgetful drunk at that! There's as good a chance as not that he has all the rocks with him."

"He's just left his quarters," said Doyle, not commenting on the character assassination.

"That's not right," said O'Connor. "I went to see Ryburn about the business with the lander, after I was outside."

"You mean your business with the lander," she corrected him.

"Yes quite, I'd better move out of here," he said looking again nervously in both directions to be sure that the corridor was clear.

"I'll check back along the way, trace back along McSweeney's steps. He could have stashed it around the airlock." He subconsciously lowered his voice to a whisper. "Can you tell me when Ryburn is back in his room?"

"Will do," said Doyle

O'Connor moved quickly. He had to avoid being boxed in

by Ryburn and his past self and so went back in the direction of the work-sphere.

As he walked he checked above, between, below and inside every piece of hardware frame, even the ones that McSweeney would have had to have lifted up to fit the trolley in. He was almost mirroring what he had already done when he was searching for his lost com but didn't remember seeing a trolley then either; then again he wasn't looking for one when he was his earlier self.

McSweeney had a habit of blasting things into space, so he searched the airlock as he wouldn't put it past him to ruin Ryburn's work the same way. He checked under the benches, in the cupboard and in the airlock itself and he was getting so desperate that he even checked behind the air tanks just in case McSweeney had unloaded the rocks behind them knowing that Ryburn would never look there. As he was pulling out all the tanks he came across his patched up tank and he pulled it out with a sense of dread. He had deliberately left it at the other airlock. How did it get over here? It seemed likely that the mystery future O'Connor must have used it. But why? He was so sure he'd never use it again so why would the future him use it when there were others to choose from? And why would he bring it back over here? He didn't like it.

A quick call to Doyle did nothing to put him at ease. All he got was a very logical point about not questioning the motives of things he hadn't done yet, if it were him at all.

He continued searching for the rocks. They were not anywhere in the airlock, nor were they in the corridor. If McSweeney had taken them, he had done an excellent job of hiding them.

Anderson's voice came through the com. "Anderson, we need your beacon open."

"Anderson please say again?" O'Connor asked back. He had heard the words but the context meant nothing to him.

"I'm sorry O'Connor," Doyle's voice this time, "please ignore Andy, he called you in error, call us back on the other setting."

That didn't sound right either thought O'Connor.

Doyle was leaning over the spare wrist com, the gauntlet shaped device sitting in the middle of the bench top. Her hands were either side of it, palms flat against the surface of the desk as she waited with anticipation for O'Connor to call. Anderson had taken a seat on the stairs in the middle of the floor. He had changed a small segment of the ceiling screen to show his burning sun and, but for the shielding, could have been sunbathing. Doyle had the ceiling screen showing the Neith station with its icon representing Sir Ryburn, Benson, McSweeney and the two O'Connors. On the far side of the station there was a white outline drawn around the past King John sitting out in space waiting for their moment to 'save' O'Connor… or what they thought was their moment.

"Doyle, Anderson, are you there?" O'Connor's voice came through the com.

"I'm here, O'Connor," said Anderson loudly, to be sure his voice carried the distance.

"He's right here," Doyle answered, motioning for Anderson to come closer.

"Have you worked out how to change the setting on the spare then?" asked O'Connor.

Anderson looked to Doyle for guidance, or a clue about what O'Connor was talking about.

"No," he replied slowly, "I've been watching the burning sun."

"I just heard you through the communicator," said O'Connor.

"No, I was quiet," Anderson assured him.

"I heard you, both of you, but it was a separate com signal."

Anderson looked to Doyle again, who shrugged.

"What did we say?" she asked.

O'Connor repeated what he had heard.

Doyle raised her hands up to her face, into a prayer like shape as she evaluated the information. "It wasn't for us," she said and after a moment, "and we leave the beacon alone."

Anderson looked a bit disappointed. "It must have been important though," he said.

"When it is your time to get the call, you will get it. I am sure of that," said Doyle with her unquestionable authority over the logic.

"What would enabling your beacon again do anyway?" asked O'Connor through the com.

"The only reason would be for a data transfer," Anderson answered.

"Just in time for that double echo of yours, wouldn't you say?" said Doyle, before adding, "Sir Ryburn's back in his room, and McSweeney has just left him and is heading back around clockwise."

"Okay thanks," said O'Connor, "I'll leave this beacon call thing with you. I'll go see Ryburn whilst he is alone and get the rocks. Radio silence again please"

"Okay, starting now" said Doyle, then once the call was cut she turned to Anderson "Let's get the timing of that echo up."

"Blast, it's going to be happening any moment now," Anderson said a moment or two after consulting the displays. He jumped to another set of controls, made another series of adjustments before they both looked up at the ceiling to await the echo. "Three seconds to go," he said. Doyle merely nodded.

Two distinct Caution of King John ships flashed into view either side on the station and then just as quickly disappeared.

"There are two of us?" said Anderson in amazement.

"Four," Doyle corrected pointing to the original King John. "Those two, our past selves over there, and us. That's going to be a tricky one for me to explain."

"At least we know what those echoes were," said Anderson as if it were some consolation prize. The situation had just become even more complicated.

O'Connor was once again using the dark corridor to reach Ryburn's workstation. He had chosen it because it was usually the less beaten path but had of late seen a lot of traffic. He dashed past the central corridor junction but in the approach to airlock-B slowed his pace mindful of not bumping into anything. Even though it was swamped in the glare of lights in the prep area, his eyes were fixed on the green light flickering above the airlock and his mind was on getting to Ryburn. However, as he approached the prep area his mind snapped back to the disturbing thought of the "patched tank" that he had deliberately left here but was now at the other airlock on the far side of the station. No one had cause to move it.

He had to check it; so he stepped into the prep area where the light seemed even brighter than normal as his eyes adjusted. A suit had been dumped onto the floor, the helmet, boots and tank dropped next to it. This didn't alarm him, as he remembered doing this when he was his original self. The green light on the control panel indicated that the internal airlock was pressurised but he knew it wouldn't be long before this whole section of the station would be lost to space. The air tanks were still as he had left them. He reached for the tank on the end, the backwards one, and manoeuvred it around on the spot. It couldn't be… but it was… he saw the patch. How could that be? He calmly turned it back around and stepped away slowly as if he was trying not to disturb a wild animal. It felt like seeing a ghost, seeing something that just should not be! How was it over here as well?

He left the airlock, rather disturbed; one thing was certain: there was no way he would be using either of those tanks. He promised it to himself, no fucking way! He should have just blasted them both into space, he thought as he passed the collection hub. In fact perhaps he would. He couldn't help but notice again the state in which Ryburn had left the collection hub. It annoyed him that it had gone back to a messy, unclean state and he wanted answers and someone to blame for not cleaning it up. The realisation that his original self had not yet cleaned it up made him smile. *Stupid linear time.*

He passed under the breech door and patted it with his palm, feeling a great sense of foreboding about the events that lay ahead and knowing that the door would have a job to do very soon. He looked it up and down as if assessing whether it was fit for purpose before giving it an approving final pat. The last time he had seen it, it was slammed shut, the internal bolts had fired and it was melt-locked into place.

Ryburn's room was just ahead, and he was nervous about speaking to him. This was going to be the first real, solid interaction he would have with the crew. McSweeney and Benson didn't really count as he didn't so much talk to them as talk at them until he could get away. This was different, he needed information and Ryburn was a clever fucker and would see through any pretence. He took a quick glance back down the corridor to be sure he wasn't going to be interrupted.

"Dr Ryburn," he said from the half open doorway, speaking just loud enough to get Ryburn's attention.

"Chief O'Connor," said Ryburn acknowledging him whilst spinning his chair around to face him. "You wish to speak to me about the landers?"

"Umm, yes I did but it can wait for now," said O'Connor thinking quickly, remembering that his original self had spoken to Ryburn over Benson's com. He had been in the central sphere checking the images of lander and checking the orbit of the station,

"Okay? You did bring it, didn't you?" asked Ryburn his eyes going to O'Connor's empty hands.

O'Connor wondered momentarily what he was talking about but then, fitting it into the complicated timing of that morning, he remembered that Ryburn was waiting for a cutting tool that his past self would be bringing over to him right now. He didn't have as much time as he thought, he had to get out of there.

"I'm sorry Dr Ryburn, I've gone and left it behind. I'll be right back..." he said thinking quickly as the little details of what he had done the other morning, the exact timings were lost to him. His heart was racing as he looked up and down the corridor, trying to recall which direction his past self would be coming from.

"And you say *I'm* losing my mind?" he heard Ryburn call from his desk.

He didn't have time to com Doyle for a direction and certainly wouldn't risk coming face to face with his past self, even though he knew that meeting never happened. Paradox or not, he wasn't going to risk it, so found himself cover behind a hardware frame within earshot of Ryburn's door.

His panic was warranted as his earlier self was right on his heels. He heard the soft tapping of footsteps from his earlier self coming to deliver the cutting tool to Ryburn and to blame him for the lander entering a collision orbit. A shadow was cast on the wall above his hiding place as his earlier self blocked the light from Ryburn's doorway as he entered the workstation. He listened to the conversation unfold, just at the very limit of his hearing. He didn't catch every word, but his memory filled in the rest. He heard Ryburn defend his position on the lander being on a collision path saying that it was a "trillions to one" chance, not knowing of course that it had not been his fault at all. O'Connor's breath caught as he listened to the misplaced placed blame being directed at Ryburn. Knowing that it was himself who was responsible for the collision orbit, caused by his effort of trying and prevent it.

The conversation went quiet for a moment, while the earlier O'Connor was showing the "evidence" on Ryburn's monitors. He remembered his anger at Ryburn, but now he was ashamed of it, the voices were raised as he heard himself say, "You think any of us want our names attached to this shit pile you've landed us in? All we want is to get home in one piece!"

"This is important, damn it!" he heard Ryburn shout, "Your little chop contract is meaningless against what I'm trying to do. You are all are meaningless compared with what I'm trying to do."

"You may be worthless. But my team is worth a hundred of you, you drunken old bastard," the earlier O'Connor replied, accompanied by the sound of breaking glass - Ryburn's drink being slapped from his hand and smashing against the wall. His past self was about to storm out.

The shadow hit the wall again as the earlier O'Connor left, muttering "Trillions to one" to himself, but the footsteps paused as the earlier O'Connor stopped and rested himself against the wall. O'Connor recalled how angry he had been at that moment and then the guilt over being angry. It was a feeling that O'Connor was now experiencing again, but now he was embarrassed for both of them. He remembered how he had wanted to turn around and apologise to Ryburn for the way he had spoken. It was unprofessional and uncalled for. O'Connor popped his head up from his hiding spot and saw his past self resting his head against the wall, still in conflict about whether to turn back and apologise or to keep his pride. Choosing pride, he left, heading to the central sphere where he was going to be calling lunarbase.

O'Connor felt disappointed in himself, Ryburn had asked for help with his prototype and his request had been ignored, but he was in a position to put things right.

"I'm sorry about that, I over reacted and let me temper get the better of me. I offer my apologies," said O'Connor as he poked his head around the door way offering an olive branch.

"Apology accepted, but I do need to get this done," said Ryburn, without looking up.

"Do you have everything you need now?" Ryburn was making adjustments to his "prototype".

"I'm fine for now." answered Ryburn, dismissively.

O'Connor was relieved. Ryburn didn't seem at all annoyed with him, so the rudeness of the previous encounter must have been in his head. Either that or Ryburn was so oblivious that it had washed right past him.

"Is that the prototype for your engine?" asked O'Connor,

with genuine interest as he couldn't believe what he was looking at. How did he transform old circuitry, wiring and Mercurian rock into the future of space travel? There had to be more to it than this… this junk.

"Yes this is it. Not much to look at. I know. But if everything plays out like my simulations there will be enough energy to–"

"Generate a magnetic field?" O'Connor interrupted.

"Exactly" said Ryburn with a smile, as if pleased that O'Connor knew where it was going.

"And it will be strong enough to move the entire station?" asked O'Connor, who still had his doubts even though he'd seen it work.

"Ha!" said Ryburn, dismissively. "That would be an impressive first implementation, but quite impossible I'd have to say. I honestly hadn't considered something so grand. Perhaps one day it could be accomplished." He trailed off.

"Perhaps sooner is better than later on this one. I'm not putting much faith in an early pickup." O'Connor felt very uncomfortable now; he didn't like Ryburn's plan: they couldn't wait until they got home. They needed this pile of junk working by the next morning.

"What makes you say that?" Ryburn asked.

"Just call it an educated guess."

"Can you explain your educated guess if you please? Some of us aren't as familiar with caretaker collection cycles." Ryburn pressed, like a dog not letting go of a bone. Ryburn held eye contact, as if searching for the truth. It crossed O'Connor's mind to leave the room and not divulge anything further, but he hadn't yet asked him where he had left the rocks and knew very well that Ryburn would not let it go until he received a satisfactory answer. If the prototype was to be working by the morning Ryburn needed some incentive and a distraction from delving into O'Connor's motivations.

Most of the time when he spoke to Ryburn he had to repeat himself as Ryburn never really listened, but this time he was sure he heard everything: or perhaps he always heard everything and just chose to be obtuse. O'Connor really wished he hadn't spoken now.

"Well, this is the way of it," he started, knowing that there was no turning back. "You have three caretakers who, let's be honest, are right at the bottom of the priority list. Perhaps second only to a disgraced scientist."

Ryburn nodded.

"If you were them, would you pick us up? But there's more you need to know," O'Connor took a breath, bracing for Ryburn's rebuttal. When it didn't come he plunged on. "Our axis has changed and we're slowly spinning toward the planet."

"Which means?" asked Ryburn.

He knew Ryburn knew what it meant. "Entering final phase will have us pointing in the wrong direction and we will end up going the wrong way."

"I see. And you didn't think to mention this before? You just wanted to soften the original blow by not explaining how badly I've doomed us?"

"This wasn't…" he started to say, but corrected himself, "… isn't your fault."

"That doesn't matter now, it's done," said Ryburn.

O'Connor could see guilt and shame in Ryburn's face, but if that was enough to get Ryburn working, O'Connor was happy to let him own it.

"I'm definitely going to need more of this iron refined. Perhaps a working prototype will rebalance the scales in our favour and secure us a lift home."

"And you have the right regulators don't you?" said O'Connor seeing that the one Ryburn was using was not the one he remembered seeing when the prototype was working later.

He picked up the sky-blue one from the desk and read out the specifications.

"Nine-gauge, eighty-two millisecond, three-gram regulator… Dr Ryburn this one's the nine-gauge," he said, holding it out to him.

"Yes it is, but it's of no use to me … nor any of the others for that matter. You can take them back," said Ryburn politely motioning and inviting the chief to help himself.

O'Connor was stuck; he couldn't tell Ryburn what component to use, he didn't really understand what he was doing. Persistence would probably just start an argument if Ryburn thought O'Connor was questioning his expertise.

"Thanks," said O'Connor, "but I'll leave them here just in case you need them, especially this blue one."

He looked over to Ryburn, but he wasn't sure he was even listening.

"It looks very useful." he said with much emphasis and little subtlety.

Ryburn was looking intently at his prototype, turning it over gently and checking each connection.

O'Connor shook his head, Ryburn would change the component to the sky-blue one soon enough, he knew it because he'd seen it already. Hopefully, he had planted enough of a seed now. He still needed to know where the ore was and this was his moment.

"What did you do with the rest of the ore?" he asked as Ryburn finished his careful inspection of the device, and was hopefully at his most receptive.

"In the work-sphere. Listen, I'd prefer it if you or Benson handled this one. I think McSweeney may feel the need for some ill-placed comedy."

"Yes of course," said O'Connor smiling to himself as Ryburn was already heading toward what he wanted to talk about next. "I'll handle this one myself, but If McSweeney was trying to be funny and hide the ore, where do you think he'd put it?"

"Yes, I've been thinking on that one since you mentioned it earlier," O'Connor didn't remember having a conversation about this type of thing but Ryburn continued. "It would have to be somewhere obvious and familiar to achieve optimal annoyance. If I were the target of the prank, he'd stash in here or back in my sleeping quarters"

O'Connor shook his head. According to Doyle, who was keeping careful eye on everyone's location for him, McSweeney hadn't gone anywhere near the sleeping quarters since the ore was brought on board. It was possible that for some reason McSweeney was not wearing his com, so O'Connor decided he would take a look in Ryburn's old quarters to be sure.

"Would he have hidden it anywhere else?" O'Connor asked,

"It has to be right under your nose. Have you looked under the dinner table?"

"Interesting," said O'Connor with a nod. He hadn't looked in the central sphere since there was always someone there but once everyone turned in for bed it would be empty.

"He stashes things in hydroponics, too," added Ryburn, "when he is out of ideas."

"Does he now? Thanks, that's good to know."

That was it, and it made sense too. McSweeney was right there in hydroponics the whole time Ryburn was refining his ore, he could have grabbed it and returned, and Doyle might not have seen it. "I'd best leave you to your work, good luck with your experiment, Dr Ryburn. Be sure to let me know when you get it working."

"Jim," said Ryburn, turning his head to face O'Connor. "You can call me Jim. Dr Ryburn is too formal and Sir Jim a bit strong."

"Very well, Jim," said O'Connor. There was no way was he going to call him sir. Where did that suggestion even come from? It was too much to just be a coincidence.

"You've been calling me it all day anyway."

"Really? I hadn't noticed," said O'Connor as he left. *All day?*

Once he was back in the corridor O'Connor called over to Doyle and explained to her the leads to possible locations for the ore that Ryburn had given him.

"You spoke to Sir Ryburn? What did you say?" Doyle asked, obviously forgetting that for O'Connor talking to Ryburn was not a big event.

"He's working on his prototype." Then he paused. "I may have told him some things I shouldn't have."

"Like what?" asked Doyle. O'Connor was sure he heard her sigh.

"That they aren't going to be rescued, but I explained it as a suspicion."

"Okay, nothing can change and I can't see how that information could be damaging."

"I also accidentally told him the axis of station had changed, meaning they can't use final phase to escape."

"But that won't happen until the airlock breach later," said Doyle.

"Then I gave him the idea of moving the station using his theory," he added, wincing as he spoke, "the thought had never crossed his mind."

"Oh no," said Doyle, but O'Connor could hear she was suppressing the urge to laugh.

"Why is that funny?"

"Sir Ryburn always credited Chief O'Connor with the concept of moving Neith. Don't you see? He always said it was you. You just did what you always had done."

"We've got some news too," she continued. "We've seen two more of us outside the station, so four of us in total." She went on to explain what had happened with the echoes and the new versions of themselves. They all agreed that there was nothing to be done about it now, and that the priority was still getting the rocks.

"Where is everyone?" asked O'Connor.

"Sir Ryburn's in his workstation, everyone else is in the central sphere, Benson on the top floor and the earlier you and McSweeney in the middle."

O'Connor remembered: his earlier self was making the call, and McSweeney was eavesdropping. This was actually a very convenient turn of events because it would mean that hydroponics, and most likely place for the ore to be hidden, would be empty.

"I'm sending the message to lunarbase, then we all sit down for dinner," said O'Connor. He left out the out the finer details, the accusations, the threats, Benson hitting the table so hard it broke; she didn't need to know all that. "I should have plenty of time to check out hydroponics and Ryburn's old room."

"Good form," said Doyle.

"After the dinner I went to speak to Ryburn. I don't know what the others did after that, call me immediately when someone leaves the central sphere. I want to avoid any more interactions."

"Will do. Radio silence, starting now," said Doyle.

Does she think that meant goodbye or over and out?

By using the lighter side of the station O'Connor didn't have to be so careful. It would take longer but, remembering how, later that evening, his earlier self would be chasing McSweeney's shadows in the corridor outside airlock-B, he wouldn't have to do it in the dark.

The crew (his earlier self included) would likely be turning in for the night after dinner, which was why he wanted to check Ryburn's old room now, and avoid any more unnecessary meetings, especially with McSweeney.

He got around to the sleeping quarters and Ryburn's old room without fuss. It would be just like McSweeney to hide the ore here, right under Ryburn's nose. The room was opposite the bunk room that he and Benson shared. He pushed the door open. The room had not been used for quite a while: it was a little dusty and it smelled stale. Compared to his bunk room this room was very spacious, but Ryburn had taken to sleeping in his workstation shortly after O'Connor and his crew had arrived and only ever returned now and then. Ryburn had been preparing to leave the station just before he got his final approval to stay and complete his work. O'Connor and Ryburn had got off on the wrong foot right from the start as O'Connor didn't want him there, and Ryburn returned the sentiment.

There was a pile of books dumped out on the floor next to a stack of moving crates. O'Connor surveyed the mess on the floor. Various personal effects and random junk looked to have been just emptied out onto the ground, but most importantly was what he had been looking for… the elusive trolley.

"Damn it!" he shouted as he planted the heel of his boot into the side of the trolley, kicking it over and letting it slam against Ryburn's old bed. The fucking thing was empty. He angrily looked around the room for any sign of the rocks. There was nothing. He let his frustrations out on one of the moving crates, sending it crashing into the wall, scattering its contents to the floor.

"I found Ryburn's rock trolley," he called over to Doyle after he had composed himself.

"Excellent, now there was an exact amount of ore processed, the discrepancy between what came onto the station and what was processed was only a couple of kilograms."

"The trolley is empty!" he interrupted.

"Oh, that is disappointing," said Doyle, the tone of her voice mirroring her words.

"I know," said O'Connor, already feeling the flush of embarrassment about losing his temper.

He searched the room very thoroughly, checking every crate and even tidying up the mess he had made. He took his time as Doyle kept him updated on everyone's location. The ore however, was definitely not in there.

"I told you," Doyle began. "I've been watching everyone's location, no one came into this room. McSweeney never even came down this…" she was abruptly cut off by a horrible, high pitched screeching noise that suddenly filled his ears. He turned his head away from the com, shielding the closest ear with his free hand and trying to put as much distance between the noise and his ears as possible.

"What was that?" Doyle called back once the interference

noise had stopped.

O'Connor's ears were still ringing.

"It happened before though, while we were having dinner, yest-" he had been going to say yesterday, but stopped as he realised it hadn't happened before, what he remembered was the exact same noise at the exact same time.

"It happened to the earlier you?" she asked.

"Yes, but through Benson and McSweeney's coms."

"What was it?" she asked.

"It was Ryburn, he said he tried to com everyone, but it went wrong."

"Why was he calling? Do you remember?"

"Yes, he was calling to say he had gotten his prototype working."

"How exciting! The other you is on the move; going to see Sir Ryburn's breakthrough no doubt."

"Yes I went to see Ryburn. He was rambling on about magnetic fields and moving the station. He was crazy… hmmm, it doesn't sound so crazy anymore, but he seemed delusional at the time. It was a messed up conversation, he knew we would be abandoned before I did."

"Because you told him before your earlier self knew," Doyle added for clarity, or for Anderson's benefit.

"And he knew about the axis change before it happened. No, he told me that it hadn't changed, I guess he had rechecked it."

"How did the conversation end?" asked Doyle.

"He accused me of blowing hot and cold," said O'Connor, recalling the exact words Ryburn had used, "said I kept changing my mind toward him and the situation."

"I guess from his point of view you had been. Do you think he suspects anything?"

"No, why would he? It's not exactly an obvious conclusion to make."

"Perhaps you aren't the only future you he has been speaking to…"

O'Connor finished checking every last possible hiding place in the room, and by then Doyle had another update for him. "McSweeney is on the move."

"Benson too?" O'Connor asked.

"No, Benson is staying still."

"Which way is McSweeney going?" O'Connor asked.

"He's on the central walkway, heading toward the airlock-B end."

"I knew it was him," said O'Connor, taking his hat off and wiping some sweat from his forehead before adjusting the hat so the unknown rip was not so prominent. He then explained to Doyle what was about to happen in the dark corridor outside airlock-B where McSweeney had done something to the airlock in a first attempt to kill him.

"He's at the end of the corridor now," said Doyle.

O'Connor could imagine him looking around to be sure no one was following before sabotaging the airlock, or perhaps he intended to lure O'Connor into the airlock before blasting him into space; it would explain why his codes hadn't worked: to prevent him from getting back in. His fists balled up at the thought of that scheming little snot.

"He's moving again," said Doyle.

"Toward airlock-B?" O'Connor asked, with certainty, waiting for Doyle to confirm McSweeney was in the corridor, effectively catching him red-handed.

"No," Doyle answered. "He's going back to the central area again."

"Going back, what for?"

"How would I possibly know that?" Doyle snapped back.

O'Connor was genuinely surprised, not that McSweeney went back, but that he didn't go down towards the airlock. He was so sure McSweeney was guilty of messing about with his past self down there but, saying that, he still wasn't convinced of his innocence either.

"Wait," Doyle called back. "Both he and Benson are moving."

"Which way?" asked O'Connor. He needed to know which direction to take so as to avoid running into them.

"They are still in the central sphere."

O'Connor looked left and right again, trying to decide whether or not to move on.

"They are heading out, the other way, in the direction of airlock-A."

"I guess that means I'll be searching the central sphere next then. Keep me updated," he said as he headed toward the central sphere.

Around the foot of the ladder was the discarded circuitry scattered about the floor after the unfortunate altercation with McSweeney. O'Connor smiled at the thought of McSweeney crashing to the floor and spilling the pieces everywhere. O'Connor looked around the room. The table, with its freshly damaged leg, was standing crooked whilst the sight of the cupboard containing those nasty meal bags caused him to remember the meal he had on the King John. His stomach actually rumbled and he rejoiced at the thought that he would never have to eat that slop again.

If McSweeney had brought the rocks here, where would he have put them? It clearly wasn't under the table as Ryburn had joked. His eyes scanned the room: there was nowhere to hide it. He wouldn't have taken it up to the top floor, where Benson had been working, as it would have been far too much effort to haul up the ladder; down the ladder however, was a different story. He could just picture McSweeney tipping the rocks out of the trolley and down the ladder wearing his stupid grin the whole time, although that would have meant he would then have taken the trolley to Ryburn's old quarters, which didn't seem likely, even for McSweeney. Be that as it may he had to check so he slid down the ladder. Hardly to his surprise, the search of this floor turned up nothing.

"Damn it," O'Connor said as he kicked a random spool of cable whilst simultaneously banging his head on the low ceiling. He cracked it at just the right place to cause spots in his vision, this earned the spool another kick as it was clearly its fault he couldn't find the ore and had banged his head.

He climbed back to the middle floor and searched everywhere he could think of including a desperate look under that table. As each location turned up nothing he got more and more frustrated and was tempted to kick something but the throbbing on the back of his head reminded him why nothing good would come of that. He took a seat at the table and was about to call Doyle when he realised he hadn't looked in the meal bag cupboard. He smiled, it was perfect, McSweeney would have put it there, knowing that Ryburn would eventually find it and he would probably be sitting right at the table for a front row seat as his prank came to fruition. He opened the door, then slammed it shut, they weren't there.

"Doyle, I've found nothing here. I'll check the hydroponics then I'll have to come back over."

"Okay, that is disappointing," said Doyle. "If it's not there we'll have to come up with another plan."

"Are Benson and McSweeney in their rooms?"

"Yes, they've turned in."

"And the other me?" O'Connor asked.

"He's in the sleeping quarters too; he spent some time around airlock-B, even doubled back towards Ryburn's room for a moment, but you already knew that."

O'Connor did remember, at the time he thought that airlock had been glitching; he had to check it was safe but his access codes had been denied leading him to manually lock the chamber to ensure integrity. McSweeney had done something but he didn't know what. "Are you certain that he…"

"McSweeney wasn't anywhere near that corridor," Doyle answered, cutting him off. O'Connor recalled the rest of his evening, and how he had had a good talk and made up with

McSweeney outside the sleeping quarters. Or at least thought he did, it certainly wasn't the case when he next saw him.

"Keep a close eye on McSweeney and the other me. Very soon they will meet outside the sleeping quarters but after that I'm not sure if he went to hydroponics. That's where he said he went but he could have gone anywhere. I want to know what he does to that airlock. Maybe I can stop him."

"You can't stop what has already happened," said Doyle obviously getting tired of repeating the mantra. "Anyway, you don't have long before that whole corridor is lost. I think it's best if you are off the station by then," she added with concern in her voice.

"Right," agreed O'Connor. "I'll get over to hydroponics. Tell me the second you see McSweeney move. He will either be going to the airlock or coming to hydroponics."

CHAPTER 14: TWO FACED

Bounding up the stairs to hydroponics O'Connor came face to face with a very unexpected person on the way down, McSweeney!

"Hi, Chief," said McSweeney with a big smile. "Did you come to help?"

"What the hell are you doing here?" demanded O'Connor, shocked to see him. Why was he here? Moreover, why hadn't Doyle warned him?

"I was just finishing up," said McSweeney still smiling, pulling off his ear phones.

"How are you here?" O'Connor rephrased, but it didn't help.

"I had a look at the air tanks too, to see if there was anything I could see that would explain the air pressure."

"Shut up, just shut up," O'Connor said, doing a poor job of suppressing his anger. How did McSweeney get here without Doyle alerting him?

"Get out of it," McSweeney joked.

"Where is your wrist com?" O'Conner demanded, this would explain why Doyle never called, and how he'd been moving around the station unnoticed.

"I didn't put it on, I just told you that and you weren't bothered," returned McSweeney.

"Well I'm bothered now."

"No," said McSweeney with a look of disbelief, that flicked on and off as he tried to work out what was happening.

"How often do you take your wrist com off?" O'Connor demanded.

"This is the only time," said McSweeney his smile disappearing.

"Have you been doing this to sneak around the station, to mess around with the airlocks?" O'Connor asked. "Answer me!" O'Connor raised both his voice and his fist.

"Or you'll what? Hit me again? Do it and I swear you'll be sorry," said McSweeney.

"Are you threatening me?" asked O'Connor, but McSweeney interrupted him.

"What about all that talk of putting my record straight and reversing the fines you've given me?"

"You have to be kidding. After all the crap you've pulled I'm going to fine you some more just for this now. Where are Ryburn's rocks?" O'Connor demanded.

"Oh, back on this again are we?" said McSweeney. "I haven't touched his stupid rocks."

"And what did you do to that airlock?"

McSweeney was two steps up on the stairwell so he was standing taller than O'Connor. In a moment of courage or stupidity, fuelled by anger and betrayal, he leaned right into O'Connor face, pushing his nose up against his and part sprayed part shouted "How about I put you out the fucking airlock!"

O'Connor pushed McSweeney's face away, sending him flying backwards and he landed awkwardly, slumped down onto the staircase, and then wiped the spittle from his face with the palm of his hand. Now it was O'Connor's turn to loom over him, but he held onto his anger this time, he didn't swing for McSweeney, although he wanted to. The only thing stopping him was that haunting warning from his future self, the words he had spoken whilst he had McSweeney up against the wall, "It wasn't his fault". O'Connor unclenched his fist and stepped back down the stairs.

"You had best get out of here, now!" said O'Connor through

gritted teeth whilst pointing toward the sleeping quarters. He sounded like an angry parent trying to hold his temper with a naughty child. McSweeney had the sense to listen; he darted past O'Connor and stood behind him at the bottom of the stairs.

"I'm going to take a look around up here," O'Connor warned, "and if I find that ore..."

"You won't, I haven't touched it," McSweeney shouted back.

"Then you have nothing to worry about do you?" said O'Connor, as he walked up the stairs into hydroponics.

McSweeney hadn't realised how vindictive the chief could be, as he watched him disappear up the stairs into hydroponics. "I'll get him," he thought to himself, all that talk about fresh starts and forgiveness. He was up to something, that much was certain. Nevertheless, he had to convince Benson, who was too loyal for his own good. Why did he keep going on and on about taking those stupid rocks from Mercury? They weren't missing, they were right there next to the smelt, where Ryburn had left them, he could see the trolley from where he was standing.

Keeping one eye on the stairs he stepped into the smelt.

"Think I took it do you?" he said, lifting up the lid on the trolley to find it full of random looking rocks. "If I'm already doing the time I may as well do the fucking crime"

He spun the trolley around and pointed it toward the door. It made a horrible grinding noise as it went over the lip of the door frame, which made him stop and look toward the stairs, waiting for the sound of footsteps, but they never came. Something crunched under his left foot as he walked through the door and, whatever it was, his right foot connected with it sending it ricocheting along the edge of the floor into the dark corner of the room.

"You will never find these now," he muttered to himself as he left the work-sphere behind him; he knew the perfect place to put them.

O'Connor coughed as the cool, fresh air hit him as he entered the oxygen farm.

"Doyle," he called to the King John.

"They haven't moved yet, they are still in their rooms."

"It doesn't matter, he wasn't wearing his com."

"What happened?" asked Doyle

"I made things worse." He took a deep breath and slowly let it out trying to rid his mind of the guilt of his overreaction. His mind went back to the conversation his earlier self had just had with McSweeney outside the sleeping quarters, how they had made peace. He continued thinking about how it would all be perceived by McSweeney, how two-faced and vindictive it must have looked.

"I'm torturing the poor boy," he finally said, cutting the call.

He focused on the vibrant green of the room, ignoring the burnt-out areas of the plants and he let the tranquil ambience of the room wash over him as he continued his search; his mind still on McSweeney and his refusal to give up the rocks. He'd never known such stubbornness from him before; usually at the first serious accusation he would promptly fold and laugh it off, usually congratulating himself on yet another "classic" gag.

Maybe he realised that this time it was very serious. Yes that must have been it, O'Connor thought as he tipped up a large, empty drum to check the inside. Where could they be? He checked under the plant beds, inside the storage areas, under the plant mass, even up above the lighting canopies. Nothing!

"Doyle, they're not here either, I've searched everywhere," he said despairingly into his com.

"Okay not to worry, we'll try again after the airlock breach. It's time to come back."

"Okay, I'll have to leave via airlock-A, my earlier self has locked airlock-B," said O'Connor and, as he would be exiting on the far side of the station from where the King John was, he added, "How good is Anderson with that tether?"

"Eye of a needle," shouted a very confident Anderson in the background.

"No problem there, O'Connor," said Doyle.

"Right, look for me on the hull."

O'Connor left the hydroponics floor, and went straight to the airlock. He had ample time to get away before the breach, but did not want to drag his feet too much. He pulled one of the space suits down from its hanger and began to dress, before choosing his tank. The patched tank was there, which still seemed very wrong and unnatural. He grabbed an alternative that had an acceptable level of oxygen and continued suiting up. At last he was ready to go. The control screen for the airlock door flashed "Denied" as soon as he punched in his code. He tried again with the same result.

"I can't get out," he called to Doyle, the frustration clear in his voice as he was rejected for a third time. "My codes aren't working; this airlock must be locked down."

He remembered Benson saying something about the airlocks earlier. He had not really been listening and anyway for him it had been over a day ago. Which airlock did Benson put the lockdown precaution on? Damn it, he wasn't sure.

"I'm going to have to get to the other airlock," said O'Connor, as he started to divest himself of the helmet and air-tank, which would be too heavy to carry across the station.

"How?" Doyle asked. "Your earlier self locked it."

"I'll have to be in the decompression, it's the only way," O'Connor answered, barely believing his own words.

"You've only got five minutes and you have to be on the airlock side of those blast doors."

O'Connor kicked off the heavy boots and started to run as best he could with the heavy outfit, toward the central corridor. He got into a good rhythm, but it was hard work as the space suits had not been designed for running. At the end of the central corridor he slowed, determined that this corner would not take him by surprise like the previous one had. The way ahead was very dark but he focused on the white light of the prep area. He clipped his shoulder on a large equipment shell sending him off balance into another shell which wobbled precariously, but didn't fall.

He entered the prep area and tested his code. It did not work but he had expected that as his past self had already used the emergency procedures to lock them solid.

"You have about two minutes," advised Doyle, sounding even more desperate than he felt.

"Look out for me," said O'Connor. "This is going to be ugly."

The imminent decompression event was going to be violent and he knew he would need to secure himself until after the effects had dissipated. He pulled on a pair of boots and tested the magnetism but they were not strong enough to hold him during the breach. He grabbed himself a tank, noticing that there were now only two to choose from, neither of which were patched. Where had all the others gone?

He connected the tank and then the helmet before looking around for a moment. There was still no sign of anything that would cause decompression but suddenly remembered that towards the breach door was that wobbly frame. That would be big enough to block the entire corridor, giving him a good, solid anchor against a bulkhead. Even if he couldn't push it over he could climb inside it and avoid being crushed by all the other debris as it was ejected into space. He gave the ceiling a quick check to confirm he wouldn't block the breach door when it slammed shut before sizing up the hardware shell. He put a hard shoulder into it and pushed until it felt as though his eyes were going to pop under the strain. Finally, it reached its tipping point, catching the adjacent shell, causing it to slowly topple over and crash into the next. The sound proofing did nothing to stop the rhythmic clanging of metal as one by one the frames slowly fell into the each other.

His shell had fallen into place against the far wall and blocked the corridor off, just as he had hoped it would. It had even slid its way to the floor, scratching the wall beams as it fell, wedging itself deeper into place. This was the best he was going to get, but then it struck him, he was on the wrong side of it! How could he be so clever and then so stupid in the same plan?

The slow clanging noise of the dominoing frames continued, like the slow beat of a drum counting down to his doom. The noise was getting further away, toward Ryburn's workstation and if he was still sober and awake would be able to hear it. Nothing could be done about that now. If that didn't wake the whole crew the decompression alarms would.

With only ten seconds remaining O'Connor's eyes searched as best they could for another option. The frame was thick, very thick, but there were small gaps in the shelving, if he could thread some type of bar through one he could use that as his brace and hold onto it like the handles of a bike. He looked around for something suitable and remembered the lever from the manual lock. He could use that! Whatever purpose it was presently serving didn't matter as that lock was going to fail at any moment. He bent down as much as the suit would allow and released the lynch pin then pulled up on the lever setting it free. The moment the lever came off in his hand he realised what he had done. There had been no failure, no elaborate McSweeney plot; it had been him who had caused the decompression. That moment hung in the air for an eternity: it was always him. He turned and got back to the overturned equipment shell and threaded the lever through the gap in the shelf before pulling his feet up into the frame, locking his boots against the inner surface and holding on grimly. He heard the dull thud of the explosives firing in the airlock doors just before the air began to stream past him, and the flashing lights around him started. The frame was lifted up and he felt it jerk as the full decompression took hold. The frame shuddered but he held on, despite feeling his right shoulder pop;

the pain was intense, it seemed to engulf his whole body, but he couldn't let go.

Suddenly the maelstrom abated, replaced by the empty calm of space and zero gravity. The seconds before the blast doors had sealed him off from the station had seemed like forever. He took a deep breath, realising that he had been holding it throughout the event. Releasing the magnetic grip, he kicked his way out of the gaping hole where the airlock had been and looking around; he could see only big chunks of hull with torn inner mesh and a sea of floating equipment frames and debris.

"I've got you," said Anderson's cool and confident voice.

"Be careful, Andy," said Doyle.

The tether cable shot past him before going slack.

"Grab the line if you please," instructed Anderson.

O'Connor used the tether and returned to the King John without incident, remembering the refracting light this time. Before he could rise from the airlock floor, where the restoration of gravity had unceremoniously dumped him, Doyle and Anderson were there to help him.

"Are you okay?" asked Doyle frantically, almost dragging the helmet off of his head, causing his neck to bend at an awkward angle and almost lifting him off the floor. He couldn't hear a word Doyle was saying but the look on her face said it all. Anderson unwound the tether from O'Connor's arm and tidied it away.

"Are you okay?" Doyle asked again as she helped O'Connor up to a sitting position.

"I caused the decompression."

"I suspected as much," said Doyle softly.

"I had to; there was no other way out."

"Are you hurt?" asked Doyle again.

O'Connor couldn't help wincing as he tried to put weight on his arm.

"No, no I'm fine," said O'Connor, which earned him a raised eyebrow from Anderson who was conveniently standing behind Doyle where she couldn't see him.

"I'm fine," he said again to which Anderson shook his head, as if to say that was the wrong answer.

Doyle, who was fussing over O'Connor, spun around to Anderson who was the picture of innocence by that point. She stood up very quickly and let O'Connor slump back down.

"Andy, would you please help Chief O'Connor up?" said Doyle, her cheeks colouring as she suddenly busied herself with nothing. Anderson did what he was instructed.

"Easy, easy," said O'Connor wincing at the pressure on his damaged shoulder.

"Bit late for that now," said Anderson.

"Bit late for what?" Doyle questioned.

Anderson didn't answer, he just smiled.

"Right, I'll start the calculations for another trip back," said Doyle.

"I thought we were going to discuss it," said O'Connor, as firmly as possible whilst fighting off a grimace of pain as best he could as he got to his feet.

"Yes we will, but everything points to another trip back. You can't get back on the station, now can you?"

"Something you object to Andy?" she snapped.

"No, not at all, the best course of action, I agree," Anderson answered.

"Good, I will start the process, tell Radcliffe we'll be dining in one hour."

She left the room, the air of authority and awkward tension leaving with her.

"I've never seen her so turned around," said Anderson, with a hint of a cheeky grin as he helped O'Connor over to the bench.

"I think I've dislocated my shoulder," replied O'Connor, completely ignoring Anderson's comments.

"Okay, let's take a look," said Anderson as he helped O'Connor out of his bulky space suit.

Once his arm was clear the damage was apparent, the normal smooth curve of his shoulder was now ugly, flat and squared where the arm had been forced forward and had popped out of the socket. The horrible looking bulge was enough to make Anderson recoil.

"We'll get that fixed," said Anderson trying his best to not look at it.

"That's quite enough," said O'Connor, once his clean jumpsuit was on and pulled up as far as his waist, "Just double it round and tie it off. This really fucking hurts"

"Very well, if you wish to look like a cave man," said Anderson flinging him his undershirt, "but let's at least put this back on please."

O'Connor, begrudging, agreed – Doyle had explained it was the height of bad manners to not wear the jump suits correctly. Mankind had been living in space for a long time now and the custom probably started off as a necessity to wear it correctly but then social behaviours evolved from there.

O'Connor did not much care for the centre of the ship. It felt like a warehouse, messy and badly lit. The medical room was through one of the many doors that led off the central hall. The lights turned on automatically as the door slid slowly open. They were bright enough to make him squint although Anderson, with his 'modified' eyes, didn't react to the sudden change.

"Didn't you have to tell Radcliffe about dinner?" asked O'Connor, doing his best to sound concerned. In truth he wasn't hungry now, just anxious about what was going to happen next.

"We eat at the same time every day," Anderson said dismissively before cheekily adding. "You've really got her turned around."

"He's quite the chef isn't he," said O'Connor, changing the subject.

"If you say so, it all comes from the same tube," said Anderson.

"Tube? You mean it is synthetic?" asked O'Connor.

"Not all of it, some of the vegetables are real," said Anderson.

"If you could please sit down in the chair," he then said, directing O'Connor to the very uncomfortable looking unpadded chair. "I'll need to..." pausing for a moment to recheck the information on the screen "...perform a diagnostic scan."

"Suspected dislocated shoulder," said Anderson after consulting another display. He unclipped his wrist from the desk and lowered down from the ceiling a large tubular device, pointing the end at the injured shoulder.

"Don't move," said Anderson, concentrating on the equipment. Once he appeared to be happy with the exact positioning he returned to the display to read aloud the next few steps on the list. Intermittent frowns of confusion did not fill O'Connor with confidence, as Anderson read aloud some of the steps until he understood their meaning.

"I think I've got his now," he proclaimed as he opened up another window on the screen and started pressing icons and moving dials. O'Connor heard the machine above his head begin to hum.

"Yes, dislocated shoulder, a serious muscle tear. Minor tendon damage."

"Can you fix it?" O'Connor asked. He didn't want to be out of action for a week or more when they still had things to do.

"Of course I can," said Anderson, the response suggesting that he took offence at the question, as if he had been asked if he could read. He pulled the device into a more central position in front of O'Connor.

"I have to measure your exact metabolism and exact constitution."

"What for?" asked O'Connor, sitting up as if to allow the device a clearer view of his chest.

"I'm not an expert at this, you understand," Anderson began, "so I don't know exactly what it measures, but it is so the auto-chemist can mix up an exact dose for you."

"Right," said O'Connor. It all sounded over his head too, but he wanted the pain to stop.

"Twenty minutes should be enough, apparently," said Anderson after once again consulting the instructions on his screen.

"Twenty minutes?" O'Connor inquired.

"The effects of the shot will last for twenty minutes but the procedure should only take two."

"You can be that exact?" O'Connor asked in amazement.

"Well, yes," Anderson answered, again like he was stating the obvious.

"So why give me twenty minutes' worth?"

O'Connor was a little cautious about drugs after McSweeney had drugged him unconscious.

"Because it says so here," Anderson said, pointing to the angled screen that O'Connor couldn't see.

Anderson began to work with the auto-chemist apparatus. It had a dozen or so input tubes all of a different colour which looked like it should have had a tidy covering to hide them from sight. As he worked at the controls the output collection tube slowly began to fill.

"Sorry about the needle," said Anderson as he pressed it through the side of the collection membrane, slowly and carefully extracting a small and exact amount of the liquid.

O'Connor tried to get a better look, his immediate thought was that of some ridiculously cartoon style plunger. He wasn't scared of needles, just wasn't sure what to expect from anything like this. The needle was of normal size, easily fitting in a hand, whilst the concoction inside was bright orange, a colour he'd seen before. The syringe looked strangely familiar too. It was McSweeney's syringe!

"Are they always that colour?" O'Connor asked.

"Yes, I think so."

"And you don't use all of it?"

"No, all of that would knock you out for hours," Anderson replied. "This amount will last twenty minutes and only on the area around the injection."

"Can you refill the syringe when you are done? I think I'm going to be needing it."

"Whatever for?" Anderson asked.

"I think I got doped with it earlier."

"Earlier? I've just made it…" said Anderson. "Oh. You know what? I don't want to know; it will only give me a headache. Let's take care of that shoulder first."

Anderson checked the instructions on the screen again before picking a spot on O'Connor shoulder. He pierced the skin just above the grotesque bulge where the ball of the shoulder was now resting.

"Here we go," said Anderson as he shot one final glance over to the instructions.

The injection was effective almost immediately and O'Connor's arm had gone so numb it felt like it wasn't there at all, no dead lump feeling and no tingling. Nothing.

He could now explain the reaction he had had to McSweeney's injection and it made sense why it had knocked him out so efficiently. It was a cocktail tailored specifically just for him.

His mind took him back to that moment: he was angry at McSweeney for lying about the rocks; had swung for him but collapsed to the floor in a heap, then taken a kicking from McSweeney, but those words that he'd first dismissed now stuck in his head. McSweeney had accused him of engineering the conflict between them, "setting it all up" were McSweeney's words. That accusation didn't sound so ridiculous now, all things considered. When the drugs had worn off he was in the airlock and in a space suit… that part didn't make any sense, if McSweeney had intended to kill him why put him in a suit?

Anderson had pulled down yet another device and clamped it around O'Connor's dead limb to begin the procedure. O'Connor knew what was going on under the hard casing. His arm was to be stretched out and popped back into its correct position.

"All done," said Anderson as he removed the apparatus and let it recoil back up to the ceiling.

"I can't move it," said O'Connor.

"You've still got a good eighteen minutes before the effects wear off," said Anderson looking very proud of himself. He lifted O'Connor's arm up and let it flop back down again.

"What about the rest of the dosage?" O'Connor reminded, not at all impressed by Anderson's actions.

"Yeah, sure," said Anderson, but he hesitated for a moment as he got the needle into position to gather up the rest of the concoction. "Do you want all of it or an exact amount?"

"I honestly don't think it matters," said O'Connor after pondering the question for a moment or two. "I'm sure whatever you extract will be the correct amount."

"What type of answer is that?" asked Anderson, looking bewildered.

"Doyle's theory," was O'Connor's answer.

"Well put," Anderson said. "She'll like that. Okay the whole lot then."

He extracted all of the liquid. After putting a small protective cap on the sharp end he handed it to O'Connor.

"Thanks," said O'Connor, who had intended to reach out with his bad arm, but it was still unresponsive, the result was a funny looking twitch of his upper body.

"Another fifteen minutes at least," said Anderson with a laugh, placing it closer to O'Connor's good arm.

"Very funny," said O'Connor. "Are there any other side effects I should know about?"

"Let's take a look," said Anderson, consulting the screen. "It makes you highly suggestible. Slap your face!"

O'Connor laughed at the absurd suggestion, before he realised he had already raised his good arm. Luckily he was able to stop himself before he slapped himself in the face.

"Must be wearing off," said Anderson but O'Connor was not amused.

All feeling and control of his arm had returned by the time O'Connor sat down for a quick snack, although the movement was laboured since there was a very deep ache in the muscle around the joint. The dining room wasn't very elaborate and looked old and very lived in. There were some old art works hanging on the wall and a scenescape of some planet with two moons looking out over a nebular that caught his eye. His knowledge of space geography was however, limited to the current system at best, so he had no idea where the planet was. The table was of an old Earth tradition and appeared to be made from wood, or at least a very convincing imitation.

"It's a fake," said Doyle, as O'Connor ran his fingers along the grain.

"I couldn't tell. I haven't seen real wood since I was a boy," he replied, still marvelling at the workmanship. He would have thought it an odd piece to have on a spaceship, but it looked like it was always meant to be here nestled in among the plants and flowers that surrounded the room.

"Are all the trees already gone in this time?" asked Anderson.

"No, they are still there; I've just been in space a long time."

It sounded sad in his own ears to hear himself say it, but the longing in his new crew mates' eyes told him it was something they knew all about. Except their longing came from generation upon generation stuck in space; a life on Earth to them was a dream. O'Connor didn't care much for a life planet side, he was always more comfortable in space, but deep down knew he'd go back to it one day. Not anymore though, it was a sombre realisation.

"There is a forest project on Cluster in some of the older orbs," Anderson said, "but they are still young trees. And even when they are of age I doubt they will be used for tables."

"What are we doing?" O'Connor asked, puzzled by the relaxed atmosphere. They had urgent things to attend to, but by the looks of it they were about to sit down to a banquet. He did not object to the thought of food, just thought that a quick bite and back to work seemed more appropriate.

"We're having our evening meal," said Doyle.

"But, shouldn't we be getting back?" asked O'Connor feeling that all the urgency of the mission had now gone.

"We can't do anything until the calculations are done," she replied. "The past isn't going anywhere."

O'Connor opened his mouth for a rebuttal, but nothing came to him that would counter Doyle's logic. He conceded that it was a valid point.

O'Connor still felt on edge, it felt as if reality had been paused allowing them a brief time out. It was a waiting of a different kind.

"It is important that we keep the traditions of old dining," said Doyle. O'Connor was staring at the yet to be uncovered steaming serving tray Radcliffe had just brought in and placed in the centre of the table he had laid modestly with cutlery and crockery which were plain and worn.

"Yes, we must keep hold of the past," O'Connor agreed, without any real conviction, his eyes fixed on the tray, since breakfast was but a distant memory. All his senses seemed to trigger simultaneously when Radcliffe uncovered the tray. It was roast meat of some type, beef or mutton perhaps, golden brown and glazed with roasted potatoes around the base. Every dish that Radcliffe uncovered was a revelation. Every vegetable that he knew of was there, but there were at least a dozen he did not recognise. A full rainbow of colours soon covered the table and the smell was intoxicating; an actual feast.

"The potatoes are real," said Radcliffe in his monotone and then continued by offering commentary on each dish pointing out the food that was "real" and the food that was "synthetic".

"And the meat?" said O'Connor as if he had been hungry all his life.

"I understand it is called Beef," Radcliffe answered.

"Synthetic," added Doyle.

"Root vegetables are commonly grown, potatoes mainly. Always plenty of them," said Anderson.

"So what is it really then?" O'Connor asked

"An extract from carefully constructed wheat and soy, with vital minerals and vitamins added."

They are just fancied up meal bags thought O'Connor.

"Anything we don't eat goes back in the tube and will be reprocessed," continued Doyle.

"That's disgusting," said O'Connor.

"It's recycling," said Doyle, "we can't afford to waste anything."

"Nothing is wasted," repeated Anderson, with a suggestive and cruel look on his face.

"I don't want to know," said O'Connor with a very uncomfortable laugh; he truly didn't want to know the full story of where his food came from. It was all he could do to stop his mind wandering to what other things were being recycled.

Radcliffe served the meal.

"Yeah, let's try some fake meat," said O'Connor, when Radcliffe reached him. He lifted up a small piece on the end of his fork and gave it a good sniff. It smelled delicious. *Just a meal bag* he reminded himself as he put it into his mouth. It tasted strange yet familiar as he sunk his teeth into it and started to chew. A bit stronger than what he remembered beef to be like, the taste was there though: rich and deep.

"So what other animals can you synthesise?" he said after he finished the mouthful.

"You name it," said Doyle, who was also eating, although with a touch more decorum than O'Connor. "Honestly, everything can be synthesised. The traditional livestock patterns are widely distributed, but the more exotic patterns are kept for those higher up in society."

"Do you have any real animals?" asked O'Connor, curious about the future.

"There is a living archive of some animals on Cluster," said Anderson.

Radcliffe was now making his way around the table with a white plastic jug of wine, filling everyone's glass up, including his own. The wine was good, thick and aromatic. *Fake*, he thought, *obviously*.

"Cluster?" asked O'Connor who had heard them mention it several times. "That's your city?"

"Yes. It's the central city of all humanity now," Anderson answered.

"More like a central prison," said Doyle, "and not all of humanity, just those of us under the heel of the Dynasty."

"What is Cluster exactly then?" O'Connor asked with genuine interest. Doyle began her history lesson as they all ate; even Radcliffe sat down at the end of the table to eat.

"Cluster is a gathering of the very large metropolis-class exodus orbs that left Earth. They were enormous arks, big enough to support hundreds of thousands of people, but they were slow." Doyle paused for a sip of her wine. "After they failed to find any liveable worlds, the generation of the day lost hope and decided to end the search and form a cluster with some of the other orbs, thus creating a central base."

O'Conner could not help noticing that the way she spoke made the story sound like a tragedy.

"All the orbs in agreement joined together at the Lagrange point between a large gas giant and its star."

"A what point?" asked Anderson.

"A point in space between two objects where their gravity is equal," said O'Connor.

"Quite right," Doyle continued. "They thought the light from the star was enough to sustain the chard levels, and the smashed up remains of an iron rich rocky planet in the system allowed mining and the on-going expansion of the cluster. Over time, some of the later orbs caught up, gave up their own searches and began to congregate in the same system. A docking ring was constructed and it was affectionately named after a planet in the original solar system because of its visual similarity."

"Saturn?" O'Connor asked.

Doyle nodded. "Saturn Cluster City, and that is where most

of known humanity now live."

"Doesn't sound so bad," said O'Connor, sinking his teeth into another glorious potato.

"Well, that was before the Dynasty truly took it over and aggressively started hunting down the other orbs who wanted no part of this false home," said Doyle. "But we can save the nasty part of history for another time," she said, returning to her meal briefly before continuing.

"You see the star they chose was older than they thought, and wasn't putting out as much chard as they expected. Over the years the reserves slowly, very slowly began to run out. Now we get just enough chard to keep the lights on."

"An energy crisis," said O'Connor in disappointment. "Sounds like some things will never change."

"Indeed," Doyle continued. "So the Dynasty came up with the Majoris project, a mission to gather up an impossibly large amount of chard from a star going nova and bring the energy back to Cluster."

"Sounds like a good plan," said O'Connor.

"It was an excellent plan," said Doyle. "I was a senior member of the team, and we executed it flawlessly."

"So what happened?"

"Their intentions were always to use the energy to maintain their dominance. There won't be another Majoris-sized nova again and that energy would be the only chance for mankind to escape that dead system. The Dynasty weren't going to take the opportunity so I took it instead, literally."

There was fire in her voice, and passion for her cause of freeing a humanity that didn't know it was trapped.

"So here we are," Doyle finished. "We've come back for an ore sample, so we can analyse it and then go back and find more so we can start the second exodus."

"The second exodus," Anderson proclaimed raising his glass, but Doyle just gave him a long-suffering look and continued.

"It's seems quite an elaborate gamble," said O'Connor,

wondering what could have possibly been the chain of events that led them to the point where stealing the light harvest and time travelling was the best option left.

"That's why we won't be going back empty-handed. We will take back hope to them all," finished Doyle indicating that no further discussion was required. "The calculations will be ready by morning; we aren't finished here yet."

"For those who have made sacrifices," said Anderson. This time Doyle did raise her glass and they shared a quiet moment, one that O'Connor did not want to intrude upon by asking for its meaning.

O'Connor reached across the table to gather up another helping; this prompted Radcliffe to stand up but O'Connor indicated for him to sit back down.

"Returning to the ore; you don't want the refined type, you need raw?"

"Yes, that's right." Doyle picked up the conversation and started to explain the chemical composition of what they knew about the ore but the very blank look on O'Connor's face cut her explanation short. "Yes, that's right," she repeated, a touch embarrassed.

"Could I not just get that by-product instead?"

"No, Sir Ryburn gave you the last raw sample. We will wait for that."

"But how can you be sure?" O'Connor asked.

"Doyle's Law," said Anderson jokingly.

"Doyle's what?" Asked Doyle, putting her fork down and looking at Anderson.

"No, this is different," said O'Connor. "You don't know for certain that what Ryburn gives me will give me the last rock sample. We can't be certain!" looking for Anderson for backup on this, then a look to Radcliffe who was looking as stoic as ever.

"What is Doyle's Law?" Doyle asked after the very long moment of silence.

"He said it," said Anderson, throwing O'Connor into the

firing line.

O'Connor gave an awkward cough as Doyle's eyes just widened with anticipation, or condemnation, he wasn't quite sure.

"It's your explanation for cause and effect being the wrong way around," said O'Connor.

Doyle raised her eyesbrows looking very unimpressed.

"When our actions are guided by the reactions, when you can't change what you already have done?" she said.

O'Connor nodded and Anderson jokingly leaned away and covered his head as if distancing himself from an impending explosion.

"I like it," she said as she returned to her meal.

Anderson looked up from his braced position. Radcliffe continued slowly eating, chewing his food, without the slightest bit of emotion.

"So, Radcliffe," said O'Connor. "Do you have a first name, or a last name?"

"Just Radcliffe, Mr O'Connor," Radcliffe responded after placing his knife and fork down very gently and gracefully either side of his plate.

"*Just* Radcliffe?" O'Connor asked.

"That's right," Anderson interjected. "In fact, that may not even be his real name."

"You don't know your real name?" asked O'Connor, finding it astonishing that anyone might not.

Radcliffe, who had just picked up his knife and fork again, returned them to their place on the table.

"Part of the indentation process, I'm afraid Mr O'Connor. I don't recall anything about my life."

"So why are you called Radcliffe?" he continued to probe.

"You will answer to the name Radcliffe, and you will serve your term upon the spacefaring vessel The Caution of King John," Radcliffe said, in the tone of someone repeating something by rote.

"Fascinating," said O'Connor, amazed by the concept. "So,

what actually happened to him?" he continued directing the question at Doyle or Anderson.

"Briefly, a series of shunts are surgically inserted into the criminal's brain, blocking the long-term memory off from the consciousness," answered Doyle. "There is a mental conditioning process they go through afterwards to prevent them from being exploited."

"You mean they're brainwashed to not allow themselves to be used as criminals," O'Connor said, remembering how Radcliffe would not assist them to remove the beacon earlier.

"Good form, that's it exactly," said Doyle. "He can't be an accomplice."

"And he serves you?" O'Connor continued, not sure how that fitted with Doyle's self-confessed energy theft.

"He serves the ship and whoever is on it," said Doyle "He was already here and was a part of the purchase agreement. That is quite unusual actually, indents usually serve the family they have wronged or are sold as labour."

"Slaves!" said O'Connor, outraged.

"No, not slaves; criminals serving their time," Doyle corrected.

"And how much time does he have left of his sentence?" O'Connor asked, he had cleared his plate now and wasn't going to be having any more.

"We don't know," she said.

"And neither does he. Watch," said Anderson. "Radcliffe, what happens at the end of your sentence?"

"I will provide seven days' notice that my sentence is ending," said Radcliffe, after placing his knife and fork down. "After that, the indentation will conclude and I will return to society rehabilitated and my penance paid in full."

"Yes thank you Andy," said Doyle who, like O'Connor, did not like seeing Radcliffe answer like a trained monkey. "Radcliffe, you may clear the table."

She placed her knife and fork in the centre of her plate. O'Connor and Anderson did the same.

"Very good, Miss Doyle," Radcliffe answered with a nod, before standing up, collecting the plates and clearing everything away.

"Is there anything in your history that could help us out?" asked O'Connor, as Radcliffe cleared the table. "I want to know why they didn't bother looking for me."

"The final account says you were lost in space and they couldn't find you."

"There's a very simple explanation for that," Doyle said, putting down her glass, "All historical accounts of you stopped after you were blasted out of that airlock."

O'Connor and Anderson both nodded.

"Well, the reason you completely disappeared without trace is because we got to you first," she said.

It was obvious after all, O'Connor nodded and a moment later Anderson understood too.

"The part in the history that will help us is what we're waiting for. According to Sir Ryburn, he gave you the ore."

"But we already know he didn't," said O'Connor.

"Perhaps," said Doyle, clearly not convinced about that.

"Did it ever cross your mind to get Ryburn instead?" asked O'Connor. "He would at least be able to help you find another Mercury in your time."

"I did consider Sir Ryburn, but there isn't a single point in his life after Neith that isn't accounted for. We know that his institute housed some ore for research purposes, but the security would have been ridiculous. No, right here, right now is the only chance we have for getting hold of it, and that chance was saving you to get the ore you didn't have."

"Did you think about going back to get Professor Chard? He would surely be of help, wouldn't he?"

"As much as it pains me to say it," said Doyle "Andy here knows more about optimising chardage now than its discoverer ever did."

Anderson beamed with pride, although O'Connor wasn't

sure how much of a compliment it had been.

"Fully harnessing the power of the light particles was an evolutionary process," Doyle explained, "and it's still ongoing even in our time, finding ways to collect more, scrape out more energy."

"We don't have enough chard stored to go back that far and still make it home." Anderson pointed out with a look of concern, as if Doyle were actually considering it.

"I wouldn't mind retiring to the past," said O'Connor, not being able to return to their bleak future didn't sound so bad. "Can't you just make me a little opening for me to jump through?"

"It's not just about creating the opening; it's about the wormhole beyond the opening too," said Doyle. "The focus point needs to be perfect. Too weak and you get nothing, too strong and the consequences don't bear thinking about."

O'Connor was about to speak but Doyle thundered right on.

"It's not as simple as just passing through it; the singularity needs to be of a certain size and strength. That size and strength determines the depth of the wormhole. We need to make it a certain age to ensure we come out at the right point in space, and we age it with chardage."

"Chardage that we don't have much of," Anderson snuck in.

"Chardage that we don't have," Doyle agreed, flicking Anderson a congratulatory glance. "And what if the other end opens inside a star? What if the gravity on the other side isn't balanced? Catastrophe is what happens!"

"If it's so dangerous, why did you risk coming back in the first place?" asked O'Connor, not trying to start an argument but merely wanting to understand the desperation behind the act.

"Because without this risk, mankind continues to wither and die, stuck on Cluster, stuck with the Dynasty and trapped in that worthless dead system, waiting for the last light to flicker out forever."

"So how does it work?" O'Connor asked.

"You know that everything in the universe is moving right?"

He nodded.

"We need to know exactly where to make the other end of the wormhole, so we need to know how old to make the singularity."

"And the time?" O'Connor asked.

"Time is depth," Doyle answered.

"Hang on, you just said-"

Doyle interrupted. "I know what I said, but that is how it works, the further you need to go in distance the older you need to make it, you want to travel back in time you make it deeper."

"What about size? What does changing that do?"

"Size is irrelevant to the process," she continued. "To establish the time we just need to know how deep."

"And that's where your dome calculations come in?" said O'Connor.

"Yes, because we only know a relative location. We need to know the exact spacial location. We work out where your relative destination actually was in space at the intended time and those, Chief O'Connor, are the bases for the calculations."

"So how do you travel forwards through time?" O'Connor asked, after a gulp of his wine.

"Same process, but you make the exit point first then invert it. Like the telescopes on the water ocean boats of your time."

"Those haven't been used for hundreds of years," O'Connor scoffed. It was a good reminder that there were at least *some* things he knew that Doyle didn't.

"Forwards is an even bigger gamble…"

"What?" Anderson suddenly drifted back into the conversation.

"Forwards into the unknown," Doyle rephrased. "We know where our future origin is so we can go back, but past, that becomes..." she paused while she searched for the best word "…foggy. Without a fixed point in space that we know about, how could we ever expect to get to where we wanted to go? Everything is revolving around something and moving around at ridiculous speeds. There are way too many factors to consider:

faint gravitational pulls from this, slight solar waves from that, supernovas explode, new black holes form. All of this has effects on the path that any planet, system, galaxy, cluster, and super cluster takes through space. Short journeys, two maybe three centuries, are all that's possible. Anything further is too dangerous."

"How do we get back then?" said Anderson, unfortunately not following.

"Because we know where we're aiming. It isn't our future; it's the future from now." O'Connor answered.

"If only we had more chard. We could go anywhere then," said Anderson forlornly.

"And to what end?" asked Doyle. "What would going anywhere accomplish?"

Anderson had no answer for that. But then his face lit up with excitement

"What if we used what we have now to travel to the point when the burning sun got angry?" said Anderson. "Would that give us some more options?"

"Assuming we do, which we won't, and assuming that the particles are numerous and potent, which they won't be, how could we collect it with the intakes burnt out?"

"Oh yeah," said Anderson.

"Anyway, that doesn't change what we're doing now: we will travel back to yesterday and O'Connor will start again, we get the rocks then we go home."

She said it, but she didn't sound convinced.

"Can't we cut our losses and just go back now?" Anderson asked. "We already have the calculations prepared."

"Okay then, let's start that then, let's jump back to just before all this happened, we can pretend we went down with the ship."

"Really?" Anderson perked up.

"No," Doyle said, with a tone that said it was an absurd suggestion.

"Why not?" Anderson asked.

"Because we don't," Doyle said. "Creating the hole and travelling that far into the future would create some crazy measurements in the Neith systems."

"So?" Anderson grunted, it was his only retort.

"There was nothing in the historical account that mentioned anything like that on any of the Neith sensors," Doyle explained, her logic sound.

"What does that matter? They say they were faulty anyway."

"It matters because it means we didn't or rather don't travel back until long after Sir Ryburn flew them to a safe distance," said Doyle. O'Connor understood that even if Anderson didn't.

"That doesn't mean we can't go now though," said Anderson.

"No it doesn't mean we can't, it means we didn't and that means we don't. Besides, there is no way I'm going back empty-handed after everything we've done to get here. And let's not forget that we have already seen two more versions of us out there! We don't because we didn't."

"To Doyle's Law," said O'Connor, raising his glass.

"You sure you want to go back to our time when we're done?" Anderson asked. "I mean there will be questions about the battery ship and what happened to all the energy, they will have people looking for us."

Doyle shrugged. "We'll worry about that when we get back. This is a once in a... in a... well, ever chance. No, we're going to do what we came here to do. People are depending on us. It will not all be for nothing, I promise you."

She placed a comforting hand on top of Anderson's.

Something must have gone very wrong, O'Connor was sure of it now, but again he didn't want to intrude.

The three of them chatted some more about Cluster while Radcliffe went about his duties. Doyle gave a very rough run down of the class system that she objected to strongly. She explained how each orb had an elected council office, which she said were all corrupt anyway. The senior members of the Dynasty were effectively a royal family running the entire city with the so called council there to take up minor matters and keep the peace. To O'Connor, it sounded very strange compared to the Earth he'd come from.

She spoke of the re-allocation and re-purposing of orbs under the more favoured members of the council. How they had slowly been stripping out entire orbs to create super dense farming areas for crops, super dense living areas, super dense everything as the population increased and the energy ran out.

They spoke well into the night in their stolen moment of time. Despite being hundreds of years apart O'Connor and Doyle found they had a lot in common. Doyle had O'Connor at a disadvantage though as it turned out that his life story had been thoroughly researched and documented after the Neith incident. O'Connor found out some more about Doyle: that she was very opinionated but her opinions agreed with his, for the most part. O'Connor was slowly coming around to the fact that Ryburn was to become a great man, shame the history books didn't have a lot to say about him before his invention. They spoke of their childhoods, their families. O'Connor spoke about losing his parents at a young age and being adopted and raised by a family friend. He spoke of how his adopted father encouraged him to seek a career in space. Doyle had antecedents who were born on one of the original exodus orbs that joined Cluster city, which was just before her grandfather on her mother's side was born. Her family went back many generations on both sides before she had an ancestor on Earth. Knowing your lineage was very important it seemed. O'Connor and Doyle barely noticed when Anderson slipped away to retire for the evening. Radcliffe continued to pop in and out asking if they had everything they needed, offering more wine when the wine jug was low, but his visits stopped when he finally retired for the night.

CHAPTER 15: ALREADY BEEN DONE

O'Connor was woken by Radcliffe knocking lightly at his door.

"Mr O'Connor," came Radcliffe's voice. "Miss Doyle has sent me to collect you, and I've brought you some refreshment, if I could please enter."

"Yes, please come in," yawned O'Conner as he got out of bed and sat down at the table, his mouth very dry. He could taste the built up of muck that had accumulated overnight in the corners of his mouth, but above all he had a terrible headache; perhaps it was one too many glasses of wine. The rough and chipped jug of water was therefore the first thing he reached for and not bothering with the formalities of using a cup, he downed the contents in one.

"Sorry," he said to Radcliffe, whose face was as blank as ever, but somehow displayed a disapproving look as he lifted from the tray a tiny silver domed cover to reveal a small paper cup and two small pills.

"Miss Doyle said you may be needing these."

"Did she now?" said O'Connor with a smile, and after swallowing the pills said "Thank you." A second later, his body shivered and his headache was gone; in fact all the alcohol related aches left him. *Ryburn could make use of these*, he thought to himself

After politely seeking permission, Radcliffe left, leaving O'Connor still wondering why he instinctively disliked him. He took a very quick shower, got dressed, and made his way to the dome. The sky view still glittered with all the trajectories and colour mapping of everything within its range. Doyle and Anderson were already there. O'Connor had been hoping to see her dishevelled, or at least with some effect from the previous night, but not a hair was out of place. She did not even look tired and was as tidy and well presented as always.

"Sorry I'm late," said O'Connor, with a well-timed stretch of his arms, doing his best to suppress a yawn as he spoke. "I must have overslept."

"I wouldn't worry about that; your metabolism will catch up soon enough," said Doyle.

"Eventually you will only need three to four hours sleep like us," said Anderson, "Part of the diet."

Doyle had mentioned the diet the previous evening, when the hour had got very late and O'Connor was being macho by not wanting to go to bed until she did.

"I only got four hours sleep as it is," said O'Connor with an "anything you can do…" expression but was then distracted seeing the Neith fully intact.

"We've already come back?" he exclaimed, to which Doyle only nodded as she was looking intently at the telemetry displayed on the screen.

She had already mapped where their first past selves would be, the white wire frame hanging in space around the first King John, whilst on the opposite side of the station a green wire frame indicated the position of the second King John.

"That's our last selves," she said, taking her eyes away from her screen and pointing up at the ceiling.

"So I'm now my third?" O'Connor asked, to be sure he understood this new numerical nicknaming.

"Yes," said Doyle, her eyes back on the screen working very intently, "we all are third now."

"Welcome to King John the Third," said Anderson, with a mockingly deep bow and twirl of his arm, as if announcing his majesty to the court. This earned him a couple of long-suffering shakes of the head.

"So what's the plan?" said O'Connor, clapping his hands together. He was quite excited about it this time around since he not only knew what to expect but had an actual plan for getting the ore. He was going to tag his original self with the tracking tag he had found in his pocket, then tag the ore trolley to track it to wherever it was hiding. He had to stop his past self attacking McSweeney too. He was not so sure about that part, it certainly did not feel like the type of thing he would do, but Doyle did not need to know that. That would be a perfect opportunity to change the past, or not change it. All he would have to do was nothing and the earlier self would take care of the rest.

"There's been a new development," said Doyle, in a tone that did not inspire confidence. "The second O'Connor has already gone back over."

"Okay?" said O'Connor, elongating the word to make it a question.

"Our plan was to have you go back and slip this tag onto your original self."

"Yes that's right, my first will be sleeping, and I just need to avoid my second taking my wrist com," said O'Connor confident that it would work. He had hoped to be able to get over there before his second self, but that was just a minor detail.

"Well, that's already happened," she said, as if somehow it was his fault. She pointed to the ceiling where two solid blue lights were showing two locations for the one tag. Once for the first O'Connor and again for the second O'Connor, who wasn't yet aware he was carrying it.

"But how?" O'Connor asked. "What's that one?" he continued, pointing to another solid light just down from airlock-B, next to the external collection hub where Ryburn would be collecting his rocks. He realised that that light must be the tag he had not attached to the trolley yet and he turned to face Doyle who was now holding another tag she had attached to some adhesive sheeting, obviously meant for attaching to the trolley. She had an even less impressed expression on her face now. "You aren't going to be there to stop your second self from getting McSweeney either."

"Does that mean he won't be stopped?" O'Connor said, not doing a very convincing job of hiding his excitement.

"Oh we don't need to worry about that," she said, having already got it all worked out.

"So now what?" asked O'Connor, this time needing an answer.

Anderson looked up from his busy work as if to say something, but obviously thought better of it.

"We know that there is going to be yet another version of us here, and we think they send us some data for something," said Doyle.

"For what, and how do you know this?" O'Connor asked.

"Andy's beacon echoes," she replied, but the bewildered look she received back from O'Connor must have told her further explanation was needed.

"When it was time," she continued, "for the echoes, for just a moment we saw two other King Johns. This means that their beacons must have been deliberately reactivated."

"Where are they now?" O'Connor asked, forgetting that it had not happened yet.

"One of them will be us," she said, then added for clarity, "well, *both* of them will be us, but we have to be one of them before we can be the other. One of them was where we are now, and the other one was there," she said, pointing out to an area of space. They all stared out into space.

"Are they there now?" asked O'Connor.

"It is quite possible," she said with a nod showing she was very seriously considering all the options. A sudden chill ran down O'Connor's spine. It was a very uncomfortable feeling knowing that you are being watched and the knowledge that it was only themselves doing the watching did nothing to ease the sensation. An atmosphere of uncertainty and disappointment hung heavy in the air - they did not have a plan.

O'Connor had been looking for the blips on the ceiling display that would have represented the location of the Neith crew, but of course Second O'Connor hadn't asked them to increase their coms range yet. The only tracking information they had was for his two earlier selves and the stationary ore trolley. The Second O'Connor had just cleared the airlock and was heading for the sleeping quarters to take the com from his first self.

"We've been running the light refractors for too long," said Doyle after what had seemed like an eternity of silence. "We're going to need to offline them and discharge the build-up."

"Won't that make us visible to everyone?" queried O'Connor.

"Like who?" asked Doyle, the tone of her voice showing that she was still very annoyed at their current predicament and his question didn't help. "Our first and second selves don't see us because we didn't when we were them. Our fourth selves, if it is them and if they are even there, know we're here." Her voice went into a cute high pitch that would have made O'Connor smile if he weren't doing his absolute best to suppress it.

"What about Ryburn? He woke me up about now with the mention of seeing something in space." He turned to Anderson, "Can you zoom in on that window?" Anderson complied.

"Is that..." Anderson asked, at a loss for words.

"That's Sir Ryburn," said Doyle in astonishment as a clear view of Ryburn, looking around the window, appeared on the ceiling display. "What is he looking for?"

"I think he's looking for Earth, or Mars," said O'Connor. "I'm not sure"

"But they are in the opposite direction," said Doyle.

"He said he saw something out of that window, that's why he called everyone."

Doyle's face lit up with anticipation, her hand hovering over the system discharge command.

"Do it!" Anderson urged her.

"There!" she said a moment later, "it's done."

"Did he see us?" Anderson asked.

"He would have only seen a flicker of a distortion, he would not know it was anything," said Doyle.

"He's lifting up his communicator," said Anderson like a child on his birthday, "he's going to say something!"

"Everyone, I saw something outside," came the sound of Ryburn's voice, coming through both O'Connor's com and the spare com on the bench. Anderson and Doyle froze. Ryburn's voice continued, sounding shaken. "I saw something outside, away from planet, out into space. I was looking out from the fourth inner X junction just a few seconds ago and it was close. Can anyone confirm this?"

"I have nothing Dr Ryburn," came Benson's voice. "I've got no alarms on the proximity sensors, I'm still seeing your hopper coming in, are you sure it wasn't that?"

Doyle and Anderson stood completely still, not even breathing.

"They can't hear us, unless we transmit," said O'Connor, putting them both at ease.

"No, Benson, this was the complete other way. It must have been close," Ryburn continued.

"He's talking about us!" said Anderson, quite excited and his face beaming with pride, "Sir Ryburn saw us."

"Okay okay, so what was it you think you saw?" said Benson.

"Well," Ryburn began, then a silence just long enough for Doyle to make rolling gesture with her hands as if to say "is that it?", but Ryburn's voice continued. "It was like something was there but I couldn't see it."

"I can't believe that he actually saw us!" said Anderson, but Doyle had her finger to her lips in an instant.

"So let me get this straight," came another voice. "You make a priority one call to tell us you didn't see anything?"

"That's McSweeney, quite the laugh he had," Doyle whispered, Anderson beamed with excitement.

"And you want us to confirm that?" asked McSweeney, after he'd finished his fake laugh.

"I saw something. This is serious." said Ryburn, sounding demanding now. "O'Connor are you hearing this? Please respond."

"Dr Ryburn," said the first O'Connor, "I'll look into it once my shift starts. O'Connor out."

"Thank you O'Connor, your support is appreciated. Ryburn out."

"I never heard that last part," O'Connor whispered to Doyle and Anderson.

"How did you know what was said if you never heard it?" asked Anderson, trying to be clever.

"My second self is outside the sleeping-quarters door listening right now."

"It's amazing," said Doyle. "All this time we were always there and were always part of it."

Anderson looked as though he might faint with pride.

"Yes, yes it was a touching moment for us all," said O'Connor, a little disappointed that the novelty of him being there had worn off.

"We'd better change the signals of our coms," said O'Connor, realising that they needed to change it to be able to continue talking without intercepting the conversation of their previous selves. He undid the access casing on each of the wrist coms, whilst showing a very unimpressed and uninterested Anderson what he was doing. "Watch, this needs to be exact or it won't work," he said. "You just generate a new random ID seed using this." He pointed to a couple of small pressure pads underneath yet another small flip panel.

Anderson put his hand over his mouth and a garbled and distorted noise came out, he was using his cybernetic voice encryption device to hide what he was saying.

"What did you say?" asked O'Connor.

"He was making fun of the technology," said Doyle. "Pay him no mind."

O'Connor changed the signals himself and reattached the casings and after a quick test they were both ready to use again.

"It is easy to get it wrong," O'Connor warned, but Anderson dismissed it with a sarcastic nod and a patronising smile.

"So we can now use them to call our past selves?" asked Doyle.

"As far as the coms software is concerned they are all different now so, yes, you can call our past selves."

"But we don't, do we?" Anderson added, putting his two cents worth in. "Because it didn't happen otherwise we would remember it, right?"

"Unless it hasn't happened to us yet," said Doyle.

"Hang on," said O'Connor, recalling the confusing message from Anderson whilst he was on the station earlier. "I got that call."

"What call?" said Anderson and Doyle in unison.

"The call from you asking yourself to turn your beacon on," O'Connor reminded them.

"That was just before the echoes too?" Doyle said. "How did we forget that?"

Anderson was now looking in every direction except directly at her.

"We never got that call though," said Anderson. "Only you did."

"And that was probably because you messed it up," said Doyle, her patience with Anderson seeming to be balanced on a knife edge, "by using your encryption, playing the fool, and not paying attention when O'Connor showed you how to use those stone age com things properly."

"So we wait for that call again?" asked O'Connor. He wasn't keen on the idea of just sitting around wasting time.

"I want eyes on that." she said pointing to the empty space where they suspected the fourth King John was.

"But if they are there, then they'll know that we know they are there," said O'Connor slowly as he wanted to be sure he actually understood what he was saying, "Why would they try to hide from us?"

"Perhaps they don't want our first or second selves seeing them," said Anderson to which Doyle groaned her disappointment and even O'Connor felt her pain. Poor Anderson, despite his genius when it came to chard yields and power dispersions, and even various criminal activities, wrapping his head around time travel was not going to be his forte.

O'Connor continued. "What I mean is, they have been us. They've been here looking out there." He emphasised his point by indicating first the floor where they stood and then to the ceiling.

"What's your point?" said Doyle crossing her arms.

"My point is, I don't think they are there. Or at least not yet," said O'Connor, not quite so sure of himself. "Otherwise it just doesn't make sense"

"Sense?" Anderson said, and laughed. "He wants it to make sense."

"It doesn't have to make sense," said Doyle. "We don't matter to them. Just like they..." pointing to the first and second King Johns in space, "...don't matter to us. We aren't trying to avoid them, we *are* avoiding them."

"Yes, but only because we know we avoid them, we don't know if we avoid our fourth selves," said O'Connor.

"No, but they know. If they didn't see their future selves when they were us, we won't see them now. The only way we will see them or talk to them is if they allow it, because they know when it did or didn't happen."

"Doyle's theory," said Anderson, not even trying to follow, just trying to relieve a bit of the tension that had built up in the room.

"Doyle's theory?" smiled O'Connor "Whatever happens, happened."

"No it is Doyle's Law," said Doyle firmly. "Whatever happened, happens."

"Okay," said O'Connor, putting his hands up to show he was backing off of the subject, or at least the argument. "So what happens now? We can't just wait until your echo or the call about the beacon."

"O'Connor's right," said Anderson, "that would be a waste of time. We don't have the chard. If we want to preserve any chance of getting back to our time, we can't waste any time. We can't be messing about."

O'Connor didn't take the statement too seriously, but seeing the look on Doyle's face changed his opinion, after all no one knew more about chard usage than Anderson. The talk of a fourth version of themselves wasn't sitting well with him.

"Go on," Doyle said, inviting Anderson to share his expertise.

"We know we jump back again," Anderson said. "That will leave us short on the journey back anyway by either time or distance. Either way we aren't getting exactly home."

"Go on," repeated Doyle.

"There can't be a fifth," said Anderson, shaking his head, "otherwise we have no hope of getting anywhere even remotely close to home."

"Understood," said Doyle, nodding. "I'm sorry, we need to make the most of our time here." Even she hesitated before saying the word time. "Do what you can to scrape every last spark of chard out of those tanks."

It was all very professional now, no arguing and no banter. She raised her finger to her mouth and begun tapping it on her lips. Then she began to pace around the room. This was a side of her O'Connor hadn't seen yet. Although he'd only known her for a short while he had never seen her without a plan; it was unsettling.

Doyle paced the room, while Anderson busied himself at one of the benches, the entire panel lighting up with various colours as he worked. The colours appeared even more vibrant as they contrasted against the blackness of the room. If it wasn't for the overwhelming glow coming in from Venus they would probably be standing in the dark.

"Go back over there and get that ore," said Doyle suddenly. She had paced around the entire circumference as she worked through the options in front of them.

"Hasn't that been the plan all along?" O'Connor asked.

"Yes," said Doyle. She was onto something. "We take the ore, I'll get what we need from it, then we travel back and our fourth selves return it."

Anderson looked up briefly, but O'Connor kept his eyes on Doyle. It was her mission and her plan.

"That's the only explanation for us travelling back again," she said, leaving O'Connor no chance to respond by moving straight on to Anderson. "Assuming we can get the ore back on board, how much chard do we have left in the tanks? I'll need an exact amount. I'll build our return calculation from that." She didn't let him respond either. "Don't answer now, we'll have to wait for the ore to be here so we know the exact times and location."

"You just want me to get it and bring it back?" asked O'Connor.

"Yes," she said in a deadpan voice before adding sarcastically, "any other questions?"

"Won't that change everything?" Anderson asked, this time looking to O'Connor for assurance. "If we take his rocks, how can Sir Ryburn invent his engine and fly them home?"

"We'll let causality figure that out," Doyle answered. "He invents his engine and flies Neith back to Earth. We know that it happened so us taking the ore won't and can't change that."

O'Connor and Anderson just looked at each other and shrugged. Doyle had just laid out a plan that made sense, at least enough that it could work. But it went against her original plan of waiting for Ryburn to simply give O'Connor the last rock sample. Had she finally decided that wasn't going to happen?

"These are the facts as we know them now," Doyle started. "The trolley Sir Ryburn used for the Mercurian ore has been tagged, so we can follow exactly where it goes." O'Connor and Anderson nodded their agreement, this was very much the Doyle show. "O'Connor, you will enter the station after the second O'Connor leaves the airlock." She pointed up to the ceiling where the light icon of the second O'Connor was in the work-sphere getting the spare com unit.

The second O'Connor's voice came through the spare com that was still sitting on the desk.

"This is O'Connor here, look I'm having some communicator problems. Could you all please dial up your ranges to maximum?"

"You sounded nervous," said Anderson to O'Connor.

"I was nervous," O'Connor replied. "I didn't know what was going to happen."

"Shouldn't you have said O'Connor out?" Doyle asked. "And why did you introduce yourself? It all sounded so unnatural."

"And rehearsed," added Anderson.

"Shut it, the pair of you," said O'Connor with good humour, although he did feel silly.

"It's looking very cluttered now," remarked Doyle as the lights representing the coms of Ryburn, Benson and Second O'Connor were added to the tracking tags of the trolley and the first and second O'Connor's. "But where's McSweeney?"

"He's on the floor above me," answered O'Connor. "I guess he never heard because he had his stupid headphones on listening to his awful music."

"So where does he go?" Anderson asked.

"Does it really matter?" said O'Connor, remembering his intentions towards McSweeney at the moment when he was the second O'Connor.

"This was when you saw another you," said Doyle "and the other you stopped you from talking to McSweeney?"

"The future you?" said Anderson. "I mean you now." He pointed a finger at O'Connor.

"It can't be me," said O'Connor, pointing a finger to his own chest, "because that is about to happen. I can't possibly get over there in time."

"The fourth" said Doyle with an all knowing nod of her head. "So what happened after that?"

"I left the station, I mean my second left the station," said O'Connor, attempting to get the locations of all his other selves right in his head. "My first was still in his room, wondering where the com was. I'm the third here and I don't know where my fourth went, assuming that is my fourth."

"And what does McSweeney do next?" Anderson continued.

"Next time I saw him was when my first went for breakfast. He was all pissy with me for something."

"What do you mean?" Doyle asked.

"He and Benson were joking about something that he didn't want me to know about," said O'Connor, starting to recall the events of that morning, events that would be happening very shortly. "I had just sat down and he was already looking to leave. He was rude for no reason and I just put it down to him not being a morning person, but something had clearly rubbed him the wrong way."

O'Connor's mind started to connect the dots. That morning he had seen McSweeney just after a future O'Connor had accosted him in the corridor. "I bet he told Benson... and I bet Benson didn't believe him," he said aloud as his train of thought ended.

"Interesting," said Doyle.

"McSweeney was in the central sphere when we started tracking his com," Anderson joined in, pointing at the appropriate space on the station display.

"That would make sense," O'Connor agreed, "Benson would have made him update his com while they were at breakfast."

"Are you certain he didn't go anywhere else?" queried Anderson.

"No," O'Connor conceded, "but in between now and breakfast there isn't time for him to go anywhere else."

"It doesn't matter where he goes at the moment," Doyle interrupted. "The ore isn't on the station yet." The frustration in her voice was obvious as she pointed out the hopper making its approach, "Nothing matters about his location until the ore goes missing, and it's not going to go missing because you are going to take it... just like your com. So you need to get back on the station and lay in wait until Sir Ryburn leaves the trolley unguarded."

"That would explain why I couldn't find it anywhere; I must have already found and taken it," said O'Connor, adding weight to her plan.

"And you won't need to worry about bumping into your second self because he will on the second King John wasting time trying to stop the lander craft from colliding with the station."

Doyle made deliberate and sustained eye contact to drive home the point that it was their foolish actions that actually caused the very problem they were trying to prevent.

"And we know I won't bump into my second because I didn't bump into my third," said O'Connor, mimicking the hands on hips stance Doyle had taken. "It's the law."

Anderson rolled his eyes and groaned.

Radcliffe had laundered O'Connor's Neith issue jumpsuit so it no longer stank. It was always the little things, the niceties, that he missed and having clean clothes was one of them. He couldn't help but give it a big sniff as he pulled it on and got ready to return to the station. Anderson and Doyle were both on hand to help him into the space suit, although with all this practice he had gotten surprisingly quick at it of late. Before he knew it he was being bundled into the airlock by an anxious Doyle.

"Get the rocks, and bring them back," were the last words he heard as the door shut fast. His celebrity status had well and truly run its course. He prepared for egress. It was more process and precaution than concern and he had part hoped he would find something wrong so he could legitimately use one of Anderson's space suits, but alas everything was operating well within the acceptable levels.

"I'm ready," he said into his com. Receiving no reply he repeated his message but still got nothing back. They had forgotten to bring down the spare com.

Doyle asked Anderson something O'Connor couldn't make

out; they were watching him through the viewing window. O'Connor walked over to the external door and was standing there waiting for the room to be depressurised before leaving the ship.

Doyle mimed something, O'Connor understood it to mean she had sent Anderson back to get the com, watching her acting it all out like a cartoon character was fun. With pedantic mime she asked him if he was ready, to which he returned a cool, calm and collected thumbs up.

He felt the gravity leave as he became weightless inside his suit, the external door slowly opened and he pulled himself out and locked his feet onto the walkway. Being out in the emptiness of space was a humbling experience: one missed step, or a grip just a millimetre out of reach could mean certain death. His experience of being blasted out into space had made him more cautious; however a fleeting thought amused him. He had a fourth, which meant no harm could come to him… he had a future. It was only a brief thought. The sound of his breathing seemed amplified in his helmet, as it always was, while he made his way over to the jump pads. He pondered their original purpose and the dark stories Doyle had told him about how they had been used to board and violently hijack unsuspecting orbs and other such crafts. He wondered if it was the soldiers, pirates or terrorists performing the actions that turned Doyle's stomach so much, or if there was any difference between the three under this so-called Dynasty.

"Much easier with sound isn't it?" came Anderson's voice. The contrasting volume of the voice and the sound of his own breathing was quite significant and he immediately dialled down the volume.

"Indeed," O'Connor answered, "You made that joke last time and it wasn't funny then either."

"Technically I haven't made the joke yet, I will be making it later, perhaps it will be funny by then," said Anderson. The shear silliness of the conversation made O'Connor chuckle inwardly.

"We've just watched your second leave the station and that's our cue," said Anderson, as O'Connor got himself into the jump position. Suddenly he was zooming through space, the gap between the King John and Neith rapidly shrinking.

"Tightening the grip," said Anderson as he applied the tether brake.

O'Connor felt the cord pulling on him from behind, slowing his approach until his feet gently touched down like a ballerina, as gracefully as could be done in those huge magnetic boots.

"Nicely done," said Anderson.

O'Connor was just thankful to have again got over without incident.

Because their King John was in a different position from their past selves his landing spot left him with a bit of ground to cover before he could reach the airlock, something he had not anticipated needing to do. The view was always spectacular from outside the station. His gaze shifted from the hypnotic clouds of Venus to his footsteps and back again. He had a good view of the profile of the Milky Way as he looked in the direction of the galactic centre.

"Which way is your Cluster city from here?" he asked.

"It's more or less straight up from here," Doyle said and started quoting constellations he had never heard of, whilst talking about location specific perspectives of other stars.

"Straight up," he interrupted, "that will do."

He craned his neck back as much as his suit would allow but wasn't sure why he did it or what he was expecting to see.

"I'll point out the system when you are back over here *with the ore*," said Doyle.

"Right, what is everyone doing now?" asked O'Connor, wanting to get a roll call of everyone and their positions on the station.

"Benson is in the central sphere, McSweeney is in hydroponics, Sir Ryburn is in his workstation. First is in the work-sphere and appears to be walking in circles. What were you doing?" she asked with bewilderment.

"I was looking for my com," answered O'Connor, now slightly annoyed and embarrassed by his past self. He'd been pacing around that room, looking in every possibly location for his missing com, at the time so sure that McSweeney had taken it.

O'Connor reached the airlock and again it was strangely surreal seeing it all back in one piece. From the external control panel he punched in his access code, still valid as it had not yet been changed, and pulled himself into the station.

"I'm going to need to get the new codes from Benson before he changes them," he said while he was waiting for the airlock to recompress.

"Just get the ore and leave before he changes them, we know they are changed sometime after Second gets back onto the station," said Doyle, as if it were obvious. "And anyway if you get stuck your previous exit strategy can be a backup plan."

He got through to the airlock and started to unclip himself from his space suit, then begun tidying it all away. He checked to see if the tank with the patch was on the end of the shelf, which it was. Why wouldn't it be? His second self had not long left it there. Once he was completely free of his space suit, he put it away nicely. He knew that although at that moment there was plenty of room in the cupboards and shelves, Second and then First would be adding their suits to the current stock, with First dumping his on the floor, yet another crime for which he had blamed the innocent McSweeney.

The corridor was quiet, still dark as ever with the only faint light being the glow from outside. The black rubber padding felt familiar under his feet."I'm going to check the trolley, he said into his com. "It will save me time if I see exactly how I am going to attach the tracker later."

"Good form," Doyle replied. "Sir Ryburn's hopper is on approach but still a long way off yet."

There was just enough light to see what he was doing without encroaching on the darkness of the rest of the corridor. The insides of the collection hub were completely clean and clear, unlike the state Ryburn had left it in after he was finished using it, which had not happened yet. The illusive trolley was parked next to it alongside the wall. He looked over the handles and inside the bucket area and then dropped down to a knee to look underneath. He ran him hands along the edge as far as his fingers could reach.

"It's not here," he finally announced to Doyle,

"It must be, your signal is right on top of it," she replied.

The trolley was heavy, but he had to be thorough. He pulled it clear of the collection chute and tipped it up on its end so he could get a really good look underneath this time. And there is was, the exact same device that Doyle had shown him earlier was attached to the base of the trolley.

"I still don't like this game," he said, hating and loving the excitement of seeing things so out of time from his perspective.

"Found it then?" said Doyle.

"Yes, it's here," he said as he dropped the trolley back down, letting it land with a dull thud before rolling it haphazardly back into roughly the same place it had been.

"I'm going to walk past Ryburn's workstation, best keep quiet for the moment."

"Okay, starting now," Doyle responded.

Just outside Ryburn's room were the shells Second hid behind while avoiding First. All of these times different events were blending together in his mind and he was losing track of them. He jokingly worried about having to hide from himself hiding from himself but that wasn't going to be for several hours yet. Could he leave Second a message? He leaned down behind the crate, in the exact spot he remembered, he could hear Ryburn in his room speaking to his computer tools.

"Execute again," was the phrase that he was picking out the most; the rest was in a low mutter, but he heard enough to know that Ryburn was speaking simulation variables at the computer programme. What message could he leave himself and how? He didn't remember anything, so it must not have happened or his past self didn't find it. Either way this line of thought was a waste of effort; Doyle's Law was clear on the matter. He didn't like his mind wandering into these circular arguments with himself. He stepped out from his future/past hiding place and walked slowly up to Ryburn's door.

"Stop. Assume unbreakable mounting. Execute again," he heard Ryburn say. "Stop. Add a velocity count to the scenario. Execute again."

He knocked lightly on the door to announce his presence and as soon as he did Ryburn stopped the programme running, preventing him from seeing his screens. He tried to move the door which Benson had moved so easily. How did he do that? That man's a freak. He attempted to move it again with all this strength and it moved slightly further into the wall crevice. He had made it worse, making Benson's later feat of strength even more impressive.

"I bet Benson could fix this for you." He offered as a half-hearted apology.

"To what do I owe this unexpected pleasure?" asked Ryburn sounding quite annoyed. Probably because of the door, thought O'Connor as he looked around the room. It was much the same as it always was. Since he rarely visited Ryburn he tried to think of the last time he had spoken to him, from Ryburn's point of view. It would have been the com that morning, briefly while he was trying to sleep. There was no sign of the prototype. The last time he had been in this room was later after Ryburn had started building the prototype and was using the wrong parts. The screens were all blank, the display windows all lowered, he couldn't see how far along Ryburn was with his work.

"Are you looking for something?" Ryburn sighed. As he spoke he was rolling his hands, obviously wanting O'Connor to get to the point of his little visit. O'Connor didn't really have a point as everything he needed hadn't happened yet, but he thought quickly and answered.

"Yes I am as it happens, how are the experiments going?"

"Experiments?" Ryburn asked.

"With the Mercurian ore," O'Connor elaborated, looking directly at Ryburn. Even as he said it he realised that it was a mistake; the original O'Connor would not have had the slightest interest in what Ryburn was doing.

"Something wrong, O'Connor?" Ryburn asked,

"No nothing wrong," O'Connor answered quickly. "Thanks Jim."

"Okay, well thanks for stopping by," said Ryburn dismissively rude as he spun his chair back to face the monitors.

"How long before the hopper arrives?" O'Connor asked, to which Ryburn replied by simply pointing to the top right screen which clearly indicated "ETA 65 minutes".

"Right, that makes sense," said O'Connor "And once you get it on board what are you going to do?" O'Connor asked. He was formulating a plan. Would he have time to get outside the station and lie in wait for the hopper, intercept the ore between the hopper arriving and Ryburn collecting the rocks? No, he recalled what Doyle had said about the weights recorded in the history matching exactly.

"Is that really important?" Ryburn asked bluntly.

"Just humour me, please?" said O'Connor as politely as he could, this would be tricky.

"Well... I'll take it to the smelt of course, but you know that because you lot are under orders not to touch it without my say so. You haven't started chopping it up yet have you?"

"The smelt is just fine. Don't panic," said O'Connor lifting up his hands into a calm down motion to prevent setting Ryburn off on an angry rant.

"Good, as agreed, it can't be touched without my say so otherwise I'll make sure none of you work any contracts for us ever again."

The threat made O'Connor smile inwardly, how insignificant those threats sounded.

"Oh I'm sure it won't come to that."

"Good, now if you please I need to get back to my work," said Ryburn, still very abrasive, but O'Connor let that go. None of this was current, it was old words and it didn't matter, it wasn't even the "real" Ryburn as the real Ryburn, in sync with O'Connor, was somewhere out toward Earth, flying home using his breakthrough discovery. Ryburn spun back to face his monitors whilst O'Connor stood for a moment thinking about what to do next. It would be an hour before Ryburn got the ore samples. Maybe he could fix it to ensure that Ryburn didn't do anything amiss with the ore. It was clear that the trolley would be used to carry the ore, it had to be because his future self still needed to add a tracker to it. What else could he do?

"One final request please, if I may," said O'Connor. This was going to be an ambitious request considering the state of their relationship at this moment.

"I don't mean to be rude, but I have very important work to attend to. Is this latest charade just to waste my time or is there some purpose I'm missing? Because if it's time- wasting you like perhaps we can talk about the cloud compositions of Venus, or the carbon to iron ratios of the outer Jupiter moons, something pointless like that?"

"With the uncertain nature of the Mercurian ore, can I get your word that you will not take it to any other areas of the station?" said O'Connor. An agreement from Ryburn would guarantee the ore would not wander whilst in his control.

"It's not that type of uncertainty," Ryburn snapped back.

"Just humour me please," said O'Connor. He just had to add enough of an argument to have Ryburn take the path of least resistance and agree… unless he wanted an argument that is. "With the uncertain magnetic properties, you do not know what effects it could have if exposed to the main systems, do you?" This was his bluff, for he had facts from Doyle, the ore was attracted to magnets, not the other way around. Would Ryburn take his concern for precautions as genuine, or would he see through the charade?

"It is clear you don't understand the nature of the ore or magnetic-"

"I agree completely," said O'Connor, after being caught on his bluff he was going to double bluff his way out. "I don't understand, don't understand any of it, which is why I don't want it being scattered about the station."

"I won't be scattering it about the station," said Ryburn defensively.

"I want your word, I want you to promise me that it won't be taken anywhere apart from the collection dock, the smelt chamber and this workstation," said O'Connor, upping the ante on his demands.

"A pointless request, those are the only places I would take it to anyway." said Ryburn.

"So do I have your word?" O'Connor repeated. This was where he had him; Ryburn wouldn't go back on his word and if it was a pointless request he would have no quarrel in agreeing.

"Yes, fine. I solemnly swear that I won't take the ore anywhere it doesn't need to go," said Ryburn sarcastically, placing his hand on his heart.

"Thank you Jim, I'll leave you to your work," said O'Connor, looking around the room again for even a hint of the experiments that would mark the beginning of this new direction of space travel. He slipped out the door into the corridor, leaving Ryburn to his work. Jim. He had just realised he'd been calling him Jim, Ryburn hadn't invited him to call him that yet… the familiarity of it would have been out of place for Ryburn. O'Connor wondered if he noticed it. Of course he would have noticed but nothing could be done about that now.

The good news was that this little conversation at the very least narrowed the locations where the ore could be. Everything was falling into place, the reason he couldn't find the ore, the upturned trolley in Ryburn's old room. It was all him, or would be all him and he just wasted a lot of his own time chasing the shadows of his future self without knowing it. That thought brought an exhausted sigh. It was hard to be angry with yourself for something you hadn't done yet. Still some warning from himself would have been nice. But that thought put him back into another circular loop of Doyle's Law.

"O'Connor, are you there?" Doyle's voice came through the wrist communicator.

"I'm here," O'Connor answered.

"What were you doing with Ryburn?" she asked.

"Damage limitation," O'Connor answered nodding to himself, then explained how he got Ryburn to promise not to take the ore anywhere apart from the collection chamber, the smelt and his workstation.

"Good form," Doyle said, "that could explain why you had no luck finding it earlier… I mean finding it later."

"Everyone will be on the lower floor when Ryburn fumbles the hopper. So I'm going to get the ore samples from the hopper before Ryburn gets to the collection hub."

He was sure that would be an ideal opportunity as he was standing just in the shadows of the collection hub. Going over it in his mind what would need to be done - simple collection job, how hard could it be?

"We've been over that idea. It won't happen," said Doyle firmly. "The logs all matched in Sir Ryburn's account, the weights matched exactly."

"It has to be now, there is no other way," said O'Connor, firmly pressing his point, "What if we alter the records?"

"It won't work," she said. "This is not the way. It can't be. Sir Ryburn's accounts were very descriptive, overly so in fact. He got the hopper in, and collected the ore from it… all of it."

"Yes but I can get all the ore first, get it off the station. You get what we need and I travel back again and return it the hopper moments after I first took it."

"Does that collection thing even allow you to do that?" asked Doyle.

O'Connor was silent for a moment. "No it doesn't, damn it,

this isn't going to work." He suppressed a cry of frustration but still was not ready to let it drop. "What if I do it from space then?"

"While First is walking around out there, you want to have Third and possibly Fourth there too?" said Doyle. "Isn't that when Second re-enters the station?"

"But I didn't see them, either time," said O'Connor, referring to when he was his first and second, "so we know I wasn't seen."

"You weren't seen because you weren't there. It is not going to happen. The plan is too messy and contradicts everything that Sir Ryburn said happened."

"Can we just check the visual feed to see if that will happen?" said Anderson, acting as the voice of reason.

"That is brilliant Andy," said Doyle with quite a lot of surprise in her voice.

O'Connor nodded his agreement, also taken aback at the simple and obvious genius of it all.

"Get on with it then," said Doyle, Anderson's moment of glory was over.

"Why would we still go to the effort of tagging the trolley?" asked Doyle, wanting to be confirmed right, before the evidence was in.

"Perhaps because we knew it had been done, so we had to do it?" O'Connor answered, with no real conviction.

"We don't have to do anything. We still have complete free choice on everything we do, and it makes no sense for us to waste time tagging the trolley if its only purpose will be to deliberately confuse ourselves," said Doyle.

Unable to think of a valid rebuttal, O'Connor could only wait until Anderson produced the proof of what would or wouldn't happen, although he pretty much knew what it would show. He played out a scenario in his head where he promised himself that if it was to be a collaborative effort, which it would have to be, Fourth would step out now and reveal himself. The corridor however, stayed empty, ergo there was no collaboration.

"Okay," Anderson began, "we have clear visual data of the

hopper coming in, once on the collection arm it moved over to the collection point." After a pause in which he was obviously checking the images very carefully he added, "No one is out there so I guess that means you don't interfere with it there."

"Okay then," said O'Connor, the hint of bitterness and even embarrassment in his voice was even clearer on his face which fortunately the others were unable to see.

"We wait for Sir Ryburn to take it to the work-sphere," said Doyle, putting O'Connor back on track. "That is our opportunity."

He agreed, for now, and left the collection hub area to walk back toward the central junction but stopped at the porthole window.

"Can you see me through the window?" he asked, his subconscious need to avoid discovery causing him to involuntarily lower his voice to a whisper.

"Yes, we can," said Anderson.

O'Connor extended his middle figure and made an obscene gesture out into space.

"One what?" asked Anderson. O'Connor laughed and wondered what type of obscenities they had in the future. Had he received any and not known?

"So I wait for the hopper?" said O'Connor, leaning into the window alcove.

"That wasn't funny," said Doyle. "I know what that meant."

O'Connor smiled.

"And stop smiling, it isn't funny," she continued.

"So where are you exactly?" he asked.

"Look up slightly," said Doyle, "now left … left. Right there."

"Can't see anything," O'Connor said.

"Good," said Doyle. "The hopper is getting close now, you won't have to wait long. We've traced what we picked up last time after everyone is on the lower deck, Ryburn goes to that collection hub and then all the way around to the work-sphere, he waits, then goes all the way back to his workstation. Look to the right, further still, and up a bit."

"Okay," said O'Connor, "what am I looking for?"

"That's where the second King John is lying in wait for the lander."

"Very good," he said. "I can't stay here, First comes this way after the impact alarm goes off." He could have actually remained there talking to Doyle for a while yet. "Where is First now?" he asked, remembering being all over the place that morning searching for his lost communicator.

"He's in the sleeping quarters again, searching in the same places again and again it would seem," said Doyle. O'Connor heard her gasp. "Sir Ryburn, he's right there!"

"Where?" said O'Connor turning left and right.

"Toward the airlock," she said.

"Okay, better go silent for a while," said O'Connor.

"Starting now," Doyle responded, as O'Connor walked quickly toward the central sphere. This was actually the last place he wanted to go since his main concern was to avoid everyone. He reached the ladder just in time to see Benson's large boots hit the rungs on the top floor and so, in a panic reaction, slid down to the lower floor and ducked out of sight. O'Connor whispered into his com, "Doyle, where is everyone exactly?"

"Ryburn's at the window now, Benson is..."

"Forget Benson," he interrupted. "Where are McSweeney and First?"

"First is in the corridor between the sleeping quarters and the work-sphere; McSweeney is back in hydroponics."

"Okay, thanks," he said, "Silence again now, nothing until I call you."

"Starting now," she replied. It was way too late to correct her on that little behavioural error, besides he found it rather cute.

He looked around and found himself a quiet place behind a large reel of reclaimed synthetic diamond cabling to make himself as comfortable as he could, then waited for the drama to unfold.

CHAPTER 16: THE COMPLICATION

O'CONNOR'S EARS PRICKED up when heard the sound of feet on the ladder. It was Ryburn, the old man's groans gave him away. It was time for him to collect the hopper. O'Connor had sat down behind a giant spool on the floor and stretched out whilst waiting. He raised himself to his knees and peeked over the top of the spool for a better view.

The collection arm controls were on the far side of the room from where he was hiding and gave him a good place to avoid the crew when they come down to investigate the impact alarms after Ryburn cocks up the collection. O'Connor had to quickly duck from view as Ryburn began looking around the room somewhat absentmindedly before finally kneeling on the floor in front of the controls. He must have been looking for a chair or something, although there was nothing of the sort left. Everything had already been stripped out as the caretakers systematically salvaged anything that might be of any value from the room. Ryburn had something up on the display screen but it was too far away for O'Connor to see clearly, but it was a safe bet it concerned the hopper.

Ryburn went through a few extension motions, obviously

familiarising himself with the sleeve device that controlled the external arm.

"Lower speed for approach," said Ryburn to the console. O'Connor felt the goose bumps on his arms rise. This was a nervous moment; this whole encounter was the beginning of the end for both the station and him.

"Apply braking, match to zero speed," said Ryburn

"Please define zero speed," he heard the console's calm female voice. That must have been the point when Ryburn made a mistake, O'Connor decided, simultaneously wondering whether he could he have stopped it. If he had helped Ryburn at that moment then it could not have been the mistake, but because he had chosen inaction perhaps it was the mistake after all. No, thought O'Connor, whether he chose to just watch or to take some sort of action, Doyle's Law dictated that the result would be the same, anything he does or doesn't do had already happened. This was Ryburn's fuck-up and he didn't want to own any of that blame.

"Define zero speed as station current speed," said Ryburn, recognising his error.

"Velocity currently below zero speed," said the console.

"Well stop the bloody brakes then," Ryburn shouted. "Increase speed, four seconds full burn".

Ryburn shouted the command a few more times.

O'Connor knew what was happening here as he had watched this twice before already. Ryburn was using the hopper's limited fuel to fire controlled thruster bursts to slow the approach. He still could not see the screen clearly, but could see a flashing red warning light.

"Zero speed achieved," announced the console.

"Another four-second burst," Ryburn repeated, "Fire thrusters again, full burn".

O'Connor couldn't see the fuel read-out but guessed it must be nearly empty, Ryburn hadn't saved enough for a controlled approach.

The alarm on the screen was beeping now, an indication that the hopper was coming in too fast.

"COLLISION IMMINENT," started to flash in big red letters and the station wide siren began to whine warning the crew to brace for impact.

"Full brake, full burn on all thrusters, no reserve," said Ryburn, loud enough to hear over the wailing siren. With his arm deep in the sleeve he flexed it again to get ready for his catch.

O'Connor could not make out what Ryburn was doing. He should have been extending the hopper's arms but instead he was just standing motionless at the controls. O'Connor's goose bumps now had goose bumps. This scene was wrong! He knew that Ryburn's last ditch attempt to slow the hopper down was to extend the beams out and use the thrusters of the landers as brakes. It was a genius idea, he'd never have thought of it – he admitted. It was the one thing that stopped the incident being a total disaster, but Ryburn was still getting ready for the "catch" seemingly unaware that the hopper was moving too fast.

O'Connor looked around in vain for something, anything that could change what was happening. Unable to restrain himself he jumped up and shouted across the room.

"The landers Jim! Use the fucking landers!"

Ryburn started shouting commands. Had Ryburn heard O'Connor shout, or was he going to use the landers at that moment anyway?

The collision alarm was still going off all around the station. Ryburn leapt to his feet and braced himself for the impact, the force of the incoming hopper was too much and he was lifted off the floor and slammed into the wall as the outside collection arm caught its jagged grip on the hopper, and although he had slowed it, Ryburn was unable to stop it completely. The velocity swung it around and it collided with the station. The whole room shook violently, the impact would have been felt everywhere, and even knowing exactly what it was this time did nothing to stop that gut-wrenching feeling of impending doom.

The sirens stopped and the room returned to its original quiet. O'Connor could hear Ryburn breathing heavily from across the room and Benson's booming voice coming from the floor above.

"What's going on down there Dr Ryburn?" Benson shouted from the top of the ladder. "Was that collision warning for your hopper?"

McSweeney was hurling swear words in Ryburn's direction whilst First was warning him to keep a civil tongue. This part O'Connor remembered, he had been in his quarters once again searching for his communicator when the alarms had started and he had run over to the central sphere where he met McSweeney who had come from the other direction. After a brief exchange they had both then followed Benson down the ladder to investigate.

O'Connor lifted his head to get a better look. All three of the caretakers had their backs to him. Benson was a big man and took up most of the view. McSweeney and the first O'Connor looked interchangeable from behind, but on closer inspection McSweeney was scrawny and wearing a baggy jump suit, whilst First completely filled his jump suit. Both of them were wearing woollen hats. McSweeney's was grey, but First's was black. Seeing his past self in his hat made O'Connor reach for his own and run his fingers along its mysterious rip. He liked the hat that First was wearing and looked at him with envy. The other minor difference was the large wrist com that McSweeney was wearing. First's forearm was empty. O'Connor remembered being very concerned about the possible damage to the station, and rightly so.

Ryburn was pacing awkwardly around the room, his legs obviously troubling him. "It came in a bit quick and bumped us a little. No damage, just a miscalculation. Nothing too…"

"Nothing too serious by looks of it," said First O'Connor from the controls, speaking over Ryburn. We will need to run checks, see if there's any damage. This, this will put us further behind schedule."

O'Connor credited his earlier self with keeping calm as he

knew full well that First was boiling inside at that moment.

"What is so damn important about these rocks of yours anyway?" asked McSweeney, the sound of his voice still triggering a bit of anger in O'Connor. "You'd better not have knocked us out of orbit, you crazy old fool."

"I don't have to answer to any of you chop-boys," said Ryburn, who O'Connor could no longer see as he was completely obscured by Benson.

"Chop-boys?" McSweeney said and, leaning against the wall, let himself slip down until he was sitting on the floor. "Is that the best you've got?"

"I've got plenty of words I could use for you McSweeney," Ryburn spat back.

"We should compare notes," said Benson, "I've got some good ones for him too."

"Dr Ryburn," said First, the voice of reason, "if we'd known you were in trouble we would have helped, you know we would have. Benson here could probably have dragged the thing in with his bare hands if you'd only asked."

O'Connor nodded to himself in agreement, hearing the cool calm voice of his past self taking control of the situation. They were all sitting on the floor now.

"Sort me out a space suit and catcher's mitt and I'll be out there for the next pitch," said Benson, his booming laugh punctuating his sentence.

"I reckon old Ryburn here would have bumped you from your spot on the team, Benson, if your coaches had seen him on the collection arm just now," said McSweeney, who as usual had his finger up when delivering back handed praise. "Saw it all on the display when that collision nonsense started up. He plucked his thingamajig clean out the air, it was magical."

"I need to get those rock samples to the smelt," said Ryburn.

"Hang on Dr Ryburn, we need to establish if our orbit is okay first, what was the final speed when it hit? It didn't breach but we need to be sure we aren't in any danger." said First.

Ryburn did not reply, he just groaned as he pulled himself back up to his feet.

"Dr Ryburn, how fast was it going?" repeated First, but Ryburn continued to ignore him.

"Dr Ryburn? How fast, damn it Ryburn! Are we okay or not?" First was on his feet now too. O'Connor felt himself colour up seeing First act in such a manner toward Ryburn. He was not proud at seeing himself raise his voice at this frail looking old man, who was about to change the world. He caught himself having this ridiculous inner argument blaming and justifying his past actions to himself. What is done is done.

"It was at two eighty six when it made contact with the arm. It slowed down as I swung it round but there would have been a slight angular change in our orbit; it dragged us round with its momentum. Our pivot would be a degree or degree point five off centre now. When it hit the hull it would have been at around fifty or fifty five, at an angle eighty three degrees to the planet and eighty one or eighty two from our central pivot axis. The bulk of the collision force was deflected along our hull so the point of impact wouldn't have breached it. At worst I've shortened our orbital life by four and a half hours. As I said, nothing to worry about."

"Have you been drinking?" said First.

"Not a factor," replied Ryburn, his little speech was condescending towards the crew and, after turning his back to them, he returned to the controls.

"What about the capacitor feeds or the panelling, or the releasing systems?" said First.

O'Connor rolled his eyes and thought to himself *just let it go, what does it matter?* He was feeling very disappointed in himself: hindsight was a beautiful thing. Ryburn ignored the questions and continued his work.

First started rattling off orders for the crew. Did he really sound like such an arse?

"Benson, get up to what's left of the control deck and check external systems. McSweeney, you help him and report to me immediately if we're in trouble. I'll walk out and inspect the impact area. Report to me immediately if we're in trouble." … "My com is still missing and the damn spare is gone too."

Oh no, O'Connor thought to himself as he raised both hands to his face, hoping the next conversation would not happen, *Now I'm going to blame McSweeney for the missing coms.*

He really wanted to jump up and slap himself but that would have been difficult to explain to the crew.

"What?" McSweeney asked innocently "Just run a trace on it."

"Yes, well funny thing the trace isn't working either; getting all sorts of nonsense back from that aren't I? All sorts of conflicts," said First causing O'Connor to hide even further into his hands.

"No one would have tampered with it, even for a joke," said Benson. "The whole station is falling apart. The trace errors are probably just another minor system failure. You know what it's like pulling these old stations apart."

"Thank you! That sounds much more likely," said a smug McSweeney.

"Watch your tone!" said First with a raised voice, "Don't think I've forgotten about your little outburst this morning. I will dock you some serious fee if this behaviour and insubordination continue!"

Let it go you arsehole O'Connor thought to himself, he could hear the anger in his voice, and remembered the anger he was feeling. He knew now that all these little exchanges with McSweeney were guiding him towards a breaking point, a breaking point that would lead to the airlock.

"Seriously, I haven't touched any of them. I swear it. Take my whole damn fee if I have." said McSweeney.

"I'll hold you to that," said First.

"I will too," Benson added.

"Okay then," said First, finally letting the subject drop. "I'll walk out without a com. So if we're in the shit you'll have to come out and get me. This shouldn't take long anyway."

Benson and McSweeney had a few things to say to each other on the way up the ladder but nothing more was said to O'Connor, who stood in the room alone with Ryburn. For a moment or two it looked like he was going to say something but instead he let out a disappointed sigh before exiting via the ladder.

Thank god for that thought O'Connor. Stepping out of his hiding place he slowly walked over to the ladder, carefully looked up the hatchway to be sure no one was there and was about to leave when he heard Ryburn speak.

"It is really important I get this ore in," he said, almost inaudibly before taking a quick look over his shoulder. Seeing O'Connor he quickly spun back around and returned to his work.

Poor Ryburn, he looked and sounded utterly defeated. With all the arrogance and rudeness he had always shown the crew, O'Connor now saw him in a new light. Perhaps now that he was so close to his goal it was all getting too much for him. He was tired and should never have been left to bring in the hopper by himself. If only O'Connor had known then what he knew now. All this blame, checking for damage that was not there, dismantling the station around Ryburn, all the little power struggles, none of it mattered. None of it. The only thing that mattered now was the ore. He felt he had to say something.

"Keep working on it Jim," said O'Connor. "But what's so important about the ore anyway?"

"You really want to know?" asked Ryburn.

"Yes I do."

"I think it could be the future," said Ryburn, as if finally being allowed to tell someone his secret.

"Don't get discouraged, keep at it. It won't be long now," said O'Connor trying his absolute best to be sincere.

"Don't you dare patronise me! You think I'm mad too don't you? I hear you talking. I know this being nice is just another silly little game of yours. Just let me finish my work in peace as you were ordered to do." This was the cantankerous Ryburn he knew.

"I'm sorry Jim, that's not what I meant," said O'Connor,

raising his hands. He was very sorry the conversation has taken this drastic turn and realised he had to show an interest in the details to prove he was on Ryburn's side and make peace. "I want to know really, please. Why does it have to come from Mercury? Tell me about the magnetism."

"Its magnetic properties are indeed baffling," said Ryburn, the bitterness on his face melting away to a soft-faced old man again. "It is attracted to solar electricity generated magnetic fields."

O'Connor of course already knew that, because Doyle had explained it to him, but it was important for him to hear the words from the man himself.

"If the attraction can be controlled, it could be a new form of propulsion," Ryburn continued.

"That's great, but why Mercury?" said O'Connor. This bit of information might be significant for Doyle.

"I don't know, maybe it has something to do with the proximity to the sun. But then we would expect to see lesser effects elsewhere..." Ryburn trailed off. "I really have no idea why."

"Okay, don't worry about that now Jim, you can work that out later I guess." He hoped that didn't sound patronising, The conversation was going on too long; there were still a lot of crew around the central sphere who could notice he was not where he should be, which was heading to the airlock to check for damage to the hull. "I have to get back to-"

"Yes yes, checking the hull for non-existent damage? Don't let me keep you from the all-important inspection."

"Yes that's right, I'll be out checking for damage" said O'Connor. It had surprised him that Ryburn remembered what he should be doing, before realising that it had only been a couple of minutes since his first self had declared where he was going. He left Ryburn to his work and quietly climbed the ladder. He needed a quiet spot to call Doyle and update her on what had happened.

"Doyle," he whispered into his com once he had found himself a quiet little alcove along the central corridor.

"Hello O'Connor," she answered. "So that was the hopper, again."

"Yeah that was it all right," said O'Connor, it was still dramatic even for a third time. "Listen, I told Ryburn to use the lander engines to slow the hopper down."

"Really?" Doyle answered, a hint of excitement on her voice. "What made you do that?"

"He wasn't going to use them, I had to" said O'Connor, justifying his actions as best he could.

"What's done is done," she said. "I wouldn't be too concerned about it; if you hadn't, that impact would have likely killed everyone."

"That's not what's bothering me," said O'Connor. He didn't need another circular explanation of him doing what he did, and not doing what he didn't.

"What's on your mind then?" said Doyle. "Anderson's not here so we can talk."

"It's McSweeney, I was a real dick to him," said O'Connor, it was hard for him to admit it.

"I don't know what that means," said Doyle.

"Oh," O'Connor said, "I've been treating him unfairly, unnecessarily so. Antagonising him, it's all out of order, but to him, to him…." He left that thought unspoken before continuing. "He didn't take my com, but I'm giving him a lot of grief for it."

"Okay," said Doyle, leading him on to continue but he kept quiet for a moment. Ryburn had just climbed up the ladder, and was heading his way. But he walked briskly past, offering just a nod of acknowledgement as he continued on his way.

"And soon I'm going to blame him for taking Ryburn's rocks."

"And it will be you taking the rocks," said Doyle, finishing O'Connor's point for him.

"Exactly," said O'Connor, with a lot of guilt. "Then my other past self, my second, will really start laying into him for it, and for killing me."

"You mean, you already did?" Doyle asked, he hadn't filled her in all the exact details of his interactions with McSweeney. "You can't stop it if it happened," she said.

"I think I do stop it though. Not all of it. Remember when I told you I saw a future version of myself talking to McSweeney?"

"Yes," said Doyle.

"Well, I was really angry, really, really angry," said O'Connor. He wasn't used to being this open to anyone. "Then when McSweeney walked past I saw red."

"Go on," said Doyle.

"I was going to attack him, really beat the crap out of him and dump him into space, just as he had done to me," he added at the end, as if it were a justification. "But my future self got to him first, and stopped me doing anything stupid."

"This was earlier wasn't it?" Doyle asked.

"Yes, it was just after my second self got the coms, and just before I came back to your ship."

"What did he say again?" asked Doyle.

"He said…" O'Connor started, "he knew why I was there, and that he was stopping me."

"The violence?"

"Yes, I think so," O'Connor answered, ashamed of himself.

"Violence that never actually happened though," said Doyle. "It's odd that your future self would be there to stop something that never happened, don't you think?"

O'Connor took the question as rhetorical and continued. "He also said that none of it was McSweeney's fault and that it was all our fault."

"Our fault?" Doyle asked.

"I think he meant just me, and the other versions of me," said O'Connor, and then there was a long silence.

"Doyle are you there?" he said after the pause had gotten uncomfortably long.

"Yes sorry, I was just looking up the historical accounts, I remember some of it but I wanted to be sure," Doyle answered. "It states here that McSweeney admitted to wanting to kill you. Claims you and he had been arguing about him trying to sabotage Sir Ryburn's work. He claimed you had been accusing him of theft, there's something about a financial dispute and an assault. Apparently you are going to punch him later."

"Already did," said O'Connor, looking at his knuckles and the little cut from McSweeney's teeth. Landing that punch felt so good and warranted at the time, but now it seemed so uncalled for. He wanted to take it back.

"And he says you set him up to drug you," she said ending the account. "What does that mean, it makes no sense... even the scholars couldn't make sense of that, because there was nothing like that on the station."

O'Connor sighed. "Later on he's going to stab my original self with a sedative."

"Really, where did he get it from?"

"I am pretty sure it is currently in your medical room, filled and waiting."

"Yes, we'll have something like that," Doyle added, not sounding at all surprised. "That is a curious turn of events, but whatever happens, happens," she said. "Just try not to make it worse."

"I think I already have made it worse," said O'Connor.

"Oh yes?" said Doyle.

"Last night, tonight," said O'Connor, getting the times mixed up again, "my first self had a good talk with McSweeney, he was on his way to do some late work in the oxygen farm. It was a good conversation, I apologised for everything I'd done out of line that day. He was out of line, but so was I but I wanted to clear the air and put it all behind us."

"Go on," said Doyle, waiting for the crux of his story.

"This was after my future self had stopped him in the corridor, after my first self had accused him of stealing the com, after my second self had punched him and accused him of stealing the ore.

He was being the much bigger man, by accepting my apology, than I ever realised. We parted on good terms that night."

"That's good isn't it?"

"But my second self saw McSweeney again, remember? I tore McSweeney a new one outside hydroponics, just before the airlock breach. I blamed him for that too."

"So what else did you say?" Doyle asked.

"I was angry that we didn't know he was there, because he wasn't wearing his com. But my first self had just told him that not wearing the com was okay. My second told him to go to bed, like he was a little child. But moments before that my first self had thanked him for the extra effort he was putting in."

The anxiety in O'Connor's voice was quite high now.

"That is quite a mess O'Connor," said Doyle slowly. "So from McSweeney's point of view you had just set him up. No wonder he wanted to kill you."

"Then the next morning he was being really rude to me again, and I didn't know why. Now I do"

"Anything else after that?" asked Doyle.

"Yeah, we had a couple of altercations over the day," said O'Connor shaking his head at his own stupid actions. "I continued to blame him for my com, Ryburn's missing rocks, tampering with the airlocks, trapping me in the corridor, that still could be him but it hasn't happened again yet."

"Anything else to add to that list?" Doyle asked.

"He gave me a good kicking after stabbing me with the syringe, he dragged me into an airlock," O'Connor continued, his memory of what exactly happened was fuzzy. "I think he was going to kill me there and then, if it weren't for Benson."

O'Connor recalled waking up in this space suit and going out into space.

"He followed me out into space, but I was onto him by then. He beat me back to the airlock. And..." he paused slightly, "well you know the rest."

"Nothing can change that now," said Doyle.

"Chief!" a booming voice called out in O'Connor's direction. It was Benson calling from the ladder. This made O'Connor jump, feeling for a second that he had just been caught doing something he shouldn't. He had forgotten himself and ironically lost track of time whilst he was confessing to Doyle.

"Sorry, Chief." said Benson. "Didn't mean to startle you"

"That's alright Benson," said O'Connor, emphasised enough for Doyle to understand that someone else was now in earshot.

"Right" said Benson "We aren't losing any air, the opposite in fact."

"Opposite?" questioned O'Connor.

"The overall pressure of the air in the ship has increased slightly and consumption is up, just a little."

"What does that mean?" O'Connor asked, carefully putting his arms behind his back to hide the com that, as far as Benson was concerned, he'd lost.

"Maybe the hopper dented the hull. That would make the insides smaller," said Benson, as he walked over to O'Connor.

"No that's not it," O'Connor answered a bit too quick, without really thinking of the time line of events, he wasn't supposed to know that yet. "I mean," he stuttered to correct himself "I'll take a good look once I'm out there."

"Or," Benson continued, "it means there is more mass on board than there was before." He scratched his head a bit, as if questioning his own conclusion.

"More mass?" O'Connor repeated. He knew exactly what that more mass was, it was the multiple versions of himself, which would explain the increase in the oxygen consumption that McSweeney had reported too. More pieces slotting into place.

"Most likely a sensor problem, you know what this place is like," said O'Connor dismissively. "Why don't you check the airlocks to be sure that they aren't reporting false positives after they open?"

O'Connor wanted those words back; the last thing he needed was Benson or anyone else checking the airlocks. They'd seen more traffic in the last few hours than they probably had in months.

"Okay I'll check them next," said Benson.

"No wait," said O'Connor, reaching out an arm to stop Benson from leaving. "What about Ryburn's rock samples, are they mass enough to match the reading?" Was that enough of a reason to explain it away, hopefully just enough to stop Benson investigating.

"Would they be enough?" Benson asked.

"They have to be, it's the only explanation that would make sense, the increased mass has to be his rocks," said O'Connor, he knew it wasn't of course, but needed to get Benson off this line of questioning.

"Just the man, Dr Ryburn," Benson exclaimed as Ryburn had just that moment crossed the walkway junction ahead.

"Dr Ryburn," Benson called again loud enough for Ryburn's attention this time.

"Yes what is it?" Ryburn called back. His body language said he would have preferred to have slipped by unseen and certainly didn't want to talk to them. O'Connor didn't want to be in this conversation either, but his eyes shot straight to the trolley, like a hunter seeing his prey after many hours of tracking. He couldn't just run over and grab it of course, he had to wait. *Let's get this over with* O'Connor thought, *minimal impact, keep it short.*

"We're getting some strange readings on the internal air pressure."

"I'm busy, what is it you want to know?" Ryburn responded.

Good, Ryburn wants to keep this short too.

"How much additional mass have you brought on board? Sensors are showing a slight increase in air pressure," shouted O'Connor – probably louder than he needed to.

"Thirty to forty litres," he shouted back. "If you need an exact figure it will just have to wait."

"Thanks Jim, that won't be necessary," O'Connor shouted back.

Ryburn didn't offer anything else and disappeared from view

with the trolley,

"Thirty to forty litres," said O'Connor to Benson and giving him 'case closed' pat on the arm.

"That would do it," willing Benson to agree and drop the subject.

"I guess so, yeah," said Benson.

"I better get a move on, need to check for that damage outside," said O'Connor, turning to leave.

"Right," said Benson. "I'll check the airlocks' tools and readings for you."

O'Connor stopped. "You don't need to, I'm sure they will be fine."

"Better safe than sorry, right Chief?" said Benson as he returned up the ladder. He wasn't trying to be confrontational on the matter, that type of intention would never have even entered his mind, but O'Connor really did wish he would drop it.

O'Connor followed along behind where Ryburn had gone, and once again found himself having to wait. The smelting process would take at least 30 minutes, and it could not be rushed. He needed to stay out of sight from everyone, couldn't risk getting involved in anything and finding out even further that it was his fault everything happened as it did. He decided to wait in his quarters and say a goodbye to the old place. He pushed the sliding door open to find the room was a mess. He had not tidied up after leaving it in such a state whilst searching for the lost com. He sat on the bed quietly looking at the room for a moment, he felt out of place again, it was his room but then again it wasn't. The mess was really annoying him. With all the drama and grief from Ryburn and McSweeney, and the news from lunarbase that they would be on their own, it was no wonder he had never gotten around to it – he tried to justify it to himself. But then again, he recalled the previous night, it wasn't messy? So he did himself a favour and tidied up the mess his past self had made.

As he was tidying up, saying goodbye to his old room, he

asked Doyle for a bit more of a history lesson.

"So how did the Lancers manage to take over?" he asked rather bluntly.

"The Dynasty? They've always been around," said Doyle.

"No, they were just a freelance firm a few years ago, now they have all the best equipment and get all the best contracts," said O'Connor. "And somehow they manage to become your Dynasty."

"They certainly aren't *my* Dynasty," she stated rather firmly, just to make that point very clear before she offered up the history as she knew it. "There isn't much information about their origins. At the very heart of it, they controlled the access to Mercury. Everything afterwards was a result of that monopoly."

"What about before Ryburn's invention?" said O'Connor, looking around the room for the next target of his tidying assault.

"The Neith Incident was a huge event for humanity and not much mattered before that. Dynasty were the first people to actually leave the original system. They'd established the fuelling stations in the Oort cloud, and would ship chard out to them in huge quantities for the exodus orbs." She had an eloquent way of telling the story of history that hadn't happened yet.

"They don't sound so bad," said O'Connor as it sounded like any other regular big contract work.

"That was hundreds of years ago, so there has been a lot of propaganda and selective whitewashing of facts since then, a lot of tweaking of history. There was an accident on the first colony."

"We had a colony outside the solar system?" O'Connor interrupted since that type of information was ground-breaking news for him.

"Yes, it was a rogue nomad planet, I don't know the scientific designation; but we know they just called it Colony 1."

"Imaginative lot," O'Connor scoffed. "What happened to it?"

He picked up the contents of his personal shelf from the floor: the scatterings left behind after his little communicator had cleared them from their regular place.

"A ship crashed into it, destroying it, the planet and everyone who lived there."

"Destroyed the whole planet?" O'Connor questioned. "Surely not?"

"According to history it was completely destroyed," Doyle answered, with little commitment.

"How fast was the ship travelling" O'Connor asked; she had his full attention.

"It had started breaking apart, which meant its own magnetic structural reinforcement had begun to fail. 4T was the standard of the day, so it would have been at least that."

"Four times the speed of light?" O'Connor said in amazement. That was a ridiculous speed to even contemplate, let alone reach.

"Yeah, those old vessels didn't travel so fast, but that was still enough to obliterate anything it hit," said Doyle. "Huge advancements in structural integrity have been made since then, of course."

"So what happened after that?" said O'Connor, transfixed by the story.

"When the distress flare-bands were picked up they reported that it was apparently a malfunction on a propulsion system that meant the ship could not slow down and so kept accelerating until impact. Since it wasn't a Dynasty ship that crashed they called it a deliberate attack on them and turned their back on the Earth, declaring themselves an independent nation, outside of Earth control. This was only a few decades into the exodus. There was an all-out conflict."

"Another war," said O'Connor to himself, disappointed but not surprised.

"I'll have to finish that story another time. Sir Ryburn is just leaving the work-sphere, he must be finished smelting the ore."

"Right you are," said O'Connor as he reached for the door, he turned around to look over the room one last time. The room was spotless; his earlier self certainly was ungrateful to not notice it later.

He jogged the short distance to the work-sphere. He was all alone on this side of the station now, so didn't need to worry about running into any of the crew. The smell of chemicals and burning hung heavy in the air. The elusive trolley was parked next to the smelt, in the centre of the room, exactly where it always should have been. Not wanting to celebrate until he was certain, he walked over to it and lifted the hatch on the top. He let out sigh of relief, the trolley was full to the top with the rocks.

"I've got them," he said victoriously into his com.

"Good form," said Doyle "but you had better get a move on; your second has just entered the station and he will be heading directly to your location."

"And he will find the room empty, just as I did," said O'Connor, as he tipped the trolley up on its back wheels and spun it around toward the door. The trolley was much heavier than he had expected the weight of a successful retrieval to be.

"Yes yes. But you really need to move," said Doyle. She sounded edgy.

"No I don't," said O'Connor, "I never saw a future me when I was him, so he won't see me now."

"Yes, very good, but I don't want any complications, just stay hidden and get it back over here as soon as you can."

"Okay, radio silence until I call you," said O'Connor.

"Starting now," Doyle responded.

O'Connor pushed the trolley back along the corridor toward the sleeping quarters, as his earlier self was heading toward him. He was going to dump the trolley in Ryburn's old room and use one of his crates to transport the rocks, which would explain the empty trolley left in the room, he would then take the ore over to the King John.

He opened the door to Ryburn's room and pushed the trolley inside, not noticing who was laying back, hands behind his head, feet up, and stretched out on the bed. He gently closed the door just in time to see the shadow of his second self dart past at the top of the walkway, heading to the smelt. He laughed at the thought of the disappointment his past self was about to experience. The sound of someone clearing their throat behind him made him turn around.

"I'm that complication your Doyle was hoping to avoid," said another O'Connor.

CHAPTER 17:

ABOUT THAT ORE

"HELLO," SAID THE new O'Connor sitting up to the edge of the bed. "Nice to meet you, I'm Fourth." He extended his hand.

"Third," said O'Connor, taking Fourth's hand and shaking it nervously. Why was his future self here waiting for him?

"Yes I know," said Fourth. "Don't worry, we aren't going to implode because we're in the same place at the same time."

"How do you know?" said O'Connor, thinking about the paradox of the same object at different points of its timeline occupying the same space at the same time.

"I've done this before," said Fourth, with a roguish grin.

"What is happening? Why are you here?" asked O'Connor. Fourth got to his feet and reached over, taking the crate and emptying the contents all over the floor, making the exact mess O'Connor recognised from earlier.

"We were never allowed to bring this much on board," muttered Fourth "yet the old crew had space for all this junk. Does that seem fair to you?"

"You know my answer to that," said O'Connor, wondering if this was some type of game he didn't understand.

"Yes I do… and I knew you were going to say that," said Fourth, his grin not faltering as he lifted the lid on the trolley and began to unload the rocks into the freshly emptied crate.

"What are you doing?" said O'Connor, grabbing him by the wrist, "we need those."

"Really? That's how you're going to be?"

O'Connor released his arm and let him continue with filling the crate, unsure what was happening.

"What are you here for?" O'Connor asked, thinking it best to cut right to the point.

"Cutting right to the point, I like that about you," said Fourth, "but your sense of humour sucks." O'Connor did not find hearing his own thoughts said back to him very amusing.

"You know what I know, because you've been me, but I'm not you yet so don't know what you know," O'Connor stated.

"Correct, I've been you, and I know what happens next," said Fourth.

"So you must know that I am wondering what the hell you want right now?"

"I want to help you to get this ore off the station," said Fourth, still transferring the rocks to the crate.

"But why?" asked O'Connor.

"Because I had help from me when I was you; it's Doyle's Law," said Fourth.

That was enough for O'Connor, who nodded his head and began to help with the rocks; you can't argue with the law.

"We have an emergency!" Ryburn's voice suddenly sounded through both their wrist coms. It made O'Connor jump, but Fourth merely raised a finger to halt him.

"What is it?" said Fourth, his voice echoing through O'Connor's com. He quickly put his other hand over the speakers and dialled the volume down to stop the infinite echo.

"We've got another proximity alert outside the station," said Ryburn.

"It's just another sensor glitch," said Fourth. "I was… I am outside the station now, checking for damage, remember?"

"Yes, quite right. My apologies O'Connor, of course you are, that would explain it."

"Chief, stay clear of airlock-B, I'm not sure it's safe, maybe that impact has made it worse," said Benson as he joined the conversation.

"I told him not to bother investigating that airlock," whispered O'Connor to his future self.

"So did I," Fourth whispered back, referring of course to the same conversation. "Yes, will do," he said into the com. "O'Connor out."

"He only checked that airlock because you told him to," said Fourth. "That was a stupid thing to do."

"You did it first," O'Connor snapped back.

"That would have been funny if I didn't know you were going to say it," retorted Fourth. "And it was much funnier when I said it."

They had placed the last of the rocks into the crate and, in unison; both flipped the lids down and pulled the locking levers into place, sealing the crate.

"Right then, you going to get your end?" said O'Connor, reaching for the front handles, leaving the back end to Fourth.

"No, we're going to use this," said Fourth, pulling a banana shaped grip handle out of his inside jacket pocket. He tipped the crate up just enough so there was air underneath it, then from the grip pulled out a thin cable and looped it underneath the crate before reattaching it to the grip. He placed his hand back on the grip and the cables snapped tight around the crate.

"How does it work?" asked O'Connor.

"Radcliffe will explain it," said Fourth, with his hand still in the grip. The entire crate floated effortlessly off the ground. "We need to hurry."

"So, it makes it hover?"

"No, it makes it weightless." Fourth demonstrated by lifting it out at arm's length and moving it around. "One of the many applications of Ryburn's work, but there is one drawback..." he said leaving it as a question for O'Connor to answer.

"That smell!" said O'Connor recognising that mysterious cold metallic odour. His mind was racing with the implications of that discovery.

"Doyle, I'm heading to the airlock with the ore," said Fourth into his com.

"Good form," Doyle replied, "Andy will be standing by ready with the tether."

"Your Doyle," said Fourth, answering the question that O'Connor was forming regarding which Doyle he had just called.

O'Connor got the door and Fourth carried the crate effortlessly out behind him.

"I don't know why it smells," said Fourth once again answering O'Connor's unstated question. "Probably a question for Ryburn," he added as he used his free arm to close the door behind them.

"Airlock-B," said Fourth as O'Connor reached the corridor, again circumventing the question that had barely formed inside O'Connor head.

"Yes it is," said Fourth, just as O'Connor was about to speak.

"That's annoying," said O'Connor.

After a brief pause, Fourth spoke again. "Go on ask, I won't answer until you ask."

So O'Connor asked what he was thinking. "You have already done all this, that must mess with your head a bit."

"Yes, but not in the way you are thinking… it is rather monotonous actually. You see, that word monotonous, I'd never have said that except that I heard me say it when I was you," said Fourth.

"So you remember everything that was said and you have to repeat it?" O'Connor asked.

"Not *have* to. I don't remember it all word for word, but I'm pretty sure I'm getting it right."

"What if you don't, though? What if you say something you didn't say before?" asked O'Connor.

"I didn't think of that; how about you try it when you are me?" said Fourth sarcastically.

O'Connor was still not amused; he turned to look at his future self to tell him what he thought but was met with a shake of his head.

"That's not very polite. I'll tell you though anyway: it's like a constant state of déjà vu," said Fourth, deadly serious this time. "You know the feeling?"

O'Connor nodded

"Well it's like that, but the haunting feeling doesn't go away. You look at your past self and you see an empty shell. You know his thoughts and his words because you were him and know that he's stuck on a course and can't deviate from what you know he will say and do." The colour left Fourth's face making him look pale and tired. "But you remember being him and you remember looking in awe at the man in front of you, and you remember the words he spoke."

"Doesn't sound so bad," said O'Connor, but his future self continued.

"And then before you know it you *are* him, that amazing you who knew your future. But it's not right, you hear the words coming from your mouth, but they aren't your words they are still his... and now it is you who is on the course and cannot falter. You've seen him walk this path before and now you can't get off it either... and that chills me to the bone."

"Wow," said O'Connor feeling his skin prickle with goose bumps then seeing the same on his counterpart. "That's pretty deep."

"Yeah, but are they my words, or did I just repeat what I heard me say when I was you? Let's move on," he said, pointing along the corridor.

Fourth O'Connor walked with confidence, O'Connor however was uncertain until his future self told him that they would not bump into anyone. The unlikely duo finally arrived at the airlock preparation area where Fourth placed the crate into the airlock and released it from his magnetic grip before returning the tool to his pocket.

"Won't I be needing that?" asked O'Connor as the device was being tucked away.

"I thought that too, obviously, but if I give it to you, that would mean you give it your past self, and so on and so."

"So…"

"So, that would mean I wouldn't have it anymore and I think I still need it."

O'Connor played that logical loop around in his head. It made sense; the device would be stuck in a time loop with no start or end point, forever being passed between different O'Connors.

"This is where I tell you the new access code and Benson's fail safe for the airlocks," said Fourth, breaking the silence and once again answering the question that was just formulating in O'Connor's head about being told something useful. "You know Benson has just changed them, or is about to change them?"

"That would be good," said O'Connor, knowing that he would certainly be needing those codes.

"Gamma gamma twenty three, then delta gamma sixty three," said Fourth. O'Connor repeated the sequence several times until it was committed to memory.

"When does Benson tell me that?" asked O'Connor, once he had it memorised.

"He doesn't."

"Okay, so where do I find it?" asked a confused O'Connor.

"Why would you go looking for something you already know?" Fourth answered as if he was reading from a script, which in a way he was, sounding as emotionally flat as Radcliffe.

"So where did it come from?" asked O'Connor.

"My future self told me."

Once the statement had sunk in and O'Connor fully understood what he was being told, Fourth once again intercepted his thoughts.

"I didn't like it when I was you and you won't like it any better when you're me, but it is what it is. Time travel can mess things up a bit. You know it because I told you, and you will pass it on when this time comes around again. I don't know where it came from."

"But you just used the opposite of that argument as a reason to not give me that lifter thing," said O'Connor, even more confused.

"I don't make the rules here," was the only explanation Fourth offered.

"This time travel is creepy," said O'Connor, trying hard not to think about it too much. He was now in possession of a piece of knowledge that paradoxically came from nowhere, he had the airlock code that had halted his second self.

"Anything else you can share?" O'Connor asked as they reached the airlock.

"Yes, actually there is," said Fourth, answering the question too quick for comfort. He picked up the suit that had been left on the floor by the first O'Connor when he had re-entered the station after investigating for external damage. "Grab yourself a suit."

O'Connor opened the overstocked cupboard and pulled out a suit for himself. It had been the accumulation of his past selves who were to blame for the mess. There should never have been this many space suits here.

"That's the suit we wore when McSweeney killed us," said Fourth without even looking.

"Really? I think I'll choose another then," said O'Connor.

"Pick which ever one you like, it doesn't matter. Because you will choose the same one I did…" he was sounding frustrated, "but that one has Ryburn's memory card tucked into the inner compartment."

"I doubt it," said O'Connor, checking the insides.

"Front right," said Fourth, again without even looking.

Sure enough, it was there.

"No, I broke this," he said, pointing it accusingly at his future self.

"True, but it hasn't happened to it *yet*," said Fourth.

O'Connor rotated the card around within his fingers, reading the words "New ventures" stamped on it. The last time he had seen the memory card was when he had snapped it. There was no reason for it to be hidden in the space suit. Ryburn never used the space suits. Why was it here? He had broken this very same card so it could not have been stashed in the suit later. No, there were two cards. Ryburn had another card, but he said it had to be fake. Or something like that, he wasn't quite sure what was said, very little of those last couple of hours made any sense.

"There was only ever the one," said Fourth, intercepting the thought.

"But I saw two, definitely two." O'Connor was 100% certain.

"You saw the same card twice," said Fourth, "and I will be needing it," he added, extending his hand.

"But what for, can you tell me that?" asked O'Connor, desperate to get just a little more information out of his future self.

"Honestly I don't know," Fourth O'Connor answered, "but I gave it to my future self when I was you so I know it has to happen."

"But what if I don't?" asked O'Connor.

"But you will, because I did."

"But if I keep it, I will still have it when I am you," said O'Connor trying to help his future self see that the loop could be broken.

"I don't have it, because I gave it to my future self," said Fourth.

"But this could be enough to prove we can change things?" pressed O'Connor.

"Please, *this is* our chance," said Fourth, "will you not just hand it to me?"

"No I'm going to..." O'Connor started but it was too late; Fourth has snatched it out of his hand and already had it in his top pocket before O'Connor realised what had happened.

"We could have done that differently," said Fourth, sounding disappointed. "I tried to get you to hand it over, which would have been different, but it happened the way it always did. Nothing changed."

"Fine," said O'Connor, admitting defeat. The thought crossed his mind to try to snatch it back or take it by force but what would be the point? How could he possibly beat a man who knew exactly what he was going to do, especially when that man was himself?

"Exactly!" said Fourth.

"Anyway I thought you were going to tell me something," said O'Connor

"I did, you just haven't realised it yet," said Fourth.

They helped each other into their space suits. As O'Connor pulled out two pairs of boots, Fourth took down two tanks from the shelf.

"I'm not having that one," said O'Connor pointing to the patched tank, like it was an abomination.

Fourth smiled. "One of us has to take it."

"Bollocks to that," said O'Connor, picking up the tank that was already on the floor, where his first self had dumped it.

Fourth sighed. "That one has no air left."

"It has plenty," said O'Connor, more than enough to get back to King John anyway. He started connecting it. "And besides, it has to have enough air left otherwise…"

"Yes, Yes, Doyle's Law. I wouldn't be here. This isn't going to play out the way you think it will," warned Fourth, as he attached his own tank to his suit.

"Yes it will," said O'Connor, so sure of himself he grabbed the patched tank.

"Really, you think it will work?" said Fourth.

"If I destroy it, it can't keep coming back, can it?" said O'Connor and he dropped it on the ground and using his big heavy boots, brought his foot down hard on the tank repeatedly, giving it a really hard stomping. Eventually the external coating gave way and the patch split, rendering the tank useless.

"It won't matter," said Fourth. "Don't forgot the connectors," he added sarcastically pointing a finger at the top edge of the tank. O'Connor smashed those beyond repair as well, before sitting back down. He looked over at his future self on the opposite bench. He looked blank and emotionless.

"What?" O'Connor asked.

"You will answer that question yourself when you are me," said Fourth. "You feel better now, I did when I was you, so at least that is something. But by the time you are sitting here it will be hollow."

O'Connor had a lot of built-up anger and that was an unexpected opportunity to release it. That patched air tank had become a symbol of the situation he had found himself in, stuck out of time. He wasn't exactly sure when that symbol had stopped being McSweeney, but giving the tank a good kicking felt just as good as when he had punched McSweeney at the bottom of the ladder that first time.

Fourth gave O'Connor the settings for his com, so they could talk once they were outside the station.

"Use the new code and confirmation," said Fourth, his voice coming in loud and clear into O'Connor's helmet, just as the words "Access Denied" flashed up on the small display above the key pad.

"He changed them already?" muttered O'Connor, disconcerted by hearing his own voice spoken back to him.

The reflective visor on the helmets completely hid the face of his future self. This time the panel said "Access Granted". He was now free to evacuate the air and open the external door.

They both pulled themselves out onto the external hull of the station, carefully bringing the crate and busted air tank with them. The two items, being completely weightless meant that they required an effort to ensure that they didn't float out of reach. O'Connor didn't want to lose grip of the tank, he wanted to be 100% certain that when he threw it away there would be absolutely no chance of it coming back to haunt him further.

"O'Connor, can you hear me?" It was Anderson, speaking to him from the King John.

"I can hear you Anderson," O'Connor answered. "I've got the ore, I've got just one thing to do."

"Who's that with you?" asked Anderson, obviously watching

him on some visual feed.

"That's my future self, he's come to help," said O'Connor, gesturing a would-be introduction to the other O'Connor.

"Of course it is," said Anderson, not sounding anywhere near as impressed as O'Connor was expecting him to be. "We've got a situation and we have to leave *now*. Just you, the other you is on his own."

"Leave?" O'Connor questioned "What's happened?"

He was beginning to worry now. He turned to face his future self. "What is going on, has something happened?"

"Yes, but it will be over soon," Fourth answered, not very helpfully.

"What will be over?" O'Connor asked, but was cut off by Anderson's voice.

"Are you ready?"

"I've got just one thing to do," said O'Connor. He cocked his arm back into his best discus position and let that patched tank fly with all his might, sending it hurtling toward the planet below. He watched for a second or two as it sped away getting smaller and smaller until it was indistinguishable from clouds of Venus.

"Will it be different now?" O'Connor asked his future self "Now that it is gone?" There was no way that tank could be retrieved now. There was no way it could get back onto the station for his original self to take over to the King John to be re-patched and reused.

"I'm afraid not. I did that and it is all the same," responded Fourth, but he didn't sound happy about it.

"But how can our past or future self use this tank now it's gone?" asked O'Connor desperately. He was sure he was right; it had to be gone forever.

"It's time," said Fourth.

O'Connor turned in time to see the small shape of the tether coming towards him from the nothingness.

"But it's gone," O'Connor repeated. "How can it come back?"

"Remember what I said about Ryburn's card."

"That I'll need it when I'm you?" asked O'Connor seeking clarification.

"Not that, there was only ever one and you saw it twice… you saw it in the wrong order."

"What do you mean?" demanded O'Connor.

"I'll leave that one for you to find out," replied Fourth. He had done all this before so he must know he wasn't being understood, which meant he was being deliberately unhelpful. Why would he do that to himself?

"Here comes your tether," said Fourth as the tether popped into reach as he blindly extended his arm sideways and caught the incoming cable.

"Is that all you are going to tell me?" O'Connor asked.

"I'm afraid so."

"At least I have the ore now," said O'Connor, taking the tether from his future self and attaching it to his suit; a moment later the slack slowly started to tighten.

"There is one more thing I have to do concerning the ore," he heard Fourth say.

"What about it?" said O'Connor, focusing more on preparing to be drawn back to the ship. He released the magnetic clamps of his boots as the cable drew tight.

"I need that too," said Fourth.

"What are you doing?" he screamed, feeling the crate slip from his grip as it was snatched away just as the tether tightened and had him flying through space back to the King John.

"You'd better calm down and conserve your oxygen," he heard his backstabbing future self say just as the oxygen alarm on his internal display started to flash.

He tried to slow his breathing down, to save on air but was too fucking angry. All that stuff about seeing the same thing twice, was that just to confuse him? It made no sense. He had just been double-crossed by himself, his own self! Why? He closed his eyes as he approached the ship in order to avoid the refracted light nonsense. He drew in one last breath and held it, the air was now all gone. He held that breath as the tether dragged him into the open airlock doors. He clenched his jaw to stop his body trying to reach for a breath of air that wasn't there as he waited for the gravity of the airlock to take hold. He clasped his helmet ready to get it off his head as soon as he felt any weight. He watched the door close as black spots began appearing in his vision. His chest begun to ache as he suppressed the urge to breathe but he wasn't going to die, Doyle's Law forbade it he hoped, otherwise he had just killed himself.

The gravity took hold and he had his helmet off before his feet had time to hit the ground. He breathed in deeply taking in as much of the air as his lungs could hold. That was the second time he'd had to do that. Why would his future self put him through that? As punishment? He had some serious bones to pick with him now. He started to get out of the top half of his space suit as fast as he could. His arms got a bit stuck but that just fuelled him on, shaking them around like a wild man trying to free them from the heavy suit. Finally he had his com arm free. He was still raging. The ore was in his hand, only for it to be snatched away.

"O'Connor!" he demanded, trying to call back to his future self, but silence was the only reply he got. That didn't help, O'Connor was sure his future self would know he was trying to make this call which meant that his future self was deliberately ignoring him and therefore deliberately fuelling his anger. It was an endless loop of infinite anger and deliberate silence. Silence? Where were Anderson and Doyle? He was expecting them on hand to help him out of his suit, as they had done every other time. But there was no one, not even Radcliffe.

"Hello?" He called out as he popped his head out through the inner airlock door. His black jump suit was there, folded up nicely on the changing bench.

"Doyle, Anderson, are you there?" he spoke into his com calling the spare unit. No answer.

He removed the rest of his space suit, but remained in his Neith issue uniform. Something wasn't right here. He took his hat from where he had tucked it into his jacket pocket and pulled in onto his head, he felt a couple of stitches pop as the rip in the fabric got a little larger. But that didn't bother him, what bothered him was why no one was there.

"Doyle, Anderson are you there?" he tried again but got nothing. He left the changing area and headed straight to the observation dome. The scent of the flowers irritated his nose as he went past one of the more densely populated stretches of corridor.

Taking the stairs three at a time he bounded up onto the dome floor. Only Radcliffe was there, standing over the desk with the spare com sitting in the middle of it.

"Radcliffe, where is everyone?" he asked.

"I cannot be certain, Mr O'Connor," Radcliffe answered in the voice which never changed pitch.

"Can't be certain? What does that mean?" O'Connor questioned, screwing his face up. He still hadn't calmed down.

"Why didn't you answer my call?" said O'Connor. The fact that Radcliffe had been standing over the com when he had tried calling just further feed his anger.

"I do not know how this device functions Mr O'Connor, besides you hadn't asked for me," Radcliffe answered in his monotone.

"What happened, what have you done to them?" demanded O'Connor, taking an aggressive step forward. *Done to them? Where had that accusation come from?*

"Miss Doyle and Mr Anderson left the room in rather a hurry," said Radcliffe. His face, devoid of all expression and emotion, offered absolutely nothing of help.

"Tell me what happened." O'Connor raised his voice and grabbed Radcliffe by the lapels, or at least he tried to. That was a mistake as before he could complete his action Radcliffe had shot both of his arms up deflecting each of O'Connor's forearms with the back of his hands, like he knew it was going to happen. The motion was causing O'Connor to stumble forwards into Radcliffe, who didn't budge an inch but instead helped O'Connor regain his balance.

"I will not be assaulted or threatened. Mr O'Connor, please refrain from such actions," said Radcliffe as he straightened O'Connor's clothing for him, even dusting his shoulders off.

"I'm sorry Radcliffe," said O'Connor, his hands felt clammy, was he nauseous? The shock of everything was certainly enough to make anyone feel ill. But he was calm now.

"That's quite all right Mr O'Connor, no harm done."

"Can you tell me what happened please?" O'Connor asked again, wanting the last few moments back.

Radcliffe nodded.

"Miss Doyle had been speaking to an image of herself on the ceiling display," he said gesturing with his right hand to the ceiling, before returning that hand to the small of his back.

"Image of herself?" said O'Connor, swinging his head around to look up. On the ceiling there was a segregated area, displaying what appeared to be the very room he was in.

"Anderson was doing the same," Radcliffe added, directing O'Connor's attention to a display on one of the benches.

O'Connor walked back and forth, looking at the displays in turn. Just to be sure it wasn't a live feed of the room he was in.

"Is anyone there?" he asked, not actually knowing whether he could be heard or not.

They can't have gone far he thought to himself.

"Has this something to do with that echo?" he asked Radcliffe.

"I'm afraid I do not know what that means Mr O'Connor," said Radcliffe, unhelpfully.

"We're moving?" O'Connor suddenly exclaimed, as he noticed the planet and station on the ceiling view were very slowly moving away. "How long have we been moving?"

"I do not know Mr O'Connor," Radcliffe responded. "I pay little attention to such things."

He may as well be a robot for all the help he is thought O'Connor. If the ship was moving it meant someone was in the flight deck and that was where he would find answers.

O'Connor reached the flight deck. At first he thought it was empty: the viewing window was completely clear, no data or information superimposed over the view of the stars. His view from the entrance archway only showed the back of the two flight pods. The screens and workstations around the sides of the pods all were all blank.

"Doyle are you in here?" he called from the door, not wanting to waste any time looking on the deck if his search was to take him elsewhere. He saw a hand flick out from the side of the pod acknowledging his presence. He walked down to find Doyle piloting the ship using the brilliant-blue orb controls.

"What's happened?" asked O'Connor.

"We're going back, Anderson how are we looking down there?" she said, speaking to Anderson who O'Connor guessed was down in the O'Connor vessel balancing the chard supply.

"We're good, levels are stable, flow is even," came Anderson's reply.

"How? I thought the calculations took hours." asked O'Connor.

"We'll discuss that in a moment," said Doyle.

"We can't go back yet. I don't have the ore," said O'Connor apprehensively before adding, "It was stolen from me."

He had expected that to have a reaction, or at the very least cause Doyle to break her unblinking concentration, but it didn't.

"Yes, we'll discuss that in a moment too," said Doyle, tipping the orb forward. "Anderson, we're on the mark."

"Mark confirmed, releasing the chard pulse," Anderson responded, going through the same process they had done before. A flash of white light caused O'Connor to shield his face from the window as the streams of chard pumped out either side of the ship to a point in front of them. The rhythmic pulsing of the white light enveloped the entire room and he couldn't see anything.

"Cutting first and firing second," said Doyle.

"Depth confirmed and chard release is all punched in," said Anderson.

Even from behind his hands O'Connor saw the drop in light intensity, but he didn't dare open his eyes yet, not until the room had gone dark again.

"Oh, O'Connor, I'm so sorry are you okay?" said Doyle "I forgot about your eyes. I didn't have a filter running." She had her hands on O'Connor cheeks checking if he was okay.

"I'm okay," said O'Connor, cautiously blinking, the white light burned into everywhere he tried to look, but it was slowly returning to normal.

"We'll get your eyes adjusted," said Doyle repeating what she's said last time he was on the flight deck. Only that time she had dialled up the visual filters to 90%.

"Why have we gone back?" O'Connor asked again. "I don't have the ore," he repeated just in case she had not heard him the first time. "It was taken from me by my future self."

"Yes I know, *my* future self told me," answered Doyle. She had her hands on his face, caressing him. His vision returned to normal and for a moment nothing else seemed to matter.

CHAPTER 18:
ENJOYING THE QUIET

THERE WAS AN air of awkwardness back in the dome and Anderson was avoiding eye contact with Doyle and O'Connor. Unfortunately he had interrupted what had looked to be the start of a tender moment between them on the flight deck. To his credit he had tried to back away before being noticed but Doyle saw him and had jumped to her feet in embarrassment. When his eyes did meet with O'Connor's they seemed to say "perfect timing you idiot".

The view on the dome looked the same to O'Connor as it had moments before and there was absolutely no indication that they had travelled anywhere. The data displays hadn't yet been initialised, though, as the computer system was in the process of restarting.

"When are we exactly?" asked O'Connor. "It looks exactly the same."

"All we know is that it is before the airlock breach," Doyle answered, offering him an affectionate smile, which he returned. "My future self transferred the complete calculation data band to us but we had no time to test to confirm the exact destination."

"With any luck we have gone back to before I walked in on

you two on the flight deck?" said Anderson, trying to make a joke and get everything back to normal and earning harsh looks in return.

"How did you know it would work?" asked O'Connor, back on the subject of the time travel.

"Because my future self said it would. Why would I lie to myself?" answered Doyle as if it were self-explanatory.

"But why are we back anyway? No one has answered that yet," said O'Connor. "I had the ore, all of it ready to go, then my future self turned up and stole it."

"I'm sure he had his reasons," said Doyle dismissively. It was important to O'Connor however, and he wanted it explained.

"I'm going to need to understand those reasons, because they will need to be my reasons when the time comes, or I swear I won't repeat them."

Doyle sighed. "It was a bad idea, doomed to failure. I knew it from the start and I was trying to force their hand into helping us."

"Who? Our future selves?" asked O'Connor.

"Yes, it was a mistake. We don't have the right equipment on board to analyse the rocks anyway."

"So why were we trying to bring them back?"

"I was hoping our future selves would have thought of something," said Doyle with a suggestion of arrogance to her words. "I'm sorry, I got desperate. We need those rocks back in our time so badly that I thought if we just got hold of them everything would somehow work out okay. I thought our future selves would help… and I guess they did, just not in the way I had hoped."

"So, you were wrong?" said Anderson. "Come on, I need to hear this."

"That's what I'm hearing too," said O'Connor.

"I wasn't wrong; I changed my mind."

She laughed as she realised that neither of them were upset.

"You mean your future self changed your mind for you?" said O'Connor.

"It still counts. It was still me," joked Doyle.

"So when exactly are we now?" asked Anderson.

"We won't know for certain until the system has restarted, but we do know where the past versions of us will be," said Doyle pointing to the three spots in space where they would be when the times came. "My future self told me that it was early enough for us to start again without compromising the trip back to our time," adding under her breath "… too much."

"Can we get the communicator and tracking information up before the whole system restarts, or do we have to wait?" said an impatient O'Connor. What the rest of the universe was doing seemed to be of little relevance.

Anderson looked to Doyle for permission, and when she nodded brought up the information on the ceiling. However, there was no information being displayed. He tried the controls again but the ceiling still showed no lights or blips.

"What does this mean?" asked O'Connor.

"I don't know," said a worried and confused Anderson as he began pushing icons on the display, and looking back to the ceiling. "Maybe something's gone wrong." After a short pause added as if trying to justify his failure to get it working, he continued. "It's not designed to be turned on and off so much."

Typically, Doyle was not worried at all. "It's fine. We're early, remember. None of the tracking is in place yet."

"Yes," O'Connor said, feeling a moment of relief, "that would make sense, I saw my future self on the station when I was my second self; he was already there waiting. If we want to avoid the need to go back again, I think we're going to need to start crossing things off the list of shit we know will happen."

Anderson looked confused.

"Good form, that's what my fourth self said too," said Doyle as she nodded her agreement. "I'd thought it was her idea, but maybe it was yours in the first place."

"Why do we need to do this?" asked Anderson.

"Everything that happened has to happen," said O'Connor,

but not answering the question to Anderson's satisfaction. He was still wearing his confused look.

"If we don't do everything this time, and we know that it has to happen, what version of ourselves will?" Doyle answered. "And besides I asked my future self and she said they hadn't seen anything to indicate that there would be any more future versions of us."

"What if she was lying?" asked O'Connor, the deception of his future self still raw.

"We can't go back again!" said Anderson firmly. "We can open up one more wormhole and what's left after that we will need to get as close to our time as possible. That's it, there isn't enough chard. Otherwise we'll be getting back to our time the long way!"

The silence hung heavy in the air, Doyle and O'Connor weren't disagreeing, Anderson spoke the truth.

"So we do everything this time," Doyle added, getting back to O'Connor's point, to which Anderson nodded his understanding.

"So..." said O'Connor slowly, whilst he put the list together in his head, "I need to plant the tracker on the ore trolley, plant the tracker on my original self, stop my second self from attacking McSweeney, then steal the ore from my third self and put it back in the work-sphere."

"You've become quite a nuisance to yourself haven't you?" said Anderson.

"It appears so," said O'Connor, realising that he had been chasing the shadow of his future self all along. "What about your double beacon echo thing?" he asked. He had his list, and they needed to be sure they had theirs too.

"That's taken care of, that is when we make contact with our thirds and, well, and we end up here."

When the computer system completed its restart Doyle was able to pinpoint their exact time which she then confirmed by adding the white wire frame of their first selves on the far side of the station from their current position.

"Just as I thought, our seconds and thirds haven't arrived

yet," said Doyle after checking the data from the control area. The control icons were always changing colour and shape and O'Connor didn't have the slightest idea what they meant.

"We'd better get a move on because they will be arriving very soon, and you need to be over there before them," she said, turning to give O'Connor his orders.

"We need to change the coms again; our thirds will be selecting these frequency codes," said O'Connor as he flipped open the panel on his and made the changes, he knew exactly which settings to pick because he had used them to talk to his future self already. He gritted his teeth as he made the change, still pissed off at his future self. The way he was completely fooled would have made even McSweeney proud.

Anderson attempted to make the changes to the spare. "Hello, hello," he said after he had changed the settings, nothing came through O'Connor's end.

"Stop, stop," said O'Connor, "what have you done, idiot?"

O'Connor walked over to correct whatever mistake Anderson had made, finding it amusing that with all the fancy technology around them Anderson struggled with a basic communicator device. "Let's take a look," said O'Connor in the most patronising voice he could manage. Anderson offered up the coms to him. Looking over the new setting that had been applied O'Connor saw what the problem was. Anderson however, wasn't paying enough attention.

"You've changed the ID, that's fine. But you've gone and called the original spare communicator," said O'Connor "this one, but when it was still in the cupboard back on the station… oh," he said, cutting himself off mid-sentence letting out a long breath, an involuntary reaction to what he'd just realised.

"What is it?" said Doyle.

"When I first got the com, my second self, I turned it on and it had a recorded message."

"What did it say?" asked Anderson.

"It was just me calling you an idiot," he said. "I didn't think anything of it at the time."

"How?" said Anderson, not getting the significance.

"It was you, you fool," said Doyle, "not paying attention again, not making the changes correctly."

"It's fine," said O'Connor, knowing it wouldn't make much of a difference. "We just need to change it to another setting, because I'm going to try to call it back and it's going to fail." He made sure that the settings were now completely different ensuring that his second self would get the "non-existent source" error that he remembered getting. "Right, that's one thing off my list."

After the new settings had been applied O'Connor was able to test both his and the spare coms without any problem.

"If you need to call me," he said to Anderson, "you select this option." He made sure that Doyle saw too, before adding, "I've moved all the old settings away to a sub directory."

That was to prevent any further mistakes from Anderson, although there shouldn't be. O'Connor would have remembered them if there were.

"I'll need the tracking tags," said O'Connor. Doyle handed them over and O'Connor tucked them into his pocket.

"My fourth self had a magnetic lifting device," said O'Connor. "I'm going to be needing it."

The looks he received didn't fill him with much confidence.

"What do you mean by a magnetic lifting device?" asked Anderson.

"Exactly what I said, it is an application of Ryburn's work apparently," said O'Connor, quoting his future self.

"We don't have anything like that," said Doyle, the balance of her expression tipping to be more of worry than confusion. "All such things were made illegal when the Dynasty recalled all Mercurian metal."

"But you must have," said O'Connor, "otherwise how would I have it later?"

"What does it look like? Maybe we don't know we have it," said Anderson.

"It had a curved handle, like a banana," said O'Connor before realising they probably did not know what bananas were. He used his hands to give them the dimensions. But they both still looked stumped.

"How did it work?" asked Doyle.

"I don't know."

"You didn't show yourself?" asked Anderson.

"No, I asked though."

"And what did your future self say?" asked Doyle.

"He said to ask Radcliffe," said O'Connor, before realising that must have been a clue, why not just tell himself though?

"Radcliffe," called Doyle, loud enough for her voice to carry over to the spot by the stairs where Radcliffe stood. "Do you know of any magnetic lifting device on board, about this big?"

"Yes, Miss Doyle. The previous owner of the King John had such a device," said Radcliffe.

"Good form, Radcliffe!" said Doyle. "Could you please fetch it for Chief O'Connor?"

"I believe such devices are outlawed, Miss Doyle," Radcliffe replied. "I am obligated to turn it over to the authorities at my earliest convenience. The previous owner had a special dispensation for the device, which I no longer think is valid and I cannot be part of any illegal activities."

"Quite right," said Doyle, "I understand. Can you please take Anderson to its location?"

Radcliffe nodded, that didn't seem to be a breach of any programmed behaviour limitation of the indent.

"Meet us at the airlock, Andy," Doyle said.

Doyle and O'Connor headed to the airlock where O'Connor began to climb back into his suit, but stopped short at his empty oxygen tank.

"It's no good," said Doyle after comparing the valves on the tank to their refilling system. "These are not compatible."

"Can I use one of yours?" asked O'Connor pointing to the nice shiny futuristic suits and tanks.

"Not without one of these I'm afraid," said Doyle, pointing to her wrist implant. O'Connor didn't bother to ask why or even how, he just accepted it, disappointed.

"What about the emergency refill canisters?" suggested O'Connor.

"It's worth a try" said Doyle, opening one of the cupboards to remove one of the grey canisters. She removed the protective casing on the sharper end and handed the canister to O'Connor. O'Connor took careful aim, lining the canister up against its target point on the tank a few times before stabbing it down onto the tank. It just bounced off. He tried again, but all it did was put a scratch along the casing; it didn't even make a dent. He tried again, harder this time but the result was the same, all he was doing was messing up the paint work. He tried again, with all his strength he slammed down onto the tank but it was the canister that buckled and bent. The tank's integrity, apart from the cosmetic damage, was untouched.

"Our tanks are lighter weight, the casing isn't as thick," said Doyle, after it became obvious that this was not going to work.

O'Connor gently ran his fingers along the scratches on the tank. Tracing each one back from the centre. He took a deep breath in, and let out a heavy sigh. He had so wanted to get rid of this tank. But here it was, the scratched up paint was the giveaway, but last time they were half covered up by the patch. It was the same tank, but before the patch.

"We will have to cut a hole, fill it, then patch it," said Doyle as if on cue. O'Connor's head dropped even further as he knew what was coming.

"Andy," spoke Doyle into her own communicator, "how are you getting on with that lifter?"

"We're bringing it back now," Anderson replied.

"Excellent. Listen, we need to patch O'Connor's tank again. Can you please have Radcliffe bring up everything he needs for that? Oh, and a large drill piece too."

"No problem, we'll be there soon," said Anderson.

"Hey, do you think this is..." Doyle started but was immediately interrupted.

"Yes," said O'Connor, shaking his head, part exhaustion, part submission, "yes I do. It's the same one."

Doyle had pieced it together too.

It wasn't long before Anderson and Radcliffe arrived. Anderson had the lifting device in his hand. He was looking it over with intrigue as he had never seen one before either. Radcliffe trotted along behind him, carrying a box containing the tools he would need to fix the tank.

"Good form," said Doyle, motioning Radcliffe to put the box down. She showed him the tank and explained where the hole needed to be.

"Quite a coincidence that Andy was able to puncture it exactly don't you think?" O'Connor said sarcastically.

"It needs to be in the exact same place as the hole in the other tank," she explained to Radcliffe, who nodded and took out the drill to begin. O'Connor watched him work. It wasn't a drill as he knew one; it was very quiet with nothing so crude as metal scratching its way through metal by rotating thousands of times per second. This device melted its way through the casing leaving a disc-shaped hole.

"How close does it look to the tank you patched for O'Connor earlier?" asked Doyle shooting O'Connor a smile.

"I would say it is exactly the same," said Radcliffe blankly. O'Connor wondered if there was even a hint of emotion or even understanding buried somewhere behind the blank expression Radcliffe always wore. If there was, it certainly never showed.

"Can you cut a patch the same size as the one you removed?" said Doyle. O'Connor guessed that even if she hadn't instructed it, the patch would have ended up the same size anyway.

"Certainly Miss Doyle."

"Does he even know what is happening?" O'Connor asked, still somewhat puzzled by the young man, the indent process was completely alien to him. The idea of having him do everything without question still seemed unnatural.

"Indents don't care," said Anderson.

"It wouldn't even be entering his thoughts," Doyle continued.

"If he even has thoughts," said Anderson, rather rudely.

O'Connor looked to Radcliffe for some type of reaction, but there was nothing; he just went on cutting a small piece of the patching material from the stock.

Doyle fitted a temporary valve over the hole and emptied the canister through it into the tank. It was a snug fit. When it was empty, Doyle unscrewed the canister from the valve and Radcliffe pressed on the patch. Doyle turned the tank around to show off the handiwork. It looked exactly the same as the tank O'Connor had originally… probably because it *was* the same tank.

"Hey, do you think that this tank is..." Anderson started but was interrupted by both Doyle and O'Connor. "Yes," they said in unison.

"That would explain why I punched through an existing patch and flush into the hole," said Anderson.

"That's how we knew where to put it," O'Connor said. "We cut where you hit, and you hit where we cut… a never ending loop."

"Oh…so that's why there was already a patch over a hole, and why the patch was only a day old," said Anderson as everything slotted into place.

"And it's why I kept seeing it at different ends of the station," grunted O'Connor.

"This tank was always going back," said Doyle, and there was a sense of inevitability about her words.

"And what about this lifting device?" said O'Connor, pointing to the device that was still in Anderson's hand. He had almost forgotten about that. They took turns trying to get it working, Doyle offering suggestions and Anderson getting it wrong.

"Radcliffe, do you know how to operate this tool?" asked O'Connor, remembering that his future self had told him to ask Radcliffe how it works.

"Yes," Radcliffe answered, he was back to standing now, his tool box under his arm waiting to be dismissed.

"Can you show us?" said O'Connor, in a tone that said that the request was already implied by the original question.

"I'm afraid that tool is illegal, I cannot be part of its use," came the flat reply.

"Can you *explain* how it works?" said Doyle before turning to O'Conner and Anderson and adding, "You just need to ask the right questions. "

"Yes," replied Radcliffe. "The safety button is on the base, that needs to be held down to release the cable clamps, those are released using the dial on the left, the anti-gravity is controlled using the dial on the right. The cable clamp has to be attached back onto the grip before it will operate."

O'Connor was taken aback by the swiftness of the answer.

"But that is aiding in the use of an illegal device, surely?" said O'Connor.

"Knowledge is never illegal," said Radcliffe. "Its application is what I cannot be part of. What you choose to do with the knowledge is up to you, I cannot presume to know your intentions."

"That's quite a loophole isn't it?" said O'Connor. "It's pretty obvious what we intend to do with it."

It was splitting hairs as far as he was concerned and the frustration in his voice was clear.

"If I've offended you Mr O'Connor I apologise," said Radcliffe.

"Apologise yes, but are you sorry?" asked O'Connor.

Doyle put her arm up for quiet as this looked to be escalating pretty quickly. Anderson however looked very amused.

"No am I not," replied Radcliffe, for someone who had no intention of offending anyone he was doing a pretty good job of it.

That seemed to be enough for Doyle. "Thank you Radcliffe, you can be on your way."

Radcliffe nodded and left, presumably to return the box and tools to wherever it had come from. O'Connor was staring daggers at Radcliffe's back as he walked away.

"He was doing that deliberately," said O'Connor. "I'm sure of it."

"He was just answering your questions," Doyle reassured him, "no more, no less. Think about it. All he gave you were answers. He has his own logic that he cannot deviate from. He's an indent; that's just what they are like."

"Okay fine," said O'Connor, letting it go.

Anderson was testing the device by lifting up the air tank.

"Smells a bit though doesn't it?" he said as the unique odour filled the room.

"It's caused by the way the metal is interacting with the magnetic field," explained Doyle, "they all smell like that, only when it is an engine it's all in the vacuum of space."

Her explanation fell on deaf ears, as Anderson was busy showing O'Connor how it worked, before handing it over for him to test out himself.

"Keep it away from your wrist communicator," Doyle said, handing it to his other hand. "The magnetic attraction is likely to fry your antique circuitry as it hasn't the compensator or shielding built into it."

"Because they haven't been invented yet," added Anderson, information that O'Connor could have guessed, but Anderson probably enjoyed pointing out the limitations of the archaic hardware of the day. They were all anxious to get what they hoped was the final stretch of their mission out of the way and now that everything was ready the other two helped O'Connor into the rest of his suit.

"Your hat!" said Doyle, he'd almost forgotten to take it off before putting his helmet on.

But as he grabbed it the last of the threads that were holding it together ripped. "That was my favourite hat," he said longingly, looking it up and down. It was unwearable since now half of it would be flapping about his face.

"I'm sorry," said Doyle, clearly trying not to stare at his bald head.

"We can fix that once we get back," said Anderson.

"That's okay," O'Connor said, before he realised Anderson wasn't talking about the hat.

"I kind of like it," said Doyle, running her hands over his head.

"Even so," said O'Connor as he handed Doyle the hat, "that was my favourite hat and I'll be need another one eventually. If I am to not stand out in your time as some type of freak, that is."

He put the helmet on and attached that cursed patched tank. Once the room was clear they wasted no further time getting him over to the station, which he entered via airlock-A as it was the closest. With his new access code committed to memory, he absentmindedly tried using it to unlock the external door. There was a brief moment of panic before he realised his mistake. He wondered what type of errors the use of future access codes would generate; could this of been one of the "strange" readings Benson had reported?

Entering by airlock-A killed two birds with one stone. First, it saved him the laborious space walk across the hull to the other airlock. Second, he could leave the patched tank here, ready for the original O'Connor to use later. He placed the tank carefully on the shelf, on the end, facing the wrong way. His suit however he just discarded all about the place, before pushing it all under the bench with his feet. Just as it was when his original self blamed McSweeney for the mess.

Stepping out of the airlock area he was fairly confident he had free run of the station. But he had to think hard on where everyone was, as there was no tracking information coming over from Doyle yet, apart from the update to say that their second selves had just arrived. He didn't have long before his second self would be entering airlock-B.

Benson would be working in the central sphere, Ryburn was likely in his room and McSweeney would be either asleep, in hydroponics or on his way there. O'Connor couldn't face another interaction with McSweeney; anything he said or did would likely increase the animosity between them. He had to have one "conversation" with him soon, but that would be after his second self arrived for obvious reasons.

The possibility of bumping into Ryburn or Benson was a calculated risk, nothing could really go wrong talking to them, but he would rather avoid it where possible. He took the central corridor and, as luck would have it, he crossed the entire station without seeing anyone. He turned right into the dark corridor leading toward airlock-B, knowing this stretch so well now he was able to navigate the equipment stacks without even thinking about it. A quick glance into the airlock told him that it was clean and tidy, the way it always should have been. The collection hub was just ahead. Upon arrival he tipped the trolley up on its end and attached the tracking device to the underside, just as he had seen it when he was Third.

"I've tagged the trolley," he said into his com.

"Good form," Doyle responded. "Your second self is still on their ship, you have plenty of time." Why did he cringe every time someone said time? It wasn't funny anymore.

Next on the list was to tag First, and he wasted no time getting over to the sleeping quarters. He opened the door quietly and saw his original self asleep in the bed with his jump suit folded up tidily at its foot. Taking out the second tag, he put it into the left leg pocket, being careful to fold the jumpsuit back up.

"Check," he said to himself quietly. Looking around the room he noticed that something was different. The door to the cupboard where he kept his spare clothes was closed. For O'Connor this would have been normal but he remembered being irritated by that door being open when he was Second. He pondered on that for a moment, was he to leave the door open for the sole purpose of annoying his past self? No, he would not do that, there needed to be a reason. He stepped toward the exit door, but looked back to the cupboard door. He should leave it, he knew he should as it didn't matter, but like some obsessive compulsion he knew he had to set the door ajar. He didn't bother to keep an eye on the sleeping First; he was confident that he wasn't going to wake himself up as that wasn't the type of thing he would forget. He opened the cupboard door, and as it swung open the first thing that caught his eye was his spare hat. It could not have grabbed his attention more if it had hit him in the face. His face lit up, the reason he couldn't find the hat earlier was because his future self had gotten there first. He grabbed the hat and tucked it into his jacket, closing the cupboard door behind him, he wasn't going to leave it open, perhaps he could change just this little detail. As he was leaving he took one final look around the room and as he did so the cupboard door gently swung open. There would be no victory over Doyle's Law here.

There was going to be a bit of a wait before he was to have his "talk" with McSweeney, and he certainly didn't want to bump into him early. What was the time now? His internal body clock was all messed up: in his head it was evening, but he knew it was morning on the station. He didn't need a clock to tell him that, as the station was always the same at this hour: quiet and very peaceful.

"Doyle," he said into his com, as he passed the work-sphere entrance. "I've tagged my original self and managed to get myself another hat."

"Oh, that is good news," said Doyle. "You've got a bit of a wait before we know where everyone is; your second self hasn't left the ship yet," she said.

This was an important detail, the arrival of his second self would be the cue for him to get into position for McSweeney.

"I'll just wait around here," he said as he reached the porthole window.

"O'Connor?" Ryburn called out. Rather loudly, over compensating for the sound proofing, but he was close enough for it to have no effect. O'Connor had just enough time to shut his communicator off, blocking off any sound that Doyle might be making.

"Oh, Morning Sir Jim, just taking in the morning Venus," said O'Connor with a laugh. He had just called him Sir without noticing, all those conversations with Doyle about the great humanitarian Sir James Ryburn had rubbed off. Judging by the look on Ryburn's face, the title confused him too.

"Oh yeah?" said Ryburn, leaning in very close to get a view out of the small window. O'Connor noticed Ryburn's body odour. Usually he wouldn't have, however he had been out and freshened up so his nose was no longer accustomed to it. It was all he could manage not to recoil. He fought the urge hard but unfortunately found that he had over compensated by not moving and was now awkwardly close to Ryburn. It was too much, O'Connor stepped back.

O'Connor scratched his nose, as he cleared the odour. "I'm just enjoying the quiet for a moment."

"The station is always quiet," said Ryburn.

"Not like this," O'Connor assured him. "How's that business with the hopper going?" he asked as he moved to his right, he had to get a bit of distance, but now found himself pressed right into a small corner of the alcove.

"It's still a couple of hours away. I'll give you the clearance to dismantle the hardware as soon as I can, however, I must point out to you that I am not behind on my timings."

"Oh don't worry about that stuff, I'm sure you'll get it finished in time," O'Connor replied. None of that mattered anymore. He looked down the central corridor, to be sure there was no danger of anyone else joining the conversation. It was taking too long as it was, He had hoped that this subtle hint of non-interest would be enough for Ryburn to finish up. He was wrong.

"Is everything okay?" Ryburn asked.

"I'm fine Jim, just fine."

"So what brings you to my window? I thought I was the only one who stared out into space," said Ryburn.

"This is my window, Jim. Yours is on the other side," said O'Connor, amused at the thought of Ryburn hiking all the way around the station to get to his window once his second self blew out the airlock.

"Not wearing your hat this morning?" Ryburn quizzed. What was with Ryburn this morning? Had the loneliness gotten to him and he just wanted to talk?

"Oh right, I've got it here," O'Connor answered, the simple pleasure of having his hat back and in one piece was very comforting for him. He reached into his inside pocket and took it out, pulling it over his bald head. "My favourite hat, not ripped either."

"Have you had a chance to look into the issue we spoke of earlier?"

Earlier? O'Connor thought, what day was that? For him it was four days ago. Wracking his brains, he remembered what Ryburn was talking about; it was about McSweeney.

"Yes. No, not yet, but I will have a word with McSweeney. He shouldn't be impeding your important work."

"Thank you, but he hasn't been that bad of late. I was referring to what I saw outside the station," said Ryburn.

"There isn't anything there, Jim. Wouldn't it be best if you concentrated on your work?" said O'Connor with a smile – he knew exactly what that flicker was.

"Perhaps you are right," said Ryburn.

"Look, about McSweeney," said O'Connor, "has he been moving stuff, taking things away just to be a nuisance?"

O'Connor was thinking about the rock samples that he would be taking from Third and would, if all went according to plan, be putting them back. But the timings were still not right in his head, if he does put them back, why would they still be missing when Ryburn went to refine them all? McSweeney had sworn blind that he hadn't taken them, but if his future self puts them back, why would they still be missing?

"No nothing like that, he's been..." said Ryburn.

O'Connor cut him off. "Are you *sure* nothing has gone missing lately?"

"No, he prefers just making jokes and getting in the way, he wouldn't take anything." said Ryburn, practically defending McSweeney.

"Damn it!" said O'Connor, raising a clenched fist in frustration. He was back to square one. Will the ore still be missing later because his backstabbing future self doesn't return it? Is this going to turn out to be his fault too, or McSweeney's doing?

"Has he taken something I should be aware of?" Ryburn asked.

"No, not that I'm aware of…" said O'Connor before a long and awkward silence. "But if he did think it was funny to hide something from you, where would you look first?" asked O'Connor. He had had a similar conversation before with Ryburn, but that would be later and he realised that explained why Ryburn had already "given it some thought".

"Hypothetically speaking, well…" said Ryburn as he folded his arms and leant back against the wall, "McSweeney is an attention-seeking clown, but there is nothing malicious in his pranks."

"Tell that to my past self," scoffed O'Connor under his breath.

"Everything he does is always about wasting time," said Ryburn. The choice of words made O'Connor smirk, if only Ryburn knew why.

"I would say he would hold whatever it was he had taken close by until you notice it is gone and begin looking for it. Then he would return it to the original position and remain close by to witness the fruits of his attempts at humour."

"Interesting, thanks Jim," said O'Connor, nodding, it made sense. If only he had some insight into what his future self will do with the rocks. "Where do you think I would hide them?" he asked, only half serious.

"Why? Are planning to take something of mine?

"No nothing like that, I'm just trying to figure him out, that's all," said O'Connor as he subconsciously pulled at his earlobe. It was all going to be over soon he thought one way or another, so what did it really matter? He could tell him everything? But it wouldn't change anything. He kept quiet and instead changed the subject.

"You've been here since the beginning haven't you?" O'Connor asked as he turned back to the window.

"Yes I have. It was a grander station back then, of course." Ryburn started to give a run down of the states of the station over the years but his explanation was long and O'Connor drifted in and out of listening. He instead found himself wondering if Doyle was watching him from the King John.

"It's sad it has to come to this," said O'Connor as he realised Ryburn had stopped talking, he turned and looked down the corridor to ward airlock-A and to where he was to meet McSweeney.

"All things have to come to an end," said Ryburn, turning to look in the same direction O'Connor has just glanced.

"I remember when we deployed this station, pride of the system," said Ryburn, "it was going to usher in a new era in energy harvesting the dawn of a new future"

"How right they were," said O'Connor. Ryburn was correct, the station would indeed be the future but not in the way they had intended. Ryburn began to laugh, O'Connor didn't know what was so funny but awkwardly joined in. He raised his hand and saw on his communicator that Doyle had been trying to call him.

"That's in a much better condition than mine," said Ryburn admiringly of O'Connor's com.

O'Connor smiled. "Don't let me keep you Jim," he said as he stepped aside making a hand gesture inviting Ryburn to leave, enough was enough, he had to call Doyle back.

"Right you are O'Connor, enjoy the view," and at that Ryburn left.

"And don't worry about McSweeney, Sir Jim," O'Connor called out after him. "He will leave you alone to get on with your important work."

He stood at window looking out into space until he was sure

Ryburn had gone before calling Doyle back. The future location of the ore was still troubling him.

"Doyle, sorry about that, Ryburn just appeared."

"That's quite all right, I thought something like that may be the case. Did you talk about the original design of the station perchance?" asked Doyle, her tone implied she already knew the answer.

"Yes we did actually. How could you possibly know that?" asked O'Connor since his com hadn't been transmitting.

"It's in Sir Ryburn's account of the events that day. The people wanted to know about the man who changed the world… and also the man who gave up his life for his crew."

It took O'Connor a second or two to realise she was talking about him.

"I didn't give up a thing, it was taken from me by McSweeney. What else does his account of events say?" O'Connor asked, he was interested in any clues that would help him be where he needed to be to make sure everything happened the way it should.

"Not much really; a lot of technical jargon, most of it about getting the hopper craft on the station and how you kept him motivated to complete his work. He says he couldn't have done it without you."

"Did that happen?" O'Connor asked himself thinking back to all the conversations he had had. "I guess it did."

All the interaction with Ryburn, since he first travelled back had always been keeping him on task. He found it strangely flattering to think that history would remember the point in such a light.

"He mentions the unknown decompression blowing out the airlock and entire corridor forcing them into a new orbit. He took responsibility for the lander course... that was in fact you." Doyle couldn't help but point it out. "He says the entire crew helped with preparing the station to fly back to Earth using his Mercurian metal. And finally says the last time he saw you was when he gave you the final piece of ore."

"Yes the ore, that's been bothering me still," said O'Connor. "If I put it back, which I will, why is it still lost later on? Is there anything in the account about that?"

"Hmm no, doesn't look like it. Oh no wait, there is something," answered Doyle and then paused while she read it to herself. "You processed the last of the ore into the metal, and Ryburn took it to the central sphere. Nothing more on the subject, I'm afraid."

"I don't know how to do that," said O'Connor.

"You'll have to find out, perhaps ask Sir Ryburn. Maybe he'll let you keep some," she said. Did she always have this optimistic outlook wondered O'Connor?

"If I'd have known I needed to know that I could have asked him just now. Or at any point over the last three days… one day… you know what I mean," he corrected himself. "Where's Second?" he asked, mindful that he couldn't miss the "meeting" with McSweeney but now wanting to try to catch Ryburn up. How would he construct that conversation so it didn't sound suspicious?

"He's in the airlock, on the second King John, he'll be coming over very soon," Doyle said.

"Okay, I'll try to catch Ryburn. Radio silence again please."

"Starting now," Doyle whispered back.

As he approached the ladder he could see Benson was in the mess area, looking through the meal bags. There was no sound to indicate Ryburn was there, and Benson would not leave him alone on the command deck. O'Connor wondered if he had the chance to get up the ladder to double check without being noticed, but that question was answered when Benson spoke.

"Morning Chief, bit early for you isn't it?" he said with his distinctive deep voice, O'Connor looked over to see the large man smiling at him, there was no suspicion on his face; this was before it all happened.

"What meal are we up to?"

Meal? Oh no, that stumped O'Connor, which bag should

they have been eating that morning? He couldn't remember since the days were all mixed together, plus he had had real food since then. Purple or green, green or purple, it was one of those. "Umm… I don't know."

"Why are we whispering, is everything okay, Chief?" Benson asked, his smile changing to a look of concern.

"Yeah everything's fine, just looking for Ryburn, was he here?" said O'Connor stepping back from the ladder.

"Yeah, you just missed him. Chief, you always know what meal we're up to."

O'Connor shrugged. "As you say, it's a bit early for me." It wasn't the same early that Benson had meant. "It's purple, Benson, we're back on the purple now," he guessed.

"Thanks Chief," said Benson returning the green bag to the cupboard. He gestured a second purple bag toward O'Connor, inviting him to join him for breakfast.

"No thanks, I can't eat that nasty stuff anymore," said O'Connor, actually swallowing back down the vomit taste that had come up at the thought of having anything from those disgusting bags. Never again. "I'll get mine later," he added to maintain the facade that he was "their" O'Connor.

"No wonder too. I don't usually see you for another forty minutes or so," said Benson with a laugh as he checked the time on his com.

"Speaking of up early, Mr Benson," said O'Connor, making this very serious now and knowing that the man would be needing to get some rest for the events that would be happening tomorrow. "It looks like you haven't been to bed at all. Have you been up all night again?"… Again, he shouldn't have said again.

"I'm a bit behind; I wanted to catch up. You see, I was checking that pressure door on airlock-A. I'm getting some strange readings and minor alarms from it. I went down and ran some diagnostics and cleaned up the internals. It took a bit longer than I thought it would. Sorry Chief!"

"Alarms?" O'Connor asked. This worried him; he had been

the only one using the airlocks, was it him entering the station that caused these alarms?

"I reckoned it's just another system failing, but I wanted to be sure." said Benson.

"What were the minor alarms?" O'Connor pressed.

"It's the strangest thing, Chief, they were showing an unknown code on the external door," Benson answered.

"On the external door? Well that's impossible, that's another system failing then. We'll have to ignore those minor alarms," said O'Connor although he knew that it was actually his fault for using the wrong code whilst trying to enter the station. He didn't need Benson poking around either of the airlocks. "In fact why not just disable all the airlock alarms? That'll allow you to get back to your assignment area," he said.

"Chief?"

"I'm kidding Benson, Just the minor ones of course." O'Connor quickly backtracked having over played his hand.

O'Connor had already spoken to Benson about airlock alarms, but that conversation hadn't happened for Benson yet.

"While we're talking about failing systems, we have sensor problems too, I have..."

"Yeah, you're probably seeing errors in the air pressure too," said O'Connor

"Yes exactly. McSweeney should be able to confirm the details. But the alerts are reporting pressure readings outside of acceptable error margins."

"When did these start?" asked O'Connor, feigning interest.

"First alert was this morning, I was worried it was connected to the airlock warnings so I-"

"More failures, this place is falling apart" interrupted O'Connor downplaying the concerns, genuine or not he knew they wouldn't matter.

"Okay but that isn't all, I'm concerned that Dr Ryburn's hopper is approaching too fast. If he fumbles the collection it could be catastrophic."

"I wouldn't worry about it, Ryburn knows what he's doing," said O'Connor, dismissing Benson's concerns. He was lying of course. Ryburn was going to really mess it up.

"Chief?" said Benson.

"It will all be fine Benson. You worry too much," said O'Connor.

"Yes, Chief," Benson answered as he sat down. He opened the nasty food bag and poured it into the bowl, the cloud of powder made O'Connor gag again. He could leave Benson to his meal, probably best if he left now before he threw up. He looked to his communicator, he needed to get an update on the location of his second self.

"Look, Mr Benson, there's something I need tell you," said O'Connor, this was likely the last time he would be able to speak to Benson in an uneventful manner and felt he needed to say something. "I want to thank you for all your work. You're a skilled and highly competent caretaker and a credit to any contract you serve,"

Benson all but choked.

"Sorry Chief?" he said, thumping his chest to clear his airway

"I just wanted to let you know how much I appreciate the work you do, it doesn't go unnoticed," said O'Connor. He wondered if he should offer a handshake, but decided that would be too much.

"Thanks Chief I appreciate you saying so," said Benson, then after the awkward moment had passed added "I'm your huckleberry," while raising his hand for a high five.

"You're my huckleberry," O'Connor laughed, understanding what that expression meant this time around and also that Benson would be explaining it to his past self in just a little while. He put his hand up to receive the high five and the slap Benson gave it was enough to make his communicator rattle.

"Anyway," said O'Connor adjusting his wrist com, "I need you to assist Ryburn in the work he will be doing over the next day or so if he asks for help. He's working on something very important. So forget about those faulted out minor alarms, keep up with the schedule as best you can, but assist Ryburn. Understood?" He spoke with positive enthusiasm.

"Sure thing, Chief," Benson answered.

"Thank you Mr Benson, I knew I could count on you. I'd better be heading off, I'll be back soon for my breakfast bag, so go easy on the sauce. I can't be eating it plain."

"Thanks Chief and will do," said Benson raising his spoon from his bowl gesturing a polite goodbye as O'Connor left him to his poor excuse for a meal.

As soon as he was out of earshot he called Doyle. "Benson has been sniffing around the airlocks, I'm going to disable the logging on them."

"Are you sure that is wise?" asked Doyle.

"The logging is active now, but later today it is not. It must have been me who disabled it. No one else would." He originally blamed McSweeney for it and once again he was innocent.

"Okay that plays out," Doyle agreed.

"Where is Second?" he asked, knowing it must be about time as he was already walking towards the altercation.

"Your past self is in the work-sphere now. He should be-"

Her voice was cut off by a new communication; calls to everyone took priority over individual calls. It was his second self talking.

"This is O'Connor here, look I'm having some communicator problems. Could you all please dial up your ranges to maximum?"

"All done, Chief," Benson replied almost instantly.

"Thank you Benson. O'Connor out," said Second, although the last part sounded awkward.

"That's my cue," said O'Connor and broke into a jog.

"Second has just left the work-sphere, still no McSweeney on the screen, just as before," said Doyle.

O'Connor rounded the bend and saw McSweeney bouncing along to his music, earphones in. McSweeney looked up and smiled, but the delight in his eyes disappeared as O'Connor grabbed him by the lapels and pushed him up against the wall, hitting the wall just as Second appeared in his view before quickly ducking behind the bulkhead.

"I know you can hear me, I know you are behind there and I know what you are thinking and this is our way of stopping you," said O'Connor to his second self.

"What are you doing?" said McSweeney as best he could whilst being stretched up against the wall with O'Connor's arm across his throat.

"And you, stay away from Ryburn," said O'Connor pulling out the earphones.

"I haven't been near Ryburn," said McSweeney as he tried to wriggle free.

O'Connor's temper was failing him and with his animosity the timing of all the events eluded him. He still had a lot of blame that needed to be dished out to McSweeney, who at the moment was completely innocent of all of it.

"Don't lie to me! We've put up with enough of your crap over the last day," said O'Connor, taking another grip of his coat and turning him around and up against the side of the arch, right in front of where his past self was on the other side "Didn't we?" he continued as he thumped poor McSweeney back against the wall again. "But it isn't all your fault, putting me out the airlock isn't your fault. We're to blame too." The last part was for his past self. "But you have to leave Ryburn and especially his rocks, alone".

"I don't know anything about any rocks, take your hands off me you psycho piece of…" said McSweeney but obviously thought better of it, he was in no position to make threats or give insults.

"Say it!" said O'Connor. "I dare you, push me, it will cost you. I've taken so much fee off you now that it doesn't matter." He easily held back more of McSweeney's attempts to get away.

"Right I've said my piece and I know it won't change anything, and you have what you've come for. I'm going to count back from 10 and you are going to go," said O'Connor.

"Ten" the count started.

"Go where, you..." McSweeney stopped short of saying something he shouldn't.

"Shut it! I'm not talking to you! Nine, move Jake!" and he heard the sound of nervous feet beating the floor as his past self took his cue to exit.

"Eight, seven," he slowly counted.

"What the hell was that all about?" McSweeney asked.

"Six, five, four, three, two, one." He let go of McSweeney who dropped to the floor and immediately jumped back getting himself a safe distance from O'Connor.

"I may have just saved your life," said O'Connor. "Now leave Ryburn's rocks alone."

McSweeney scampered off. O'Connor didn't like it, he hated what he had just done. Were those his words, or was he just repeating what he heard his future self say? That smile McSweeney had given him at first was so genuine. Before that incident, before that point in time, they had gotten along so well. They had never been friends but they certainly weren't enemies. But as that smile faded away from his spotty face he realised that he had put the first straw on the proverbial camel's back, and it was a pretty big straw. It played heavily on his mind as he entered the airlock to disable the logging systems. Both airlocks ran off the same basic systems, so he was able to disable everything from this one junction box. He unclipped it from the wall and punched in his access code, authorising all minor alarms and history to be ignored. It was going to be a long wait before he was able to check the next item off his list. There was plenty of time to build up more feelings of guilt about McSweeney as he went through in his head over and over again the order of the interactions he had had from McSweeney's point of view.

CHAPTER 19:

ON THAT ROAD

DOYLE HAD KEPT O'Connor up to date with all the tracking information. First had just left his sleeping quarters, Second was at airlock-B. The ore trolley was still at the collection hub waiting for Ryburn to move it. The second and third King John had just been joined by the original. Including themselves, there were now four of them lurking in the darkness like vultures.

"Don't go that way," said Doyle, as O'Connor started toward the sleeping quarters, "your first self is coming that way."

"I don't like this," said O'Connor, ducking into the entrance to the work-sphere and watching himself walk past. Even though he knew that he wasn't going to be found by his past self it was still nerve racking to see him walk past. Even more disturbing was knowing that several times he had been within spitting distance of a future version of himself. It sent a shiver down his spine just thinking about it.

"What don't you like?" asked Doyle

"I can't move anywhere, I'm feeling trapped," O'Connor replied, looking up the corridor to see his past self disappear around the curve of the corridor. "I have to come back over," he said, thinking of the airlock he'd just left.

"Not yet, you need to get the smelting instructions from Sir Ryburn"

"I can't do that now; my third self will soon be arriving and talking to him, before going to the central sphere. I can't stay here as McSweeney will be back along and I can't be anywhere near him. My first self will be all up and down here, effectively blocking off these corridors searching for his com."

"You can't leave, you won't be able to get back," said Doyle emphatically. "Too many of you will be using the airlocks; there's just too many of you here for you to be productive," said Doyle, agreeing with him finally, but making it sound like it was her point.

"Okay. I'm just going to have to wait for Third to deliver the ore to me in Ryburn's old room," said O'Connor, thinking that he could do with a lie down and it was the one place he knew he would not be disturbed.

"Good form," said Doyle, "at least then we will have one less version of ourselves to avoid."

O'Connor walked down the corridor to the sleeping quarters and opened the door to Ryburn's old room. For him it was only a couple of hours since his future self had betrayed him, and here he was about to enact the same event from the other side, he wasn't sure about this. He sat down on Ryburn's bed, infinitely more comfortable than his rock hard bunk but not a touch on his new bed on the King John.

Those new ventures guys sure had it good, he thought as he stretched out, looking around the room. So much more personal baggage was allowed compared to the single crate he brought on board. And books, actual books made of paper. How did they get away with such a blatant disregard for the conservation of weight? O'Connor stopped partway through that line of thought since none of it mattered any more. He thumbed through some of the books, admiring the myriad of subjects they covered.

"Why do I always seem to be waiting around for that damned hopper?" he joked to Doyle after he had run out of things in the room to criticise. They chatted for a while, before O'Connor finally got around to asking a serious question.

"Did Anderson lose someone?"

"Yes, during the hijacking, we lost some good people."

"I'm sorry," said O'Connor.

"They were supporting Andy when he flew in with the King John and latched onto the O'Connor."

"What happened?" O'Connor asked.

Doyle hesitated a moment. "They were outside operating the clamps…they didn't make it."

"Who were they?"

"His two closest friends. They were like family, he won't speak of it."

"I'm sure he will when he is ready," said O'Connor

"It's in the past now, nothing can be done," said Doyle.

O'Connor stopped the conversation when he heard his first self come back to his room to check for his com. It was quite a convenient way to change the subject. He could hear his original self swearing and cursing through the door. O'Connor silently smiled along but was very ashamed of his past self, he was not aware of how he sounded or acted. He had had the unique perspective of being able to see and hear himself a few times now, and he did not like what he had witnessed.

"Your third self has just left Sir Ryburn's workstation," said Doyle, adding a couple of minutes later, "He's standing by the window, I remember that."

O'Connor smiled; she had been watching him through the porthole window at that particular time. After the swearing from the O'Connor on the other side of the wall had stopped, she continued to update him on the progress of events: Ryburn was heading to the central sphere for the hopper whilst Third was already there waiting/hiding behind a spool of cabling.

"So what do we know of the next events with our future selves?" asked O'Connor.

"Andy and I were watching you on the ceiling, you had just left the work-sphere with the trolley and gotten to where you are now. We heard Sir Ryburn's call come through about his ghost on the outside, and you replied."

"That wasn't me, it was my fourth self," O'Connor answered, not wanting the ownership of that just yet.

"Then it was quiet again."

O'Connor nodded along to that. "Well I got to this room to find my fourth waiting for me... just as I am doing now. We then loaded the crate with the rocks. He then called you pretending to be me."

"What did he say to her?" asked Doyle.

"What, don't you remember?" asked O'Connor.

"I never got that call," said Doyle, "it must have been to his Doyle."

"He lied to me," O'Connor realised, although he didn't know why. "I asked and he was very clear that it was to you. The third Doyle."

"Well I got the call from my fourth, telling me it was time for the beacons to go on…" said Doyle but wasn't able to elaborate on that any further. O'Connor silenced her as he heard the first O'Connor had returned to his room; he was still cursing and still searching for his com.

"Why did you keep coming back?" Doyle whispered.

"Because I knew it had to be there," O'Connor whispered back. "How was I to know that I had taken it while I was asleep?"

The lights in the room started to flash red and the sirens started to sound. It was collision time. He heard his first self bolt out of his room, heading straight for the central sphere.

"Not long now," he said to Doyle, leaning back on the bed waiting for the sirens and lights to stop. It wasn't so dramatic for O'Connor this time around, he even found the energy to yawn and stretch out on the bed some more. The impact happened, there was the shaking, but all in all, it seemed to be over and done with a lot quicker this time around.

Doyle kept him informed as the crew left that bottom deck.

"Sir Ryburn came pretty close to you again," said Doyle at the point where his third self has been talking to her at the window.

"Yeah that's when I was talking to you about McSweeney."

"How are you feeling about that now?" Doyle asked.

"Pretty shitty to be honest with you," O'Connor answered. "When I had him against the wall, I just made it worse. That was when it all started for him. I saw it in his eyes."

"I guess so," Doyle responded in a very sombre tone. "Benson will be interrupting us soon," she said changing the subject back to what Third was doing, before giving him the run down on everyone else; McSweeney was back in the hydroponics, First had left the station for his inspection. "Your fool Second has just hit the stray lander," she added.

She loved to bring that up and O'Connor secretly enjoyed the mocking, although he would never admit it to her. They continued their banter for a while before getting serious again with the news that Third was now in the sleeping quarters.

"What are you doing in there?" Doyle asked.

"Tidying up," O'Connor answered, a little bit embarrassed.

"Why?" Doyle asked with a laugh of disbelief.

"I'd left it in a mess while looking for my com, I figured I owed it to myself and Benson not to leave it in such a state." O'Connor was only half joking: the real reason was that at that moment he was trying to get his mind off the shame he had been feeling after seeing how he had behaved towards his crew.

"Did you notice it was tidy when you were your first self?"

"No I didn't," O'Connor laughed, "I'm an ungrateful sod."

"He's left now," said Doyle, "I remember telling you to get back to the ship because we didn't want any complications."

"Right, I'll call you when we have it."

"Trolley is moving, I'll wait for your call," said Doyle, she was quite excited about this. O'Connor on the other hand was dreading it, haunted by words of his future self.

"Let's get this over with," he said to himself.

The door opened and the trolley came hurtling in. Third shut the door behind him as the shadow of Second running past blocked the light above the door.

I can't believe I didn't notice me he thought as he cleared his throat to make his presence known. "I'm that complication your Doyle was hoping to avoid. Hello, nice to meet you, I'm Fourth" he said as he sat up, extending his hand for Third to shake.

"Third," said Third as he shook his hand looking completely baffled.

"Yes I know," said O'Connor. "Don't worry, we aren't going to implode because we're in the same place at the same time," he added remembering what his third self was thinking.

"How do you know?" asked Third.

"I've done this before," said O'Connor, smiling, he remembered saying that.

"What is happening? Why are you here?" asked Third.

O'Connor ignored the question, in truth it was because he didn't want to lie to his past self. He stood up, grabbed a crate down from the top of a stack, and emptied the contents all over the floor.

"We were never allowed to bring this much on board, yet the old crew had space for all this junk. Does that seem fair to you?" he asked the question, although it was rhetorical as far as he knew his own thoughts.

"You know my answer to that," said Third, right on cue.

"Yes I do… and I knew you were going to say that," said O'Connor, this was actually quite fun, nothing like what his future self had described. He flipped the lid on the trolley and began transferring the ore.

"What are you doing? We need those," said Third grabbing his wrist and preventing him from unloading any more rocks.

"Really? That's how you're going to be?" said O'Connor.

"What are you here for?" Third repeated.

O'Connor remembered how he just wanted a straight answer. "Cutting right to the point, I like that about you," said O'Connor trying to make light of the situation with a joke, but seeing his past self very un-amused added, "but your sense of humour sucks."

"You know what I know, because you've been me, but I'm not you yet so don't know what you know," said Third.

"Correct, I've been you. And I know what happens next," answered O'Connor, he was beginning to understand what his future self had meant about the discomfort of seeing his past self repeating everything that had already been said as if he had no thoughts of his own. It was as if he were reading from a script.

"So you must know that I am wondering what the hell you want right now," demanded Third.

O'Connor could not believe how rude his past self was being to him, he knew it happened because he remembered it, but was that really how he sounded and looked? It was at that moment when the feelings of guilt about putting one over on himself all faded away. This rude, arrogant past O'Connor in front of him had this coming. "I want to help you to get this ore off the station," he said, whilst still transferring the rocks to the crate.

"But why?" asked Third.

"Because I had help from me when I was you; it's Doyle's Law," said O'Connor not needing to explain it any further.

"We have an emergency!" Ryburn's voice suddenly filled the air, causing Third to jump with surprise.

"What is it?" O'Connor said. His voice echoed back through Third's com and he slapped his hand over his speaker to stop the echo, before turning the volume off.

"We've got another proximity alert outside the station," said Ryburn.

"It's just another sensor glitch," said O'Connor. "I was… I am outside the station now, checking for damage, remember?"

"Yes, quite right. My apologies O'Connor, of course you are, that would explain it." said Ryburn.

"Chief, stay clear of airlock-B," Benson said, his voice coming through. "I'm not sure it's safe, maybe that impact has made it worse."

"I told him not to bother investigating that airlock," whispered Third.

"So did I," said O'Connor with a patronising nod of his head before speaking back into the wrist com, "Yes, will do. O'Connor out"

"He only checked that airlock because you told him too," said O'Connor. "That was a stupid thing to do."

"You did it first," Third snapped back.

"That would have been funny if I didn't know you were going to say it. And it was much funnier when I said it," said O'Connor, who remembered this whole conversation. Were they even his words he was speaking anymore?

"Right then, you going to get your end?" said Third reaching for the front end of the crate as they closed the lid.

"No, we're going to use this," said O'Connor, pulling the lifting device from his jacket.

"How does it work?" asked Third, in a demanding tone that grated on O'Connor's ears.

"Radcliffe will explain it," said O'Connor. He knew it was an unhelpful answer, but knowing it would be enough. Was that really the reason for the short answer, or was it because that was the only answer he had been given? Was that a distinction without a difference? He didn't like this feeling, he was stuck on that road just as his future self warned. He was his future self now; it was chilling.

"We need to hurry," said O'Connor as he picked up the now weightless crate. It felt awkward in his left hand, but he was keeping it away from the com, just as Doyle had warned.

"It makes it hover," said Third in amazement.

"No," said O'Connor correcting him, adding "it makes it weightless." He swung the crate around the room. "One of the many applications of Ryburn's work, but there is one drawback," he added remembering what was coming next in the conversation.

"That smell!" said Third.

"Doyle, I'm heading to the airlock with the ore," O'Connor said, making the call that would set his betrayal in motion.

Back on the King John, Doyle had brought Anderson up to speed with the new information and the plan. In turn Anderson explained what he remembered from his role in the situation.

"Good form," she replied when the call from O'Connor finally came through. "Andy will be standing by with the tether ready." She was standing with her hands flat on the bench, one either side of the wrist com.

She took a deep breath, "Andy how do you change the call on this thing."

"Oh it's easy," said Anderson, with a delusional sense of confidence.

"If you could please set this up so I can call our past selves," she asked, she thought she would know how to do it, how hard could it be? The tech was hundreds of years old. Nevertheless, she did not. It turned out that O'Connor had set it for them each time and it was too late to call him back to ask for instructions. Anderson flipped the lid up on the side panel and made the adjustments. "Anderson, we need your beacon open," was all he got out before Doyle grabbed the com away from him and killed the call.

"I make the call," she snapped. "Do you remember getting a call from yourself? No you don't." She looked at the settings.

"Anderson please repeat that," came O'Connor's voice.

"Which O'Connor is that?" Anderson whispered.

"I'm sorry O'Connor. Please ignore Andy, he called you in error, call us back on the other setting." she clicked the button to end the call. "That was the second O'Connor…and that was the call he said he got from us that we never made." She wasn't happy. Anderson just looked away in shame, both of them wishing he had paid closer attention when O'Connor was showing him how it worked.

"Doyle, this is Doyle we have a situation over here," she said, after correctly calling their third selves.

"I'd been expecting you, are you the fourth?" Third Doyle answered.

Doyle shot Anderson a glance to get the message across that *this* was how it was done.

"We're the fourth," Doyle said, "and I know you were expecting our call. But this isn't going to go the way you think."

"Oh? You are calling to tell us it is time for the beacon correct?" Third Doyle answered.

Do I always sound so patronising? Doyle thought to herself, but was careful not to vocalise that question to Andy. She could guess what his answer would be. She remembered being very aware that it was close to the time for the beacon double echo to happen. The one they had blindly recorded the first time and witnessed the second time. Their thirds were about to be one half of the echo, just as they had been. And now they were about to be the second half, just as they had witnessed their future selves being.

"What do you need the beacon on for then?" asked Third Doyle.

"To establish a visual link and data stream connection," she answered, as she continued to stare intently at the com on the bench.

"Okay, we will get right on that," said Third Doyle. Doyle remembered herself clicking her fingers in the air and giving Anderson all sorts of looks and gestures to get him to move.

"Good, once it is on we can establish a link and get away from this cave man wrist com nonsense," said Doyle, scowling at the device.

"Does Andy have any problems with reactivating the beacon?" asked Third Doyle.

"No, your Anderson is fine, it's my idiot that is the problem," Doyle answered, still a bit raw about Andy's mistake.

"Yes problem," said Doyle, remembering that Third Anderson was silently questioning her past self on what she had meant, "Now get a move on Andy."

"Yes, I'm talking to you," Doyle shouted through the com,

again remembering that Third Anderson was silently asking if she was talking to him.

"That was funny," said Third Doyle, "He won't understand how you did that."

"He still doesn't," said Doyle. "I'm looking at his confused little face right now."

Anderson was indeed looking very confused, looking as if he'd just seen behind the curtain of a magic show and still didn't understand the tricks.

"Open your beacon exactly when your countdown runs out," said Doyle. She had her own countdown running too, the same countdown she used when she was her third self. "Once the beacons are open, our respective ships will perform their locator handshake and the visual and data link bands can be established and maintained. The beacons can then be shut off, the process will only take a moment, and hence the reason why the double echo only flashed for a second before disappearing."

The countdown hit zero and Doyle entered the commands to establish the link, knowing her counterpart was doing the exact same thing.

"That's more like it, much more civilised," said Doyle, looking at a small section of the ceiling that had now been converted to the visual link to their third selves.

"What can we do for you?" asked Third Doyle, who was now looking at her ceiling too.

"We're here to take the ore and put it back," said Doyle. "Our O'Connor is in the process of retrieving it from your O'Connor." Doyle was beginning to dislike the experience of talking to her past self as it was very unnatural. Her words kept plucking at her memory. She could not quite remember the exact words her future self had said. But every time she spoke it was disturbingly accurate.

"I see," said Third Doyle, looking unsurprised yet grateful. Doyle remembered the feeling of relief when she heard this, she knew she had no real plan at the time, only to try and force their future selves into action; it worked, but was bitter sweet.

"I will spare you the explanation of why we're doing this, as you already know," said Doyle, remembering perfectly well how her third self had absolutely no means of doing anything productive with the ore. That technology remained back in the future. "Thank you," said Third Doyle with a polite nod. "But you are calling my bluff though, I forced your hand… my future hand."

"Yes, good form," Doyle concurred, it was a good plan and it had indeed worked. But if only she'd have known the repercussions. "This is where it gets fun, there are too many of us here and our O'Connor cannot complete his list in such a crowd. So you are going to jump back to allow him the freedom of movement on the station he requires."

"Okay, I'll start the calculations immediately," answered Third Doyle.

Doyle remembered this part all too well, and it still gave her the chills.

"No need for that, I'll transfer them over to you," she said, transmitting the calculations over to her past self.

"Thank you, this is a time saver. When do I prepare these?" asked Third Doyle as she received the transmission.

"You don't," said Doyle "I got them from my future self, and now I'm giving them to you." She left that statement stand for itself. The few hours since she had been her past self had done nothing to help her come to terms with it.

"So where did they come from?" asked Third Doyle. It was rhetorical, there was no possible answer to that the question.

"It is a genuine paradox," said Doyle.

"There no such thing as a…" Third Doyle began, but did not finish. Doyle remembered immediately accepting the wisdom of her future self on the matter and also remembered that she wasn't going to let it go.

"Where will it take us?" Third Doyle asked, she was cautious and rightfully so.

"Back to the beginning where you are to start checking things off your list of known anomalies to ensure that you don't need to travel back a fifth time."

"What anomalies?" Third Doyle asked.

"Every event that involved some interaction from your future self," Doyle explained.

"Do we succeed completing the list?" Third Doyle asked.

"I don't know yet," answered Doyle honestly, "But so far there is nothing to indicate that we have a fifth, so we haven't failed yet."

"Okay, thank you," said Third Doyle. "What happens now?"

"You go to the flight deck. You need to be at these coordinates at this time to get through." Doyle said as she sent through the information. She mentally braced herself for the reaction her past self was about to have, she remembered all too well. She watched as Third Doyle calmly reviewed the data before jumping back from the screen.

"This can't be right," she said and put her hands up to her head, running her fingers through her hair. Doyle remembered that she had very serious doubts about whether they had time to collect their O'Connor and get to the coordinates provided.

"Why did you make it so tight?" Third asked.

"You will have time to collect him; this information didn't come from us remember, but it is good information…otherwise I wouldn't be here." Those were the words that she remembered convincing her, although she also did not have much choice. Third Doyle ran from the dome, heading toward the flight deck as fast as she could. Doyle found herself surprised by the complete lack of empathy she had for her past self. Even though there was very little margin for error in what her third self was about to do, just knowing that this had already happened made the whole situation bland.

She addressed Anderson now. "Andy you are to prepare the tether. My Andy here will tell you what is to happen. He knows it because he has done it before."

Anderson instinctively put his hand up over his mouth and

activated his voice encryptor "So," he said to the image of himself on the ceiling.

"So," Third Anderson spoke back, after activating his voice encryptor to "What do you want to talk about?"

"I don't really know," Anderson replied, this was embarrassing. His mind had drawn a complete blank and he had no idea what to say any more, he couldn't remember and couldn't think.

"How's the mission going?" Third Anderson asked.

"Good," Anderson replied.

"So when do we jump back and become you?" Third Anderson asked.

"Your Doyle has gone to start the process now," Anderson answered, remembering the answer. "Once you get O'Connor back over you will need to get down to manage the chard levels and dispersion, I'm going to start it for you."

"I don't need any help," Third Anderson answered, and Anderson remembered that he felt that he was being insulted.

"Do you want help with the chard or help with the tether?" said Anderson back to his past self, it was an empty question he knew exactly what was going to happen next, maybe this time around he would actually find it funny. "Choose carefully," he joked.

"But you know what I'm going to choose," said Third Anderson. "And either way I will end up doing both."

"So…" Anderson said, inviting his past self to choose.

"Can you do the tether then?" Third Anderson said, and Anderson remembered that he had been deliberately trying to change the future by doing the opposite of what he was told.

"No, I can't. Not from here," he laughed, although the laugh sounded forced. Why did he laugh? It still wasn't funny.

Third Anderson did not think it was funny, just as he remembered. After a moment of very awkward silence, his third self asked a good question. "So… have they hooked up yet?"

Anderson had been waiting for that question and answered with a bottled up enthusiasm. "Oh no, but they were so close, it is so hard to watch, both of them are as bad as each other."

"You're telling me, all that busted shoulder nonsense," said Third Anderson.

"That was just embarrassing," said Anderson and they both began laughing at their crew mates behaving like nervous teenagers.

Doyle looked on with one of her looks. She cleared her throat rather loudly reminding them that, although her Third had left, she was still there. Both of the Andersons didn't need a decryptor to understand it meant "get on with it!"

Anderson released the voice encryptor and started to instruct his past self on what needed to happen. "Get the tether ready and call your O'Connor, he will be on the hull outside airlock-B, get him back over as soon as you can otherwise he will die."

Anderson remembered hearing those words and how he had said them. It seemed an odd choice of phrase since he knew that O'Connor didn't die. Why did he say that, and why did he say it in such a dead pan way? He sounded like Radcliffe.

"Die!" said Third Anderson in astonishment.

"Don't worry he doesn't die, but as soon as he is back and you re-pressurise the airlock you need to get down below to take over the chard dispersal. I'll start preparing it all remotely from here." He gave Doyle a nod, which she returned with approval of a job well done. Anderson began preparing the chard systems remotely. There was a certain amount that could be done but most would still be down to the past Anderson, who he of course had complete faith in – because he knew he didn't fail.

"When will O'Connor be ready for me to bring him back?" asked Third Anderson.

"Right now please Andy," said Doyle.

"I'm on it," said Third Anderson and he shuffled down the next desk and started to work on preparing the tether.

Doyle continued to watch and listen. "When did this link finish?" she asked.

"It was wasn't cut; it broke" said Anderson. "Connection

severed when we, they, travelled back I guess" said Anderson.

Doyle continued to speculate as she watched Third Anderson go about his task through the link.

"O'Connor, can you hear me?" Third Anderson spoke into the com to his O'Connor. "Who's that with you?"

"That's my future self, he's come to help," came Third O'Connor's reply.

"Of course it is," said Third Anderson. "We've got a situation and we have to leave *now*. Just you, the other you is on his own."

"Are you ready?" Third Anderson said.

"I've got just one thing to do," said O'Connor.

Unfortunately, for Doyle they did not have line of sight with the two O'Connors so could not see what was happening.

Back on the hull of the station, O'Connor was watching his past self launch the freshly battered patched oxygen tank towards the planet below.

"Will it be different now, now that it is gone?" Third asked.

"I'm afraid not," O'Connor responded.

"But how can our past or future self use this tank now it's gone?" queried Third.

"Third Anderson has just launched the tether," interrupted Doyle, "you should be able to see it now."

"It's time," said O'Connor nodding inside his helmet, although no one would have seen. He pointed at the incoming tether.

"But it's gone, how can it come back?" Third asked.

"Remember what I said about Ryburn's card," said O'Connor.

"That I'll need it when I'm you?" Third asked.

"There was only ever one and you saw it twice… but in the wrong order," said O'Connor, thinking it was suitably cryptic to get his past self to think, which it had.

"What do you mean?" Third asked.

"I'll leave that one for you to find out." O'Connor replied, knowing that it would leave him stumped until he realised he was talking about the air tank. "Here comes your tether," he added and reached out to the side without looking and caught it. He knew it would work because he had already seen it. He thought he'd be more pleased about such a feat, but instead it was haunting, he was still on that road and couldn't deviate.

"Is that all you are going to tell me?" Third asked.

"I'm afraid so," said O'Connor. Deliberately or not, his past self had been rude and obnoxious to him. Taking the ore back now felt like a suitable retribution.

"At least I have the ore now," said Third as he attached the tether and it started bringing him back to the ship.

This is it O'Connor thought, and then out loud, "There is one more thing I have to do concerning the ore."

"What about it?" he heard Third answer as he released the clamps of his boots and started to float away.

"I need that too," said O'Connor as he snatched the end of the crate from Third, leaving him hanging in space for a moment before the tether begun to draw him back over to the King John.

"What are you doing?" shouted Third.

"You'd better calm down and conserve your oxygen," said O'Connor, knowing that Third's oxygen alarms were about to start. "Doyle, I have the ore."

"Good form," said his Doyle. "We just watched Third Andy tear away from the dome."

"I was heading down to the airlock to re-pressurise it to stop you from dying... again," said Anderson.

"I'm going to put it all back in the work-sphere," said O'Connor, talking about the ore. "Then I will go to see Ryburn about how to smelt it. I'm going to turn my com off for a while, my past self has some pretty choice things to say to me that I don't want to hear."

O'Connor glanced up to where his past self had been taken back to the ship. He remembered the anger he had towards himself at the time. How ridiculous that anger was; it solved nothing. At least he had been right about being deliberately ignored by his future self.

With the crate in hand, O'Connor slowly made his way along the outside of the hull. He had to go all the way back to airlock-A and to make matters slower he had to avoid the central sphere. He found the situation ridiculous and amusing as he thought of his original self taking the opposite path across the exterior of the station. The clip, unclip of his boot was growing ever more monotonous as he made the long walk around the station. It crossed his mind that the third King John could probably see him if they were looking, but he was coincidently avoiding line of sight with both the first and second. It was a calming change of pace compared to what his past self would be going through. As he reached the apex of the external walkway, Doyle called him.

"What was all that business with Radcliffe about?" she asked.

"Has that just happened?" said O'Connor as he had hoped that it was long gone since it felt like he had been outside on the hull for ages.

"No, the thirds are all gone," said Doyle. "I thought I'd wait for Andy to leave the room before I asked you."

O'Connor took a deep breath in, before explaining himself, Doyle didn't sound angry or upset, the bulk of her tone was concern.

"It was something that had to happen," said O'Connor.

"Why though?" Doyle asked.

"I've been watching myself, seeing how I talk to and treat people," O'Connor explained, then after a pause "I don't like it, I was raised better than that," he added. "When I am there, in the moment it seems so justified, but being able to see myself act that way, it changes everything. I overreact."

"So what happened with Radcliffe?" she asked again, like a psychiatrist delving deeper.

O'Connor did not answer. He had a great view of Venus from where he was. It was so tranquil. He instead changed the subject

"Where are all the crew?"

Doyle, letting go of the Radcliffe matter, gave him a rundown of the locations of everyone. It had not been long since Second and McSweeney had crossed paths in the central corridor and O'Connor grimaced remembering the punch all too well.

"I've got the new codes. Good thing too as I think that's when Benson changed them," said O'Connor, after hearing that First had finished his inspection and had since been in the central sphere with Benson.

"Oh good form! I had forgotten about that little detail," said Doyle.

"Well, yeah, funny story, I never actually got them," said O'Connor.

"Ah, your future self?" asked Doyle.

"How do you always know?" O'Connor joked. "Yes, he gave them to me, and I gave them to my past self, just before I took the ore from him. Where do you think that knowledge came from, if I never actually found it out properly?"

It was a poor choice of words but Doyle must have understood what he meant.

"The same place the calculations for this last jump back," said Doyle. "They were always there, stuck in some strange paradoxical loop, never found and never needing to found... time is creepy."

He finally got to the airlock and using the new codes to open the external door, he pulled himself inside with the crate, gently pushing it to the floor so it would not suddenly drop and break, or worse, alert the crew, when the gravity took told.

"Is it safe to come out?" he asked Doyle.

"You're clear," she responded.

He dragged the crate out of the airlock. It was heavy and it clunked as the back end cleared the foot of the doorway.

He removed his space suit and hung it up carefully, taking note of the patched tank that was now ready and waiting for his past self, when his time came.

The lifter made moving the crate simple so it created no

problem… but that smell! He knew that Second would be along to check Ryburn's old room for the ore and, therefore, he had to wait for himself to search the room, get angry and have a little fit and leave, before moving on.

A horribly loud, high pitched noise suddenly burst from his com. He jumped in alarm as the noise somehow disengaged the lifting device sending the crate crashing to the floor. If it weren't for the rubberised panelling on the floor, it would have caused such noise that it would probably have damaged his ears if they weren't already ringing from whatever it was that had screeched through his com.

O'Connor could have kicked himself, despite Doyle's earlier warning, he had been using his right arm, his communicator arm, to control the lifter and the noise was probably the internal circuitry of the device being swamped by the unique magnetic field being generated and causing a massive distortion across the network and all communicators that were currently connected to it.

"Sorry about that," he said as he called Doyle, and to test it was still working.

"What was it?" Doyle asked.

"My com was too close to the lifting mechanism. My com must have caused the feedback noise."

"Well, at least we can cross that one off the list now," Doyle replied.

O'Connor would have been happy if he hadn't heard her voice distort as it came through on his end.

"Doyle, can you hear me okay?" he asked.

"I can hear you," Doyle said, but her voice was twisting, changing pitch and speed.

"I think I've fried my com," he said after banging it against the edge of one of the wall beams. What the caretakers called "a technical fix".

"Okay, we'll use it sparingly," said Doyle, her voice clear this time.

He was close enough to drag the crate the rest of the way to the sleeping quarters, where Second was already in Ryburn's room. He could hear him talking to his Doyle about McSweeney's movements. Once Second had left, O'Connor entered Ryburn's room and shut the door. The trolley was turned over sideways against the wall, where his past self had kicked it in a moment of rage. He transferred the rocks from the crate back over to the trolley as fast as he could; it was a laborious task for one. The last distorted update about everyone's locations was that McSweeney, Benson, and First were on the central sphere but would soon be on the move and heading this way, most likely to turn in for bed. He didn't want to see McSweeney again, not before he had to. The combination of his first and second past selves would soon inadvertently do much more damage to their relationship, and even when he tried to make it better it made it so much worse. He wanted no further part of that downward spiral.

He left the room, pulling the trolley up onto its back wheels for extra speed as he pushed it along the corridor. He swung it into the work-sphere and brought it to a stop exactly where he had found it earlier. He looked at the controls on the smelt. Just in case smelting the ore into the Mercurian iron was straightforward… it was not; there were absolutely no clues as to what option he was to select. The ore was to remain as it was for the moment.

He stepped out and asked Doyle for the exact location of his past selves but his communicator needed another crack against a beam before her reply could be understood. Second would soon be taking advantage of the empty central sphere, to search in vain for the lost ore as he would still be blaming its disappearance on McSweeney. First was with Ryburn. O'Conner started along the corridor towards Ryburn's workstation.

When he arrived he could hear talking. He closed his eyes trying to remember why he was talking to Ryburn at that moment, it seemed so long ago. First had just informed Benson and McSweeney about the reason for calling home, then Ryburn had wanted to see him. Ryburn had the prototype working! That realisation was much more significant to him this time around. He crouched down, back in his familiar eavesdropping position and listened in on the conversation waiting for his past self to leave.

"Look Ryburn, I believe that you think you can do it, and that's fine. But I'm going to wait, they won't just leave us here!" said First.

"So you don't think we're expendable now?" asked Ryburn

"I should have a band back from lunarbase by morning. We'll know what is what then," his past self said. O'Connor ducked down to be sure he was out of view as his past self tried to unjam the door again.

"You think it will do any good, waiting for their reply?" Ryburn asked.

O'Connor sat putting everything into chronological order from Ryburn's perspective and realised that Second had already told him they were on their own which explained Ryburn pessimistic attitude.

"They'll at least confirm what our options are," said First.

"You mean that we're on our own?" said Ryburn

"I'll speak with the others and make sure they are aware of the importance of your work. They won't give you any trouble," said First, and O'Connor remembered that it was a bluff, he only said that to keep them all away from each other, in the fear that McSweeney would do something stupid.

"They were already supposed to understand the importance of my work," Ryburn said.

"Reiterating the fact wouldn't hurt though, especially to McSweeney. We have to think positively… that they won't leave us here," said First obviously trying to convince himself

Ryburn muttered something, but O'Connor couldn't make it out.

"And what is that supposed to mean?" O'Connor heard his past self snap; he sunk his head, waiting for more embarrassing behaviours from his past to haunt him. Had Ryburn said something he couldn't hear?

"You O'Connor, you are what is interesting. You swing hot and cold so quickly, one minute you are interested in what I'm doing, the next you couldn't care less. One minute lunarbase is going to arrange our collection, the next we're on our own."

To First's credit thought O'Connor, he had held onto his temper that time, remembering thinking that it was Ryburn who had flown the cuckoo's nest. He changed the subject back to "thinking positive".

"Nothing much we can do now anyway. We should have a reply back by morning," said First.

"Do you want me to stay up working on a solution or not?" Ryburn asked, sounding like he was all set to down tools and continue his work back on Earth.

"Do whatever you like Dr Ryburn," said First dismissively, "they won't leave us out here; you mark my words! Worst case we float out and have to wait a few weeks for collection."

O'Connor couldn't help but smile at that statement: his words would indeed be marked. Marked wrong.

"I rechecked our axis, we're still within tolerance," said Ryburn. This pricked O'Connor ears, the axis of the station wouldn't change until the airlock breach. He had told Ryburn earlier about the axis change, in an effort to encourage him to keep working on his engine. And when the axis actually changed his original self remembered Ryburn had already been investigating it. Oh, what a messy loop he had created.

"Our axis?" original O'Connor questioned.

"The hopper incident, it didn't put us in a spin after all," said Ryburn.

"Okay thanks Ryburn," said First as he left the room without anything further to say. O'Connor caught a glimpse of his face as he walked out; he looked as confused as he remembered being at the time.

O'Connor jumped up quietly and stuck his head in the door.

"Thanks for rechecking the axis for me Jim," he said, trying to restart the conversation as smoothly as possible. Ryburn turned to look at him. It was the same Ryburn but he somehow looked different. He had seen him so many times now out of sequence that he couldn't remember if they were on good or bad terms, he was gambling on good.

"That's okay," said Ryburn, turning back to the prototype. The first thing O'Connor saw was that it still had the wrong component at its core. He needed the blue regulator but the floating device still had the bright orange piece. All the spare and wrong components were still on the desk untouched from where his second self had left them. The subtle hint of positioning the sky-blue one at the front had gone unnoticed.

"Do you mind if I take these ones back?" he asked Ryburn, pointing to the wrong spec regulators.

"Be my guest," said Ryburn.

"Thanks" said O'Connor. He pulled off his hat to use as a makeshift bag but as he put the first piece in he stopped suddenly as a flash of déjà vu hit him. He recalled the ripped hat full of broken components that Ryburn had shown him. He had seen this before, as his first self after the airlock breach. This was going to come back to sting him somehow.

"Jim, let me help you out," O'Connor suggested, taking a break from loading up his new hat. "The ore is down in the work-sphere; let me set it smelting for you, save you a job."

Ryburn turned back to look at him with surprise…and suspicion "that would be very helpful, what do you want in return for this?"

O'Connor smiled, perhaps the terms with Ryburn weren't as good as he'd hoped "Only two things," he said. Nothing he said now could change anything, but if Ryburn's final account of events were true, perhaps his words mattered.

"Go on," said Ryburn folding his arms, obviously expecting a ridiculous request.

"I want you to seriously think about how you will fly the crew home; we've got plenty of power and diamond chard cables... we could run the cables through the ship, blow out the corridors we don't need..." that was enough he thought, a huge piece of bait to get him thinking.

Ryburn scoffed, but O'Connor could see the wheels inside Ryburn's head begin to turn.

"Perhaps you just need a different regulator," he added as he continued putting the rest of the wrong parts in his hat, leaving the bright blue one on the desk. He placed the last one into his hat and felt the rip it as a jagged edge sliced. He lifted it back out revealing a small but familiar rip in his hat. It was only a hat he told himself, it didn't matter, much.

"And your second caveat?" asked Ryburn.

"Which cycle do I run to refine the rocks?" said O'Connor, as he continued to inspect his hat.

"I've got it saved, it's under cycle 27," said Ryburn. "Put all the ore in and the machine will take care of the rest."

"I'll get that done for you, I'll have it ready by morning," said O'Connor. That was it, the last bit of info he needed.

"I think this regulator may be faulty," Ryburn said to himself.

That was enough for O'Connor and he slipped out the door, but his smile turned quickly when he looked back to his hat, which was his last hat too. There wasn't going to be another one. He ran his fingers over the all too familiar rip. "Bollocks to it," he said, throwing it along the corridor, hearing it hit the frames then land on the floor. It crunched under his boot as he stepped on it, before he kicked it up against the wall. His lack of concentration however meant he was marching directly toward his original self and the dark corridor.

O'Connor called Doyle and heard her try to reply but all he got was a distorted noise. He gently tapped his wrist against the wall and spoke again, but her reply was again inaudible. The corridor was dark and he was not paying attention to where he was going. He slammed his communicator into the side of another metal shell, it clanged against the next, and since they all had hard backs, the sound carried all the way along the corridor. First's shout barely carried to where he was, but as soon as he heard it O'Connor knew what was happening. He couldn't see First because the dim white light above the collection hub was obscuring everything behind it. He turned his communicator off, as it would be just his luck for Doyle's voice to come through clearly.

"Is that you Ryburn?" he heard his past self shout, loud enough to avoid his words being swallowed up by the sound proofing. "Benson? McSweeney? I don't have a light, come on guys, what's going on?" He did not quite catch the next part. His heart skipped a beat at the next sentence. "You want me to fine you a couple of hours work McSweeney?" More blame and threats for McSweeney. O'Connor stood in silence remembering his actions and words.

"I'm not in the mood," shouted First. O'Connor could hear a bit clearer now, which meant First was walking towards him. "Have you been hassling Ryburn again?" he was definitely closer this time.

O'Connor, with his chest pressed up close to the wall, stepped past the light, trying to stay hidden. He couldn't see anything in the darkness ahead but he could hear footsteps rapidly coming toward him. He remembered! He ducked, missing the wild swing from his past self. He then stepped to the side, avoiding the kick at ankle height that had been thrown in an attempt to hit a McSweeney who was never there. O'Connor hadn't known how close he had actually been to making contact. It was too close and he ran silently toward the airlock leaving his past self flailing in the dark. As he now knew this path all too well, he remembered to sidestep that bastard shell that he had tumbled over. First would not be so lucky and unfortunately for him would be colliding with it at knee height. That knee was still a little tender too. After a quick look over his shoulder to see if First was in sight, he swung into the airlock prep area. He needed to get back over to the King John and as this airlock wasn't going to be around for much longer, now was an opportune time.

He had a little time before First would realise, or suspect, that someone was in the airlock so using the new codes, he unlocked and opened the airlock door, grabbed the first of each of the space suit items, including the helmet that he'd left on bench, and bundled them all into the airlock before shutting the door behind him. He pulled on the suit as quickly as he could, surprisingly fast now as he had had a lot of practice of late. He hit the controls for decompression. The indicator light changed from green to red. He took a deep breath in, the last before he would have the helmet on, put on his sleeves and secured the front of the suit. When he plugged the helmet into the tank. It filled with a brief mist of air allowing him to breathe normally. As the gravity released him, he opened the outer door, pulled himself through and, pulling the tank through behind him, quickly shut the door again. He saw the airlock light change back to green meaning the airlock had re-pressurised and he paused to take stock of what had happened. He now knew how close his past self had been to catching him. He pulled the tank close and clipped it into its correct place on his back.

Fortunately the audio system in the space suit didn't utilise the same system as the broken com, just piggybacked on the transmitting system. Doyle's voice came through loud and clear.

"What are you doing on the hull?" she asked.

"I didn't want to be caught."

"By whom?" asked Doyle.

"By First coming back from Ryburn's."

"Do you remember catching yourself back then?" she asked.

"I panicked," he replied, knowing his reasoning was preposterous as he already knew he didn't catch himself, and the rush out of the airlock was unnecessary. It wasn't the smartest move either considering First would have sealed the airlock permanently by now.

"What about the smelting did you get all the info you needed from Sir Ryburn?"

"Yes, I know the cycle to select."

"Good. We need to get you off of there; the whole section

you are standing on won't be there for much longer."

"Oh fuck," was all he said, increasingly realising that it certainly was a stupid move to come outside the station. "Can you get a tether to me?" he asked.

"We're on the far side" she responded.

He started moving along the hull. He had to get just close enough to his King John for Anderson to shoot the tether over to him.

"How come we didn't see me out here earlier?" asked O'Connor.

"We weren't looking I guess" said Doyle.

"That's was lucky."

"Not really, our firsts had no reason to, and our seconds didn't have line of sight, the direction you are taking is away from them… actually I suppose that is lucky."

He was making good progress but space walking was still slow. There was nothing that could be done about it, the magnetic boot locks had about a five centimetre attraction range, and if he missed that, he would simply float awkwardly away. He moved as quickly as he could, once or twice perhaps he came close to missing a footing.

"Your second self is outside the work-sphere; he's on his way to hydroponics," said Doyle.

"And McSweeney?" said O'Connor, who had just rounded the bend on the outer hull. Not long now, until he left for airlock-B.

"How much further before you can get me?" asked O'Connor.

"You are still too far, you need to get past the sleeping quarters," replied Doyle.

O'Connor started to build up good speed, all things considered. The sleeping quarters were just ahead, but he was going to take a short cut. He unclipped both boots and let his momentum carry him toward the sphere, flying through space with his arms flailing before locking his boots on impact, coming to a full stop before setting off again. One more gap to clear to reach the outer walkway.

"We've lost the tracking on the trolley," shouted Doyle suddenly.

Her words snatched away all of his attention, causing a mistimed release of his left boot. With his direction slightly off he was flying in the general direction of the walkway, but not its centre. He came close to landing on it, but close didn't matter in space. A near miss might as well have been a light year. He reached his arms out instinctively and frantically tried to grip something, anything. They found nothing as he floated past the edge of the outer corridor and off into space.

"Do you need some help?" said Doyle sarcastically; she had seen his jump attempt, O'Connor wasn't sure if he was thankful or not.

"Yes," O'Connor said. "Can you see me yet?"

"I see a fool floating in space," said Doyle. He couldn't tell if she was concerned or amused. "Don't worry, Andy has you."

"What was that about the ore?" but she didn't reply.

"Doyle, are you there?" he asked.

"She's gone down to meet you at the airlock," said Anderson. "I'm getting the tether prepared now, just working out the aim."

"What happened to the ore?" he asked again.

"All we know is that the tracking stopped," Anderson said, before adding. "Your second self is at that doomed airlock."

O'Connor knew what was coming next; he spun himself around to watch the breach. His failed jump had carried him out far enough for the central sphere to no longer obscure his line of sight. He'd seen the aftermath of the breach, he'd been at its centre and felt it, and now he was going to witness its destructive splendour from afar.

In complete silence the airlock doors ruptured, a torrent of air rushed out bringing with it all the equipment shells mixed in with big chunks of wall and hull and then it was over. It had happened so quickly, but stuck in the middle of it seemed to last forever, especially after his shoulder had popped. In the suddenly restored stillness he saw the small space man drift out into the nothing, following on behind all the debris before changing speed and direction rapidly as his tether took him back to the second King John. A moment later, the grey blur of his own tether came into view. He clipped it on and was soon being drawn back to his King John

CHAPTER 20:

ONE LAST TIME

"WE LOST THE tracking on the ore trolley. It started to move from where you left it and the signal stopped as it went through the door way of the work-sphere," said Doyle the moment O'Connor removed his helmet.

"So, you are telling me we're really back to square one now?" said a frustrated O'Connor. He was about to throw his helmet across the floor, but didn't. Knowing that it wouldn't help, he instead took in a deep breath to calm himself.

Doyle put a calming hand on his shoulder; he suspected she knew what he was trying to do but also half suspected she was staring at his bald head. His suspicion was soon confirmed.

"I thought you got another hat?"

"I did, but Doyle's Law got to it."

Doyle smiled, briefly, before getting back to the more urgent topic of the once again missing ore.

"You have to get back over there and find it." She wasn't talking about the hat.

"I can't go searching for it all over again," said O'Connor. The thought of turning the station over yet again actually scared him since he knew that every single potential hiding place would have to be checked because all previous locations were before it was lost.

"You have to," said Doyle.

"I can't, not again, there isn't time," said O'Connor in despair, defeated and looking at the floor.

"The ore is smelted by you, Sir Ryburn said so," said Doyle. "You have to find it."

"When did you lose the signal?" asked O'Connor, exhausted.

"Just as Second went into hydroponics," she answered.

"That was after I tore McSweeney a new one," said O'Connor, suspecting that he knew what happened.

"Your man McSweeney must have taken it after all," said Anderson, who had just arrived and was winding up the last of the tether.

"We don't know that," said Doyle, looking at O'Connor, obviously not wanting to aggravate the McSweeney situation.

"Ryburn was still complaining about it not being in the work-sphere; he was in the work-sphere," O'Connor said, trying his best to remember what was said. The problem was that at the time he was more concerned with their immediate predicament and not crazy rambles about missing rocks. But he was sure something was said about them being missing.

"I was talking to Benson and McSweeney, when Ryburn called about it. McSweeney swore he hadn't touched it though. I remember that part."

"And he was probably telling the truth, same as he had been doing all day," said Doyle.

"No," said O'Connor slowly wracking his brain, "he did have it, I went for him, he said he'd put them back." That memory was still fuzzy, probably a side effect of the drugging. He slid his hand down to his side to where McSweeney had stabbed him.

"The syringe," he exclaimed.

"What syringe?" Doyle asked.

"Of course! I'll get it," said Anderson, his face lighting up, before he shot out of the room.

"What are you talking about?" said Doyle; she certainly didn't like Anderson understanding it before she did.

"One of the last things that happened to me on the station was McSweeney drugged me, with a concoction that Anderson is probably making right this very moment. Second Anderson, on the second King John. Our Anderson has just gone to get it."

"Why?" Doyle asked

"I messed my shoulder up pretty bad in the airlock breach," said O'Connor, giving Doyle a sideways squint, as he reluctantly came clean.

"You said you were fine," said Doyle "Why would you..."

"Oh, you idiot," she exclaimed affectionately.

Anderson arrived back with the syringe in hand, the bright orange liquid sloshing around in the vial.

"And you..." said Doyle, pointing her finger at Anderson and adopting her stern voice, "Don't keep information like that from me in future; he could have been seriously injured."

Anderson looked dumbfounded. "Yes Doyle, I apologise." said Anderson, "It won't happen again."

O'Connor smiled, enjoying the benefit of the double standard. Anderson handed the syringe to O'Connor who carefully checked that the stopper was secure.

"What are you waiting for then?" said Doyle after O'Connor had stowed the syringe inside his suit.

"Nothing I guess," said O'Connor as he picked his helmet up. "One more time."

"One more time," repeated Anderson

"One *last* time," said Doyle, improving the sentiment.

O'Connor was launched back over to Neith. The aim was a little off this time and instead of landing flush on the walkway section of the outer hull he landed just short and found himself on the wall between two of the windows. It wasn't a concern, it just wasn't perfect. He was near the airlock so he didn't bother walking himself to the roof of the hull and the traditional space walking path.

As he stepped over one of the windows he saw Ryburn walking past.

"Doyle, Ryburn's in the corridor," he said, almost accusing her of not keeping him informed.

"He's in his workstation," replied Doyle, who was back in the dome with Anderson.

"He just walked past me."

"He must have left his com behind," said Doyle. "We're only tracking coms remember"

"Yes I remember," he remembered all too well; it was what caused one of the clashes with McSweeney. He tried to peak through the window to confirm if indeed Ryburn was missing the com, but he couldn't see him anymore, the angle was all wrong. He continued his walk and soon reached the airlock door.

"I'm going in," he said to Doyle. "Where is everyone else?"

"All in the central sphere," she said with the same sense of urgency he had.

O'Connor punched in the access code and entered the airlock. Getting the external door shut as fast as he could, he re-pressurised the airlock and crouched down out of view to undress in the actual airlock since he didn't know for certain where Ryburn was on his journey to and from the work-sphere. Once out of his space suit, he popped his head up slowly and, since there was no sign of anyone, he opened the inner door, leaving the space suit in the airlock.

"Benson, are you there?" Ryburn's voice came clearly though his com.

"Benson here, what…?" replied Benson's voice but the message distorted at the end. More noise came through and he gave the com a bash on the wall. The next message was clear enough to understand.

"I need the rocks back, has anyone moved them, by accident or purpose? I don't care, but I need them back."

"The smelt hasn't been touched yet to my knowledge," came Benson's distorted reply.

"Someone has been in here! The crafting unit has been moved, it's down by the airlock I'm going to need some help getting it back in here and set up."

O'Connor glanced along the corridor toward the hardware Ryburn was talking about. That was going to be a bugger to move, it was heavy, really heavy. His thought led him to his front pocket and the lifter. That nasty déjà vu hit him again. He was the one who was going to move the unit. He remembered that his first self had McSweeney in a choke hold at that moment and was about to speak through McSweeney's com. His com messed up the next couple of exchanges, all he got was garbled nonsense, but enough to know the voices, Ryburn, Benson, Ryburn again. Another bash on the wall cleared it up enough to hear his own voice clearly, and he sounded very put out.

"That's enough Ryburn! A crew wide com is for emergencies only."

"This is an emergency, we need those rocks. How many times do you need me to say it?" Ryburn met the anger with some of his own.

"Do either of you know where they are?" said O'Connor, addressing his crew.

"I don't know anything about any stupid rocks," said McSweeney. Then the com ended and everything was silent. He remembered McSweeney giving him his word that he knew nothing of the rocks. That *must* have been a lie.

O'Connor stepped out of the airlock prep area and walked to the crafting unit. Ryburn's voice came through the com again, only a little bit twisted now.

"Hello?" said Ryburn but meaning, "I'm still here and waiting for an answer."

"Ryburn, Benson here, McSweeney knows nothing about..." the crackling noise went silent, the call was over...or the com was completely dead.

O'Connor crouched down behind the crafting unit; it was big. He pushed his face to the ground to find enough of a gap to get the lifter cables underneath it. They shot through the gap and connected the end all the way over the hardware and back to the handle. He remained ducked down as Ryburn stomped past on his way back to his workstation.

He slid the device into position and gently lifted the whole unit up. It was off balance and lunged to the side hitting the wall before he managed to regain control. He spun it over in the air, so his arm was stretched out. The cold smell was strong now and he had to resist the urge to sneeze. He pushed it along the corridor but it was a very clumsy operation, nothing like the earlier ore crate.

The smell seemed to be getting stronger; perhaps he was overloading the device. It almost got away from him a couple of times, crashing into the other hardware shells sending them clattering out of place, the once tidy walkway now a mess. One hardware frame fell over on top of the crafting unit, the force of it caused the whole thing to slide into the floor, tearing the distinctive gouge marks that he had seen before into the rubberised flooring. He pulled the whole device slowly up, tipped it on its edge and let the frame topple back against the wall with a thud. He floated it up at arm's length in front of him again and carefully walked the rest of the way to the work-sphere avoiding the remaining hardware. He looked like he was flying a cuboid shaped kite. Upon reaching the work-sphere he swung it down to the floor in a randomly chosen spot in the middle of the room. Unclasping the cables, he let them retract back into the grip.

O'Connor looked at his handiwork, and was not at all surprised to find he had haphazardly chosen the exact spot he remembered. Next, he had to connect it to the room's power source and that was no problem because he knew the exact panel on the floor he has to look under to find the cables. Using one of the crowbar devices from the edge of the room, he selected the panel and popped it up, separating it from the floor along the seam and revealing the clip point on the cable. He smiled when he found it, but that was almost immediately replaced with a quizzical smirk. The knowledge of the location was yet another piece of information stuck in a never ending loop in time. He had marvelled at the precision, when he thought it was Ryburn, but instead it was a paradox of knowledge, just like his door codes. He only knew where to look because he had seen it; he had only seen it because he knew where to look. He withdrew a suitable length of cable and clipped it into the socket on the crafting unit. A little jiggle of the cables and he felt the slight vibrations as it powered up.

In his mind's eye he could see himself standing exactly in this spot, wondering what it was that Ryburn was building inside the unit. He ran his hands over the smooth surface, drumming his fingers, the exact way his past self had done. The whole machine was for the scrap heap. The display screen didn't work and just flapped loosely, over where the controls had been. It was going to craft two large scale regulators Ryburn needed for his plan. The slot for the memory card was empty but from his pocket he retrieved the memory card containing the schematics and instructions. He pushed the new ventures card into the slot. The screen was completely dead, but that didn't seem to matter, the gentle vibration and humming from the machine told him that it had started doing something. O'Connor was confident it was going to work, his original self will be taking both the card and the two regulators back to Ryburn. He stepped back from the unit looking it over; it was now picture perfect, ready for his past self.

As he got to the door, crowbar device still in hand, he saw the fixed position communicator that Ryburn had just used; he must have done because he didn't have his com. This wasn't right, because when he had tried to use it, it wasn't working. It had been deliberately disabled, another realisation. Using the crowbar he popped open the casing and grabbed a big handful of wiring and pulled them out, sending sparks flying around the surrounding area. Once it had gone dead he tucked the loose wiring back into the casing before closing it back into position, nice and tidy. Without looking over his shoulder, he threw the crowbar device, confidently knowing exactly where it would land on the floor.

He didn't need to put much thought into hiding from his original self; he stood still next to a large equipment shell. O'Connor had complete confidence in knowing that he wouldn't be found as he watched himself walk past, sniffing at the air like a blood hound following the strange smell. There was one more thing he needed to do, to ensure that his past self stayed away. He selected a large shell, one with a full and obstructive back to it and tipped it over. It landed with a thud that he felt shake through the floor. Using the lifting device, he quickly stacked up four more shells on top of the fallen one, blocking off the entire corridor. The last shell took a bit of effort as he really needed to wedge that one in and completely close up the space. He didn't want to make it too easy on his past self; he hadn't been shown that courtesy. Doffing an imaginary cap at the newly created barrier and mocking his angry past self who would soon be coming up against it.

He jogged all the way around to Ryburn's workstation where he found the legend of humanity slumped down in his chair.

"What's wrong, Jim?" he asked

"Forget it, Chief," said Ryburn, not bothering to look up, "without the ore I can't do anything, which I guess is irrelevant anyway because without the crafting unit I can't build the regulators. We'll have to enter final phase and hope for the best I'm afraid."

"There isn't going to be any 'best' to hope for," said O'Connor, putting himself back into Ryburn's time line. "The message from lunarbase was as expected, we aren't going to get any help."

"We're doomed?" Ryburn said looking up, over his half-moon glasses. "I'm sorry."

"You aren't doomed, you still have your 3MP engine, and your plan to fly home."

Ryburn just grunted.

"Come on Jim; imagine the looks on the faces of every bastard who wronged you when you take the station home. Wouldn't that be the slap in the face to all the slimy bureaucrats who left you here to rot? It will work Jim! I know it, you got the right parts now," he added pointing to the floating prototype and the blue regulator at its centre.

"How did you know I had the wrong part?" asked Ryburn, with distrust in his eyes.

"I don't know what you mean," said O'Connor, playing dumb, had he said too much? Ryburn looked on at him suspiciously.

"Your plan to fly the station back to Earth," O'Connor pressed, swiftly changing the subject back to the task at hand. "We need to get the station moving as soon as possible."

"The ore has gone." Ryburn said, shaking his head, "I can't even build the regulators we need."

"I've moved the crafting unit. I'll bring you the regulators. Next time you see me I'll have them, I promise… one on each hip," said O'Connor.

"Just like you promised to have the ore refined down?" Ryburn snapped back.

"I'm working on that one, McSweeney has it, I'm sure of it. I just need to convince him to do the right thing."

"That is going to be tough, the way you've treated him today," said Ryburn. "I saw the split lip and the bruising, whatever he did it didn't warrant violence."

"There is nothing I can do to change that now, I was very wrong."

"What did he do to you?" asked Ryburn.

"Forget it, assume we get the ore refined and you have your regulators, what next?"

"Why the urgency? We have weeks," asked Ryburn.

"Not so. You only have hours," said O'Connor. "The airlock put us in a spin and pushed our location into the path of the stray lander's next pass."

"Let me check that," said Ryburn as he brought up his own calculations. "You told me that earlier, and you were wrong."

"Fine, check, but the ore, how much of that needs to be processed?" asked O'Connor as Ryburn busied himself at the monitors.

"We will need all of it processed, every last gram," said Ryburn firmly, looking O'Connor in the eye to be sure he was understood.

O'Connor's heart sank. That pretty much put an end to Doyle's idea that he would simply give up a large sample.

"All of it?" O'Connor asked. "Surely a kilo or two wouldn't matter?"

"All of it," Ryburn repeated and switched screens and brought up the calculated yield of the remaining rocks. "And that is using a generous ratio," he pointed out. "We might get lucky but it doesn't seem like that type of day."

"Okay, okay, all of it, I got it. What next?" said O'Connor knowing he would have to break the news to Doyle somehow.

"We need to run the chard cables from the central sphere all along the... we can still use them, yes?" said Ryburn.

"Yes, as much as you like," said O'Connor, instantly. Salvage didn't matter anymore. "You work out the details I'll work on McSweeney," he said, slapping Ryburn on the back and leaving him with a re-found motivation to get this done.

"You are right," said Ryburn as his simulation of their new axis and orbital path clashed with that of the stray lander. "How did you know that was going to happen?"

O'Connor left the question unanswered leaving Ryburn to fine-tune his plan. He had to talk to McSweeney next, he would still be in the central sphere with Benson, likely still fuming from their last encounter, for McSweeney it was only twenty minutes ago but for O'Connor that encounter was days ago.

He had to put his mind back to that encounter, it was an ugly conversation in which Benson and McSweeney had accused him of sabotaging the salvage contract, all sorts of accusations were flying about. But as he recalled the details of the accusations he slowed and had to lean up against the wall as the wave of everything rushed over him. It was like being shot. McSweeney blamed him for the airlock breach. They had brought up proof that he had disabled the airlock systems and had been leaving and entering the station unchecked. They had accused him of ignoring vital warnings on key systems, ignoring the concerns about the hopper. McSweeney accused him of violence and docking his fee. He had denied it all of course, but it was all true. He had done all of those things, he just hadn't done them in a linear order.

This upcoming conversation was going to be harder than he thought. Where did he leave it, what were the last words he said? He had told them that they had three weeks left before they would need to enter final phase: the last controlled jettison of the outer walkway, which would give the station enough momentum to leave orbit and float out toward the rendezvous point.

He took a deep breath and climbed the ladder to where Benson and McSweeney were, for them he'd not long left. Instantly McSweeney gave him a look that could have burned a hole in the hull, Benson on the other hand gave him a sombre yet cautious look.

"Guys, please I need to discuss something with you," he said with his hands open and to his sides. "I mean no harm."

"We're preparing for the final phase as you asked, you bastard," said McSweeney.

"No that's fine, I deserved that," said O'Connor. "Look, forget final phase; it's too late for that."

"Too late? Why?" asked Benson.

"Our rotation is wrong. We don't have time to prepare for final phase anymore. And even if we did we would go the wrong way. Final phase will drop us into the gravity of the planet."

"What?" Benson and said McSweeney in unison.

"Final phase isn't going to help, you're leaving orbit now instead." said O'Connor.

"How?" asked Benson in disbelief.

"Ryburn is going to fly you clear. McSweeney, I need those rocks back, I know you have them."

"We've been through this already, several times," said McSweeney.

"I know," O'Connor said, "and I'm sorry, I'm sorry I accused you of taking them. But I know you have them now, hidden somewhere around here. Without the rocks you are all going to die."

"You mean 'we', don't you Chief?" queried Benson, looking worried now.

O'Connor hadn't realised his poor choice of words, that didn't make the situation better.

"You know Ryburn's been working on a new engine? That is our only hope now," he said, trying his best to sound like a reasonable person, which was a tall order considering what had just happened from their perspective.

"Ryburn's flying rocks? You can't be serious," said McSweeney.

"Please both of you," pleaded O'Connor.

"Nothing you say will convince us you aren't a lying, scheming, violent thief," said McSweeney, the hurt in his voice overpowered his words.

"But you can show us the message you received from home," said Benson, "that would put us at ease."

"The message from home?" O'Connor questioned, what was in that message they thought he was hiding.

"Yeah, show us that you haven't been plotting all along for this to happen and for you to somehow profit from it all."

"And that will be enough?" asked O'Connor "You'll return the rocks?"

"It will be a start," said McSweeney looking like he was trying not to spit in O'Connor's face. Their last conversation had effectively had O'Connor backing away as both his crew men stood up to him.

"Okay then, the message from home," said O'Connor, walking over to the terminal and bringing it up after typing in his personal encryption key. He hadn't showed them this out of concern they would take the news out on Ryburn but it may work in his favour now.

A video flashed up showing a man wearing a cheap suit and tie with the Lancer company emblem all over it. There was absolutely nothing noteworthy about the man on the screen, he was just a nameless company stooge by all accounts. Unfortunately, though, this was their new employer. O'Connor had no doubt whatsoever that the words he was about to listen to again were not from the man who was talking. He was likely a poor pleb sent to read the company statement.

"Chief Jake O'Connor," the man said, his eyes trained left to right giving away that he was reading from a prepared prompt. "I must take this opportunity to inform you that the Lancer Consortium have purchased your current salvage contract for the Venus orbital station designation Neith. Your message was received and your request has been denied by the new owners of the salvage contract. You will not enter final phase early, you are to proceed as planned. If the salvage is lost, compensation will be made payable to the company from you and your crew's final remuneration. In the event of your deaths, anything left will be passed on to your next of kin as stated in your final intentions agreement. I repeat, you are not authorised to enter final phase ahead of schedule. The risk of significant damage to the station has been deemed acceptable. Your priority is to complete the salvage contract. No more communications on this subject will be heard. The Lancer Consortium would like to thank you and your crew, Benton and McSween." The screen went black without so much as a wave goodbye, and the text "message ended" flashed on the screen.

"There, we're on our own," said O'Connor. "We've been bought out and being left out here. They don't give a shit about any of us, they couldn't even get your names right."

It took a moment for Benson and McSweeney to process the information.

"This is all Ryburn's fault," said McSweeney, wanting someone to blame.

"Ryburn's the one person who can get us out of this mess," said O'Connor. "His engine can fly us back home." He remembered his pronouns this time.

"With his magic rocks," McSweeney scoffed.

"Yes, but not unless you go and get them," he said, meeting McSweeney's eyes.

"I never said that I had them," McSweeney said, stubbornly folding his arms.

"Go and get them," said Benson softly.

"Thank you," O'Connor said. "Benson, Ryburn is in his workstation; can you please go and get instructions from him about what needs to be done?"

Benson stepped in the direction of the ladder but McSweeney stopped him.

"No, no, it's not that simple" said McSweeney, "You aren't going to leave me alone with him. I want some assurance from you that all your bullying will stop. You've put me through hell yesterday and your nasty streak ends now."

"I wish I could," said O'Connor, but that wasn't going to be enough.

"I want your word," McSweeney demanded. "And I want you to witness this." he said to Benson

"I swear that my poor behaviour and my stupid temper all stops today," said O'Connor, he was making the promise to himself, more than to McSweeney.

"On your life?" McSweeney demanded.

"On my life," O'Connor promised. He knew what that meant, he saw it in McSweeney's face, his body language and that damned pointing finger. It was a threat that McSweeney would follow through on.

"Sure it's in the..." McSweeney started but O'Connor cut him off raising up a hand.

"You know what, I don't even want to know where you've hidden it. I just want it all back in the work-sphere," he said.

"Will do, Chief," said McSweeney, there wasn't any anger or hate in his voice or on his expression, it again felt like the air had been cleared between then and that made what was going to happen next even more difficult.

"Then come back to me here when you have returned it. I will have another task for you."

"Will do, Chief," he said, offering a wary mock salute and adding a cheeky "See you soon Benton," before climbing down the ladder.

"He's going to call me that forever now," said Benson, shaking his head.

"Most likely," O'Connor agreed.

"What do you need me to do now?" Benson asked.

"Go to see Ryburn. He will have a plan."

"Will do, said Benson and then added nervously, "It will work, won't it Chief?"

O'Connor smiled and placed a hand on the big man's shoulders as he descended. "Ryburn knows what he's doing"

O'Connor considered what was happening elsewhere. His original self would have been free of the barricade by now and would have gone to see Ryburn.

"Doyle," he said into his com, "McSweeney's going to get the ore."

"Good form. It's going to be all over soon," she said back, her voice distorting.

"I spoke to Ryburn," he said. "There will be no spare rocks, he needs it all."

He had to bash his com to hear the reply, asking her to repeat it.

"I said, are you sure? Could he be wrong?" asked Doyle.

"He's sure," he replied, shaking his head. Ryburn wouldn't be wrong, not now.

"Okay then." O'Connor could hear the sadness underneath the words.

"What are we going to do?" O'Connor asked.

"We wait for events to play out," said Doyle. "McSweeney's on his way back, he's been to the work-sphere, he had been at..." but the sound distorted and he didn't catch the information about where McSweeney had been.

"Radio silence," he said, as he saw the scruffy blond figure of McSweeney climb the ladder. He heard another garbled noise; he assumed it was Doyle saying, "Starting now".

"All done" said McSweeney as he approached, beaming.

"Why so happy?" asked O'Connor.

"I'm happy we're getting along again," he said and somehow the smile widened, it was a real genuine smile that shone in his eyes, they even sparkled with a sense of relief.

He had missed seeing that smile and that made what he was about to do very hard. "I need you to take something to Ryburn," he said and reached into his pocket.

"Make sure you give this to Ryburn when you see him," he said handing McSweeney the syringe with the orange liquid, the custom built sedative to perfectly match O'Connor's metabolism. "Hold it like this," he added flicking off the stopper and placing it in McSweeney fist, needle end sticking up. "Don't drop it, keep it in your hand."

"Will do Chief," McSweeney said, looking at the orange liquid, it was bright. "What is it?"

"Some magnetic strengthening agent," he lied

"Whatever the hell that means," McSweeney laughed.

It was the McSweeney he remembered knowing. He patted him on the shoulder and with a tear in his eye he said "I am very sorry for everything," before pulling him in for a hug.

"Easy, Chief" McSweeney said, pulling away. "Don't want to stab you with this, do I?"

"I mean what I said," O'Connor called out to McSweeney, causing him to turn around "I swear on my life, it stops today."

McSweeney nodded, smiling again before heading off on his way with a renewed spring in his step. He would be seeing O'Connor again in just a moment and it wasn't going to be pleasant for either of them.

CHAPTER 21: THE DONKEY AND THE CRAYON

O'Connor followed McSweeney at a safe distance, sticking to the shadows. He had to see this one last lesson in how not to conduct himself. He didn't have to wait long.

"Chief!?" said McSweeney, turning to look back and gazing almost directly at O'Connor in the process. For a heart stopping moment he thought he had been seen but then realised that original self was there too, it was time.

O'Connor could not recall exactly how this played out as his memory of the event was a like a dense fog. He remembered being angry that McSweeney had lied about the rocks and that it ended with a needle in his side and a good kicking.

"How did you... do that?" said McSweeney looking past O'Connor and back along the corridor.

"Are you in on this too?" he heard his past self shout.

"What?" McSweeney asked, sounding puzzled but, from the tone of his voice, still happy. "I've done nothing, I've put them back in the work-sphere just as you asked, and I've got that thing for Ryburn, how did you get..."

"You better not be talking about what I think you're talking about. What did you put back?" demanded First.

McSweeney looked back along the corridor, still missing O'Connor who was standing in the shadows and speculating that McSweeney was trying to work out how the chief had got in front of him without being seen.

"Ryburn's rocks… just as you asked," said McSweeney.

"You lying little..." said First, clenching his fists ready to attack.

"This is another set-up, isn't it?" said McSweeney stepping backwards and looking down at what he had clenched in his hand. "You've set this all up, you swore on your life," he said, his voice trembling almost as if he was about to cry. O'Connor found it difficult to watch, but like a car crash he couldn't look away.

First began to advance.

"So you hid the ore and then lied to me."

The quiet tone of First was more disturbing than shouting would have been.

"This is a set-up, why do you do this?" McSweeney shouted back while slowly retreating like a deer from a lion. "I'm only doing what you asked." He was frightened now and his next word was a scream. "Benson!" he started to raise his com hand up, but First was quicker.

In one fluid motion First slapped down McSweeney's communicator and swung his right fist directly at his subordinate's unguarded chin. The shot however, landed short and limp on his shoulder and both men toppled to the floor in a heap. McSweeney scrambled up, kicking the dead weight of First's body off of him in the process. In the light O'Connor could see the shiny streaks on his cheeks where one or two tears had fallen. He felt McSweeney's pain, especially considering their last conversation.

McSweeney was standing over the fallen First. It was his turn to rage and he began kicking the body all the while screaming at the crumpled chief. From his hidden vantage point O'Connor looked away. He'd seen enough. The kicking and shouting continued until McSweeney was out of breath. McSweeney reached under First's arms and tried dragging him, but he was too heavy for him to move any distance and he had already exhausted himself. He gave up and instead dumped the carcass roughly behind a crate where it was hidden from view.

"I'll leave you here were you won't be found," growled McSweeney, giving First another kick before straightening himself up, gathering his composure and walking off toward Ryburn's workstation.

O'Connor left; he still had to refine the ore. There was no need to check on his past self; he knew the outcome. In the worksphere he had never been so happy to see that ore trolley. That damned ore had caused him so much grief and wasted so much of his time, time that was wasted more than once. He knew he was the culprit who stole the ore and had later returned it. He also knew that it was his constant accusations to McSweeney that had made him take it too. Now it was back, and that was what mattered. He began unloading the rocks into to the collection chute of the mini smelt. The rocks were of all shapes and sizes. The last one, of reasonable size, two kilograms maybe, made him pause. Surely this was his moment?

"Doyle," he called through the com.

Her answer was broken and distorted.

"I've got the last rock in my hand" said O'Connor, "what do I do?" there was a long pause. Nothing. He bashed the communicator on the side of the smelt and then tried to call Doyle back. Nothing. Not even static. He looked over to the cupboard where the spare had been but it was empty- his fault. He looked over to the fixed position com on the wall but it was broken- also his fault.

"Whatever happens happened, my crew *will* get home," he said to himself and dropped the ore, watching it disappear down the chute before he slammed the lid shut. Bringing up the settings on the control screen he selected cycle 27, just as Ryburn had instructed, and started the processing. All the ore had gone, there was none left for Doyle. He hoped he had made the right choice.

Meanwhile, over in his workstation, Ryburn was trying to explain to Benson and McSweeney his plan to use the 3MP to move the station.

"Let me put it this way," said Ryburn to their looks of bafflement, "It's like dangling a carrot in front of a donkey that you want to pull a cart." He was trying his best, but found it very hard to keep the irritation out of his voice. They hadn't understood the hard scientific explanation and so now was trying to use something a little more colourful… more crayon. "The donkey sees the carrot and starts walking to reach it."

"I still don't really understand how that will move the station," said Benson. "Where's the chief, anyway?"

"The chief won't be coming," said McSweeney firmly, the corners of his lips curling up.

"Do you think he's been acting very strangely as well?" Ryburn asked McSweeney. Ryburn and Benson had just witnessed the chief behaving very abnormally. He was talking nonsense and throwing around the weirdest accusations, claiming not to remember most of everything that people had spoken to him about. Then to top it all, he bolted for the door like a madman. Benson had thought that he was feverish or something. Something was very wrong with O'Connor's behaviour of late. Ryburn however suspected something more peculiar.

"O'Connor is a nasty, evil piece of shit," said McSweeney with clenched teeth. "And I want nothing more to do with him."

Benson gave McSweeney a questioning look but McSweeney just shrugged. Ryburn looked to Benson for an explanation but Benson's look said "don't ask".

"Very curious," muttered Ryburn to himself as he started using random items on his desk as props to try and help them to understand how his plan was going to work. "The donkey keeps pulling the cart but because it is attached to the cart he can never reach the carrot," he smiled a toothy grin, but only received a blank look from Benson and a monkey-ish head scratch from McSweeney. "It's too stupid to realise that it can't get the carrot and just keeps walking, pulling the wagon," said Ryburn, his frustration taking over.

"Are we the donkey in this?" Benson asked.

"We're the cart! The metal is the donkey and the magnetic field is the carrot," said Ryburn. It was hopeless, even with the prototype floating in front of them they just couldn't see it working.

"Here, hold this," said Ryburn to Benson, handing him the prototype, choosing him because of how big he was. "Hold it tight, both hands."

Ryburn extended the small prongs so they were not being crushed between Benson's fingers. "Now, do you know about chard and energy?" he asked as Benson had a good hold of the device. Both of them nodded. "Right, I'm sending just enough energy through to light a small light bulb; don't let go."

Benson felt his arms being drawn upwards.

"Try to fight it," Ryburn encouraged, but even with Benson leaning all his weight on the device, it kept climbing, until he was dangling two feet off the floor.

"Why don't you jump on too?" he said to McSweeney, who leapt up and grabbed onto Benson's back. They hung in the air for a moment, looking ridiculous. "That was barely enough to start a light bulb," he reiterated, as he lowered them back to the floor, "Now imagine what we can do with all the chard reserves in the station."

They had not understood the theory but Benson and McSweeney were easily convinced by the practical demonstration. Ryburn began to show them the plan for the station again but this time they listened intently. His plan was to essentially turn the station into a giant version of his prototype. The thick diamond cables would be connected to the chard reserve capacitors in the central sphere and then be run all the way to each end of the central corridor. The cables would then need to be attached to some sort of sturdy poles sourced from the salvage. The blast door at each end of the corridor would be deliberately released and the porthole window of each removed allowing the poles to be threaded through forming the prongs on his prototype.

Once the prongs were in place and the blast doors were sealed, their windows would be filled and the outer corridor would be detached final phase style; abandoned to a fiery death in the Venus atmosphere. The refined Mercurian metal would be packed tight into the frontmost point inside the central sphere then, using the regulators, Ryburn would create and maintain the magnetic field.

"Any questions?" said Ryburn; it was like he was teaching in some university somewhere. He had rattled off a large plan before asking the dumbfounded students if they understood.

"I think..." started Benson but Ryburn interrupted.

"The thinking has been done, what's left is the doing," he said before going on to explain further just how they were to achieve this in the short time they had left.

Pleased with the ease that Benson and McSweeney had understood the construction plan he had explained, Ryburn realised to his surprise that maybe the two weren't such ignoramuses as he had always thought.

"Where is O'Connor?" he asked at last. "We need as many hands as possible, and another set of eyes on this wouldn't hurt."

"If we see him we'll let him know," said McSweeney dismissively.

From his familiar hiding spot O'Connor had been listening in, he had to stay well away from McSweeney for the rest of this last sojourn on Neith. He stayed hidden and let McSweeney and Benson leave without interruption. Ryburn was putting various personal effects, pictures of his family, his world cup cricket ball, the odd book, into a small box. O'Connor coughed to get his attention.

"O'Connor!" said a startled Ryburn, before staring at him intently and adding, "I hope you have composed yourself."

"Yes, I'm sorry about before," said O'Connor, keeping it short.

"I think you owe me more than that?" said Ryburn.

O'Connor didn't know what to say but thought quickly, "I'll explain my behaviour when we're on the way home. What's the plan?"

"Here is the plan," said Ryburn, putting the box down on his desk and bringing up the schematic display of the station. "I trust you will find it preferable to entering final phase."

O'Connor could feel Ryburn studying him watching for a reaction, any reaction. The screen showed a wire frame of the central sphere and central corridor "Good, it all looks fine." It was exactly how he remembered seeing it in real life when he was outside with McSweeney and Benson.

"Is that it?" said Ryburn with suspicious eyes.

"That's it, the rest of the ore is smelting away. I guess you are all almost ready to go."

"'We' O'Connor, you mean 'we'," said Ryburn looking like he'd caught him out.

Damn it thought O'Connor. He'd done it again. "Of course I meant we."

"Did you now?" said Ryburn. O'Connor stayed calm and cool.

Ryburn shifted his box to the left and, as he started to gather up more junk from his desk, revealed the ripped hat. Without thinking O'Connor reached for it. Ryburn caught his arm by the communicator.

"I fucking knew it!" said Ryburn, looking O'Connor right in the eyes, as if searching for the identity of the man behind them. "That isn't your hat, remember? And you lost your communicator. Who are you?"

O'Connor was stumped, his mind raced trying to think of something to say. Nothing came to him.

Ryburn fired in a question "How did you know I needed the nine-gauge, eighty-two millisecond, three-gram regulator to get my prototype working?"

Of all the possible questions, this was Ryburn's most pressing issue. O'Connor couldn't help but laugh "That's your question?"

"Answer it then," Ryburn demanded

"Very well. I didn't know the specs, I just knew you needed the blue one," answered O'Connor.

"How?" Ryburn demanded, standing back and putting himself out of arm's reach.

"Because that's the one I remember seeing three days ago, when you showed me it working" O'Connor said, no way he could bluff his way out now, the game was up.

"That was only a couple of hours ago," said Ryburn.

"Three days, couple of hours, same event," said O'Connor, dusting off the loose pieces of glass and metal from his hat and pulling it over his head. The rip was larger now but was still most definitely wearable.

"You are out of time, aren't you?" said Ryburn, for the first time really looking at him.

"Yes," said O'Connor, smiling at Ryburn's choice of phrase. "When did you begin to suspect?"

"The memory cards," said Ryburn. "They were the same card."

"Oh, yes the card. I almost forgot I still need that," said O'Connor, extending an open hand toward Ryburn, "May I have it please?"

"But why do you need it? The parts are done," said Ryburn, pointing to the nice shiny large regulators on the desk top.

"Well, earlier today I bumped into a future version of myself who showed me where to find it and I gave it to him. A few hours later, when I showed my past self where to find it he gave it me. I used the card to build your regulators."

"That's how they were built before I even loaded the schematics and instructions to it," said Ryburn, nodding to himself.

"My past self broke it, ending it. And you saved the instructions to it, starting it," said O'Connor.

"You are lucky, I'm probably the only person who could have

followed that statement."

"And now I need it back, I have to stash it so my past selves can find it," said O'Connor.

"I get the picture," said Ryburn offering the card. "What if I keep it, and break the loop, though?" he said, snatching his hand back.

"Nothing will change; you do what you were always going to do. Go ahead, keep it, you'll see I'm right."

Ryburn handed it over "But why are you out of time? You haven't answered that yet."

"In the future, they've lost Mercury. They came back to analyse your rocks so that they can find more of the Mercurian metal."

"How do you lose a planet?" asked Ryburn, like it was the most ridiculous thing he'd ever heard.

"I don't know, humanity leaves and can't come back or something, they kind of glossed over it," said O'Connor. "The fact is they needed the rocks."

"They?" Ryburn said. "They are outside the station. The flickers in space are them?"

"Yes," said O'Connor, relived to be able to share this now.

"I told you I wasn't going mad, I knew it," said Ryburn excitedly with a celebratory clap. "All the talks I'd had with you that you hadn't had with me yet. I have to ask, have you been able to change anything?"

"No, not a single bastard thing. Nothing changes and if you try it all stays the same only worse than ever before," said O'Connor, shaking his head.

"What did you try?" asked Ryburn.

O'Connor laughed "I tried to change the lander's trajectory so it wouldn't be on a collision course with the station."

"And what happened?" Ryburn asked, with bated breath.

"I accidentally put it on the collision path, if I'd done nothing everything would have been fine," said O'Connor, not sure what type of reaction he would get from that confession.

"Ha!" Ryburn exclaimed with glee "I knew it was impossible.

And flying home, that was your idea too wasn't it?"

"Only because I'd seen it happen," said O'Connor with a smile to match Ryburn's; he had never seen him like this. "So I have a question for you," said O'Connor after Ryburn had come back down to earth. It was all out in the open now so he had nothing to lose.

"Anything," said Ryburn.

"I've processed all of the ore," said O'Connor, leading him in slowly "Just as you asked, there is none left."

"That's right, we need all of it," said Ryburn, repeating what he has said earlier.

"So if it is all gone, why would you put in your official account that the last thing you did was give me a chunk of it?"

"I haven't written a final account," said Ryburn, then he caught himself "I wouldn't lie in it when I do. Why is this important?"

"Because that is why they came back to save me, because I was meant to have the last rock sample on me."

"Save you?" Ryburn said, sounding very worried now. "You won't be coming back with us?"

"No, but I know you will make it back safely, although I don't envy any of you being stuck so close together," said O'Connor, trying to make light of the fact that he wouldn't be with them on their triumphant return.

"And they saved you, will save you, because you have the last piece of ore."

"Well no, I didn't have it," said O'Connor.

"Not him, you" said Ryburn, clarifying he meant the O'Connor in front of him, not any other O'Connor.

"Yes, but I don't have it either…" said O'Connor, "because it is all gone."

"Not all of it," Ryburn admitted.

He turned to his bookshelf and picking up the rock that he had brought back from the smelt at the same time as the refined brick. "I liked the way the iron veins went through it so I kept it, I guess you better have it."

He threw the lump over to the chief, who caught it.

"Good form, Jim," said O'Connor, sounding like Doyle now. He turned the rock over in his hands, taking it all in before awkwardly putting it in his jacket and zipping it shut.

"You know, you could've just asked for it," said Ryburn "When you first time travelled, I would have believed you. It would have been a lot easier than all that has transpired since."

"I'll bear that in mind," said O'Connor, then after noticing Ryburn tightly closing his eyes. "What is it, what's wrong?"

Ryburn hesitantly opened one eye "I was waiting to disappear. Won't you now travel back and change what you did?"

He was joking of course, Ryburn joking! Imagine that.

"So what happens now?" said Ryburn, standing up with his box putting the regulators on top, he was ready to leave his workstation for the last time.

"I'll help you prepare the station and then slip away," said O'Connor, motioning to the door. Ryburn had a million and one questions as they walked fairly briskly along the corridor. O'Connor answered them as best he could, which mostly consisted of him confirming which "him" it had been at various points over the last day.

They got to where McSweeney had dumped his unconscious body, it was still there. O'Connor stopped. Ryburn didn't notice, he carried on a couple of steps ahead before turning back.

"Why am I still here?" O'Connor asked out loud, it was rhetorical. "He should have taken me to the airlock by now." He had no idea how long he was unconscious for, all he remembered was waking up in the airlock.

"Who is that?" asked Ryburn, stumbling backward with shock at seeing a body.

"Don't worry, it's only me," said O'Connor.

"Are you dead?" Ryburn asked, then quickly apologised for the question. "Is McSweeney trying to kill you?"

"Yes, but I don't blame him. I drove him to it… and I'm not dead," said O'Connor adding the last detail as an afterthought.

"How did it come to this?" said Ryburn, shaking his head in equal parts disappointment and disbelief.

"I need you to use your com, Jim," said O'Connor. "Mine's fried."

"Are you going to call them?" said Ryburn offering the chief his arm.

O'Connor popped open the small access panel and made the necessary adjustments. "Doyle are you there?"

"O'Connor, thank the stars, what has happened?" asked Doyle.

Ryburn looked like he was going to melt with excitement, hearing the voice of a time traveller.

"Doyle, listen. I'm here with Ryburn I've told him everything. Well he figured it out," said O'Connor.

"Sir Ryburn, really?" Doyle asked.

"Yes, but listen…" O'Connor began.

"Can I speak to him?" asked Doyle with trepidation.

"He can hear you," said O'Connor, in a tired "just get it over with" tone.

"Sir James Ryburn, it is truly an honour to have this opportunity to speak to you sir," O'Connor could picture her curtsying and laying the pomp on extra thick.

"Hello," said Ryburn, finally at a loss for words. "Nice to meet you, I've given the chief the last raw ore sample. He told me that you've travelled a long way for it."

"Sir Ryburn, we all thank you. You may have just saved humanity for a second time."

"Doyle, listen. My original self is still in the corridor. How long before he needs to be in the airlock?"

"A little over 30 minutes. We've had to move out of the way of our original selves, they are in position now. Their Anderson is on the jump pad."

"That's a bit early isn't it?" O'Connor asked.

Doyle laughed as she responded. "Yes, I had him out there for hours waiting, we didn't know exactly when you would be lost."

O'Connor could just imagine Anderson perched there like an eagle ready to swoop.

"Does McSweeney come back for me, my original self?" asked O'Connor.

"Let me check the tracking," said Doyle.

"And I will be knighted?" Ryburn whispered.

"Yes you will apparently," said O'Connor.

"You called me Sir yesterday morning; which O'Connor was that?"

"That was me, and it was an accident," said O'Connor.

"This has turned out to be a good day for me," said Ryburn, jokingly straightening some imaginary lapels.

"I just wish it would finally end," said O'Connor.

"O'Connor," Doyle called back. "No, McSweeney is on the far side. He stays there until the airlock incident."

O'Connor looked around. He wasn't disappointed or confused but he was out of ideas. Doyle spoke again, "but I am seeing that Ryburn and O'Connor go to the airlock at the same time."

"Really?" said O'Connor, looking at Ryburn accusingly. "When?"

"In about 5 minutes," said Doyle.

"Okay, we got this. O'Connor out," said O'Connor. He grabbed his past self underneath the arms and indicated to Ryburn to get the feet. They began to move the heavy lump down to the airlock. O'Connor held most of the weight whilst Ryburn managed as best he could, but he was far from his physical peak.

They carried the unconscious O'Connor to the airlock and dumped him onto the prep-area bench. Ryburn stood up awkwardly stretching his back, looking at the two men… no not two men, the same man twice.

"He's not aware of any of this is he?" asked Ryburn.

"No, none of this," said O'Connor; it certainly wasn't something you would forget. "The first thing I remember is you and Benson woke me up."

"Okay, let's hope I'm here for that," said Ryburn with a hint of sarcasm. "I'll go and collect the processed metal, it should be ready now. Correct?"

"Yes, I ran cycle 27 just as you said," said O'Connor.

Ryburn stretched his back out again and then he left toward the smelt.

O'Connor opened the airlock door and picked up the suit he had left behind. Throwing it back through the door it landed at the feet of his other self, who fell forward off the bench landing face first on the floor. O'Connor rubbed his forehead in an empathic gesture to his past self, before lifting him back up on the bench. He was face to face with him now, he could see that his eyes were flickering slightly, trying to open but not being able to. His hat had fallen off when he fell, O'Connor picked it up. The perfect hat, no rips no tears.

"I'll be taking that," he said, swapping it for his ripped hat. "Sorry about this" he added as he put it on… but he wasn't sorry at all. He put the ripped one onto his past self and it looked as silly as he had thought. He took it off, having a little sympathy for his past self, and tucked it inside his jacket pocket instead. He started to put his past self into the space suit. He had never had to dress anyone like this before; it was awkward with the loose limbs flopping around offering no resistance as he tried to get arms and legs into the suit.

"What's going on in here?" asked Ryburn, poking his head in seeing O'Connor in a very compromising looking position. He was trying to get his past self's legs into the suit, but from the door it looks like something else entirely.

"I have to dress him. When I woke up I was already in my space suit," said O'Connor.

"Did all of it process okay?" O'Connor asked, upon looking up and seeing Ryburn was pushing the ore trolley.

"Yes, more than enough, a purity higher than I expected. I'll take it to the central sphere and start securing it in place."

"I'll be along shortly," said O'Connor, as he finally popped the second foot into the end of the trouser leg. That was the hard part over; the rest of the suit should be relatively easy to put on. However, it still required a lot of effort, which really tested O'Connor's patience as his unconscious self was no help, arms just flapping and always dropping down and getting in the way. Once the suit was finally on, he slid Ryburn's card into the small compartment, ready for his Second and Third, crossing another item off the list. He attached the gloves, and then the heavy boots. He selected a helmet and placed it next to himself on the bench. He pulled down that damned patched tank and took a deep breath. It felt like the ceremonial passing of a torch. His adventure was ending, whilst for his past self it was just beginning. He leaned his past self forward, connected the tank and then leaned him back against the wall giving himself a "Good luck" pat on the shoulder.

He left the airlock and headed toward the central corridor to see where he could make himself useful. He met Benson at the junction; Benson had been running from the central sphere with a long amount of cabling wrapped across on shoulder, a large metal beam under the other arm. In each hand a cutter tool and a tube of emergency sealant. But when he saw the chief he dropped everything and stopped, cautiously watching him. O'Connor had to think, the last time Benson had seen him was when he had fled from Ryburn's workstation and no doubt McSweeney would have filled him in on their little encounter too.

"Forget what's happened, let's just get this done we don't have much time, How can I help?" asked O'Connor.

"We need to get this door lowered so I can cut out the window" said Benson, pointing to the ceiling in the direction of Ryburn's workstation. He looked at it carefully then his eyes traced along the wall to an access panel, which he ripped off using the edge of the cutter to reveal the manual release for the door.

"Give me a hand," said Benson and they slowly lowered the door by turning the crank wheel.

"What about the other side?" asked O'Connor.

"McSweeney's got that one," said Benson. "Best stay clear of him, Chief." It was good advice, and Benson's eyes told him that it wasn't a suggestion either.

"That will do," said Benson, when the door was about three quarters down, not wanting it all the way to the floor as they would still need to get to the other side.

Benson cut around the frame allowing the window to come out in one piece. Hand over hand they both threaded the synthetic diamond cable through the hole before, pushing a third of the metal beam through. O'Connor ducked under the door while Benson held the beam in place. Once O'Connor had taken the strain on the other end, Benson applied the sealant, filling up the gaps with the rapidly expanding gel and making it air tight. If it wasn't they'd soon know about it when they trigger the corridor release.

Benson ducked under the door and he and O'Connor looped the length of cable around the protruding pole, wrapping it tight and holding it in place with the sealant. They both ducked back under, Benson dusted his hands off. "That's that part done," he said.

"Can we close the door then?" asked O'Connor.

"I think so," said Benson before seeking confirmation "Dr Ryburn," he said into his communicator. "We've got the beam and the cables in place, are we clear to seal the door?"

"Yes Benson go ahead... no, wait!" Ryburn called back. But in the brief moment, O'Connor had already hit the door release and it was slowly lowering the door, an irreversible process. Benson reacted fast and got his hands under, he was holding it, just.

"What is it Dr Ryburn?" Benson said his voice strained as he held the door, the vein in his head popping out under the exerted force. The door mechanism was relentless it would keep trying to close.

"The regulators, they are still in my box, it's just along the corridor," said Ryburn. "We need them, or this won't work!"

"I have this," said O'Connor, and slid under the door.

"I'll hold it as long as I can," Benson groaned, dropping down to one knee.

"Benson, are you there?" Ryburn called back, but Benson couldn't respond, all his focus was on not letting go of the door.

The corridor had never seemed so long, as O'Connor sprinted down to where Ryburn had put his box down when they had moved his past self. He grabbed the regulators and turned back without slowing down. As strong as Benson was, he could not hold that door forever and when O'Connor got back to it, it was too low for him to fit under. He slid the regulators underneath just as Benson's grip failed and the door slammed into the floor.

A horrible thought came to O'Connor. Was this his end? He had nothing left on his list. His past self was in the airlock ready to begin his journey. The station was all set for Ryburn to fly home. He looked around the corridor, the small amount of light seemed to be closing in on him, and there was nothing that could be done. He tried his communicator, it was still dead, but at least it was still transmitting his location so Doyle and Anderson would be able to collect his body and retrieve the last of the Mercurian rocks.

Was this one more piece of inescapable history? Was this really where he died?

CHAPTER 22: O'CONNOR DAY

"Don't seal the door yet!" Ryburn yelled but he arrived just in time to see Benson's strength give out and the door hit the ground. "We need the regulators." he added before surveying the scene, which now had Benson sitting exhausted.

"He went to get them, but I couldn't hold the door up," gasped the shattered Benson and, pointing to the grey-coloured components on the ground added. "I held it up just long enough for him to get the parts under."

"O'Connor!" Ryburn shouted, but it was no good, the sound could not get through the door. "Was he wearing a space suit?" asked Ryburn, trying to establish which O'Connor it was behind the door.

"No, he was wearing normal uniform," Benson answered, trying and failing to get some purchase on the bottom of the door with his hands.

"Is this the way of it?" Ryburn asked himself, whilst Benson continued to try and find a grip-able edge on the door. Ryburn tapped his bottom lip the way he always did when he was thinking. He looked to the open panel, down to the cutting tool, then back to the door.

"We need to cut," he said to Benson at last, "cut through this, here."

Benson jumped into action, grabbed the cutter and pressed the cutting edge against Ryburn's target.

"Now here," said Ryburn pointing at another spot. The glowing metal cut-off hit the floor, soon another chunk joined it. "Turn the crank," ordered Ryburn and Benson wrapped his large hands around the handle and heaved with all his might. Ryburn did not know whether the door or the crank would give way first, but it was the only option they had.

O'Connor was leaning back against the wall, wondering how much longer he had before they jettisoned the corridor and the thought crossed his mind to go back to Ryburn's room and make himself comfortable, but rapidly concluded that there was no point. When the door behind him started to creak he thought his time was up.

There was a loud cracking sound, and then the door lifted slightly, just high enough for the persons on the other side to insert a metal wedge. The door then lifted again and another makeshift brace appeared. This continued until there was enough clearance for him to get through. O'Connor got down and began to crawl through the gap and suddenly felt the weak, but well meaning, grip of Ryburn's hands on his arms pulling him through. As he emerged he saw Benson, dripping in sweat with his hands on the crank wheel. Ryburn helped him up to his feet and O'Connor winked at him, just to let him know which O'Connor he was.

"Your day is not over yet it would seem," said Ryburn.

"Not just yet, but I did wonder for a moment," replied O'Connor. He was shaking.

Benson turned the crank wheel, lifting the door just enough to allow O'Connor and Ryburn to kick the blocks out before he let go and the door slammed to the floor.

Ryburn hit the button and they heard the explosives go off

inside the door, firing the bolts into the walls and ceiling and melting it all into place. On the opposite wall was the manual release mechanism for the corridor. O'Connor pulled the levers down one at a time, entered his code and hit the release button. There was a creaking noise. Benson had the sealant in his hand in case of any leaks, but it wasn't needed. The corridor on the other side of the door had been released.

"Is that it?" asked Benson.

"We won't know for certain until you are outside. Can you go check on McSweeney and see if he needs any help. I'll meet you at the airlock," said O'Connor, meaning that his past self would meet him.

"I'll catch you up," said Ryburn as Benson left, and then waited until he was sure Benson couldn't overhear.

"If the other you is still asleep, give him this," said Ryburn, handing O'Connor one of his sober shots. "I won't be needing them anymore, all my synth was in that box."

O'Connor nodded and smiled. "Thanks. I'll follow them out over the station to be sure nothing goes wrong. I'm heading in that direction anyway."

Despite all the panic and chaos, the station seemed quiet again. O'Connor took his final walk along the corridor to the airlock, perhaps slower than was needed. This corridor would be sealed and released as soon as Benson and McSweeney were back from their space walk. He was taking it all in one last time and ran his hand along the wall, as if saying goodbye to the old girl. He stepped into airlock area, his past self sitting eerily still on the bench and not showing any sign of moving. He pulled one of the last two suits off its rack and started putting it on once again, taking his time to do so. He was getting nostalgic, his emotions all over the place. Not often does anyone get to relive the last moments of their life, after all.

"This will wake you up," he said to his past self as he gave him the sober shot in the neck. His past self immediately began to stir. O'Connor stepped out of the prep area, back into the corridor.

His movements were laboured in the space suit but he got out of the doorway and out of sight just as he heard the footsteps of Ryburn and Benson on the rubber flooring. He heard them enter the airlock prep area.

"Sorry Chief. Didn't mean to startle you," said Benson to the original O'Connor, who was now awake, but in a highly suggestible and obedient state due to the medication from the King John.

"I'm fine, where's McSweeney? Why are you winking at me?" he heard his past self say.

"Nothing, just checking something," said Ryburn.

"Where's McSweeney?" his past self repeated, he remembered he was remembering being worried about McSweeney, but not knowing why.

"Oh don't worry about him," said Ryburn.

"Good job you're all suited up. We don't have much time, you've got to come with me," said Benson.

"Suited up?" past O'Connor repeated.

"Only one left," said Benson. "Come on Chief."

O'Connor heard the dull thudding of air-tanks and helmets and waited patiently whilst Benson was getting into the space suit and checking the oxygen levels in the tanks.

"I guess this will have to do," he heard Benson say. "It will be enough."

"Enough for what exactly?" said the original O'Connor, his voice still sounding slow.

"To angle the prongs toward the front of the station," said Benson.

He heard the airlock door close, and then watched the light go from green to red and back to green as his past self and Benson left the station.

"Jim," he said softly into the prep area. "Is there anything you need me to do out there?"

"Do they make it back?" asked Ryburn, looking at the closed door of the airlock.

"Benson and McSweeney do, I would have been last in, but McSweeney decompresses the airlock and I get blown out into space… that's when he does it"

"There aren't any suits left," said Ryburn. "McSweeney isn't going anywhere."

O'Connor looked around the floor then checked the cupboard. There were no more suits, all that was there was the helmet for him.

"Are you certain he has to go out there?" Ryburn asked.

O'Connor closed his eyes as another flood of realisation washed over him. "It was me, I have to go now" said O'Connor. Goodbyes weren't his strong suit. "There is nothing more for me to do in here now."

"Good luck Chief," said Ryburn, extending a hand. "I cannot thank you enough."

"Good luck, Sir James Ryburn, the man who will take us to the stars," said O'Connor taking his hand and shaking it, as best he could, through the space suit.

He stepped into the airlock and Ryburn closed the door behind him. Once outside O'Connor pulled his way up to the top of the walkway where he could see Benson at the junction ahead, looking across to the far side.

"I've got this Benson," he said through his helmet com to the big man, "Don't worry about me, you get back inside."

"Chief, I'm nearly out of air, I gotta get back." Benson slowly turned toward the direction of the airlock. "McSweeney must have been sent out to help us I see him coming up from the airlock."

Benson had mistaken him for McSweeney, O'Connor realised, a fair assumption he concurred, he'd just been with the original O'Connor. Why would he think otherwise? Keeping up the charade that he was McSweeney, and just in case Benson was trying to talk to him, he waved to him, then tapped the side of his helmet, "Right you are, I see him," said O'Connor, now pretending to be the voice of his past self, all for Benson's benefit.

"I guess his helmet isn't working either."

He and Benson crossed paths as they headed in opposite directions, O'Connor's face hidden beneath his visor. O'Connor slowly walked his way to the first junction. He looked out over the edge seeing their previous handiwork. This prong was solid, but along the walkway his past self was moving slowly, much slower than he recalled. He remembered his mind getting clearer at about this point. The effects of Anderson's injection, the suggestibility side effect wearing off. His past self turned back around slowly. O'Connor remembered that he thought the figure approaching was McSweeney. He waved at his past self, making gestures for him to turn around. He pointed to his oxygen display, just as he remembered seeing McSweeney do. Except of course that he now knew that it wasn't McSweeney, it never was; it had been him all along. His past self stopped, letting him catch up. He was thankful the visors on the helmets weren't transparent from the outside. He pointed again to his oxygen supply indicator; his dial was green whereas his past self's was red. His past self got the message and started heading back. The prong needed some attention; the diamond cabling had started to loosen and unravel, its end floating aimlessly in space.

The whole prong looked bent, most likely getting caught on something when the corridor was released. He pulled the length of cable in and re-wrapped it and then after a little effort bent the prong back into position.

"Doyle," he said, "I'm ready to leave."

"Good form," replied Doyle. "Andy has you, but you need to clear a bit of distance from the hull."

O'Connor launched himself into space and looked back over to the station. He could see the figure of his past self walking along the far side and disappearing from sight as he pulled himself down toward the airlock. A moment later he saw the same figure shooting out fast and away from station, spinning uncontrollably, getting further and further away. McSweeney had got him.

His gaze shifted back to the station, the release of the

remainder of the outer corridor had caught his attention. All that was left broke free in one single, semi-circular chunk. The airlock, the work-sphere, sleeping quarters all jettisoned to burn up in the atmosphere.

His eyes went back to his past self and appearing out of nowhere hurtling toward him was the figure of Anderson. The two figures collided before being drawn away into the ready and waiting, original Caution of King John.

"Hello," O'Connor said through his com, it was a broad message so everyone within range would be hearing it.

"Chief we can't get you, we're locked down," said Benson.

"That's fine Jerry, don't look back," said O'Connor.

"There is nothing we can do Chief, I'm... I'm sorry." said Benson; the big man was starting to sob.

"Let me get this out." said O'Connor "I've been proud to work with every one of you. Jerry Benson, you are the best human being I've ever met. Seymour McSweeney we've had our ups and downs but let me have the last words, it was all my fault, all of it. I do not blame you for what happened, I had it coming."

"Bye Chief," McSweeney said, not offering anything further

O'Connor continued. "My actions over the last... three days didn't make sense I know, but it was all leading here, leading to this, to getting you all home safely. Jim, Sir James Ryburn, you are mankind's greatest hero now."

"I appreciate that Chief, thank you. If there was anything we could do we would."

O'Connor continued. "I'd say to split my fee between the three of you but trust me when I say none of you will need to worry about money ever again."

Ryburn spoke again. "Jake, we have to go now. Good luck to you."

"That's fine, now fire that engine up and let me see the lights again, one more time."

"Goodbye, Chief," said Benson.

"O'Connor out."

Doyle put her hand up over her mouth and looked toward Anderson with one of her looks. To which he predictably lifted up his hand, and using his encryptor he checked off the last outstanding item from their collective list and completed the final piece of O'Connor's speech with his words.

"What? It was word perfect"

Doyle closed off the communication. "Yes it was" she said to Anderson. Anderson did not follow her meaning for a moment, then he understood.

O'Connor watched the station as two large balls of light grew from each of the prongs, before each one flashed two bolts of lightning out to in front of the station. The lightning flashed away again as quickly as it appeared. Each of the prongs began to glow and framed perfectly against the backdrop of the planet below as the station began to fly itself clear.

"That was a good speech," said Doyle, her voice coming only to him.

"Don't give me that, you've heard it a thousand times before," O'Connor joked.

"Never like that, that time it had real meaning," she said. "Hurry back; there is something important you need to hear."

O'Connor was greeted in the airlock by Anderson who helped him out of his suit and promptly took him up to the dome where Doyle was waiting. She was smiling.

"While you were on the outside on the station with your past self we received a call from Sir James Ryburn. Listen to this." she said as she played the conversation.

"Doyle, can you hear me?" the recording of Ryburn said.

"Sir James, you shouldn't be calling," said Doyle.

"I know, but I have some important information for O'Connor."

"You need me to relay a message to him, Sir Ryburn?"

"No, tell him this once it is all over and we're gone," said Ryburn. "I've circumvented the airlock controls. McSweeney cannot do anything. It will not change the result, but the details are another matter. It will be me who will be blasting O'Connor out, not McSweeney. Can you be sure he gets this information?"

"Of course, but why are you doing this?"

"I thought it would help O'Connor to know that McSweeney will not have done anything extremely stupid out of anger. Something he would regret. Of all people O'Connor will understand and appreciate this."

"I'm sure he will," said Doyle, "but what about you?"

"I feel no guilt, because I know he doesn't die. The success of today was all because of him, this is the least I could do. Good luck to you Miss Doyle. Ryburn out."

"So it was Ryburn all along." O'Connor smiled. Ryburn was right. O'Connor did appreciate the gesture. His actions had not condemned McSweeney and made him a murderer and that was a huge victory for him.

"Are we ready to go back now?" said Anderson.

"If we hurry we can use our original calculations, the ones our first selves were going to use when they thought they would be retrieving the rock," said Doyle. "Speaking of which…" she added extended her hand out to collect her prize.

"You mean this rock?" said O'Connor, holding out the ore given to him by Sir Ryburn just as she had said all along. He handed over the heavy lump of Mercurian ore that he had finally been able to bring back, but as she took hold he pulled his arm back and her along with it and planted on her lips a long passionate kiss, and she kissed him right back.

Anderson looked as happy as anyone could; he had watched them tiptoe around each other ever since O'Connor first arrived. However, even for him the kiss went on a bit long, "Come on Radcliffe," he said, turning to the blank as ever indent. "Let's leave them to it."

THE END

…THE BEGINNING

Printed in Poland
by Amazon Fulfillment
Poland Sp. z o.o., Wrocław